JACQUELINE NEW

SINS
OF THE
FATHERS

VINCI
BOOKS

By Jacqueline New

DCI McNeill

Vinci Books

vinci-books.com

Published by Vinci Books Ltd in 2025

1

The EU GPSR authorised representative is Logos Europe, 9 rue Nicolas Poussion, 17000 La Rochelle, France
contact@logoseurope.eu

Prologue

THE STREETS LOOKED slick with oil. Orange lights reflected in shimmering puddles. Rain drummed loudly on the roof of the van. The windscreen was a sheet of water; occasional scrapes from the wipers losing a battle against the deluge. He wore an oversized black hoodie. No marks of branding. A cheap garment from China bought online and probably manufactured unethically. Something he would have to make amends for. It was a single drop in this Edinburgh rain storm though. A lot more on the list before unethical consumerism could be addressed. The hood was pulled up, casting his face into deep shadow. He knew it did because he'd double checked in the mirrored wardrobe door at home. Ensured his face couldn't be seen, even in the full glare of the electric light.

The garment felt conspicuous and unnatural to him, but he knew it blended into a modern urban landscape perfectly. No-one would notice another hooded figure in this city. Even in broad daylight, they could be seen, heads down and faces covered. Under the hood he wore a dark coloured surgical mask, the kind of disposal face covering that had proliferated during Lockdown. They'd littered the streets, the parks and the woodland then, and he'd picked them up to prevent wildlife from being snared. Not so many anymore. Disposable vapes were the latest pollutant. Ironically, he reached for the packet of cigarettes in the side pocket of the driver's door. Then remembered the mask. He left the craving alone, clenched the steering wheel instead. The street was a canyon around him. A bridge ahead carried South Bridge from left to right. He was parked on Cowgate, running underneath South Bridge east to west. There were cheap hotels along here. Trendy looking bars. At least they appeared trendy to him. But his knowledge of such things was limited. The stonework was black and sooty, rendered impenetrably dark by the current soaking and harsh shadows formed by the streetlights. To the right was a tall fence of wooden boards, covered in adverts. A section was a gate, secured with a padlock. On the other side was a row of three tenement style buildings that had been demolished, left derelict and neglected. The developer who'd bought the site had run out of money during the pandemic and the site remained vacant. It was a gaping hole of dirt and accumulating garbage. Including the human kind.

But in this weather, he expected it to be empty. Even the junkies, degraded and less than human, preferred not to abuse themselves in such conditions. He closed his eyes, mumbling under his breath, dismayed at his own callous thoughts. Compassion. He took a deep breath, feeling his heart racing as it had been since he'd stopped the van. That had been half an hour ago. It was always the same. The act itself was the work of a moment. Quick and efficient. It was the most primal of instincts. To kill. To inflict violence. To punish. A choice to unleash the bestial, forget reason and any other civilising principles. But the disposal of a body required nerve. Especially in a city like this. There were always eyes in Edinburgh. Always a potential witness. That was why his discovery of the old cellar in one corner of the abandoned building site had been so fortuitous. The cellar and the even older passage, long bricked up but opened by the violent teeth of the excavators. A gateway to another world.

Time. There was a body in the back of the van that needed to be removed. He had a schedule to keep, and the ritual was calling. He took a breath, feeling the mask adhering to his lips. Then he picked up the bolt cutters from the passenger seat and got out of the van. Forcing himself to walk the ten yards to the locked gate was the most harrowing part when every instinct was to run. A running man would draw attention, whereas a walking man would be ignored, filtered out of the perception of anyone who was looking. Reaching the gate, he put the cutters to the newest padlock. It was replaced regularly. This one must have been added this morning. A moment's effort, including a frisson of panic that he might not be able to break in. Then the lock was open, and the gate swung in. He strolled back to the van, got in and started the engine, driving down the dirt slope into the excavated crater before returning to close the gate.

Edinburgh stood with its back to him, as though turning a wilful blind eye to what he was about to do. The buildings towering all around revealed their fire escapes, their unpainted backsides, previously hidden by the huddle of buildings that had once been behind them. Now exposed. Peeling paint, stained concrete. Rust. He opened the doors at the back of the van and hauled on the dead weight wrapped in heavy plastic. He was not a big man, neither in height nor mass, and it took him a heavily straining minute to move the corpse. Then it was sliding towards him. He crouched, hauling the weight over one shoulder. Muscles already screaming with pain, he began walking towards the cellar and its uncovered portal. Several times he tripped on the uneven, brick strewn, muddy ground. Each time he saved himself from falling and being pinned to the ground by the body he carried.

Sweat mixed with rain on the exposed part of his face. He wore a small rucksack on his back, a modest weight but now feeling ten times heavier. It was an achievement to finally stagger into the exposed cellar, two walls of which stood, broken brick clawing at the sky. In the far corner of those two walls was a brick-lined, oval hole of utter blackness. He had spent the last four nights clearing it. Finally finishing the night before, widening it from an initial crack of just a few inches. Hard work, but thrilling for the possibilities it offered. Having ventured inside, it proved more than he could have hoped for. A secret world free from prying eyes in which he could carry out his work. Brick dust replaced water as he stooped. Steps led downwards, uneven and worn.

He was reaching the last vestiges of his strength now but once he reached the foot of the stone stairs he would rest, putting down the dead man he carried over one shoulder, knowing there was no-one down here to see him. That thought was a goal to be reached, a respite for protesting muscles, aching back and sweating body. He couldn't see the vaulted ceiling above him, but knew it was there. Once upon a time, this had probably been a close. A narrow street hemmed in by buildings, effluent running through it like a stream. Then the South Bridge had been built, connecting the ridge of land that carried Edinburgh's famous Royal Mile. The vaults that held up the bridge sealed the fate of the small streets that clawed their way up the hill. Burying them and creating a dark, subterranean world.

He lowered the body as gently as he could and stood up, hands at the base of his aching back as he stretched his spine and worked out the kinks in his neck. Taking out his phone, he used the torch to inspect his surroundings. Ten yards into the passage. Rain pattered against the top of the stone stairs. Not far enough. Still a chance of a homeless person wandering in. Or an addict. The ritual was important, vital. The need to complete it burned in him, overwhelming the pangs of the nicotine addiction that had sunk its claws deep into him more than a decade ago. Muttering under his breath with fervent passion, the sounds indecipherable but the meaning clear in his mind, he bent once more to his task. Lifting the body from the ground was agony, but the pain was fitting. He almost didn't make it, but this wasn't the first time, he'd had practise at this act.

He plunged further into utter darkness, feeling the way with careful, probing steps and one hand against a damp wall. The feet of the body thudded jarringly into a protrusion on the left, almost knocking him off his feet. Turning and putting out his hand, he felt brick barring his way on either side with a lintel at shoulder height, a very small doorway. Crouching, he picked his way over a cluster of rubble. Something squealed and squirmed away from his feet. Something else tickled his outstretched hand. Could have been a spider's web. Could have been a spider. His skin crawled and prickled with cold sweat, but the ritual beckoned, drew him on. Everything here was a trial to be endured. The reward would come at the end. A satisfaction of sorts. A quenching of the craving. At least for a while.

The ceiling on the other side of the doorway was low, and he had to release his burden and resort to dragging it by the feet. More than once he thought about turning back. The ritual couldn't be completed in the tunnel, and he did not know how much longer this passage would stretch for.

The decision was made for him as he sensed the ceiling vanish suddenly. He straightened cautiously, reaching up but unable to find it. He was aware, standing in the impenetrable darkness, that he had entered a larger space. Taking out the phone, he shone the torch around. His heart almost stopped. Panic gripped him as three people were illuminated, standing in the far corner, huddled together as though whispering. It only took a moment to realise they weren't people at all. They were mannequins. Dummies. He laughed at himself. They were dressed in a style of clothing from a few hundred years ago. Sweeping the torch from side to side revealed other antique artefacts, or at least replicas. Items of everyday life from a previous age. Pots and pans. Tools. Furniture. Boxes of fabric were revealed to be more antique clothes, though the labels inside showed them to be modern reproductions. At the far end of the room was a doorway covered by a metal grate. Beyond was a cobbled street. Washing hung between buildings. Untouched by moving air for two hundred years or more.

He chuckled to himself and silently gave thanks. He recognised this place now. Had visited it once during the day as a tourist. It was part of Mary King's Close. A tourist attraction made out of a buried street. He'd known the ancient passage he'd discovered in his quest for a quiet, secret place for his ritual, most likely connected to the warren of vaults under South Bridge but hadn't realised it linked up to the most famous part of Edinburgh's underground world. This was far enough. He dragged the body into the room, a storeroom out of sight of the visiting public, he judged. Unwrapped the plastic carefully. The man was naked and cleaned of the blood that had poured from his opened throat. The foam and vomit that had spewed from his mouth when the poison had been administered was also gone. Taking the rucksack from his back, he opened it and took out a small fresh loaf, wrapped in paper, a can of lager and a pewter tankard.

He opened the can and poured the beer into the tankard, setting it on the floor beside the body. The bread was placed on the naked chest. He knelt beside it, head bowed. Now the moment was here the excitement was almost sexual. The demand for release clenched his stomach. The anticipation of the feeling that would overcome him. In this day and age, evil was just a word, the province of fanciful movies about possessions and hauntings. When it came to real life, it was an unfashionable word, one from the dark ages of human ignorance. Call a child molester disturbed. A wife beater the product of childhood trauma. A serial killer insane. But he knew evil was real. Knew that it had a taste, a weight. Knew because he'd felt it settling on him. Tasted it in his mouth and down his throat. Raising his head, he reached for the bread and broke off a piece. He ate, repeating the same words over and over in his mind. Another piece. Another. Each bite was harder to swallow than the last. He was consuming much more than just food.

When he'd swallowed the last of the bread, he drank the beer, draining the tankard in a succession of gulps. Finally, it was done. The ritual was complete.

Chapter One

CALLUM MCNEILL, Mac to almost everyone who knew him, wanted to throw the phone across the room. He wanted to smash in the face of a dead man with the butt of the gun that had killed him. He got as far as raising the phone in one hand. Hard floor. Bare wall. Corner of the hi-fi unit. All hazardous to a delicate smart phone. Except this one wasn't delicate. It was a model he'd never heard of, but Detective Sergeant Kai Stuart informed him it was a leading make of rugged phone. That was a thing, apparently. Rugged phones. It felt like a military grade radio handset, encased in rigid rubber and plastic. And smashing it would leave him at a dead end. No closer to finding the killer of his sister than at any point in his life. He lowered the phone and dropped it onto the beech wood coffee table in front of his black leather sofa.

The phone told him it was just after three am. Sleep hadn't come tonight. A room that was usually occupied by only a single sofa and a hi-fi rig was now home to three large whiteboards. Two were wall mounted, the third stood on a collapsible metal stand. It was stolen, property of Police Scotland and taken from a station he had been based in three months ago, working on a murder case. All three whiteboards were covered in marker pen of different colours. Strings of text and numbers were written in neat block capitals with lines connecting some and crossing out others. Behind him was a pile of take away containers and wine bottles. A half empty bottle of red and a stained glass stood on the coffee table. A stack of washed laundry next to him on the sofa had collapsed into an untidy pile while in the washing machine was full of a load that had been washed three times and forgotten about after every cycle. The floor needed hoovering. Had done for a fortnight.

The mess would normally be like steel thumbs pressing into the meat of his brain. Impossible to ignore and impossible to function until it was resolved. That compulsion to bring order to the chaos was still there, but it was subservient to the need to solve this riddle. Six months ago, he'd come into possession of the phone. Thousands of messages. Tens of thousands of files and hundreds of thousands of folders. None of it clearly labelled. At least not in a method that was clear to anyone other than the person who had devised it. The white boards showed the first hundred or so folders, each containing sub folders. He'd decoded some of it, had quietly leaked the information to informants and journalists, letting it filter back to the police with no way of tracing it back to him. It had led to arrests, the breaking up of county lines and distribution networks. But he hadn't found the information he wanted. The information that would lead him to his sister's murderer. The information that had been promised to him in exchange for a man's life.

Mac sat back, running his hands through unruly dark

hair. His jaw felt rough, coarse with stubble. He was naked except for a pair of boxer shorts, chest taut with muscle and a light covering of black hair. A vein was visible running down the middle of each bicep. He didn't care for gym culture or working out, but recognised the importance of staying in shape. Even a DCI had to chase down a fleeing suspect occasionally. A workout at midnight in a twenty-four-hour gym removed the danger of any social encounters or pestering by personal trainers. His blue eyes went back to the board, and he stood, stretching hands above his head to free himself of the ache that had set in from sitting too long without moving. It was legwork more than detective work. Slogging through each folder, trying to identify the names and places detailed within. His police work took up the daytime. This work took up the nights. Hayley had gone, sacrificed on the altar of Mac's obsession. He hadn't spoken to Clio in…how long? He couldn't remember and in a moment he had forgotten the thought.

His eye was drawn by initials he had noted on one of the boards and circled with a question mark. JC. Suddenly, he thought he remembered a name that might fit those initials. But where had he seen it? At work? In the maze of folders stored on the encrypted phone? Or maybe it had been in a conversation with an informant. His train of thought was cut off as his own phone rang. Mac looked around the room, momentarily disorientated. He saw the light from the buzzing phone's screen, sitting on the break-fast bar that separated his open plan living room / kitchen. Walking over, he picked it up, not recognising the number.

"Hello," he said, swiping up on the screen.

"Callum. Ben Musa."

Mac was silent for a moment.

"Working late, Musa?"

"Celebrating actually. Got a big arrest today. I think I owe thanks to you."

There was the sound of drink in DCI Benjamin Musa's voice. A slight slurring. A too bright tone.

"Don't think so, Musa."

"Come on, Callum. Don't be modest. Why do you never call me Ben, anyway?"

Definitely drunk. The question was asked with a tone of injured pride.

"I know the case you wrapped up today, Musa," Mac said, emphasising the use of surname. "But it was nothing to do with me."

Ben Musa was a media darling and counted the Deputy Chief Constable as his mentor and sponsor. English with a private school education and a degree. Also, bent as a three-pound coin and, if Mac's informants were to be believed, a nonce as well. Trouble was, none of that could be proved. Musa's political connections were bulletproof.

"Callum, Callum, Callum. You and I both know that's not true. My team has received a lot of cases in the last six months from investigative journalists or snouts with really crucial information. Information we've been after for months. Someone is leaking this stuff and I've been catching the windfall. You were the last one to see John Lowe alive, weren't you?"

"I was in the room when he was shot," Mac said. "It's late, Musa. Is that all you wanted?"

"You've made my job a lot easier. And I'm not talking about police work," Musa said, suddenly sounding sober and serious.

"You're certainly not talking sense," Mac muttered.

"What?" Musa challenged.

"You either phoned to brag or to threaten. I'm not interested in either."

"How are you getting all this dirt, Mac?" Musa asked, the mask slipping away as he reverted to the nickname everyone used.

He'd been called Mac so often and for so long, he sometimes forgot he had a first name.

"I don't know what you're talking about."

"Thing is. If it were me. I'd be using that dirt to elevate myself. But your career has stalled, hasn't it? While Reid is out of action, you're not the golden boy anymore, are you? That's a wasted opportunity, Mac. I hate to see it."

"You afraid of what I've got on you, eh?" Mac said, leaning against the breakfast bar.

Silence. "You have nothing on me. There is nothing on me," Musa said flatly.

"I've got a witness to your sexual preferences. I know you're paying to keep them quiet. I also know you're trying to take over John Lowe's empire," Mac said, keeping his own voice level and matter of fact.

That would land better with a man like Musa. Far better than losing his temper. Again, his words were met by silence.

"Be careful, Mac," was the eventual reply.

Musa's voice was dead. There was the sound of liquid sloshing in the neck of a bottle. Another sound. A male voice in the background.

"That what you called to say?" Mac replied.

"Yes. AC couldn't prove you were the one that shot Lowe. Or that you didn't facilitate it. Who are you working for, Mac? Hance Allen? The Hungarians? The Russians? There's a lot of players out there now, but I'm the biggest, swinging dick of all of them. Got it?"

Mac laughed. "Got it. Enjoy your swinging while it lasts. I'm about to cut your balls off. See you in the office sometime."

He hung up and dropped the phone. His chest was heaving and his hands clenched into fists. Truth was, he had nothing solid on Ben Musa from the encrypted phone. A few possible coded references was it. He hadn't found the name of the man who had supposedly confessed to murdering a teenage girl on Skye back in the nineties. All he'd found were the names of a few dealers and contract men. He was failing. Looking around the room, he added his own life to that failure. It felt like he was falling to pieces. Behind on his counselling sessions, not sleeping or eating properly. Hiding behind work to avoid the few personal relationships he had.

Picking up the phone again, he scrolled to a chat with Clio. Three messages from her read but not replied to. She kept messaging, though, refusing to give up on him. Mac recognised the instinct in him to just shut down, focus on work. Work was easy. It was the relationships that were difficult. Hayley had drifted away from sheer neglect after a month or two. It had been pretty good. Probably because Mac had been on suspension and there was no work to interfere. Once that ended and he was back in the thick of it, she'd been pushed to the sidelines. He thought maybe she'd been into him, too. It was hard to tell. He tapped out a message to Clio. It felt empty, but he needed to at least make the gesture. She wouldn't see it until the next morning, so he wouldn't have to deal with an instant response. Still, he hesitated before hitting send. Once it was away, he switched the phone to silent. Then walked back to the whiteboards, picking up the encrypted phone as he went.

The notion occurred to him that there had been a

contract man called Creed. First name…James? John? He'd done time at Saughton and got his sentence reduced. Lowe pulling strings with parole services. Lowe had a lot of contract men, people ready and willing to carry out assassinations for him. Do major time in return for major rewards. Contrary to the Hollywood image, a hit man wasn't a high skilled position. It just took someone willing to stick a knife in and twist.

Why would Lowe pull strings to reduce a sentence for this one? Maybe because he'd turned up information that Lowe knew would prove useful. Information on the murder linked to a copper's family? Mac began scrolling through the maze of folders and files, trying to find where he'd seen the name before. The initials had appeared in connection to the police. Possibly, this Creed character was involved in paying off coppers. That was why Mac had highlighted it on the board. It was a connection to Reid, on medical leave, but also under investigation for corruption. The tall floor to ceiling windows of his Leith apartment lightened unnoticed behind him as he worked.

Chapter Two

MAC FELT brittle as he stepped out of his apartment, artificially bright from too much caffeine. He wore his customary uniform; black suit and shirt. No tie. Open collar. Against the promise of cold and rain, he wore an overcoat with a sheath of evidence bags in one pocket and latex gloves and a face mask in the other. A vape rode in the inside pocket. The last six months had seen him fall off the nicotine wagon and DC Isla McVey had given him the vape to help him get back off the cigarettes. It was nowhere near the same, but it was habit forming and Mac hadn't smoked tobacco for six weeks now. His apartment was at the end of a hallway of neutral colours and a floor of neat, ceramic tiles. A window at one end looked out over a golf course. Another three apartments shared this floor. As he strode towards the staircase at the far end of the hallway, the last door opened.

A woman in her mid to late-thirties stepped out. She carried a laptop bag slung over one shoulder and wore a neat, expensive looking suit. Her blonde hair was piled up on her head, revealing a long neck and the collar of a soft, white blouse. She glanced up as he approached and smiled.

"Morning," she said.

"Morning," Mac replied, meeting bright blue, expressive eyes.

"I've just moved in. Stacey Campbell," she said, putting out a hand.

Mac took it and gave the required brief squeeze of the fingers.

"I've seen you in court," Stacey said. "You're a police officer?"

She was turning to follow him along the hallway, and Mac nodded.

"I am. Don't think I've seen you. You work there? Solicitor?"

"KC," Stacey replied.

Her accent was from somewhere higher up north. Maybe Aberdeen. Mac nodded.

"Don't think you've ever cross-examined me or I would have remembered," he said.

"Me too," Stacey replied with a chuckle. "When I took the flat, the agent said there was a police officer living in the building. Like it was a selling point."

"I don't do private security," Mac said, dead-panned.

Stacey laughed at the not-all-that-funny joke in the way people do when just being polite. The hallway turned ninety degrees to the right. Lift was at the end of corridor, stairs were dead ahead. Mac turned the corner, deciding when Stacey stepped towards the lift that he would head for the stairs this morning. She was pretty, but his head wasn't in that place. As he reached the stairwell door, his phone rang. Stacey had just opened her mouth to say something as Mac fished out the device. It was DI Melissa Barland.

"Sorry. Work," Mac said by way of explanation. "I'll catch you later."

Stacey smiled. Her lipstick was shiny and subtle; the sort that looked natural. Her face was round with high cheeks and a full lower lip, giving her a pout that was enticing. But Mac was already focusing on the call, the job. He turned to the stairs and shoved the door open with his shoulder.

"Mel, good morning."

"Morning, guv. We've got a body. I'm en route. So are Kai and Isla."

That was Mac's team of detectives. An inspector, a sergeant and a constable. He'd promoted Kai himself, brash and overconfident but a technical whizz. Isla was an over-achiever that he'd lured over from supercop, Ben Musa. He was glad he'd made such a good impression that she'd requested the transfer. She was a good officer and didn't deserve to be tarnished by Musa's corruption. Not that anyone could see it at the moment.

"Where?" Mac said, taking stairs two at a time.

His shoes echoed off the concrete staircase.

"Mary King's Close. You know it?"

"The tourist place under the City Chambers?" Mac asked.

"Aye, that's it. The manager spotted it when he was opening up, getting ready for the first tours. A naked man in a storeroom. Throat cut."

Mac left the building by the rear door, feeling fat drops of rain as he crossed the car park. His car was an Audi, black. Mac didn't like to waste time making decisions on frivolous things like colour choices. A wardrobe of dark suits and shirts. A dark car. A flat that was, apparently, Scandi minimalist. To Mac, it was just empty of everything he didn't need. Getting into the car, he dropped the phone to the passenger seat and started the engine. Waited for the Bluetooth to kick in.

"I'm just leaving now. Who's on call for forensics?"

"Stringer. I called him and he's on his way."

"Good. This place is a tourist attraction, so we're going to be drawing attention. Get all the uniforms you need to establish a decent perimeter. I don't want tourists traipsing through my crime scene," Mac said, starting the engine and pulling out of his parking space.

"Of course," Mel replied without a trace of reproach.

She was a pro and didn't need to be told the importance of keeping the public out. She also didn't give a hint how much of a dick she thought her boss was being. Mac put his foot down as he turned out of the car park and headed towards Leith Walk, which would take him south towards Waverley and the Old Town. He'd never visited Mary King's Close, but had lived in Edinburgh long enough to know the location of one of the city's most famous tourist attractions. After the Castle. He considered his words for a moment, spoken without thought and no concept of how he sounded. He'd learned a lot about himself in the last few years, more recently helped by Clio. Understanding he was autistic and how it affected the way he dealt with people.

"Sorry, Mel. Didn't mean to micromanage. I know you'll have the scene locked down," he said, feeling as though he shouldn't have to say this, but knowing to anyone but him, it was required.

"Thanks, guv," Mel replied, a smile in her voice, "I'm almost there. Lot of traffic this morning. There's road works on Leith Walk. You might want to detour."

Mac was already seeing it ahead, the traffic clotting the city centre artery. He made a quick decision and turned right, swerving in front of oncoming traffic and earning an angry blast from a bus driver. A couple in all weather gear and backpacks jumped back to the safety of the pavement as Mac's car darted into the mouth of the side street they'd been about to cross. Mac was thinking a dozen turns ahead as he put his foot down. Rush hour would be chaos throughout the New Town and Waverley Bridge. No point diverting around the road works only to drive into that mire. He headed west through the outskirts. The Castle appeared on the skyline to the left between tall Georgian townhouses. Judging he was past the worst of the tailbacks building along Princes Street, he turned left, not paying attention to road names but keeping the Castle ahead of him.

Skirting Princes Street Gardens, he turned left again with the rock and its medieval fortress looming overhead and the streets choked with tourists craning their necks. The rain had passed and there were traces of blue appearing in the sky between scudding clouds. The city looked drenched and washed clean by the ferocity of the rain. Soon, the sky was obscured by the concrete and stone canyons that were the narrow streets of the Old Town. Johnstone Terrace became Lawnmarket, then High Street, cobbled and rumbling. The famous Royal Mile with the Castle at one end and the palace of Holyrood at the other. In between, dozens of shops selling cheap tat or overpriced crap. Tartan, wool and whisky abounded. The pavements were clogged and Mac was forced to slow to a crawl as pedestrians stepped on and off the high kerbs, clumping together like weeds. The Mound passed on the left. Ahead was St Giles Cathedral competing in terms of ornate grandeur, with the saltire waving City Chambers opposite.

Except, this morning Police Scotland were drawing all the attention and cameras that were usually pointed at Edinburgh's gothic architecture. Uniform officers, bulky in stab vests, stood resolutely outside two innocuous looking wooden doors in a building to one side of the grand portico entrance to the City Chambers. A forensics van was parked on the pavement beside the entrance to the close. A marked car had been driven up onto the pavement on the other side. Mac could see more white police vehicles in the Chambers' car park, separated from the street by a succession of archways and reachable by car from the far side of the building. Mac just stopped in the road opposite the uniformed officers. He slapped his police parking badge on the dashboard and got out. Cameras were pointed at him and the building he walked towards. His overcoat was open, and he thrust his hands into trouser pockets as he walked.

The press were always quick enough to report, even when it was one officer visiting a residential property. When it was multiple vehicles and officers with a major tourist attraction thrown into the mix, they would be all over it like flies on rotten meat. A loud American voice was demanding the police sort out the refund of the ticket he'd booked for Mary King's Close. As Mac looked up, a fat man wearing an oversized sports jersey and the ever present rucksack blocked his way, face belligerent.

"Hey, buddy. You in charge here? I paid…"

He cut off as one of the uniforms stepped up, putting an arm between Mac and the tourist, and then shunted the man aside by the simple expedient of refusing to stop moving until the man was backed up at least twenty yards. Mac didn't look back as he went in. First impressions were that no-one could bring a body in from the Royal Mile, even in the middle of the night, through this door without being seen, whether by organic eyes or digital. Which meant there was at least one other means of ingress. A trestle table had been set up just outside the entrance and Mac picked up a paper suit and shoe covers. He put on the gloves he carried in his pocket along with the mask which he left hanging from his ears for the moment.

Beyond the door, Mel was hurrying forward. A ticket office stood to one side, closed, and Mel swiped a card to open a disabled gate in the ticket barrier that barred further progress. She gave him a smile of hello. Mac managed a twitch of the lips in return, looking beyond her to where large displays of the history of Edinburgh flanked the tourist's path into the exhibit. The light in there was dim and orange, like firelight. The displays were islands of white. Mel was fully kitted out in forensic gear, hood back and mask in one hand. She had brown hair, tied back, and her face was open and expressive. In interviews she was always the choice for good cop next to Mac's glowering aggression. It was a partnership that worked a lot.

"Looks like quite the scrum out there," Mel said.

Mac grunted. "Where was the body found?"

"Down there. It's an entire street, you know. Quite steep. They've got houses and shops, all kitted out like it would have been hundreds of years ago."

"You ever been here as a tourist?" Mac asked.

"Never. You?"

Mac shook his head.

"There are rooms at the back of the buildings which the company uses as storerooms, out of sight of the customers. The body was left in one of those."

"Show me."

Mel led the way through the exhibit. They passed the information placards and the display cases holding interesting relics. The light dimmed to a dull titian glow and ahead of them was a series of steps. Mac wondered how disabled access was managed as he traversed the stairs and set foot onto a steeply sloped, cobbled street. Looking up, he saw a stone sky, knew it was the foundations of the City Chambers. For the rest, it was as though they were walking along an alleyway. It could have been any ginnel in the city except for that stone ceiling. The atmosphere was impressive. The buildings were tall and narrow. Washing had been hung on lines running from window to window above them.

The air felt thick, heady with the smell of food and something else. Something unpleasant. Not a decomposing body. Mac knew that sickly sweet odour well enough. He suspected this was something they pumped into the air to give an authentic historical atmosphere. It occurred to him the period this time capsule was supposed to encapsulate was probably one pre-dating plumbing. Presumably that's what the smell in the air replicated. He tried to ignore it.

"Heard from Clio and Maia lately?" Mel asked as they walked down the hill.

"Haven't seen them much since they got back from visiting Clio's dad. Just text messages," Mac replied.

Time was, he wouldn't have taken kindly to a personal question. Even from Mel, who had been with him longer than any other member of his team. But he'd mellowed. He still resented the need to allow others some insight into his personal life, but recognised it was all part of getting along with people. Mel had an interest in Clio more than most because she and her wife had looked after Maia when Clio had been wrongly arrested for murder. For that reason more than any other, Mac indulged the intimacy. Had Kai asked the same question, he probably would have been on the receiving end of a bark for which Mac was justly famous. His bite was just as bad.

Mac didn't need Mel to point out where the body had been found. Spotlights had been set up on tripods, trailing cables up the subterranean street. People of indeterminate gender in white paper suits, hoods, and masks were moving in and out of a narrow doorway. Flashes announced the presence of a photographer inside. Mac drew the mask over his lower face and pulled up his hood. He suddenly felt claustrophobic, but pushed the sensation to the back of his mind. In front of him was a room made to resemble a residence from whatever century this was supposed to be. In a corner of the room was another door. Mac went through and saw a barred gate at the far end. It was standing open and beyond, illuminated by the ferocious lights, was the body.

Chapter Three

MAC KNEW IMMEDIATELY which of the three masked figures standing around the body was Derek Stringer. The paunch was a giveaway. A head turned toward him and gave a nod of acknowledgement. Mac carefully moved into the room, watching the floor for any forensic markers. There was one within a chalk circle at the body's left hand. Several other markers were scattered to either side, accompanied by much smaller circles, millimetres in diameter. He took up a position on the opposite side of the body to Stringer, looking down and trying to put aside any preconceptions. It was important to take in the scene with an open mind, observing without colouring it with his own emotions or thoughts. He was a recorder. The difference between him and the photographer crouching at the body's head was that Mac was processing the images he saw using methods of reason and logic, not merely capturing them.

The man was naked and severely underweight. Ribs standing proud, the stomach a recessed hollow between them. Legs were darkly hairy, with prominent knees. Those knees were abraded, the skin rubbed away in a couple of places. Mac noticed scratch marks on either side of the gaping wound in the throat. It yawned wide, conjuring an image of Kermit the Frog. Mac mentally shook away the wholly inappropriate picture. Hair was dark. High cheeks and a protrusive forehead. Shadowed jawline. Swarthy would have been the old-fashioned description for him. Maybe Slavic ethnicity. Maybe Russian or Polish. Even Turkish.

"I don't think the cut throat was the cause of death, though it certainly happened while he was still alive. The blood was cleared away after it had stopped flowing. If you get closer, you can distinctly smell the cleaning product used. Not soap. Nothing you would use on yourself," Stringer said.

"What was the cause of death, then?" Mac asked.

But he'd already crouched beside the body to better observe the bluish tinge around the mouth and lips. Suffocation perhaps?

"Could have been a plastic bag over the head and then the throat cut, as he was literally breathing his last as a coup de grâce," Stringer said. "Definite evidence of cyanosis. Strangulation, possibly with the blade applied below the ligature. Notice the scratch marks on the throat where he clawed at the skin."

Mac nodded, eyes moving up and down the body.

"He was on his knees," he said.

"On a hard surface and struggling, I would say. Concrete or brick would have made those abrasions," Stringer said, eyes following Mac's to the man's knees.

Mac didn't need to look around to know the man hadn't been killed in this little storeroom. There were mannequins and other objects stacked against the walls. If a struggle had taken place, they would have been dislodged. Even if the killer had tided away the evidence of struggle, it would have been the work of a full day to get rid of that much blood. And there would still be traces for the tech team to find, particularly on the fabric of the mannequin's clothing, which couldn't have been removed without it being obvious. There wasn't so much as a single drop. He pictured a scene. This man, not heavy or strong, attacked from behind. A bag over the head or cord around the throat. Then a blade. Arterial spray jetting out but missing the killer who was behind.

"How long ago?" Mac asked.

"Up to twenty-four hours, I would say," Stringer said after a moment's thought. "Brought here. Not killed here."

"Aye, I got that," Mac said. "What else can you tell me? What's this?"

He pointed at the larger of the circles marked beside the body, a few inches from where he crouched.

"Alcohol. From the smell, I would say beer, though I'm no expert on that particular beverage. A ring of it on the floor. As though someone had put down a wet bottle or glass. Maybe they'd opened it here, and it dribbled down the side."

Mac frowned, bending his head closer to what he could now see was a wet circle within the dry circle of chalk. It did indeed smell of hops and wheat. A sharp tang.

"I'm no expert either, but I'd agree," he said.

"So nice to have my theories peer reviewed," Stringer said acerbically.

Mac gave him a look, then his attention went to the smaller circles marked with forensic flags.

"Those?"

"Crumbs. White in colour. I would say from bread. I

also found some on the body. On the chest. I left them for you to see."

Mac looked to where the pathologist was pointing. There were crumbs amid the dark hair furring the chest. White under the lights. White bread.

"Someone had beer and sandwiches down here?" Mac said incredulously, thinking aloud.

"That's what the physical evidence suggests," Stringer replied. "The beer could have been there already, although in my expert opinion I'd say it's unlikely, but the breadcrumbs, if that's what they turn out to be, obviously were left after the body was placed here."

"Eaten by the killer as they stood over the body," Mel said from behind Mac.

"No, we don't know that. That it was the killer, I mean," Mac corrected without looking over his shoulder. "All we know is someone dropped crumbs on the body. The killer, possibly. Someone else, maybe. Any chance of DNA from either?"

"Maybe," Stringer said, slowly and non-committally. "If one of those crumbs was dropped from the diner's mouth rather than from the bread before it was eaten. We'll do our best."

Mac nodded.

"Any sign of sexual activity?" Mel asked. "Given the victim is naked."

"Nothing visible," Stringer said. "Of course, anything to the contrary will go into the report. Welcome back, by the way, DCI McNeill."

Mac glanced up, then stood. "You heard about that, eh?"

"Yes. I think Doctor Blackwood should have had the book thrown at her, but then it is my profession."

"She thought highly of you. Called you pre-eminent," Mac said.

"Did she?" Stringer replied, in a tone that was ever so-slightly preening. "Well, it doesn't excuse obstruction of justice."

"That was never proved," Mac replied.

"Ah, yes, I heard a rumour about the two of you," Stringer said, primly, moving to the door.

Mac resisted the urge to grab his arm, instead choosing to ignore him and allow the mask to hide his gritted teeth. The two other forensic technicians were also leaving. Mel took up a position on the other side of the body. The instinct to defend Hayley was still strong despite the end of their relationship. Mac was aware of a feeling of guilt. Once his suspension had ended, he knew the job had taken over. It had happened with Siobhan. It always happened. And he let it. Hayley hadn't deserved that. He forced his mind back to the case, shutting off the guilt for the moment. Add it to the tally. Face it later. The dead body before him deserved his undivided attention.

"Do we know how they got the body in here? I presume that gate was left unlocked?" He nodded at the gate they had entered through.

"Not according to the manager. A Mr. Devi Darwash. He's the one who found the body. This gate was locked. I think they must have brought the body in through there."

She pointed to a corner of the room where there was a low brick passageway. Mac moved to it, peering in but unable to see anything but blackness.

"Could you move one of those lights?" he said.

Mel obliged, scraping the metal tripod legs of one of the spotlights and then tilting the light so that it shone over

Mac's shoulder. He saw a brick-lined passage which stretched away beyond the reach of the spotlight.

"Any idea where that goes?"

"Mr. Darwash doesn't. Didn't even know it was there. He said this room was full of boxes until last week. I looked it up on Maps. Where we are now is somewhere between the Royal Mile and Cowgate. There's a building site just adjacent to Tron Square. Here."

She showed him her phone, pointing to a spot which Mac tried to relate to the roads he knew above. It was difficult to think of directions in three dimensions. He sighed.

"Only one way to find out. I'll call you from the other side," Mac said.

He took out his phone and switched on the torch, holding it out ahead of him. Then, bent double, he began walking along the passageway. Mel didn't argue with him. She knew better, though Mac sensed she wanted to go with him as backup. But Mac needed someone on the end of the phone to direct the uniforms and forensics to seal off wherever this passage came out. A body had been brought through here. It all had to be scoured for evidence. Mac grinned to himself at the thought of the prissy Derek Stringer having to do his job in these conditions. The walls and floor were damp. He could feel it cold against the paper suit as his back rubbed against the ceiling. A thought occurred, and he stopped, ignoring the discomfort of his awkward position, and shined the torch on the floor. There, in the muddy, mossy slick that was covering the brick, was a broad swathe where the moss or fungus or whatever it was had been torn away. Something large had been dragged through here. Shining the torch at the ceiling, he saw similar marks.

A person bent double and dragging a body behind

them. From the width of the swathe cut through the moss, it had to have been dragged by the feet, with the shoulders in contact with the ground. The back and shoulders of the person moving the body doing the same on the ceiling. No sign of this wet crap on the body that he had seen and Stringer surely would have commented. Either it had been cleaned from the body or the body had been wrapped in something. Sheeting? Tarp? The dull ache in his back was becoming a shrill scream, and he decided to push on. The passage couldn't be too long. Someone had dragged an adult male body through here. He continued, praying the passage would, in fact, prove to be short, gritting his teeth against the pain running down his back and into his tensed thighs. Despite the agony, he stopped. There had been a sound ahead of him. Something moving. The torch showed more rotten brick and predatory darkness.

He listened, closing his eyes to block out everything but sound. His breath was loud. His heart was loud. Nothing else. Mac swore, shining the torch ahead and behind, feeling as though something was creeping up on him.

"Thank god I have little imagination," he muttered to himself.

He was reminded of a scene from a movie he'd seen a long time ago. Might have been Alien. This was right about the time he turned around and the creature jumped out at him. All teeth and slime drooling jaws. Not hearing a repeat of the sound, he turned his phone over. No signal. Under several thousand tons of stone and cement, what did he expect?

"Callum, this is the stupidest thing you've ever done. This is what we pay uniforms for. Jesus Christ!"

He kept shuffling forward, wanting to kneel and take the pressure of his quads but not wanting to stop for the sake of his back. The floor became strewn with rubble, forming a small slope that he had to climb, squeezing himself through the reduced gap. Then the pressure of his back against the roof was lifted. He groaned as he straightened, putting a hand to his lumbar region to massage away the knots. The torch showed him a squat shaped passage, a few inches taller than he was but wide enough so he couldn't touch the walls with outstretched arms. Suddenly, a shadow at the furthest reach of the torch moved. Mac reacted instantly, swinging the light back towards the movement and glimpsed something crouched scurrying away.

"Hey! Police!"

His voice echoed hideously in the confined space, rebounding on his ears painfully. He started running, slipping on a loose stone, and slamming into the wall with his right shoulder. Pain lanced into his arm, but he ignored it and pushed away from the wall. Around the bend, the passage went straight for a few yards. There was a crouched figure running at the outer limit of the torch. Mac got a glimpse of dark clothes. A hoodie with hood pulled up. He growled as he resumed the pursuit, slowing his pace after almost cracking his skull on a sudden protuberance from the roof. The passage turned sharply to the right up ahead. Mac stopped, not wanting to blunder around the corner if there was a killer waiting for him. What the killer would be doing hanging around, he couldn't imagine. But he couldn't fathom someone eating a snack over a dead body, either. Actually, on second thoughts, he could. And none of those he knew who were capable of such an act were the type of men he would want to run into in a dark, underground tunnel.

"I'm a police officer. DCI McNeill. There are more

police officers behind me. It's not worth it. Just talk to me, eh?"

He tried to sound friendly, but it was a tough ask. He was in pain and with a growing sense of claustrophobia induced panic held barely in check. It made Mac aggressive, sharpening his anger against the individual who was forcing him to run in a reeking tunnel. There was no sound from around the corner now. No running. No breathing. Mac edged forward, pressing himself against the wall and holding the torch out to the side, trying to see around the corner. There was a split second warning. The light caught a shadowed hood pointing right at him, features invisible in the blackness. Then his prey became the hunter and rushed at him, a raised brick in one hand.

Chapter Four

THE NARROW CONFINES of the tunnel saved Mac's skull. His attacker swung with a brick in his right hand but it caught against the roof, slowing the momentum, and giving Mac the chance to get his hands up. He found himself gripping a thin wrist, greasy skin slipping beneath his fingers. The force of the attack bore him backwards and his head struck the brick behind him, rebounding and reducing his vision to white spots against inky blackness for a moment. Blinded, he tightened his grip on the scrawny wrist as its owner tried to wrench it free. The man was keening like an animal and Mac could smell foul breath, feel spittle hitting his face. Taking one hand away, he punched the man hard in the gut, only able to get a few inches of room to pull back. It was enough. The pressure holding him against the wall lessened and Mac shoved hard, sending his assailant flying back into the passageway. He was strong but feather light.

Mac realised the man had only overpowered him

initially because of his momentum and the element of surprise. The man ended up on his back but immediately scrambled onto hands and knees, feet scrabbling for purchase as Mac lunged after him. Mac's phone was on the floor, torch pointing towards the ceiling. The man's frantic foot came into contact with it and it skidded into a wall, flipping over. Mac grabbed at a leg, holding on, feeling the fabric of joggies. A shoe caught him in the mouth and the leg was freed from his grip. Mac fell back once more but, fired by pure anger, pain and frustration now, powered himself forward. The light from the torch was wasted, facing downwards, and Mac didn't waste time grabbing it. He followed the sound of desperate, panting fear. The scrabbling, scraping footfalls.

He kept low, running like a sprinter, but with hands out front to feel for walls that were now invisible. He tripped and fell, kept getting up, kept following. Then his hands hit against stone steps a second before he kicked the lowest hard. Looking up, he saw the daylight above. A figure briefly silhouetted against a hemispherical entrance. It stopped, bent, and picked something up. Too late, Mac realised what it was. He covered his head with his arms as the figure hurled a brick down the stairs. It struck Mac's left forearm hard enough to numb it, sending a nauseating stab of pain from wrist to shoulder. Keeping his arms around his head, he launched himself up the steps, grazing his knees and shins on the steps as he charged ahead, bull-like in fury and screaming expletives at the man he had been chasing. More bricks hit him, but he was too fuelled by anger to stop.

As he reached the top, he saw the man ten yards away, sprinting across dark, uneven ground. All around them towered the backs of buildings. Then blue strobing lights announced the arrival of the cavalry. The wailing police car bounced down from street level, debris crunching beneath its wheels. The man was pinned by the headlights as the vehicle skidded to a halt and two officers leapt out, hitting the ground at a dead run and converging on Mac's assailant. Mac stopped, lowering his arms, and breathing deeply. The feel of cold air on various parts of his body told him both the forensic and his own suit were torn in several places. Blood was running from his shoulder and down his back. Or maybe it was sweat. His left arm ached, and he carefully flexed his fingers, checking none of them were broken.

Slowly recovering his breath and easing his aching back, he walked towards the scrum on the floor where another officer had now piled on. All three were fighting a whirling, biting, scratching fury of a man who screamed at the top of his lungs. Mac wanted to hit him hard in the face until he shut up. He thought all three of the struggling uniforms would likely turn a blind eye.

"Guv?" Mel was getting out of the car, jogging over to him.

Mac put aside the half serious thought of dealing out some resisting arrest injuries. He raised a hand, then winced at the stab of pain in his shoulder.

"I'm OK. Met that freak down there somewhere. Came at me."

The attacker was under control now, his arms pinned by two of the officers who were turning him onto his front to apply handcuffs.

"There's evidence in the tunnel a body was dragged through from here. Get forensics down there and seal off this area. What is this place, anyway?"

"Building site, I think," Mel said. "It's fenced off and gated, but the lock has been snipped. Recently too, by the look of the metal."

Mac took a torch from the belt of one of the uniforms, switching it on and shining it into the face of the hand-cuffed man. His hair was greasy and matted, as was his thick beard. Wide eyes stared from a dirty face and he snapped at those around him like a wild animal.

"I think we need to talk to someone in mental health services," Mel said. "No good taking him to A&E in this condition."

"Must be off his face!" a constable snarled.

At that moment, one of the uniforms slipped. He staggered and lost his hold on the man, who lunged for him. Before anyone could react, the man was on top of the hapless constable, teeth snapping at his throat. Mac grabbed a handful of slippery hair and yanked back as hard as he could. The head turned mouth wide to bite down on his arm and Mac swung, catching him on the jaw. The man went down in a heap and Mac felt as though he'd just broken every bone in his hand. He turned away, clutching his fist, and swearing loudly and continually.

"I don't care what you do with him. Just get him in a van and a straitjacket, then get him out of my sight before I kill him," he snapped.

———

MAC SAT at his desk with a bag of frozen peas wrapped in toilet roll resting on his left hand. It was the closest thing to an ice pack the staff canteen at Brunswick Road Police Station could produce. A vending machine coffee was by his right hand on the desk. He'd downed four paracetamol to combat multiple pains. His suit jacket was over the back of his chair, along with his shirt. Mel had applied iodine to several cuts and abrasions Mac had sustained, refusing to allow him to shrug them off, citing the filthy underground conditions and the risk of infection.

"If I didn't know you were married and gay, I'd think you had a reason for getting my shirt off," Mac muttered with a grin, eyes skimming emails as Mel worked.

"In your dreams. I'd rather just take you to A&E, but as you're being such a baby about it," Mel countered.

Mac barked a laugh.

"That's all done, I think," Mel said, standing back. "How does it feel?"

"Bloody sore," Mac grumbled, reaching for his shirt. "But thanks."

Mel smiled, putting the iodine back into the first aid kit she'd brought into Mac's office.

"Duty mental health officer has just arrived," Kai said, after knocking once on the open door.

He looked from Mel to Mac and the absence of expression on his face was as good as a wisecrack. Mac raised an eyebrow, daring the joke. Kai cleared his throat.

"Duty sergeant took her right in. He's having kittens with that lunatic in the cells. Wants him out and into a padded room. Says the guy's been claiming to be a vampire?"

Mac stood, buttoning his shirt. A nutter hiding underground and believing he's a vampire. A body with a slit throat. Could he really be that lucky? Sometimes that's how it went. He grabbed his jacket as he strode out of the office and into the larger open plan room where his team had their desks. It was half empty. Mac had three officers under his command. The rest of the room had once been occupied by DCI Musa's Organised Crime Taskforce, but they had ascended into the political stratosphere and now had their own building somewhere near Haymarket. Another DCI hadn't been moved in yet to replace them and Mac was glad. He hadn't enjoyed sharing space with either of the DCI's he'd been neighbours with. Both had tried to screw him over through politics. At least the first, Akhtar, had been straight. Musa was all kinds of crooked. He ran his hands through his hair, pushing it back from his forehead.

Isla McVey, red curling hair tied back from her pretty, smooth-cheeked face, was setting up the image boards Mac liked to use on his cases. Pictures of the body and the crime scene in full, glossy colour were up. He stopped, casting his eyes over the boards. Isla stepped back, waiting for a nod of approval. She was young and a promising DC but Mac wanted her to be more independent. He thrust hands into trouser pockets and walked closer to the boards, running his eyes over the pictures.

"Probably worth letting the duty officer do their assessment before heading down there, eh guv?" Mel said.

"Aye, I was just thinking that," Mac said. "Look at how the body was placed. Arms by its sides, feet and legs together, head upright. Does that look like the work of the Tasmanian devil downstairs?"

Mel shook her head. "Now that you mention it, no. But maybe he was in an agitated state because you'd found him. He could've been calm when he did this."

"He really tried to bite Neil Gibbons?" Kai asked.

"Yeah," Mac said, distractedly.

He hadn't known the name of the uniform who'd almost had his throat bitten out. Kai knew everyone.

"Maybe he was interrupted by our lot turning up, and that's what made him so mad," Isla suggested.

Mac looked at her, the idea taking root. She returned his stare steadily, not blinking or looking away. Mac's mouth twitched, realising he was glowering though he hadn't been seeing Isla at all. His mind was racing.

"He went to all the trouble of placing the body just so. And it would have taken him a lot of effort to get the body where he did, through those tunnels. He was interrupted and couldn't finish whatever it was he'd planned to do next. So, he goes mental. Plausible?"

He posed the question to the room, but was looking at Isla.

"Could be. If he was heavily invested in what he was doing."

"If the killing was planned, he would be invested emotionally," Mel said.

Mac nodded. "True, but Stringer said the victim was killed about twenty-four hours ago, give or take. Why would the killer come back and risk being caught?"

"Maybe he had something important left to do and didn't realise the body would be found so quickly?" Kai suggested.

"Aye, that's possible. We need to start by identifying both the killer and the victim," Mac said. "Mel, you chase up forensics for the DNA results. See if there are any matches in the database. If our luck holds, he's been processed at least once in his life and we'll know who he is already. Kai, the usual. We've got a ton of CCTV around this crime scene. You get to ruin your eyesight by staring at it. Find our victim or our vampire and trace their movements. Isla, you and me are going to see Count Dracula."

Isla beamed and forgot herself enough not to hide it.

Her predecessor, Nari Yun, who had defected from Mac's team to advance her career, would have hidden that eagerness behind a cool exterior. Mac found Isla's enthusiasm refreshing. He jerked his head towards the double doors at the far end of the room and Isla followed him out.

Chapter Five

"YOU'VE REVIEWED the initial facts. Give me your take," Mac said as they walked to the lifts.

Isla had a bag slung over her shoulder and reached into it for her small, reporter style notebook, flipping a few pages in.

"From the pictures, the body was carefully placed, but the location suggests a desire to conceal the killing. At least for a short time. If the killer had really wanted to conceal the body, they could have left it further away from Mary King's Close."

Mac nodded, stabbing the button to call the lift. "The passage behind the storeroom must have been a hundred yards long. In the middle of that, no-one would have found it until it started to stink. So, why put it where it would be found imminently after dragging it all that way?"

The lift arrived, and he stepped in, followed by Isla. He was verbalising his own thoughts, but also wanted to give her the chance to show her own deductive ability. Once he had considered himself as good a guv'nor as he was a detective until one of his team had transferred to another DCI. Mel had diplomatically pointed out how Mac could be difficult to work for and he'd begun making adjustments.

"I haven't seen what it was like in the tunnel you were in. I imagine it was dark and cramped?" Isla said as the lift bumped its way down to the basement level where the cells were housed.

"Very," Mac said.

"The killer wasn't just looking for somewhere to hide the body then. Otherwise, they could have dumped it in the middle and left it there."

Mac nodded. The doors opened. The corridor floor of the custody level was tiled, and the walls were concrete painted white. Secure doors had winking digital keypads next to them and wire embedded in the glass that made up the top half.

"Makes sense. They wanted or needed an open space for something and the most suitable was right at the far end."

"Space for what, though?"

Mac swiped his ID card and heard the heavy door click. He pulled it open and let Isla precede him.

"Something," Mac said, his mind returning to the scene.

The body laid out. The crumbs littering the dark hairs of the chest. A circle of beer on the floor beside it. A tableau. He had seen them before. Killers who presented their work as though it was an exhibit in a gallery. What was this tableau intended to communicate? Was Mary King's Close chosen specifically, or was it just a convenient, secluded space where it was unlikely he would be interrupted?

"Morning, sir. Heard you had a run in with Dracula this morning?" said Sergeant Maxwell.

He stood before the custody desk in front of a bank of monitors, giving him CCTV images from each cell and a personal computer. Maxwell was short and wiry with grey hair, a large nose and had been a fixture at Brunswick Road nick for as long as Mac could remember.

"Yeah, forgot my holy water and garlic, eh?" Mac replied with a half grin.

"Well, he's quietened down some since the shrink arrived, thank god," Maxwell said. "She's in the cell with him. Number two."

Mac nodded, not questioning the wisdom of letting a lone female into a cell with a violent man. Jim Maxwell would have made sure there were plenty of bodies on hand to help her if needed. Mac and Isla walked along the cell corridor, turned a corner, and saw two men standing outside cell number two. The door was closed, but they looked on edge, taking occasional discrete peeks through the observation slot. Maxwell would be watching the CCTV like a hawk as well. They stepped back to give Mac room, and he stooped to look in. The man he'd arrested wasn't visible, but the duty psychiatrist was sitting on the concrete bench that served as a bed, looking towards a corner of the room beside the door. He estimated her age to be roughly late thirties or early forties, hair a dyed auburn and cropped close to the scalp. She was talking softly, her voice smooth and controlled, bearing a hint of Scots and a flavour of the African continent.

Her eyes lifted from her patient for a moment and met Mac's. She gave the merest movement of her head, a shake. Mac gave a salute, finger to temple, acknowledging his understanding. He stepped away from the slot and put a finger to his lips, eyes moving around the two uniforms and Isla. The man in the cell had been as violent as any drunken hooligan Mac had ever encountered. On a par with many a gangster thug. If the psychiatrist had managed to talk him down, Mac was sure the slightest provocation would send the man back into fight or flight. Probably fight. A raving lunatic was no use to him. Questions needed to be answered. DNA obtained. Mac leaned back against a wall of the corridor, hands in his trouser pockets, staring at the wall opposite. Waiting.

When it was safe, the woman in the cell would come out and tell him if the suspect was ready to be interviewed. Or if he needed to be hospitalised. Mac didn't care if the man was locked up in a rubber room and the key thrown away, as long as he got his answers first. It took a few minutes before there was a soft knocking on the metal cell door. One of the uniforms unlocked it and the psychiatrist stepped out. She closed the door behind her, taking care to do it softly, and the PC re-locked it, taking equal care. She gently slid the observation window closed, looked at Mac, and pointed down the corridor. He nodded and led the way, with Isla bringing up the rear. When they were back in the main custody area, he stopped, turning to face her.

"What's the verdict?" he asked.

"I'm Melody Onayemi from the NHS Lothian Crisis Mental Health team. May I know your name and rank?"

Mac smiled thinly, disguising his impatience. She had spoken precisely and politely, but her dark eyes and unblinking stare made it feel like a challenge.

"I'm Detective Chief Inspector Callum McNeill, Serious Crime Unit. The man you've been speaking to was found near the location of a crime scene. A murder."

Melody nodded. She looked at Jim Maxwell. "May I have my pad and pen, please?"

He handed over an A4 sized notepad and biro to her.

"I considered it wise not to take anything in with me that might be used as a weapon," she explained.

"Aye, them paper cuts can sting like a bugger, eh?" Maxwell said.

Melody smiled brilliantly and chuckled. Mac felt himself warming to her a little. Despite her formality, it seems she was willing to have a joke. Maxwell grinned back. For a moment, Mac envied him his easy way with people. Melody opened the pad and made a note.

"Is that Mac or Mc?" she asked.

"Mc, two l's."

"OK, Detective Chief Inspector…"

"Just Mac, please. We'll be here all day if you're pronouncing my rank every time."

Melody nodded with a small smile. She held Mac's eyes as she spoke, which set up a rising discomfort in Mac. He held her stare for a count of three in his head before glancing away, masking the discomfort. He could stare down a hardened gangster without the blink of an eye, but this was different. Maybe she was flirting? No. Trying to assert herself in a very male environment? Much more likely.

"Mac…I'm familiar with the person you're holding. Is there somewhere private we can speak?"

Mac nodded and indicated the corridor that led off the custody suite.

"Thanks, Jim," he said over his shoulder to the Sergeant.

Mac led Melody to the lifts and the three of them ascended one floor, then turned into the nearest empty interview room. Isla slid over the sign on the door from Vacant to Occupied before closing it behind them. Mac took a seat and Melody sat opposite, where a suspect would normally be seated. Isla took a chair next to Mac. Melody opened her notebook, flicking through a couple of pages.

"Their name is Jacob Danzig. I have assessed Jacob on several previous occasions. They are suffering from paranoid schizophrenia with a number of other related conditions and have been in and out of institutions for the last decade."

"Wait," Mac said, holding up a hand. "They?"

"They identify as non-binary. I would strongly advise against addressing them as Mr or sir. It could easily provoke a violent response. Their gender identity is deeply linked to their psychosis. It has become a trigger for them."

Mac nodded slowly. "Understood. They. Them. Got it."

Melody raised an eyebrow, and Mac grinned. Full on rogue, trying to be disarming. "I had training last year," he said.

She gave a small chuckle. "I'm afraid Jacob has regressed since the last work I did with them fifteen months ago. That was when they were last hospitalised. Since then, they have come off their prescribed medication, become homeless and begun abusing drugs and alcohol. It seems they were involved in an altercation with another resident at the sheltered accommodation they were placed in and then evicted. Subsequently, falling off our radar and...falling apart is the best description."

"Is he...they dangerous?" Mac asked, leaning forward.

"Yes, when in the middle of a psychotic incident. If not, they would simply be frightened of their own shadow. Timid and introverted. You were unlucky to stumble across Jacob while they were deeply in the grip of an episode."

Mac shook his head. "If this man is so dangerous, how is he on the streets?"

Melody's eyes didn't shift from Mac's face, but her face seemed to harden.

"They," she reminded him. "Better to get in the habit now if you intend to speak to them."

Mac sat back, running a hand through his hair, and trying not to look impatient. He didn't think he was doing very well.

"We need to speak to Jacob about why he was underground. What he might have seen. Or done," Isla said, then stopped herself. "They. Sorry. This is quite difficult."

Melody smiled. "It is. And if you are in a room with them and make a slip like that, it will be the end of the interview. I can promise you that. They will react badly."

"I have a murder for which Jacob is currently my primary suspect. Is...are they in a state in which I can interview them?" Mac asked.

"Right now, yes. But I would recommend speaking to Jacob in the cell and changing out of your suit. They also react aggressively to authority figures, uniforms of any description. That is why your officers had such a hard time with them. A suit is perceived as a uniform in this context. In answer to your next question, yes, Jacob could be capable of killing. At the worst point of their psychosis, they might not even know what they were doing. May I ask how your victim was killed?"

"His throat was cut," Mac said.

Melody nodded slowly, considering. "One of Jacob's paranoid fantasies revolves around vampires. Specifically, the belief that they have been infected with some kind of parasite that is turning them into one of the undead."

"Jesus," Mac said, looking at Melody but seeing straight through her to the person who had come at him from the darkness with a brick in his hand. Had tried to bite the throat of a police officer.

"I am going to ring around to see if I can find a bed for them. They need to be under twenty-four-hour care."

"He's a murder suspect and at the very least carried out a serious assault on two police officers," Mac said, stirred from his reverie. "He's not going anywhere."

"*They* are. If I can find a room somewhere," Melody replied. "My assessment is that Jacob is unstable and a risk to both themselves and others."

Mac saw his chance slipping away. Once Jacob was in a secure unit under the care of doctors, it would be nigh impossible to get to question him. Even if there was a window where he wasn't sedated. Mac stopped his train of thought, mentally correcting himself. They. They. The last thing he wanted if he was to take the chance now to talk to Jacob was to trigger a full on psychotic break.

"You said Jacob is calm now?" Mac said, standing.

"Yes…"

"And I might be able to talk to them if I ditch the suit?"

"Yes, I would need to be there with you. They trust me…"

"Isla, ask Kai if I can borrow his gym stuff. He keeps it in his locker," Mac said.

Isla didn't question, but hurried from the room. Mac held Melody's gaze, daring her to make a joke. He felt ridiculous, hoping Kai wasn't the type to workout in Lycra. Mac could get away with a pair of shorts and a football top.

"Anything else I should know?" Mac asked.

"Don't make direct eye contact. Use their name, and if they ask if they know you, just say yes. And if I indicate the interview needs to end, don't argue."

Mac wasn't used to being secondary in a police station

to a civilian. Nor did he like interviewing someone with so many restrictive rules. An interview was an art form for police and the environment set up to put the questioner in a position of power. This would be different. This person was dangerous and might be a killer. Even if they were, a misstep from Mac and Jacob Danzig could escape to a hospital and an insanity plea. Danzig would be off the streets in that instance but it hardly felt like justice.

Chapter Six

KAI'S WORKOUT gear wasn't Lycra, thank god, and it just about fitted Mac, who was a few inches taller than his Detective Sergeant. The trainers Kai had in his locker were too small, so Mac found himself padding to the cells in his socks, feeling like a prisoner on suicide watch. As he entered the custody suite, Melody following, he glared at Jim Maxwell, daring a comment. Maxwell glanced up from his monitor briefly, then did a double take so swiftly he might as well have shouted his thoughts out loud.

"I'm going to see the prisoner in number two," Mac said, not volunteering why he was dressed in shorts and t-shirt, with Isla carrying his suit.

Maxwell's mouth quirked, the grin being promptly disguised as a cough.

"Right, sir," he said, stepping out from around the desk and picking up the keys he wore on a large, heavy duty key-ring on his belt.

Stopping at the door, he uncovered the viewing panel and looked in.

"Can't see…" Maxwell began.

Mac could hear the 'him' coming and stepped in.

"Fine. Forget protocol. I'll take the risk," he whispered.

Maxwell turned to face him, prepared to exercise his authority regarding custody matters, even over a superior officer. Mac looked him in the eye and lowered his voice further.

"Trust me, Jim. This one's delicate."

Finally, Jim nodded and unlocked the door, turning the metal handle with a loud thunk. Mac stepped in, knowing if Jacob couldn't be seen, then they must still be in a corner of the room. Melody followed him in. Mac walked to the bench and sat down, hands clasped between his knees. Melody sat next to him, knees together and hands carefully placed upon them. This close Mac could smell a faint, subtle perfume. He dismissed it, focusing his attention on the figure crouching in the corner. Jacob was barefoot. The odour from him filled the room, sweat, dirt and urine. Sour. He was looking at Mac from beneath a shock of matted, filthy hair. He sat with knees drawn up to his chin, bony arms wrapped around them. Dark, unblinking eyes.

"This is Callum, Jacob. Do you remember him?" Melody asked.

Mac forced a smile, alarmed that Melody seemed to be trying to trigger memories of his underground meeting with Jacob.

"No."

"You've met before. A while ago," Melody assured him.

Mac wasn't sure if it was his imagination, but Jacob seemed to lessen the tight hold he had around his knees.

"Oh, sorry. I don't remember."

"No worries, Jacob," Mac said. "How've you been?"

Melody had told him the best way to earn Jacob's

trust was to play the part of someone who knew him. He would be distrustful of strangers but inclined to be more open if he believed there was already a relationship in place.

"Not good. The meds don't work anymore. The parasite is too strong," Jacob said.

Mac nodded, as though seriously considering the information. Sudden inspiration grabbed him.

"That's why you were living in the tunnels, eh? Don't like sunlight?"

Jacob's hands went to the floor, and he stretched his legs out, folding his hands in his lap.

"That's it. You get it. Think I remember you now, Callum," they said.

"Mac. Remember? Everyone calls me Mac, Jake."

It was a gamble, shortening Jacob's name like that. But Mac wanted to build trust quickly, before something triggered Jacob. It was a reasonable guess that they might have shortened their name to Jake or Jack.

"Mac. Yeah, I remember," Jacob said, eyes flicking to Melody, then back to Mac.

"How long since the parasite made you go underground, Jake?" Mac said, diving into the fantasy world Jacob had built.

"Not long. About a week ago, I noticed the sun was hurting my eyes. Maybe three days ago I found the wee hole in the ground. Thought I was lucky."

"Oh yeah? You were. Could have been stuck outside in daylight if you hadn't," Mac said, leaning back and putting a foot up on the bench, clasping his knee with both hands, affecting relaxation.

"It wasn't luck," Jacob said, voice suddenly going flat.

Mac picked up on the danger signal even before Melody

pressed the back of her hand against his leg, a sure signal for him to stop.

"I thought it was, but I was drawn there by the Master," Jacob intoned, pulling his knees back up and lowering his chin until only his eyes were visible.

Mac noticed the sudden tremble in Jacob's arms as they tightened their embrace. The hand pressing against the outside of his thigh increased its pressure. Melody didn't like where this was going, but Mac needed answers before Jacob completely flipped.

"Who's he? Assuming they are a he?" Mac said.

Jacob's head lifted, and they actually smiled. "Well done, Mac. No assumptions. I don't know if the Master fits our human definitions of gender. It isn't human."

"Was it down there with you?" Mac asked, remaining in his casual pose, praying that Jacob would mirror him.

"I saw it," Jacob said. "With a victim. Who knows how many more of them are down there? It had drained him dry. Opened his throat."

Mac nodded and looked away from Jacob around the room, not wanting to reveal his sudden eagerness.

"You know what it looks like?" he asked.

Jacob watched Mac for a long moment and Mac wondered if he had triggered something, tensed against a sudden rush of violence.

"No," Jacob finally said. "It was hooded. But I got a good look at its victim."

Mac wondered if this was true. Had Jacob seen the killer? Or was Jacob the killer and this story an attempt to distance himself from the act, psychologically if not legally?

"Strange thing was it didn't just drink their blood. It ate human food too," Jacob said.

"What kind of food?" Mac asked.

"It put bread on the man's chest then ate it," Jacob said, wonder in their voice.

Mac mirrored the expression of puzzlement that he saw on Jacob's face.

"Odd, eh?" he said.

Jacob nodded eagerly. "Isn't it? Why would a vampire eat bread? Why would it need to? And why pray over your victim?"

"Pray? It prayed?" Mac asked.

Jacob nodded. "Aloud. Said a prayer before eating the bread."

Mac raised his hands in a silent shrug. "I'm no expert," he said. "Have you seen it before?"

Jacob gave an emphatic shake of the head. "No. It hadn't revealed itself to me before. I think what I witnessed last night was a message."

"Mac, we have to go," Melody said brightly. "Remember? We're late already."

Mac glanced at her, no intention of leaving when he had Jacob talking. Her eyes held his wide and insistent. She reached out and rested her fingers against his forearm. When Mac looked back, Jacob was standing, hands braced behind them against the wall, fingers splayed. Mac experienced a momentary thrill of fear. He hadn't heard Jacob move. Now, Jacob was breathing hard, head down, and Mac could feel the pressure building. He stood and found the door opening for him before he had taken two steps. Maxwell was on the other side, face serious. Melody followed Mac out. Her grip tightened on his arm and she pulled him with her down the corridor.

"Those are physical signs of an impending breakdown. Had we stayed in that room, they would have become violent. I need to get them sectioned. They are too unstable."

"He's a witness," Mac pointed out.

"*They* are a volatile paranoid schizophrenic lost in a fantasy world. I don't know want substances they might also be under the influence of right now on top of that. You've got everything you're going to get out of them."

"I need a DNA sample," Mac said. "To eliminate them from our inquiries."

Melody shook her head emphatically. "They won't let you near them, and if you try and force them, they might never come back. I will make a formal complaint about excessive use of force if you do."

"Did you hear what they were saying, Melody?" Mac demanded, raising his voice. "They are either an eyewitness or a killer. They don't get to disappear into some hospital for the rest of their life!"

"What do you want, Mac?" Melody demanded with just as much fire. "If you push them, you get nothing. Back off and maybe you'll get a lucid moment later. My priority is not your case, but what's best for Jacob."

Mac suddenly saw the absurdity of the situation. Standing in the station's custody suite in his socks and someone else's gym gear, arguing. He ran a hand through his hair and sighed.

"OK, Melody, you win." He considered for a moment, "Will you be in charge of Jacob when they've been committed?"

"I can request that I be assigned as their consultant, yes. I will have to move my caseload around."

"Would you mind doing that? I need a contact in the system."

Melody looked at him for a long time. This time, there was no discomfort holding her gaze. Mac was in police officer mode, and Melody was the key to his only witness. He wasn't going to back down. Eventually, she nodded.

"I'll do what I can," she said.

Reaching into her bag, she took out a card and handed it to him. Mac patted his borrowed pockets and then grinned.

"I won't lose it," he promised.

"I need to make some calls," she said, suddenly brisk and efficient.

———

MAC WENT BACK into the locker room to change. Isla followed him, hanging his suit on one of the pegs above the bench seating in the middle of the room. Mac stripped off the t-shirt and picked up his shirt. His mind was racing, and he didn't stop to think that he was half naked in front of his subordinate. Isla showed no sign of being aware of it, either.

"Jacob's talking about prayers being said over the body. Assuming the whole thing wasn't dreamed up," she said. "I was listening from Jim's control room."

"A ritual. That's what they were talking about," Mac said, buttoning his shirt. "The body laid out just so. Cleaned of blood. A prayer said over it. It's ritual. Which means the bread was significant. It was part of it. Possibly the beer too."

Isla was writing on her pad. "I'll start researching any funeral rites involving..."

Mac had stripped off the shorts and picked up his

trousers now. "No. Don't waste your time. Focus on the police work. I know someone who's better placed to tell us about rituals. I want you making yourself an expert on Jacob Danzig. Pull anything and everything we have on him and then fill in any blanks. Give his full description to Kai, so he can add him to the CCTV checks. Friends, family, hospital inmates. Anything you can find out."

Mac sat to lace his shoes, feeling more confident by the second now he was back in his own uniform.

"Is Jacob Danzig still a suspect?" Isla asked.

"He's a… christ, they're a nutter. So, yeah, they are," Mac said, standing. "Go back and speak to Jim Maxwell on the custody desk. Have a cup of tea sent in to Jacob. We can obtain his DNA from that to check against whatever forensics find at the scene."

Isla frowned. "Guv, not sure we're allowed to do it like that. I think we need permission."

Mac grinned boyishly. "Like I said, they're a nutter. They don't know what day it is. We'll tell them we asked. But don't tell Melody Onayemi, for god's sake."

Isla laughed, still writing. "Right, guv."

She left the room as Mac gathered up Kai's things and put them into a holdall he'd left on top of his locker. By the time he got back to his office, Isla was at her desk, phone at the side of her head. Mel wasn't there, and Kai was engrossed in the three large monitors that surrounded his workspace. Mac went through to his cubbyhole of a private office and closed the door. He skimmed through his text messages and saw a reply from Clio. Chiding him for letting work absorb him. Asking him about Hayley Blackwood. Offering a coffee after work. He checked the time. She'd be at work by now, at the university. But then this was police business. He hit call.

"Clio, how're you doing?" he said as she answered.

"Hi, stranger. So, what do you need my help with this time?"

Chapter Seven

MAC SAW CLIO'S CAR, a pale blue Nissan Leaf, as he turned into the car park for Holyrood Palace. He pulled up alongside, both cars facing out onto Queen's Drive, with the mass of Arthur's Seat looming over them. She got out of her car as he did, looking serious and folding her arms. Mac felt a frisson of guilt at leaving this for so long, and then meeting only when he needed Clio's help with police work. As he approached, she tried to maintain a stern face towards him, but the pink, hand-knitted bobble hat and matching scarf wasn't helping. He walked around the back of her car, approaching her and giving her the full-on rogue.

"Don't even think about it," Clio said.

She pointed at him with woollen, fingerless gloves.

"I said I was sorry, Clio," Mac said. "It is good to see you, though."

"You've been up to your old tricks. Living to work and cutting out anyone who isn't part of your police world. Maia has missed you."

Mac stopped a few feet from his friend and tried to look sheepish.

"I've missed her. Missed both of you."

"You could have called. Or text. It's been three months!"

Clio slapped her hand against his chest, half-playfully.

"That's assaulting a police officer," Mac said.

"Good!" Clio replied. "Arrest me. Then maybe I can get some quality time with you."

Mac was trying to think of a witty retort when Clio threw herself forward, hugging him tightly.

"You stupid man," she whispered.

Mac returned the embrace, enjoying it for a moment in silence. Then Clio was pushing him to arm's length.

"Can we get in the car? It's bloody freezing out here!"

She got into the driver's seat, lifting a sheaf of papers from the passenger side. Some spilled into the footwell and Mac scooped them up as he got in. There was barely room for him to stretch out his legs. Clio hesitated about where to put the papers for a moment and then dumped them onto the back seat. She started the engine and put on the heater at full blast, holding her hands out to the vents.

"Nice motor. All electric, must have cost a bit," Mac said.

"It was a present from my dad. The Polo was costing more to run than I paid for it and as I was driving back up to Scotland with Maia, he wanted to make sure I had a decent car. He wanted to buy me a Range Rover. I had to talk him down to this."

"A Range Rover? Maia put her foot down about that one then?"

Clio laughed. "She did. I wouldn't have taken it, anyway. Ninety plus grand for a car! That's obscene. But, there's no way she would be driven in a gas guzzler even if I was OK with it. Which I wasn't."

"Good for her," Mac said. "How's school?"

"When I was staying at dad's he paid for a private tutor. A real hipster. Piercings, tattoos, Oxford educated and as gay as anything. She loved him. Now she's back at Cramond Secondary and…well, feels like we're back to square one. Teachers don't know how to deal with her. Other kids are little…"

Clio swore, a word that Mac didn't even think she knew.

"Sorry, I haven't been there for you," he said. "Since last year I've…"

"Had a lot on?" Clio finished for him.

"It's not that. Not just ordinary work." He stared out of the windscreen at the mottled green hill opposite and the slate gray sky around it.

A few cars went by in both directions. A brave hiker was climbing the slope in hi-vis colours and hiking gear. For a moment, he found himself looking for anything that would indicate surveillance. Kenny Reid had been under investigation by Anti-Corruption after evidence emerged he had taken money from a crime boss named John Lowe. Reid wasn't bent. He'd been trapped, debt making him vulnerable, not knowing where the money was coming from until it was too late. Now Mac had the means to completely exonerate him if he could decode the contents of the encrypted phone. If AC didn't get to him first, that was.

"I'm going to tell you something nobody else knows. I mean it, no-one," Mac said.

Clio nodded, sensing his seriousness. She took off her woolly hat, shaking out her shoulder length dark hair. For a moment Mac was struck, as he always was after not seeing Clio for a while, at how beautiful she was. She'd let her hair grow since he'd last seen her. It suited her. He pushed the thought aside brutally. There was no room in his life for women and Clio's was complicated enough without any deeper involvement with him. Besides, their friendship was the only good thing he had outside of his job. He wouldn't risk that for the sake of lust.

"Last year, I was involved in a case linked to a gangster named John Lowe. I ended up with…some information on an encrypted phone. It was his entire business, his entire operation. Messages, files, spreadsheets, names, addresses. Clio, he claimed to know who killed Iona."

Clio's eyes widened, and she took his hand, holding it tight.

"If that's true, it's…huge. But how did he know?"

It was the question Mac didn't want to examine too closely in case it turned out to be a bubble easily burst.

"He said one of his boys was inside and another inmate confessed to it. No way either of them knew who Iona was in relation to me. I'm guessing it was just one guy telling another about a girl he raped and killed on Skye. Lowe must have done some digging on me and put two and two together. Iona's murder made the papers so it wouldn't be hard to find references to her family. I didn't change my name or anything. So…it could be true."

He wanted it to be true. Desperately. Not least because he'd done something to obtain that information. Something that went against everything he stood for as a police officer. Something that would get him fired and prosecuted if it came to light. One more secret to keep. One more weight to carry. Sometimes it felt like the burden of those secrets would break his back.

"What makes you think he was telling the truth?" Clio asked, softly.

"He had a gun to his head."

Clio's squeeze got tighter. Mac gave a half grin. "Not me. It's a long story. He was talking for his life, thought I would save him."

"And you didn't?"

Mac thought about coming clean. Telling her he had walked away and heard the two gunshots. One bullet for John Lowe and one for the man who had killed him turning the gun on himself. How he had condemned a man to death at the hands of a serial killer. Just for a phone. As he looked into Clio's eyes, though, he realised the thought of seeing her disappointment was too much to bear. What difference did one more secret make to the ones he already carried?

"I couldn't," Mac lied. "I got shot, well, you know that much, and before I knew what was happening, Lowe was dead and the man who killed him had shot himself."

"Christ!" Clio whispered. "I knew you'd been shot. You said it was an armed robbery."

"I lied. I'm sorry," Mac said. "I didn't want you to worry. The whole mess was just…"

He trailed off. That much was true. It was a bloody mess and not one he was proud of. The shame and guilt had hit him like a sledgehammer even as he'd walked away. Now the phone was in the inside pocket of his suit jacket. In his office, it got locked in a drawer. Isla had carried it for him when he'd been forced to change out of his suit, though she'd had no idea. Mac took it out, showed it to Clio.

"This is it. With the information I've managed to decode leaked to the right people, I've caused a few dozen pimps, dealers, and contract men to go down. And it's occupying my every waking hour. Trying to save Kenny Reid and trying to find the man who killed Iona."

"I don't understand," Clio said. "Why not just give it to your tech people?"

Mac grinned, a rogue's smile. "No-one knows I have it. If I declared it, then the Organised Crime Taskforce would seize it. And their boss is as corrupt as they come. I can't risk him getting his hands on it."

He put it back into his pocket, eyes scanning the vehicles passing by and the pedestrians heading along Queen's Drive to Holyrood, or crossing to attempt Arthur's Seat. He lingered over anyone who might be watching or listening, knowing the technology AC could deploy to overhear distant conversations. There wouldn't be large aerials spinning on top of a Bedford van or a hiker crouching behind a bus pointing a high-powered microphone at the car. It would be invisible. But the risk had to be taken. He needed Clio.

"Thank you for sharing that with me. I know it doesn't come easy," Clio said, still holding his hand.

Mac was in no hurry to take it back. He gave a shrug, instinctively relapsing into a facade of casualness. "Easier than with anyone else,"

Clio laughed. "You're so smooth, aren't you? Hero cop and romantic matinee idol all rolled into one."

Mac barked a laugh. "What's a hero, anyway?"

"Oh, but you'll take the matinee idol, though?" Clio said, punching his shoulder.

Mac's answering grin was the kind that turned heads, male and female alike. Clio was immune, though.

"So, what do you need from me?" She asked, picking up a cardboard coffee cup from a beverage holder. "I got one for you, by the way. It's from Toasty, their special Ethiopian blend."

Mac picked up another cup and sipped at the lukewarm

coffee. It had a hint of citrus underneath the brutal bitterness.

"A body was found this morning inside Mary King's Close, you know it?"

"Of course. I've been there with Maia. Fascinating slice of history."

"Thought you would. A man with his throat cut. The body was laid out on the floor, naked, and positioned too perfectly to have been dumped there. There were bread-crumbs on the body and we think beer had been spilled next to it. I'm wondering if there's a historical context. I just don't know what. Mean anything to you?"

He was deliberately sketching out the crime scene in the barest detail, not wanting to prejudice Clio's opinion. Tell her he believed there was a ritual element and she might automatically start thinking along those lines only. He sipped the coffee, watching her face as he considered the problem.

"The breadcrumbs didn't get there by accident? I assume you wouldn't have mentioned them unless you thought they were significant," Clio said. "They were mostly found on the chest of the body?"

Mac's heart almost stopped. His lips twitched in a smile and he took another swig of coffee. The familiar thrill of the hunt surged up within him. It was what made him get up in the morning and go to work. That rush when a lead presented itself, or a solution became visible in a previously opaque puzzle.

"They are significant, I believe. And yes, on the chest. How did you know?"

"Just from the historic connection. Nothing to do with Mary King's Close per se, but certainly the period. In fact, right up until the early twentieth century. It's a practise called sin-eating," Clio said. "Individuals, usually the poor, would become sin-eaters. There was one in every district, and they were sent for by the deceased's family and friends. They would take on the sins of a person who had just died through a ritual performed over the newly dead body. Bread was placed on the chest or the face, an incantation said, then it was eaten by the sin eater. A drink was also consumed. Usually beer because it was readily available and cheap. The act of consuming food and drink led to the sins of the deceased being ingested, thus freeing their soul to ascend to heaven, cleansed. They literally ate the sins of the dead. They were also paid a small value coin."

Mac frowned. "Isn't that a lot like the...what do Catholics call it? Host?"

"Don't let the Catholic Church hear you say that. They would consider it a corruption of the sacrament, or Eucharist, where worshippers consume the wafer and wine, which they believe contains the body and blood of Christ. The Church hated sin-eating. Everyone hated them because the practitioner was carrying around the sins of every person they'd performed the ritual for. They were outcasts, pariahs. But they were invited to every funeral. No-one wanted a family member to go to hell because they hadn't been unburdened of their sins. The last sin eater died in the 1900s, I think."

Mac had frozen with the coffee cup at his lips, looking at Clio and hooked by her story. It fitted perfectly. Both the evidence and the account given by Jacob Danzig. Mac wondered if Danzig knew about sin-eating. If his belief in vampirism was linked to that somehow. It just made him an even stronger suspect in Mac's eyes.

Chapter Eight

MAC RETURNED to his car as the rain began again. The sky went dark and Arthur's Seat became ominous. He resisted the urge to hunch his shoulders as he walked, hands in trouser pockets, holding his coat open. As the pelting began in earnest, he turned, sweeping hair from his eyes to raise a hand to Clio. She beeped as she drove past him and made a gesture with the thumb and little finger of her left hand that either represented heavy metal, or call me. Mac waited until she was out of sight before getting into the Audi. Checked his phone. Email from Mel entitled DNA results. Email from Stringer, preliminary forensic findings. SMS from the same person, unrepeatable language. Seems he wasn't happy about crawling about under the city. Mac smiled, then saw the missed call from Kenny Reid. For a moment, he decided to leave it, check in with the team first. Then he thought better.

Docking the phone, he started the car, pulling out of the car park and heading east along Queen Drive. He brought up the contact list on the interactive dash display and pressed Reid's number. It rang once.

"Mac, I called you."

"I was working, guv."

"Yes, thought as much. Why do you think I'm being so polite?" Reid answered gruffly.

"How's things?" Mac asked.

He was following the contours of Arthur's Seat, working his way east and north, past St Margaret's Loch, towards the A1. From there, it would be ten minutes back to Brunswick Street.

"Limbo, that's how they are. The Commissioner has made me an offer I can't refuse. Let the investigation half-heartedly drag on and I'll retire with a full pension in six months. At which point AC will move on from me. Lowe taking a bullet has slowed them down, but Akhtar won't be persuaded to drop it."

"He's by the book. It was Akhtar that investigated me when Lowe was killed. All kinds of pressure from above not to come down too hard on a hero cop or his own niece for that matter, but he stuck to his guns. Two people dead and a murder case screwed. Someone senior had to pay."

Detective Chief Superintendent Omar Akhtar headed up an Anti-Corruption Unit that was in charge of both Mac's recent disciplinary and the ongoing investigation into Reid. His niece was DCI Hafsa Akhtar, formerly a colleague of Mac's until a wrongful arrest had slowed her climb up the greasy pole.

"Aye well, shouldn't have been you. Even Mayhew was forced to say nice things about you to the press," Reid said.

"Mayhew never saw a bandwagon he didn't want to ride," Mac said.

He didn't know if Deputy Chief Constable Mayhew

was corrupt, or just a politician. But he was DCI Musa's chief patron and a major reason for Musa's meteoric rise. Mac had posed for pictures with Mayhew when he'd been commended, upon his return from suspension, for his heroism.

"Listen, I found something I wanted to run by you. Might be nothing. You know anything about a contract man named Creed?" Mac asked.

"Aye, from Glasgow actually. An old lag, as they used to say. Knew what he was doing but got unlucky," Reid said. "What of it?"

"I found the initials on Lowe's phone. Lowe said one of his boys was told by someone he was inside with about a murder on Skye."

"Jon, without the h. Short for Jonathan. Hebrew. Not that you would know it. Doesn't exactly go to synagogue. I know he got out way too early. Should have done a twenty but served less than half."

Reid's information echoed what Mac had already guessed, but before he could say more, Reid interrupted.

"Have you found anything more on that phone about me?"

Mac hesitated. "Lowe admitted the paper trail Akhtar was following was faked. There is no evidence against you, guv. Is there?"

He waited a moment. Reid didn't reply for a long time.

"Look, son, I just don't want something to blindside me when I'm about to cash in my pension, right?" he said, belligerently.

Mac remained silent, wondering if there was more to be found.

"You weren't on the take though, right guv?"

"I got paid, but it was a scam. I wasn't on the take, but

that doesn't mean my name didn't appear on the books," Reid said. "I did none of the things they asked me to do."

"Which was?"

"Intelligence. I gave them nothing."

"You got any way of getting in contact with Jon Creed?" Mac asked.

"Maybe. I'll dig through my files. One of my old snouts might have a way of getting hold of him."

"I'll see what I can dig up my end. Make sure there's nothing else incriminating to you."

"Mac, just because the Commissioner wants this swept under the carpet doesn't mean Akhtar is going to let it. He's likely to go for it before I retire."

"That's what I would do. That's what you would have done," Mac pointed out.

"Didn't say it wasn't the right thing for AC to do, did I?" Reid barked. "Just don't put me on a back burner yet, eh, son?"

"Don't worry," Mac told him. "I don't actually think you're bent, so I'm not about to let you get fed to the wolves. Gotta go. I'll be in touch."

He hung up before Reid could reply. It felt like some small progress. As he hit the end call button, his eyes were drawn to a car that had taken up position right behind him. It was a dark coloured BMW. Two people inside. Both men. As it came closer, he thought he could see the LED lights concealed in the front grille. Unmarked coppers. It kept coming until the radiator grille was hidden from the rear-view mirror, as were the headlights. Glancing in the side mirrors showed them driving on his rear bumper, almost close enough to touch. The two men stared straight ahead, no conversation. No expression. Not AC surveillance. They would be driving to the letter of the law, inch perfect. These two were trying to intimidate. Which meant they were Musa's boys.

His phone rang. The number that appeared on the dash was not withheld. He took the call.

"Mac, Ben Musa,"

"Your boys radio in they'd found me, did they?" Mac said.

"Yeah, actually. Popped downstairs to talk to you, no-one knew where you'd gone. Know you were just on the phone to Kenny Reid, though."

"What do you want, Musa? Thought you'd be hung over today."

"What?"

It was an unguarded moment that Mac wished he could experience again. He grinned.

"Check your phone," he said.

Ahead, a gap in traffic was opening, and he began to accelerate. The car behind matched his speed. Mac knew there was a turning coming up on the left, a double-back that might catch his tail by surprise.

"Mac, we need to talk," Musa said. "Come and see me."

"I'm heading back to the office now. You could have emailed me."

"I'm not in the office, mate."

Mac reached the junction with Blenheim Place and swung the wheel, stamping on the brakes and slewing into a u-turn. Then he was back on the accelerator and the car was rumbling over cobbles, heading back in the opposite direction to the one he'd been driving. In the mirror he saw the BMW was braking, having missed the turn, and now backing up. But more cars appeared behind it, blocking them on the road they were on. Mac slowed, heading along

Royal Terrace. On one side was a succession of impressive, black stained Georgian buildings with paved bridges connecting their front doors to the pavement. Steps led down to basement level properties beside each one. Mac stood on the brakes as a car suddenly pulled out in front of him, blocking the road. He had been doing fifty and was forced to swerve, yanking on the handbrake. The Audi came to a rest parallel to the car, which now blocked the road. Mac watched DCI Benjamin Musa get out of the passenger side.

The driver also got out holding what looked like a plastic bag. Musa was tall with dark glasses and an athletic frame. He wore an expensive gray suit with tie and scarf. Gold glittered on his wrist. Mac got out, slamming the Audi's door.

"What the hell are you playing at?" he demanded, striding towards Musa.

"Now, now, Mac. People are watching," Musa chided. "Lots of solicitors and barristers with offices around here."

"Get out of the road then," Mac said.

"Would you blow into this bag please, sir?" said Musa's driver.

He held up a breathalyser. Mac stared at it.

"You're kidding me."

"Nope. Drink driving is a crime, Mac. Senior officer or not," Musa said pleasantly. "And you were doing fifty in a thirty zone. Good reason to pull you over."

Mac laughed. "I didn't realise the task force was so hard up for work since I got rid of Lowe for you. You're doing traffic stops now?"

Musa grinned, a shark's smile. "Did me a favour, mate. Don't worry about the bag. We've already got a reading well over the limit and your DNA on the mouthpiece."

The driver put the breathalyser kit into an evidence bag and stepped back. Musa stepped close to Mac.

"You're a difficult one, Mac. I like to know weaknesses, you see. Like to know where to apply pressure. I was doing alright with Lowe until you stepped in with your size twelves. Like a bloody bull in a china shop. Months of careful work and you dropped a nuke on it."

"I'm a hero, remember?" Mac said, refusing to back down from Musa.

"Yeah, I heard. Long way to go before you've got the inches I've got. Column inches," Musa replied. "Now, we're both busy men, so I'll keep this short. I wanted to speak to you away from the office. I'm going to get back on track with my plans, mate, but you're still dropping bombs, aren't you? I know it's you. You're dismantling parts of Lowe's operation before I get the chance to step in and take over the levers. What I want to know is how you know who to go after? I'm thinking you've got a name. Someone deep into the operation who's feeding you intel."

Mac thrust hands into his trouser pockets and shrugged.

"What the hell are you on about?"

Someone was approaching along Royal Terrace, slowing as they saw the road blocked. Musa's driver approached them, holding up his badge.

"Less of the attitude, Mac. You're not doing yourself any favours. I've given you time, given you a chance to see sense…"

"And now you're piling on the pressure because you're scared. Why else would you call me at three am? Dutch courage was it?" Mac said, shoving a finger into Musa's chest.

He saw the effort on the other man's face to control a

spasm of anger. Musa took off his sunglasses and Mac saw the bloodshot irises.

"You're messing with the wrong person, Mac. I've got a name for you. How about an exchange? My name is Clio Wray. Want another one? Maia Wray. What have you got?"

Mac stared, jaw firming as his teeth clenched. He wanted to hit Musa but the other man had height on him and the build of a rugby player. Besides, with his DNA on an over the limit breathalyser, taking a swing at another officer in public wouldn't look good. Nor would showing Musa that his barb had hit the mark.

"Who're they?" Mac asked.

Musa was the first to break the poker face. His teeth bared as he grabbed the lapels of Mac's coat.

"Don't!" he hissed. "Do not insult me! I'm going to give you twenty-four hours to give up your informant and then I go after your girlfriend…and her daughter. Got me?"

He turned and stalked away, getting into the car and slamming the door. His driver was quick to disengage from the irate member of the public, now joined by another. Musa's car reversed at speed, mounting the pavement, then roared away eastward. Mac returned to his car more slowly, ignoring the sounds of impatient motorists. He got in and pulled to the side of the road, staring out of the windscreen. There was no secret Clio had helped Mac on an investigation. Her contribution had formed part of the evidence used by the Procurator Fiscal in their prosecution. And he supposed Clio's involvement in another case was probably widely known. What he hadn't realised, and should have done, was that anyone had made a personal connection between them. Musa had seen that connection and considered it a worthy extortion lever. Mac's hands tightened on the wheel until his knuckles were white. Rain spattered the windscreen, and he felt the old familiar tension rising within him.

Anxiety coloured with anger. Flashbacks danced before him. Not images, though. The smell of rotted wood and wet grass. Disturbed soil and the copper tang of blood.

"I am here in this moment. I am a police officer on a murder investigation. There is a body in the morgue and a suspect. That is the present."

The mantra had been given to him by his therapist, helping him deal with the panic attacks triggered by memories of that night on Skye. The night he had almost killed a man. Was Mark Souter in the encrypted phone? It was the first name Mac had looked for. Hadn't found it yet. The mantra wasn't working. The panic was subsiding, but the anger that made him want to chase Musa's cars through the thronging streets and ram them into the side of a building was rising. He closed his eyes tight, feeling the overwhelming weight of secrets and their consequences. He wanted to hurt someone.

Chapter Nine

"EVERYTHING OK, GUV?" Mel asked after knocking once at Mac's office door.

"Fine," Mac replied.

"Did you see my email? We…"

"No, Mel, I didn't. Just tell me, will you?" Mac snapped.

He'd returned to Brunswick Street in a mood that he was finding it difficult to control. The anger within him needed to be released, but there was no target for it. He hated the killer whose twisted ritual had made this the perfect case for Clio to consult on. It could have been a motiveless stabbing. Or a pub fight. Or a drug deal gone wrong. But no, it had to be something that needed the talents of a historian. He hated the victim for allowing himself to get killed and most of all; he hated himself for dragging Clio into danger. Clio and Maia. How easy it would be to go up to Musa's office, stab him through the eye with a pen and then just let himself be taken down. No more Musa. No more danger to Clio. Life in prison would be a small price to pay. Mel didn't bat an eye, which meant she had taken the comment on and was deliberately choosing to ignore it. Isla would have flinched, and Kai would have made a joke. Mel was the only one to take it to heart. Which just made Mac feel worse.

"We've matched the victim's DNA to the police database. His name's Adam Glebe. Not long out from a sexual assault charge. He was a repeat offender with one previous conviction for sexual offences. He did seven out of a ten-year stretch."

Mac digested the information. "How long had he been out?" he asked.

"Three weeks," Mel replied, cool tone stripped of emotion. "I'm chasing up known associates and family. He went down for sexual assault against his partner. She was named in the trial, so I'm looking for her."

Mel made to leave, but Mac stopped her. "Wait. Come in. Close the door."

She did and stood before his desk, hands clasped in front of her.

"I'm sorry, Mel. That was uncalled for. I...I let my emotions get the better of me. Under some stress right now," he said, feeling as though the words were inadequate but unwilling to involve Mel by giving her more.

"Anything I can help with?" Mel asked, her tone softening now that Mac had apologised.

He smiled, knowing for open-hearted Mel it was all that was needed. He shook his head.

"Personal stuff. Don't usually let it get in the way, but it blindsided me," he explained.

"You can talk to me anytime, guv," Mel told him.

"Yeah, I know. Thanks, Mel. OK, get on with it, eh?" Mac said, putting a touch of mock gruffness in his voice.

Mel winked and left the room. Mac forced his mind

back to the case. An ex-con sex offender recently released. A ritual murder with the purpose of cleansing his soul. Who would care enough about a sex offender to want to relieve them of their sins? Unless the ritual was a smoke screen. Someone with just enough intelligence to know about sin-eating. Or someone who'd seen a documentary on YouTube. Screening a different motive. Revenge? The family of Glebe's victim? Her current partner? Assuming that Danzig wasn't the killer. Or maybe he knew Glebe? Mac growled. Too many strands. Too many questions. They needed to narrow it down. He stood, pulling his jacket from the back of his chair where he had flung it just a few minutes before. The sensible strategy was to review the paperwork his team was generating and review the case progress, prepare a situation report for acting Detective Chief Superintendent Carmichael, Kenny Reid's stand-in. Mac was sure that Gavin Carmichael was in the fifty unread emails in his inbox, and probably at least one missed call.

But Mac wasn't happy being sensible. He wanted to be active, not stuck in a cupboard. Out in the field he could clear his mind, zero in on the facts he needed. Come up with a solution to Benjamin Musa. He pulled open the office door and strode out; hands already in pockets as he walked to the boards on one side of the team's cluster of desks.

"Mel, good work on identifying our victim. Any joy with Jacob Danzig's DNA?"

"Not found on the body or in any of the samples taken from the room it was in. Plenty of…evidence he'd been in the tunnel, though, for several hours," Mel replied from her desk, turning in her swivel chair.

Mac stood before the boards, letting his eyes once more

roam the crime scene pictures and his mind de-focus, waiting for something to pop out.

"Kai, what does Big Brother tell us?"

"Big Brother, guv?" Kai asked.

Mac looked over his shoulder. "It's a book…never mind."

Kai shrugged with a grin that said it was all over his head and he didn't care. "Got a vehicle parked up on Cowgate last night and a man approaching the gates of the site where Jacob Danzig was arrested. All in black, hoodie with hood up and a face mask. Can't see the reg. I've tried a few different cameras around there. None of them got a good look. It's a white van, transit type. One of a million. Anyway, this guy had some kind of tool, bolt cutters I think. So there was a lock on the gate. Clips it and opens the gates, then drives in."

"Any cameras in the site itself?" Mac asked.

"Not one."

"What about Jacob Danzig? Have you seen him gaining entry to the site?"

"Not yet. Isla and I are still looking," Kai said.

Mac saw the brief gleam in his sergeant's eye. Of course Isla was helping him; he had a habit of developing crushes on female colleagues in the team. Nari had been the first, but Isla seemed to have completely turned his head. He had thought Kai had a girlfriend, though. But then, knowing him, he probably still did. Mac had a wicked thought then.

"No, I want Isla with me. We're going to Saughton Prison. Isla get them on the phone and tell them I'll want to interview anyone who knew Adam Glebe. Staff or prisoners. Tell them we'll be up there within the next hour."

Mac suppressed a smile at the look of mild chagrin on Kai's face as he turned back to his CCTV slog, now deprived of his pretty co-worker. Mel looked at him side-ways and he winked at her. Taking action felt good. Too much of a DCI's work was collating evidence gathered by other officers, holding press conferences, and liaising with bosses who used words like optics and actionable tasks. The governor of HMP Edinburgh needed some lead time to establish which staff members or prisoners would be best to talk to the police. Mac checked the time on his phone. While Isla gave them notice, he would tackle the new boss, brief him, take some stick for not being more prompt, and then be free to get on with his actual job.

————

HMP EDINBURGH, still known locally as Saughton Prison, was much like any other modern prison. Corporate and soulless. Parking in the visitor car park, Mac and Isla crossed to the glass-fronted main entrance. The extensive accommodation halls were visible behind the main building, home to almost a thousand men. Mac never felt comfort-able visiting a prison. For him, it was similar to an airport, a place that induced tension and anxiety, that overwhelmed with its visible security and labyrinthine system of rules. One foot wrong in a place like this would mean trouble magnified beyond any consequence that would take place outside. They checked in their possessions, walked through a metal detector before being given visitor passes. The governor, Elaine Kirkpatrick, greeted them once they'd passed through security. She was on the upper side of middle-aged with greying hair and a lined face with no makeup and thin lips.

"I've assigned a room for you to do your interviews in. It's usually the family room but we don't have visits until later in the week, so it's free," she said with a highlands accent that held traces of Scandinavia.

"Are there many people that knew Adam Glebe?" Mac asked as he followed Kirkpatrick through a security door locked by a digital keypad and along a corridor.

"A few. He'd been a long-term prisoner. He shared a cell for about a year while we were short on space because of building works. Most of his sentence was spent in segregation as a sex offender. Though as his crimes weren't same sex and didn't include children, he wasn't as vulnerable as some to attack from other prisoners. His cellmate has been released, but I've found one prisoner who knew him, worked with him here. He wasn't well liked. Not a very pleasant individual to be around, in fact, particularly for my female staff. It led to him getting into a few fights."

"I thought you said he wasn't vulnerable?" Isla said.

"Not as vulnerable, I said," Kirkpatrick replied. "Some of the prisoners, especially the younger ones, can bond with the female staff. It leads to them feeling protective and when someone is leching over a staff member…well, justice is dealt."

She almost sounded as if she understood the motives of those young prisoners. A woman in an overwhelmingly male environment. Maybe she thought it was justice after all. Kirkpatrick led them into a large room filled with plastic tables and chairs. It had tall, barred windows and a high ceiling, giving a sense of light and air. Seated at one table was a man dressed all in black; shirt, trousers, socks and shoes. One foot casually resting across the knee of the opposite leg. He was reading a book and didn't look up as they entered the room.

"Father Nick, there you are. I've been looking for you," Kirkpatrick said.

The man looked up in surprise. He had a long, thin face with expressive brown eyes and short brown hair, worked into a neat side parting on top. As he turned, Mac saw the dog collar. Father Nick looked to be in his thirties. But with a youthful face, so could easily be five or ten years older. Good looking, but serious. He seemed the kind to have an acoustic guitar on hand for a chorus of 'Matthew Row the Boat Ashore.' He stood and walked towards them.

"Were you? I was just taking a moment for some peaceful reflection. Lucky I was here. You found me," he said brightly.

His voice was pure English, from somewhere down south if Mac was any judge. Well educated.

"This is Father Nicholas Cass, our chaplain. He probably spent the most time with Adam Glebe while he was here. Adam was Catholic."

"Adam?" Father Nick asked.

"Adam was found dead this morning, Father Nick," Kirkpatrick said. "These people are the police in charge of the investigation."

Barely allowing the news to land, she stepped back. "I'll have the other staff sent up once you're done with Father Nick." Then she was walking away, phone retrieved from a pocket and clamped to her ear as she walked.

Cass looked to Mac and Isla. "Adam's dead?"

"Yes, murdered," Mac said. "We're here to find out whatever we can about him, given how long he'd been inside."

"Of course, of course. My, that is very sad news. I honestly thought he had turned a corner."

Cass sat down and Mac took a seat opposite with Isla at his side.

"Governor Kirkpatrick said you knew Adam?" Mac asked.

"Yes, well…when I say knew, I mean as well as anyone in a prison environment can be known. Everyone here wears a mask for their own protection. Even the staff keep secrets. But I was his confessor, so I suppose I was the one getting the actual truth from him."

Mac's ears pricked up at that. He suddenly realised what a stroke of luck it might have been to find his victim had been Catholic. What might he have confessed that would shed light on why he was killed? He sat forward keenly.

"I need to understand what made him a target. Is there anything he confessed to you that might give me some insight? A crime he hadn't been convicted of, for example?"

Father Nick's face was serious, and he prodded the table with a long finger.

"The confession is sacrosanct, officer. I can't repeat anything that was told to me in the confessional."

Mac frowned, not expecting the response. "I'm talking about murder…" he began.

"And I'm talking about his immortal soul. And mine, for that matter. I can't do it. I'm sorry."

"I could get a court order…" Mac began, knowing it was in vain, but he had to try.

"You could apply for one. But I assure you it would be thrown out. Look…I'm sorry I don't even know your names."

Mac introduced himself and Isla. Father Nick looked at both with an expression of infinite patience.

"I'll give you chapter and verse on what I thought of him as a man, as a Christian, as a sex offender. I'll tell you every conversation I overheard by or about him, but nothing that was confessed to me as his confessor. Now, for example," he prodded the table again and then stammered over his next words. "Did, did you know, he was almost killed last year? Stabbed. That was what brought him to God, near death experience and all that."

"Governor Kirkpatrick didn't inform us, no," Mac said as Isla wrote furiously.

"Well," Father Nick said, drawing out the word. "She's a busy woman. I'm sure she would have mentioned it eventually."

"Who stabbed him and why?" Mac asked.

"Mickey Plant. Bit of a tearaway. He was doing three years for burglary and got caught smuggling drugs in. Got moved to HMP Shotts, I believe. He's probably still there."

"And the why?"

Father Nick made a face, tilting his head from side to side as though searching for an answer.

"Well, Mickey was never one to talk to the police or 'screws.' Or me, for that matter. But I heard he knew the woman Adam had attacked. Although I don't know if that's true."

So an attempted murder inside for revenge. Was Mickey Plant out of prison? Or did he know someone on the outside who could get done what he hadn't been able to? But this young tearaway didn't sound the type to be versed in obscure pseudo-religious funeral rites. So where did that leave Clio's sin eater? Father Nick had placed his hand upon the book he'd been reading, which Mac saw unsurprisingly was a Bible. The priest was frowning at the tabletop. Then he looked up, face brightening somewhat as though he had come to a decision.

"Look, there is maybe something else I can tell you. Towards the end of his sentence, he was talking to me a lot about repentance. About sin. Almost obsessively. None of this comes from the confessional, of course. This was just me and him talking, in between chatting about football and the Quo. I got the impression there was something on his mind."

Mac wondered if the priest had seen the error of his earlier moral certainty, decided to try bending the rules to help with a murder investigation. But looking into that earnest face, he dismissed the idea. This man was secure in his vocation. Convinced of his own righteousness. It probably took that much moral certainty to function in a place like this.

"Repentance," Mac said. "Like a crime he hadn't been punished for, you mean?"

Father Nick spread his hands. "I can't say. He didn't tell me. Look, Detective Chief Inspector..."

"Mac's fine."

"Right, Mac, thank you. I'm Nick. Look, what was I saying...oh yes. I don't think for one minute that most of the men in here give a stuff about guilt or sin. They make all the right noises about seeing the error of their ways. Show suitable remorse, do their time and go out and re-offend. You know that and so do I. But every so often someone genuinely sees the light, and that's what makes my job worthwhile."

"Are you saying that Adam Glebe...saw the light?" Isla asked.

Father Nick smiled. "Oh, I was hoping so. I really was. The way he was talking to me about his faith, I had high hopes. But I suppose we'll never know now."

"Do you, or any of the other men you work with, have information about other illegal activities Adam may have been involved in?" Mac asked. "Even a rumour?"

Father Nick shook his head slowly. "I'm sorry, Mac. I can't help with specifics."

Mac looked at him hard and got his own glare mirrored back. Except Father Nick did it with a touch of serenity and humility. There was no aggression or testosterone in his steadfastness. Merely certainty. Mac had his own certainty. Adam Glebe had confessed something. Someone else knew about it and had metered out the ultimate punishment. Another certainty; Father Nick would never tell him what it was.

Chapter Ten

NONE of the other staff could provide more insight into Adam Glebe than Father Nick. A handful of prisoners spoke, but only to say the usual inanities. He seemed OK. No-one had a grudge. Except Mickey Plant. But no-one was willing to talk about him. No-one admitted to seeing the attack or knowing anything about it. The prison officers who worked the wing Adam Glebe was housed on were similarly reticent. They quoted their own incident reports no matter how many different ways the question was phrased. It took three hours after speaking to Father Nick for Mac and Isla to get through the rest of the staff or inmates corralled into speaking to them. Three hours of shrugs, official quotes and 'he was alright.'

"I thought we'd get some insights from the staff. More than we did anyway," Isla said as they walked out into brittle sunshine and a fresh wind. "I mean, I thought they'd know the prisoners they're looking after."

"You're assuming they care to take an interest. Or that they don't have their own secrets to hide," Mac told her, pressing the central locking button for the Audi as they walked towards it. "Some of them will be smuggling contraband in and not want to say too much in case they expose themselves. Others won't care. They just think whatever happens to a prisoner is what they had coming to them."

"At least we have a lead we didn't have before. Mickey Plant," Isla said.

They got into the car.

"Aye, Mickey Plant. Get onto HMP Shotts and see if he's still an inmate. If not, find out what address Parole Services have for him. It doesn't fit the ritual part of this, but we need to chase it down."

"Ritual?" Isla asked. "I know we talked about the body being positioned carefully, but what's the ritual?"

Mac remembered he hadn't shared the insights he'd gained from Clio with the team yet. He opened his mouth to speak, but then thought better of it. Musa's threat was uppermost in his mind. He had already thought of a way of buying time, but he didn't want Clio any closer to the police now than she had to be.

"I did some research. I was curious about the bread over the body thing," Mac lied. "Turned up an old funeral ritual called sin-eating. Google it will you and prepare a briefing for the team, give them an overview. It's something we should bear in mind."

Isla was making notes. "Some kind of occult thing? Like devil worship?"

"No, it's religious, but not the sort of thing the church would endorse. A priest wouldn't do it."

She nodded. "Blasphemous or something?"

"Something like that."

He pulled out of the Saughton Prison car park and headed northeast along Gorgie Road back towards the centre of the city. Clio needed to be removed from the investigation. She could feed information to Mac and Isla could brief the rest of the team so they were at least on nodding terms with the practise of sin-eating. Assuming it wasn't all a smoke screen. He didn't see some ned coming up with that to disguise a revenge killing. But you never knew. Maybe Mickey Plant was a history buff. You could learn a lot online these days. Still, it didn't seem to fit. As they drove back to Brunswick Street, Isla began making calls. Mac didn't hear her carving her way through the red tape to get the information she needed. His thoughts were on Clio. Musa wasn't the kind to make idle threats, of that Mac was positive. He couldn't get police protection assigned to Clio and know for sure the officers assigned weren't bent. Even if he did get the overtime signed off by Carmichael. A threat would have to be present, and Mac couldn't prove there was one.

He would have to do it himself. And Clio would have to be warned. She would take his word for it and would take no chances with Maia. Would she leave Edinburgh? Probably best if she did, somewhere random she couldn't be traced to. But Clio had already taken a leave of absence from her job as department head at the University of Edinburgh. And Maia had already been taken out of school. Wouldn't work. He would have to be staying with them to make sure they were safe. It was the only way. The idea was not an attractive one. Clio was one of the few people Mac would label as a friend. But the prospect of being somewhere other than his own environment, where he had total control, was...unsettling. Clio and Maia, together, were a force of nature, living in a state of perpetual semi-chaos. He tensed at the thought of being in that chaos for a prolonged period. He needed to deal with Musa.

"Guv?" Isla said.

Mac realised she had been talking to him and rewound the last few minutes in his mind.

"Sorry, Isla. Mickey Plant, he's out, you said?"

"Yes, released early for good behaviour. The stabbing was never proved, so wasn't added to his tariff. Parole Services have him staying at an address in Stenhouse. We're not far from there if you want to take a look now."

"Why not," Mac said, taking the first left turn he saw.

Isla read out the address and Mac hit the Sat Nav button on the dash display. She put it in and Mac steered them back in the general direction of Stenhouse and Saughton. It took a few minutes to reach Stenhouse Drive. A succession of bland, anonymous roughcast clad blocks of flats. They didn't even have the distinction of being tower blocks to make them stand out. Just rows of grey boxes with red lockups on the ground level and open stairwells for each floor. Almost as if designed to give the desperate somewhere convenient to jump from. Mickey Plant lived in a box within one of those boxes. Opposite the rows of flats was scrub ground, more brown and grey than green with metal fencing beyond that. A train shot by, hidden by the cleft the tracks ran through, but audible. Next stop Haymarket.

They found the right building based on the flat numbers, signposted on the gable end of each row and made their way to the communal entrance in the middle of the building. A group of boys, primary school age by the looks of it, were kicking a ball against a wall. They stopped and stared at the Audi as Mac and Isla got out. Mac beckoned to one who had picked up the ball and stood furthest out from the group. Obvious leader. He took out a tenner.

"That's my motor. I like it. Another tenner if it's just like I left it when I get back."

"Twenty," the boy replied, reaching for the down payment.

Mac held it up out of his reach. "Twenty and not a scratch. Or I'll come looking for you."

"Alright, polis," the boy said, reaching for the money again.

Mac gave it to him with a grin. The boy turned back to his pals, pocketing the money, and kicking the ball back to them. He sauntered towards the Audi, taking out a phone and began texting. As they approached the main entrance, Mac noted a cluster of tracksuited figures just ahead, a group of four or five loitering around a car, who scattered in as many directions at their approach. He and Isla might as well have had a neon polis sign flashing above their heads.

"If he's straight, he'll be in," Mac said as they entered the building.

The glass on either side of the double doors had streaks of blue graffiti on it, and the lock was broken. Inside was a lift cordoned off behind a plastic barrier with an out-of-order sign handwritten on a piece of card stuck to the doors. There was a staircase ahead with a black plastic handrail and bare concrete steps. Isla glanced at a sign next to the door giving the flat numbers.

"He's in 17. Second floor," she said.

There was the sound of running footsteps ascending the stairs ahead of them. Then banging, followed by the slamming of a door. Mac grinned.

"Someone's bricking it."

"Think we should call for backup, guv?" Isla asked, sounding slightly nervous.

"Nae, the sharper locals will already have figured out this isn't a raid and they'll be spreading the message those idiots outside didn't figure out. Two plain clothes coppers aren't coming to take someone away. We'd have brought a van if we'd wanted to do that. Things will settle down in a minute."

He walked up the stairs, taking his time. Every half floor, there was a stairwell with a concrete wall but otherwise open. Glancing down the first one, he saw his car's bodyguard still in place, kicking back a football that had been aimed at the car and then swearing at the kicker loudly. At the second floor landing there were four flats, two on one side of the building and two on the other. A lanky man with a mullet and a trackie, all in red, was leaning against the handrail at the top, an unlit roll up hanging from his mouth.

"Alright, mate," he drawled.

Mac ignored him, heading for number 17.

"He's no' in, mate," the man said. "Got a lighter?"

Mac knocked, but there was no answer.

"Told you, eh?"

"Where is he?" Isla asked.

"How would I know, hen? No' his brother, am I?"

Mac swore profusely and strode up to the loiterer. "Look, I don't want to be here any longer than I have to. I've got some money for Mickey. From the boss, eh?"

The man grinned, revealing rotten teeth, and then spat. "Come on, polisman. I'm nae daft."

"You'd be dead. Yeah, we're polis, but we work for the big man. The Black guy. You know who I'm talking about?"

The man's eyes weighed and measured. He knew who Mac was talking about. The name Musa wouldn't be used, and it was a stab in the dark that he might be known for his size and skin colour. The big Black guy who was taking over John Lowe's patch. Even if this area was under Hance Allen's control, or someone else, it wouldn't make a difference to the people on the streets. They would report that one of Musa's boys had been sniffing around. That would make trouble for Musa, which Mac was more than happy to do. A door opened behind them with a soft click. Then another. Mac turned. Number 17 stood open and a middle-aged man with dark stubble on his head and tattoos under his chin was watching them, one hand hidden by the door. The flat opposite was open as well. A guy in a baseball cap and trackie, this one sky blue with white piping down the seams, also hiding one hand behind the door.

So, two armed in front, and the one behind almost certainly armed himself. Even if it was just a Stanley knife. Mac could feel Isla tensing beside him, but he stepped forward nonchalantly.

"You Mickey Plant?" he said.

"Aye. And the big man disnae owe me nothing," Plant said.

"Don't care mate," Mac said. "Just want to talk to you about Adam Glebe. You chivved him at Saughton, remember?"

"Not me, pal," Plant replied.

"Yeah, yeah," Mac said. "I'm not here for you or anything you've done. Just want to find out about Glebe. Can we go in, or do you want to do it out here?"

"You don't work for the big man, then?" said the man at number 16.

"Just want to talk to Mickey. Now close your door before I see something I can't ignore, pal, eh?" Mac said.

"You, alright, Mickey?" the man said.

"Aye. I've got nothing to hide," Plant said, stepping back from the door and moving his left hand behind his back.

"Just get rid of whatever that is while we're not looking,

right?" Mac said, stepping into the flat and brushing past Plant.

Isla followed and Mac was pleased to see she put on an air of total disregard, almost sauntering past Plant and his pals. Just the right attitude. Give people like this a copper who looked nervous, and they'd take advantage. Inside, Mac looked into and quickly away from a bedroom filled with boxes that looked to be phones. Plant closed the door.

"In there," he said.

They stepped into a living room that stank of cigarettes. A TV was on in the corner, paused on a football match. Mac noted the teams and wished he followed the game so he could spoil the final score. Juvenile.

"Don't bother sitting down. What do you want?" Plant said, picking up a packet of cigarettes from a coffee table strewn with an ashtray, a half depleted six-pack of cheap lager and three more high-end smart phones. He casually gathered the latter up and put them in the front pocket of his tracksuit top.

"I already said. Adam Glebe. You got transferred from Saughton to Shotts after he got stabbed," Mac said.

"And?"

"Listen, pal. You want me to come back with a van and half a dozen uniforms? You want your mates to see you dragged down to the station?"

"I've done nothing since I got out. I'm clean."

Isla glanced around the room. Then at the square bulge in Plant's pocket where he'd stashed the phones. He shifted, turning away.

"You want a cup of tea or what?" he said, suddenly hospitable, licking his lips.

"No, we don't. So, you haven't heard about Adam Glebe then?" Mac said.

"Heard what?"

"He's the body that was found in Mary King's Close," Mac said. "And from what I'm told up at Saughton, you had issues with him."

"No, no, no. You're not pinning that on me," Plant said, backing away.

Mac raised his hands and then took a seat in an armchair with threadbare cushions and ring marks on the arms.

"Ok, I don't like you for it, anyway. But you knew him inside, so I need to know what you know. Just calm down."

"I suppose I'll just make that cup of tea, shall I?" Isla suggested, picking up on her boss's tone and mirroring it.

She smiled prettily at Plant. An obvious ploy to Mac's mind, but Plant visibly relaxed, edging back into the room. Mac had spotted the flat's tiny galley kitchen and didn't envy Isla going in there. He doubted she'd find a clean cup, anyway.

"You really work for the big man?" Plant asked, dropping his voice almost to a whisper.

"You don't?" Mac said.

There wasn't much tea making noise coming from the kitchen, but Mac caught a stealthy sound from the opposite direction. Isla sneaking a look into a bedroom. Plant closed the living room door, oblivious to what she was doing, and walked over to Mac, leaning over. Breath steeped in tobacco and cheap lager washed over him.

"He pays for information, aye?"

"He does. You got some, Mickey?" Mac said.

"Maybe. What's it worth to him?" Mickey said, greed and fear warring across his face.

"More if you give me what I need to know about Adam

Glebe. The big man doesn't want that kind of distraction going on, eh?"

Plant's face was liquid with relieved honesty. He grinned.

"Seriously, mate. I didn't have nothing to do with his getting killed. I chivved him in prison 'cause I found out he's a nonce who was fiddling his step-daughter. He deserved it. But, I haven't gone looking for him since I got out of Shotts."

"Where were you last night?" Mac asked.

"Doing business, eh?" Plant winked. "But my dad will give me an alibi."

Mac ran a hand over his face, chuckling. Mickey Plant's alibi was that he'd been out house breaking, but his dad would lie for him, anyway. Trouble was, Mac believed him. This was a low level crook, a thief. Just because he'd stabbed Glebe inside didn't mean he'd do it on the outside. More likely there was someone else in Saughton, an old lag with seniority that had put him up to it.

"The big man doesn't want to waste his time on a snout that gets banged up for murder. What use are you to him in Saughton, Mickey?" Mac demanded.

"I swear I didn't do it. But he needs to know who's looking to take over Mr. Lowe's turf over here. Look, get the CCTV checked on Mr. Android, phone repair shop on Murrayburn Road, just down from the bus depot. They've got a camera at the back. No faces, but someone went over the back wall at just after one this morning. How would I know that if I hadn't been there, eh?"

Mac sighed. There was a kind of twisted logic there.

"If I find out Mr. Android didn't have a break-in last night, I'm coming back," he said, standing.

"Weren't me," Plant said automatically, apparently

forgetting his alibi for murder depended on just the opposite.

"Tell me what you want the big man to know," Mac said, playing along.

"The Russians are moving in. Starting to see some of their boys on the streets. I got some names."

Isla appeared in the living room door, sans tea. Mac glanced towards her and she gave a small shake of the head.

"He'll be in touch, Mickey. Keep your head down, eh?" Mac said, brushing past him on the way to the door.

Chapter Eleven

"ARE you going to report him to Robbery?" Isla asked on the drive back to headquarters.

"No, he could be a useful snout. I'll keep him in my pocket for a bit. I don't think he's our killer."

"Nothing I could find in his bedroom. No bloodied clothes. Nothing that could be used to wrap up a body," Isla confirmed. "Is that ethical, though? Turning a blind eye to a crime, I mean?"

"Not really. But if we arrest him, the commissioner just gets another number added to the crime stats and we lose a potential source who could help us bring down bigger fish."

"Mind you, I can't talk about ethics when I've just stolen from him," Isla said with a cheeky grin.

She reached into her shoulder bag and came out with a chef's knife, holding it with a latex glove wrapped around the handle.

"This is what he stashed behind the door when we came in. So, it's got his DNA on it. If he wasn't involved, it shouldn't show up anywhere and we can check this blade against the wound in Adam Glebe's throat. If we eliminate Plant, we don't have to waste any more time on him."

Mac grinned broadly. "I shouldn't really encourage that sort of behaviour but you'll go far, constable. Bloody good work."

She carefully put the knife back. Then looked at Mac directly.

"Who's the big man? The Black guy?"

Mac considered his reply, staring at the road ahead but conscious of Isla's eyes on him. She was sharp, wouldn't be where she was if she wasn't. Having previously worked for Musa, did she suspect something? If she didn't and Mac told her what he suspected, she might just think Mac was being absurd and tell Musa. It could sound like a conspiracy theory or plain old jealousy.

"I've been hearing about a new player. Muscling in on John Lowe's old territory. Black guy. Don't know that anyone calls him the big guy, but he is, so it seemed likely. Just thought I would chance my arm to get in with Plant. Sorry, should have told you I might try that if we ran into trouble."

He smiled, looking at Isla and hoping he looked contrite. She looked back.

"Oh," she said. "Would have been nice to know, guv. I was a bit worried for a minute there."

"For what it's worth, you didn't look it. You improvised well."

Isla nodded, still frowning though.

"Got a name for this new player?" she asked.

"Why, your old boss looking for intel?" Mac replied, unable to keep the edge from his voice.

Isla looked at him, and when he glanced at her, he could see the question on her face.

"No. Just would be nice to know what you know. I don't work for DCI Musa anymore," Isla replied levelly.

Mac shrugged. "OK, no name, just the description. But Mickey Plant and his mates seem to know. So, looks like it's more than just a rumour I'm hearing, eh?"

"Looks like it. Just clue me in next time, guv."

"Will do. When we get back to the office, get onto Mr. Android and check out Mickey Plant's alibi," he chuckled. "Can't believe the moron tried to alibi himself with another crime. I'm ninety percent sure he isn't our sin-eater, but let's just put a tick in the box, eh?"

"Right. I'm on it. What about the alleged child abuse? Kirkpatrick said his crimes didn't include kids. Want me to track down Glebe's ex and see if there's any truth to it?"

"I'll get Mel on that," Mac said.

It was their next best angle. He wondered if that's what Adam Glebe had felt so guilty about?

"Is that what he confessed to Father Nick, do you think?" Isla asked, echoing Mac's own train of thought.

Mac snorted. "If it did, then the guy's got a lot to answer for."

"A priest can't break the sanctity of the confessional. I grew up Catholic…" Isla said.

"It amounts to protecting a paedo," Mac cut across her. "There's no excuse."

"You're not suggesting Father Nick…?" Isla began.

"No. I'm not," Mac snapped, suddenly angry. "But some religious bollocks shouldn't get in the way of catching a criminal. Whether that's a killer or a paedo. His conscience might be clear, but what about the girl Glebe was abusing?"

"Allegedly," Isla said.

"Aye, allegedly," Mac sighed. "We'll find out soon enough."

He knew his patience was thin at the best of times and Isla had brought up the very subject that would snap it. He had no concept of how Nick Cass could put the rules of his faith ahead of protecting a child. Man-made rules too, he was pretty sure. Unless there was some proven divine instructions in the bible telling the Catholic Church how to run confessions. Isla might be a believer and might even be offended by his attitude, but he had a hard time feeling any kind of guilt about that. The case had moved on, though. They were looking for potential child abuse as a trigger for the killing. Revenge still seemed likely. As they neared the Brunswick Road headquarters, Mac realised Isla had been quiet for a while. He grudgingly accepted he might have snapped a little hard.

"Good work on that knife, by the way," he said, gruffly, not meeting her eye as they pulled into the car park to the rear of the building. "That was quick thinking. Maybe take it to the lab personally and get it done as a priority. Walk it through. Might lessen the chances of anyone asking awkward questions about where we got it from. Once it's locked up in the evidence room, no-one's going to ask questions."

Isla smiled. "Right, guv," she said in a tone that Mac took to mean all was well.

At least he hoped so.

———

MAC TRIED Clio several times that afternoon. He got her voicemail and couldn't do more than tell her to call him urgently. This might just be how she felt being friends with him, having more conversations with voicemail than the actual person. She had a career too, but he selfishly assumed his was the only job that could take over your life, pushing people to the periphery. A text from an unknown number had arrived not long after he had got back to the office and finished briefing Kai and Mel about the developments of the case. It had just contained an image of a clock. Simple message. Clock is ticking. No surprises for guessing who the sender was. He began a text to Clio and discarded it. If she was too busy to check voicemail, she wouldn't be replying to texts. Unless something had already happened?

That got him half out of his chair, wanting to drive immediately over to Old Moray House, where Clio had her office. Then he sat again, grinding his teeth in frustration. Putting his phone down on the desk, he took out the encrypted one, unlocking it from memory. Give Musa some red meat. Give him a name. And get Clio to safety while Musa was chewing on it. Someone on the phone who had it coming to them. A name came back to him: Doug Griffiths, a fixer and formerly an armed robber. Assault, domestic abuse, murder. Griffiths had spent more time inside than out in his life and was a rabid sectarian bigot, to boot. His name was on the phone for some cover-ups that Lowe had orchestrated for him. That was just the scumbag to throw to Musa as a grass.

Mac picked up his own phone and called the unknown number. It would be a burner. Musa wouldn't want to have conversations on a traceable line. Not when he was sober, anyway. It barely rang once before it was answered.

"I've got a name." Mac tried to put some kind of submissiveness into his voice. "Hello?"

Nothing but breathing.

"Just leave her alone, ok?" Mac hated even pretending to fear Musa.

The truth was, though, he was scared. Not for himself, scared of what Musa could do to Clio and Maia. Scared of what he would do. Mac didn't think there were any limits to Musa. Not if he was serious about his ambitions. That fear just made Mac angrier. More resentful. He hadn't always been an entirely honest copper. He'd never exactly been bent, just not always in agreement with the aims and values of Police Scotland. A dead gangster was preferable to one locked up for a finite amount of time. Although carrying a little guilt, he'd lost no sleep and had no nightmares about John Lowe. Walking away and leaving him to a serial killer. John Lowe had been hurried on his way to hell and deserved it. Musa deserved it too. He felt pain in his fingers, realised he was gripping the phone so hard the corners were digging in.

"I'm listening," Musa replied.

"Dougie Griffiths," Mac said, after hesitating for just long enough to make it seem it was being dragged out of him.

There was a chuckle at the other end, then the line was dead. Mac slammed his phone on the desk. The screen was already cracked. Mac had a bad habit of breaking phones. There were fifty-three unread emails. Another one joined the pile. Meredith Blakeley from Police Scotland PR over in Glasgow. Mac felt trapped by the tiny office, by the chains of administration. Clio and Maia were in danger. He itched to be out and doing something. Screw it. He pushed his chair back so hard it banged into the radiator on the wall behind him. Grabbing his coat, he dropped the encrypted phone into the inside pocket. He snatched open the door, leaving it wide open as he strode out, shrugging on his coat as he walked.

"I'm away out. Call me with any developments," he said to the team at large.

Isla was over at the University of Edinburgh Hospital where forensic labs were maintained for police use. Kai and Mel were at their desks. Kai held his hand up, thumb uppermost.

"Guv, did you see the email from DCS Carmichael...?" Mel began.

"Saw it. Will deal with it," Mac called over his shoulder, raising a hand over his head in goodbye, not stopping.

"It was marked 'response required'," Mel called out.

Mac turned as he shouldered through the double doors to the corridor. Rogue's grin.

"Aye, but it never said by when."

It occurred to Mac that heading directly for Clio's place of work was a good way to confirm to Musa that she was important to him. If Musa had someone following him, anyway. But if she wouldn't answer her phone, he didn't know what else he could do. He drove too fast, circling out to the east of Holyrood to avoid the traffic heading that way from the direction of the Castle and the Royal Mile. Arthur's Seat loomed over him to the left as he took Queen's Drive, getting briefly up to sixty before catching up to a string of traffic. There was a sizeable gap behind him, and as he slowed, his eyes flicked from the road ahead to that behind. As the traffic concertinaed, he saw nothing that looked like an unmarked police car. If Musa was having him followed by non-police, there would be no way to spot the vehicle, anyway. Approaching a junction, he turned without indicating and, finding himself on an open, if narrow road, floored the accelerator.

Brightly coloured tourists in Day-Glo Hi-Vis and woolly hats turned to look as the Audi roared along the section of Queen's Drive that circled Arthur's Seat to the east. No sign of another vehicle in his rear-view mirror, though anyone following would know exactly where Mac would end up. There were no turn offs on this road. It circled the hill. A mini roundabout forced him to slow, and he changed direction again, circling back around the east side of the hill, passing Duddingston Loch in the blink of an eye. At that point, the city was screened from view by the hills to either side of the loch. He might have been in the highlands. For the few seconds it took to pass the loch, Mac was tense. No traffic and little footfall, the perfect spot for an ambush. Or maybe his paranoia was working overtime. Then Edinburgh was roaring towards him again, the hills to the right disappearing with their scrub grass and heather to be replaced by residential streets, which had the air of a village absorbed by the city.

He sped past terraces of eighties houses in white and black roughcast and timber fronts, then sandstone. The road narrowed and Mac was forced to keep his eyes ahead, reducing his speed down almost to the limit. In his career, he'd completed advanced driving courses, and it had added to a sense of confidence on the road that would probably end up in a fiery wreck one day. In the meantime, he drove on his instincts. No sign of a tail and he didn't think anyone could have predicted his route in order to get ahead of him. He worked his way back toward Holyrood more by instinct than accuracy, keeping the hill to his left until he'd almost reached the point where he had raced off on his diversion.

Splats of rain began to hit the windscreen, and Mac felt the familiar tightness of the chest. He squeezed the steering wheel purely for the sensation of the warm leather, blasted the AC up to get a hit of cold air to his face. All were sensations to anchor him to the present, to ward off the ghost odour of wet soil and rotten wood that always came with the sight and sound of rain.

"Should move to bloody Jamaica then," he muttered to himself, angry at his own perceived weakness.

He was getting close to Old Moray House now, turning onto Canongate after passing the palace with its ever-present screen of tourists in front. As he saw the ancient building come up on his left, he bumped the car up onto the pavement and stopped the engine. Hands would be shaking if they weren't white knuckled on the wheel. Someone harangued him about his driving, but he ignored them. Didn't even register if it was male or female. A mantra went through his head, a reminder of the present. A shield against the past. Mac had never wanted a cigarette more. His hands trembled as he took out the vape and drew long and hard on it.

"I'll get him, Iona. I'll get him," he promised to the ghost that was never far from his side.

Chapter Twelve

"EXCUSE ME, you can't go in there. She's in a meeting!" said the receptionist, whose desk was in a small anteroom in front of the door bearing Clio's name and title.

Mac registered the title of doctor spelled out in neat black lettering against the white painted door. He knew Clio had her doctorate. It just never entered his consciousness. She wasn't Doctor Cliodna Wray, faculty head, Centre for Celtic Studies. Just Clio. He rapped sharply on the door once, then opened it. Clio sat behind a desk in an office marginally larger than the cubby her receptionist used. Two people sat before her desk, both holding large A4 notebooks. A man with greying hair, tweed and scuffed brogues and a woman with an array of ribbons tied into her dark hair and glasses on a chain. Clio was in the middle of speaking and, for a moment, just stared at Mac, openmouthed. He grinned, full on rogue, trying to take the edge off.

"Hi Clio, can I have a word?"

"I tried to stop him, Doctor Wray; he just barged right

past me," the receptionist said. "Should I call the police or something?"

"He is the police," Clio said, sitting back.

She wore a blouse and trousers instead of her customary jeans and tee. Like an office worker. The room was furnished with tall bookcases, their shelves tightly packed. A laptop sat open at an angle facing Clio and her hands had been hovering over the keyboard.

"I'm in the middle of a faculty meeting, Mac. Can it wait? Maybe we can grab a coffee later," Clio said.

"No," Mac said, hands in trouser pockets, eyes locked on Clio. "We need to talk."

He could feel the curious stares of the others. Could almost feel the pressure of the questions they had. He realised he was behaving badly, throwing his weight around unnecessarily. It wasn't as if anything was going to happen to Clio in broad daylight and in front of her colleagues. But what about Maia? That was what drove Mac to charge into Clio's workplace. An anxiety that Maia was vulnerable, and it was because of him.

"I'm sure we do," Clio said. "Well, I won't say no to the police when they need help. It doesn't happen often."

Despite calling him Mac, Clio was adopting a cool tone, behaving as though Mac was just a police officer. Not a friend.

"Malcolm, Cynthia. Could we pick this up tomorrow? Speak to Andrea about times. I really want to hear about the Rotterdam Conference, Malcolm, and the paper you have for The Journal of European Celtic Studies, Cynthia."

"When it is convenient," Malcolm said with an edge of testiness to his voice and a side look at Mac.

He got up and Mac took his seat the moment he was out of it, making himself comfortable. Clio was frowning as she stood and shook hands with Malcolm and Cynthia, who were ushered to the door by the receptionist. When the door was closed and they were alone, Clio stormed back to her desk and swung around on Mac.

"You've got some nerve. Not a word from you for months and then you're disrupting my work, making demands on my time as though you're the most important person here. You're like a bloody bull in a china shop. What was that all about? Are you trying to get me fired?"

"If it was just you, I'd have waited outside. It's Maia…"

Mac had intended to finish by saying that she was fine in all likelihood and that he was just playing safe. Something in him didn't register the fact that the words 'it's Maia' would set off an unstoppable chain reaction of anxiety in Clio. She gripped the desk.

"What the hell do you mean? Where is she? What's happened?"

Each word was pitched higher until she was almost shouting by the end. Her eyes were wide with fright, and Mac regretted not being more circumspect. He grimaced.

"She's fine. Nothing's happened. It's…"

"Jesus Christ, Mac! Don't do that, you bloody idiot!" Clio raged; face momentarily falling into shaking hands.

Mac sat forward; concerned he had scared her, but not seeing how he could have started the conversation any other way.

"I know nothing has happened to Maia because, if it had, you would be all official, and probably not alone. You're not. You're barging into my office, throwing your weight around. Basically, being you. But, when a policeman starts a conversation with a mother by saying 'it's your child,' the immediate reaction is fear and panic," Clio said, letting her hands fall. "Just think about that, will you?"

"I'm sorry, Clio. Nothing's happened to Maia," Mac said, biting his tongue over the word 'but' that wanted to break free.

Clio waited, folding her arms. Her dark hair was tied back in a ponytail, looking severe and professional. Neither of those looks suited her. Mac saw Clio as something akin to a spirit of nature. He was the opposite, a city boy who liked the security of concrete under his feet and the knowledge that anything he wanted was an app away, no matter what time it was.

"Do you want a cuppa?" Clio asked, giving him a tight smile. "I have someone to make them for me now."

"Aye, thanks," Mac said, recognising a peace overture.

Clio pressed a button on an intercom on her desk and asked for two teas. Then she sat in the chair next to Mac.

"Tell me," she said.

Mac had rehearsed this explanation in his head on the drive over to Clio. How he would explain that because he was trying to solve the mystery of his sister's murder, he had now endangered both Clio and her daughter. There was no hedging. He wouldn't insult Clio by trying to put a spin on it. It was his fault. Had he behaved entirely by the book, then the encrypted phone would have been submitted as evidence and Musa would have no reason to go after him. But Mac had wanted John Lowe to receive punishment for all the misery he had brought to the city. For all the people whose lives he'd ruined with his drug dealing and prostitution and all the other sordid and heinous crimes he was involved in. One blind eye led to another. Allowing a man to be murdered led to keeping another secret, which led to another. Now he was burdened with their weight and about to share it with Clio. He felt like a piece of crap.

"I told you about the…phone," he said. "Well, the head

of the Organised Crime Task Force wants it. They don't know it exists, but they do know I have a source of intel that has led to multiple arrests. They want that intel and they're now applying pressure on me to give up my source," Mac said.

"And this is the corrupt officer you mentioned before?" Clio asked.

"Right."

"How does that affect Maia and me?" Clio asked.

"Because he knows there's a connection between you and me," Mac said, stating the fact as plainly as he could.

He watched the realisation dawn on Clio's face, and it made him cringe inside. It was the dawning of horror and the visceral fear of a mother for her child. The kind of fear you don't get to experience until your life is completely in someone else's hands. Someone with reason to watch it all burn.

"This…officer. He's dangerous?"

Mac nodded a single, sharp motion. Clio laughed bitterly, swearing repeatedly and with gusto.

"I don't believe this. This is my reward for helping you. Mac, I can't take another sabbatical. I'll lose my job. Maia needs stability as well. We've had to move house recently. After Karen…left and I got her job, our home life isn't the same. I'm struggling to give her the time she needs. I'm already hanging on by my fingernails and now you drop this shit on me?"

Mac took the blows, feeling every word like a baseball bat to the head. She was right. He wouldn't hide from it. This was the consequence of corruption. Just because he'd acted with the best of intentions didn't change what it was. He'd let a man die so he could find out who killed Iona. That was wrong. It was corruption, and he deserved to lose his job. At that moment, if coming clean to Carmichael and handing over the phone would call off Musa, Mac would have done it without hesitation. But he doubted it would. Musa would only be stopped when he was inside or dead.

"I've bought us some time. Given him a name that'll take him time to chase down. I want you and Maia to go somewhere he won't find you."

Mac was avoiding using Musa's name, wanting to keep Clio's knowledge small to make her as little of a threat to the unscrupulous bastard as possible.

"I can't go anywhere, Mac," Clio said, an edge of hysteria entering her voice.

There was a knock at the door and the receptionist brought in two cups of tea, holding the mugs together by the handles in one hand, a pot of sugar packets, and UHT milk in the other. Clio cleared her throat, smiling her thanks and waiting for the receptionist to leave before turning back to Mac.

"How can I go anywhere? I'm not about to go running back to my dad for money and if I take time off, I'll need it. I don't have a choice but to be here."

"And I can't get you police protection. That would be an official request and would require evidence of a threat, which I don't have. You and Maia will need to move in with me," he said.

Clio scoffed. "No, that's not going to work. Maia needs stability, I told you. I can't think of a way to explain why we're leaving our home to move in with you that won't scare her."

"Just tell her it's a wee holiday..." Mac began, not convinced this part was as big a problem as Clio was making out.

"She's fourteen. She's not stupid," Clio said.

Mac ran a hand through his hair. That had seemed the simplest plan to him. He would know exactly where Clio and Maia were and could protect them. He hadn't expected Clio to push back.

"Alright, I'll move in with you. Tell Maia my flat's being redecorated," he said with exasperation.

"You wouldn't last five minutes at my place," Clio said. "It's chaotic at the best of times. You'd go mad."

"I'd cope."

Mac leaned towards her, holding her gaze. "Clio, this is my fault. There is nothing I won't do to protect you."

"Give up the phone," Clio said.

Mac pulled away, turning his head. He didn't want to say it. Didn't want to make a liar out of himself because he'd meant it. But surrendering the phone wouldn't eliminate the threat. He knew too much.

"That won't work," Mac said, quietly.

"You mean you don't want to do it," Clio said, her voice unusually hard.

Mac looked at her, seeing the stony resolve on his friend's face. He realised when it came to Maia, friendships didn't matter any longer. There were only two people in Clio's world. Her and Maia.

"I mean it wouldn't work," Mac said, harshly. "I know too much, right? Until I can neutralise this guy, until I can figure it out, you and Maia are in danger. So, I will protect you, ok? Decision made."

He was angry, but not at Clio. He was angry at himself and at Musa. Clio was taking the brunt of it, unfairly. He sighed, putting his face into his hands for a moment before berating himself for his weakness and straightening up. Clio had tears in her eyes and the sight cut him to the quick.

"I'm..." he began.

"Don't," Clio said, holding up a hand. "Don't say you're sorry. I know you are. It doesn't help. My life is thrown into turmoil again because I'm friends with you."

"So walk away," Mac said. "Your dad can help both of you make a fresh start. A long way from here. Get out while you can."

Clio was silent for a long time. Mac half hoped she was about to agree. Lean on daddy and use his money to start again without the drag effect of Callum McNeill in her life. Only half though. The idea of losing Clio left him feeling empty.

"And leave you to face this shit on your own?" Clio said. "Do you really think I can?"

"Don't worry, I'm used to it," Mac said.

Clio punched his shoulder and put some real effort into it. Mac grunted, just biting back an actual yelp. She was glaring at him.

"The Mac I know doesn't wallow in self-pity," she said. "Pull yourself together and start thinking of a way out of this where we all survive."

For a moment, Mac glared back at her with a ferocity that matched her own. Then laughter welled up in him. His mouth twitched. So did hers.

"You're such a…" Mac began.

Clio raised an eyebrow.

"Good friend," he finished.

"You're lucky to have me," Clio said, smiling. "Maia is going to be bouncing off the walls when she hears Uncle Mac is coming to stay."

Chapter Thirteen

THREE DAYS PASSED in which Mac found himself, strange as it was, settling into the kind of domestic life he hadn't known since Siobhan. Clio and Maia had not long moved from the village-like suburb of Cramond to Corstorphine. A distance of just a few miles closer to the city, but still firmly in leafy suburbia. Their house was a bungalow in a cul-de-sac with SUVs and large German saloons in the drives. Cottage gardens and white-haired dog walkers abounded, making Mac feel as though the city he knew was a long way off. This was not a place to be afraid of bent coppers or deranged ritual killers. He expected it to make him feel antsy. Instead, it felt as though a weight were lifted from him. Maia had short, spiky hair dyed jet black to match her eyeliner and clothes. When Mac arrived on the first night, she had been wearing a Black Sabbath t-shirt and had an acoustic guitar in one hand. Two years previously, she would have rushed him and hugged him tight enough to make his ribs creak. Now she nodded an acknowledgement and tried very hard to be cool.

"How long do you think you'll be staying for?" Clio asked him on the third morning.

Maia had left for the bus to school a few minutes earlier. Mac had wanted to drive her, but Clio didn't want Maia thinking there was something wrong. Something she needed to be afraid of. Maia put on a brave face, acting older than her years, but Mac could see the chinks in the armour and the scared little girl underneath. He had offered to intimidate any teacher who was giving her a hard time because of her ADHD. Clio had looked like she wanted to slap him. Maia had seemed to consider the option. Mac was only half joking.

"I thought a week. While I figure out how to manage things," Mac said, sipping the black coffee carefully.

"Not that I don't enjoy having you here. Maia certainly does. She's not been out of her room this much since we moved here. Though I blame you for her musical tastes."

Mac grinned. "I've gone to some trouble not to be followed here and I've seen no sign of surveillance. This street is ideal for spotting anything out of the ordinary. No through traffic."

Clio shuddered. "It gives me the shivers to think someone might be watching us."

"I don't think they are. This guy isn't the sort to make empty threats, but the lead I gave him isn't one he'll get to the end of quickly. I'm sorry to have put the two of you in the middle of this."

Clio waved away the apology. "I'm mostly over it. I only resent you a little, like when I notice the same car behind me for longer than five minutes. Or I think someone is looking at me oddly. Or if I can't remember whether I locked the front door…yeah, only a few dozen times a day."

"I'm glad to hear it," Mac dead-panned. "It won't be forever, Clio. I'm just being careful."

"I know. And part of me thinks that if this is what it takes to see you more than once every three months, then it's worth it. Almost," Clio replied, so poker-faced that Mac couldn't be completely sure she wasn't being serious.

He decided not to mention the blue Vauxhall hatchback he'd noticed the previous evening. It had caught his eye a few times as he'd driven from the office to his flat to pick up some clothes. Then he'd spied it again as he headed west across the northern outskirts of the city towards Corstophine, the Firth of Forth to his right, heavy and leaden. He'd headed to Clio's house via the scenic route to test if he was, in fact, being followed. It had vanished by the time he pulled into the airport at the end of a long detour. There had been no sign of it when he headed back towards Corstorphine. But he'd noted the reg and had it checked on the ANPR database. A rental. Made sense for it to be near the airport then. Maybe a tourist at the end of their holiday had decided to see a bit more of the city before catching their flight.

"You haven't noticed anything that I need to know about?" Clio asked after a moment's silence.

She looked at him, eyes sharp and focused. Like she could read his mind. Even Siobhan hadn't been as canny as Clio could be.

"Nothing," he lied.

No sense worrying her. They both left a few minutes later. Mac felt the familiar weight firmly settling itself onto his shoulders as Clio locked the front door and he looked up and down the street from the end of the garden path. The same cars parked on the same drives as were always present at this time of day. A pickup truck with the name of a gardening service on the door and a trailer full of tools was parked half on the pavement, two doors up. A man with a baseball cap and overalls was unloading a wheelbarrow, and he called out a good morning when he caught Mac's eye. Clio was the one to return it, using the man's name. Mac dismissed him. He followed Clio's Nissan into the city, keeping far enough back to note anyone who might be tailing her. No sign of the blue rental or anyone else lingering for too long. When Clio was pulling into the car park of Old Moray House, Mac drove on, heading for the palace and then turning left to head north towards Brunswick Street.

Kai and Isla weren't at their desks when Mac arrived. Mel Barland was. Mac glanced at the desks across from hers and she shrugged.

"No idea, guv."

"What? Where the hell are they? Didn't they leave a message? Have you called them?"

Mel just looked at him.

"Of course you've called them. Just ignore all that. I'll deal with them when they decide to show up. So, where are we with the Glebe case?" Mac asked.

"I went to see the next of kin that Saughton had on file. His ex-partner is Jennifer McCrae. She's in Livingstone now, used to live in Sighthill when she was with Glebe. She didn't know he had given her name as next of kin and wouldn't let me in the house. Said she hadn't seen him for years before he went inside and he's now in hell where he belongs."

"Motive then," Mac said, sitting in Isla's empty chair.

"Yes. From the limited interaction I had with her, she really seems to hate him."

"We need to go back out there and establish her whereabouts at the time of the murder. Also, Glebe was stabbed in prison because of a rumour he was sexually abusing his step-daughter. That needs confirming."

Mel nodded, making notes.

"Is she religious?"

"She was wearing a rosary, so I thought Catholic," Mel said. "I paid a visit to the nearest Catholic church I could find. Tracked down the priest, Father Michael Trent. He confirmed that Jennifer and her daughter are part of his flock. The daughter has been confirmed and they both attend mass every week. She has a criminal record for assault and disorderly conduct going back twenty years, when she was a teenager. Nothing but a couple of cautions for disorderly conduct relating to drink since then. Last one was about five years ago, got into a fight on a hen night."

"Sounds promising," Mac said. "Let's pay her a surprise visit today and give her the choice of talking to us at home or coming in here to do it."

"Actually, guv, I'll reach out to Father Michael first I think. He has some influence with Jennifer and her partner Brendan, it seems. It was her partner who brought Jennifer back to the church, apparently. Anyway, the local priest might be able to smooth our way a bit?"

Mac nodded, liking the idea. He wouldn't have thought of it, just turned up with his badge and bullied his way into the house with a threat to come back with blue lights and uniforms. Mel had, as usual, found the softer approach.

"Who's the partner?" Mac asked.

"Brendan Halloran. Born in Belfast and according to the PSNI, he had a record over there for possession and did some small time for it. Came over here to work as a brickie and has been clean ever since," Mel said, consulting notes.

"Any history or capacity for violence?" Mac asked.

"No record of it," Mel said. "And I didn't get to meet him. Father Michael said he volunteers at a local boxing club for kids, though, so I'm assuming he knows his way around a ring."

"So Jennifer McCrae had a reason to want Adam Glebe dead and a boyfriend who used to box. Enough to be pursuing, eh?"

"What about Mickey Plant? You haven't been too clear on why he's out of the picture as a suspect," Mel asked.

She'd raised it at the briefing after Mac and Isla had been to see Plant and Mac had dismissed the question, not wanting Plant looked at too closely.

"He's not the type to dress up a revenge killing. Doesn't have the imagination or intelligence. Nothing but a burglar who gets caught a lot. He's not our man," Mac said, meeting Mel's eyes briefly before using the boards behind her as an excuse to look away. He got up, hands in trouser pockets and walked up to them, running his eyes over the crime scene pictures and new images of their latest suspects.

"His alibi checks out," Mel said. "Isla checked the CCTV. Mr. Android was broken into and there were images on CCTV of someone going over the back wall of the property. Can't prove it was him, though. His dad and his dad's girlfriend and two of his dad's friends all gave statements putting him at his dad's house in Slateford when we believe Adam Glebe was killed. Obvious lies if Mickey was breaking into a shop that night but…"

"But hard to prove otherwise. It's not him. His DNA wasn't found at the site and the knife taken from his flat wasn't the murder weapon. There was an obvious nick in the blade that would have left a mark on the wound," Mac said, restating the forensics findings that Isla had reported back. "We've covered this, Mel. Let's move on."

Mickey Plant knew something about Musa. The 'big man,' as Plant called him. Mac had referred to him as the 'Black guy' to be sure Plant and his pals were talking about Musa. Now, Mac didn't want Plant lifted. But he couldn't tell Mel that. She was watching him. He could feel it. He turned to look at her. She wasn't convinced, opened her mouth to speak, and the doors opened. Kai and Isla came in.

"Afternoon," Mac called out drily, grateful for the distraction.

"Sorry, guv," Isla said. "Car trouble."

"Car share, was it?" Mac asked.

"Isla gave me a ring when her car wouldn't start. I picked her up," Kai said, looking Mac in the eye in a way Isla was struggling to.

Mac nodded. "You know the rules. I don't care what you get up to in your own time. Just as long as it doesn't affect the way you do your jobs. That includes being here on time. If you're going to be late, then you call in. Understood? We're in the middle of a murder investigation here. I don't need to be wasting my time wondering where you two are and what you're doing."

Kai nodded, and Isla blushed. Mel glanced at Mac. Of course, she knew the two of them had paired up. Mac was always the last to figure out these things. Truthfully, he didn't care, though part of him hoped Isla wouldn't go the same way as all of Kai's other girlfriends. She was a decent girl. He put it from his mind. It wasn't relevant. Not at the moment, anyway. If it compromised the way the team worked, then he'd have to step in.

"How did you get on with tracking Adam Glebe's movements before he died?" he asked Kai, who was hanging up his overcoat.

"Not great. He stays at a scatter flat from the council out in Wester Hailes. None of his neighbours wanted to say anything about him, even the ones who could speak English. To be honest, guv, they don't really know him. He hasn't been there long enough."

He sat down, swinging his suit jacket over the back of his chair.

"Did he have a job to go to or has he signed on? What about his social worker meetings?" Mac said.

"He received a subsistence payment on release. Application for universal credit was made shortly after," Isla said, fishing a notebook from her bag and flicking back and forth through the pages. "Paperwork was also going through for a Community Care Grant from the Scottish Welfare Fund. He didn't have a job yet but had applied for Jobseeker's allowance."

Mac nodded. "And the social worker?"

Isla flicked over a couple of pages. "Angus Douglas. He met with Glebe when he was released and took him to the flat. Sorted out the money and paperwork I mentioned before and saw to it he had enough food. He was supposed to meet Glebe again the following week but had an emergency, so couldn't make it. He called Glebe to rearrange and Glebe told him he was taking a week or so away. Mr Douglas got the impression it was some sort of holiday. He was supposed to be back already, but Angus Douglas didn't hear from him. Went round the flat, but there was no answer."

Mac felt a familiar tingle of excitement. His subconscious telling him this was significant. For the moment, all thoughts of Musa, Clio and even Iona faded to a background hum. The scent was suddenly strong in his nose.

"Convenient for the killer that Glebe was going away

and wouldn't be missed for a while," Mac said. "Gave them a good window of time to kill him and arrange disposal of the body. Who would know Glebe was taking a break somewhere?"

"Obviously, Angus Douglas," Isla said.

"Any mates he had? Although I haven't found any yet," Kai said.

"Anyone he was meeting while he was off?" Mel suggested. "People take holidays to see family or friends they don't normally get a chance to."

Mac looked at Kai, who shrugged. "If he had any, I couldn't find them. No social media. No messages or calls other than spam on his phone."

"He's only just out of prison," Mel said. "I doubt he'd have any of that in place yet. His old friends might not still be around. I'm still trying to find family members."

"So, he was alone. God knows how he filled the days," Mac said, thinking aloud. "Wait, was he going to church?"

He got blank looks back and clenched his teeth. They'd all forgotten that Glebe was Catholic. So had he, which was the only thing stopping him from losing his temper with them. Too much on his shoulders. Too much in his head, crowding out the basics of an investigation. He ran his hand through his hair, giving himself a few seconds to calm down.

"He discovered his faith inside, 'saw the light' apparently, and was making confessions to the padre in Saughton. We have to assume he kept that up when he got out. The local priest might know more about him than we do."

"Want me to ring around the Catholic churches near where he was staying, guv?" Isla asked.

"No, I'll do it," Mac replied, still irritated, and snapping his answer more than he'd intended. "Speak to Angus

Douglas again; see if you can find out where Glebe was going on his week off. Kai, try and track down any old friends or acquaintances and any family. He must have been going somewhere and seeing someone. Mel, you're on Glebe's ex, get her to tell you where she was at the time of Glebe's death. Throw the partner in for good measure and prove the child abuse rumours one way or another. OK, as our new boss is fond of saying, we all have actionable tasks. Let's circle back before the end of the day."

Kai groaned at the cringey management-speak and Isla chuckled dutifully. As Mac headed for his office, he felt Mel watching him.

Chapter Fourteen

THE THIRD PRIEST Mac called recognised the name Adam Glebe as belonging to his parish. He was Father Neil Fitzsimmons, and the church was St Aiden's. He grabbed his suit jacket, checked the encrypted phone was in the pocket, and headed out of the office. Mel's suspicions were added to the weight he already carried. She was a good detective and adept at reading people, him especially, and he couldn't give her a good enough reason for not liking Mickey Plant for the killing of Adam Glebe. Nothing apart from the fact that Mickey Plant was a typical ned criminal from a family that considered the polis to the be the enemy. It didn't fit his character or criminal history to be carrying out rituals. But Mel knew as well as Mac that someone could have paid Mickey to do it that way. Mac thought it unlikely. His gut told him he was looking for someone else, but Mel was a professional. She followed the evidence.

It was a problem for another day. Mac wasn't about to give up a snout who knew something about Musa and his takeover of John Lowe's criminal empire.

"I'm away to see a priest. Call me with any updates," he said to Mel as he passed her desk.

"Right, guv," she replied, almost sounding like her old self.

"Later, guv," Kai replied without looking up from his screen.

Mac didn't hear Isla or notice the omission. Mel had been deputised to give Meredith Blakeley a press conference. It kept the press officer off Mac's back. The last thing he wanted at the best of times was to appear in front of cameras. Mel didn't like it any better. Mac checked his phone for messages from Clio as he descended in the lift. A thumbs up to signify she'd arrived at the office safely. Mac checked on Maia's phone. Clio had given him the sign in details to track her. They hadn't told Maia for fear she would do something rash out of sheer teen rebellion. Like ditch the phone or the SIM. The tracker showed her at school. Mac wondered if Musa had caught up with Dougie Griffiths yet. Dougie would deny being a grass of course, but Musa would have access to more powerful means of interrogation than Mac. He wouldn't just take Dougie's word for it. Mac thought it would be several days before Musa decided Mac had lied. Shame for Dougie Griffiths, but he had it coming from way back.

Heading out onto Brunswick Street, Mac noticed the blue rental car within a minute. He'd memorised the reg. Could be a different customer by now. But what were the chances two different renters would be going the same way as him? Mac considered his options as he joined the traffic on Leith Walk, heading south towards Waverley. Tram lines ran down the middle of the two lanes. The buildings were neat terraces of sandstone, blotchy tan of varying shades. The pale brick in between the tram lines looked bright and new, giving the street the appearance of cleanliness. His follower made it out of the junction two cars behind him. At this time of day, traffic oozed along towards the train station. Mac had time to think. Neither he nor his tail were going anywhere. No side streets to dive down until they got to the Playhouse. That gave Mac an idea. There was a back road that ran behind the theatre. There were blocks of flats down there and service entrances to others on Leith Walk.

As he came up to the junction, he indicated in plenty of time, wanting the car following to see the turn. Seconds later, the other driver indicated. Mac had taken the opportunity to look at the man following. Baseball cap shadowing the face. Mac had an impression of round cheeks. Grey hoodie. Nondescript, giving nothing away. Making the turn, the road dipped into a u-turn, running behind the buildings Mac had just driven past. Behind and at a lower level. One side was impassable, with trees and thick undergrowth held back behind an ancient stone wall. The other side was the concrete edifice of the theatre's backside and a covered car park. Mac put his foot down, seeing a layby come up on the right and swinging the Audi into it. He got out and ran across the road into an alley opposite and crouched behind a small skip size wheelie bin. After a minute, the blue car appeared, drove past the mouth of the alley and the layby before stopping, the driver obviously having seen the parked Audi.

Mac moved quickly from his cover to the passenger door of the blue car, opened it, and got in. Very bloody risky! A good way to get stabbed if he'd misjudged the kind of man who was following him. But he didn't think a contract man or any serious gangster would kick about in an airport rental. Musa's boys would be travelling in pairs and this man was alone. So, a bloody risk was right, but a calculated one. Mac snatched the man's hat from his head. He was looking into a green-eyed face that could have been twenty-five or thirty-five. Boyish and round, smooth-cheeked. The kind of face owned by a man with a skin-care regime. His hair was short and fair, styled and coloured, not barbered. The hoodie and matching bottoms looked new. Mac stared for a moment. He'd seen him before, a long while ago, but couldn't place him. He took out his warrant card.

"DCI McNeill, Police Scotland Serious Crimes Unit. But then you already know that, don't you? Park up just behind my car and let's have a chat."

To his credit, the man didn't panic. After a brief instance in which his eyes widened to the size of saucers, he nodded and carefully reversed, parking the car behind Mac's. A phone was held in a cradle attached to the windscreen. Mac realised the phone was filming the driver. A dashcam was also present, connected via a USB cable.

"I need to inform you I am recording for my YouTube channel," the man said calmly, with only the slightest hint of a tremor in his voice.

"Well, you'll need to rethink that, pal, because I'm not about to give consent to be filmed," Mac replied. "Who are you, and why are you following me?"

"It's not a crime."

"Didn't say it was. But I'm a senior police officer and you've been stalking me. You're lucky it was just me hiding behind a bin and not a tactical response team. Now while I'm holding onto my temper, gonna tell me who the hell you are?"

"Don't you remember me? My name is Ramsey Jones. I'm a journalist," the man said.

That name slotted into a niche in Mac's memory, clicked into place with a resonance he felt through his body.

It took a second for him to see the full picture and what it related to. The last time he'd seen this man was in an interrogation room, a terrified snivelling wreck. A far cry from the well groomed and put together man sitting before him.

"You were the one that bought crime scene pictures of—"

"Suicide. Not a crime scene. It was a suicide. I was *given* the pictures by a police officer. A secret drop off point. I never met him." Jones said, quickly.

Mac glanced at the camera. He was in shot.

"Fine. You *obtained in breach of confidence,* scenes from a young man's suicide. Now, why have you been following me?"

"This footage is automatically backed up to the cloud. Even if you take or destroy my phone, it will still exist," Jones said, as Mac glanced at the phone again.

Mac sighed, leaning back against the passenger door, and raising his hands.

"Happy? I'm not going to touch you or your phone. I know following me about isn't breaking the law unless you are actively threatening me. What I want to know is what you're after, eh?"

Jones still had his hands on the steering wheel. He swallowed and nodded. Then he reached up and turned off the dashcam. He stopped the phone recording, taking it out of its cradle and slipping it into a pocket. Mac knew Jones was trying to avoid incrimination. His heart rate stepped up a notch, waiting for the revelation. Was Jones investigating Musa? Or Lowe's business operations?

"You found a body in Mary King's Close," Jones said.

"As everyone in Scotland knows, thanks to STV," Mac replied.

"There was evidence of someone eating and drinking

over the body. Specifically bread and beer," Jones said, licking his lips and glancing at Mac.

Mac didn't reply. Nor did he take his eyes from Jones. The journalist was slender, a touch below average height. He had an English accent, northern, and spoke like an educated man, avoiding colloquialisms and dialect. There was a sense of entitlement to his actions that made Mac think of the elitism associated with public schools. Someone who decided their goals justified any action. Within the law, anyway. Mac decided to lean into Jones' obvious nervousness.

"Mr Jones, I must make you aware that you do not have to say anything, but anything you do say may be given in evidence…"

"I'm not recording. You don't have to be so official," Jones protested.

Mac went right on reading him his rights.

"Consider yourself under caution, Mr Jones. Now, explain in detail what you've just said."

"You mean about the sin-eating?" Jones replied, a touch of defiance in his voice.

Mac sighed, running a hand through his hair, and looking out of the window for a moment.

"You just keep digging, don't you? Where and how did you hear that term?"

"It's called an education Detective Chief Inspector. I researched it."

Those pale green eyes were fixed on Mac's dark stare. Mac wasn't about to back down.

"You want me to arrest you on suspicion of murder?"

"You want me to get a solicitor?"

"Go ahead. You'll spend the next twenty-four hours in a cell. Or we could just stay here and you can tell me how you know something only my team and the killer know," Mac said, anger colouring his tone.

Jones stared back defiantly but spoiled it by swallowing and shifting in his seat away from Mac. Mac leaned closer, putting one hand on the steering wheel to remind Jones of his proximity.

"Lukasz Burksi," Jones said. "Killed in June 2021. Murdered. Bread was found at the scene. Crumbs on the body and a chunk of it soaked in blood on the floor. There was no evidence recorded of the presence of beer, but I surmised it must have been there even if no trace was left."

Mac watched Jones until the other man looked away, running a hand over his face. The name Lukasz Burksi wasn't familiar. If it was murder, then it hadn't happened in Edinburgh or Mac's team would have been assigned.

"Where?" Mac asked.

"Glasgow," Jones replied. "He was found in his flat in Drumchapel."

"And how would you know about it?" Mac asked.

But he already knew. Details of forensics reports would have been purchased, either from a technician on the take or from a copper. It happened frequently, which is why people like Meredith Blakely were paid as much as they were. Police Scotland worked hard to control the flow of information.

"I'm not recording, and I'll deny it if you charge me."

"Obviously."

"I paid for the forensics reports. I won't name who. But I was already investigating Lukasz Burksi over the Amanda Holly case. You know it?"

Mac nodded sharply. Of course, he knew about Amanda Holly. A twelve-year-old girl who went missing on the half-mile walk from her home to school. A half mile through residential streets of an affluent Edinburgh suburb. She'd never been found. It had been five years and Amanda was almost certainly dead. But there was no shortage of amateur sleuths keeping the case alive online and in the media. Mac sneered. Too many self-appointed detectives who were only in it for the publicity. For a podcast or a YouTube channel. For the likes and the follows. They prevented the family's wounds from healing. It was one thing for a member of Amanda's family to refuse to let the case rest. But, for a journalist, it was self-serving. He felt a powerful urge to punch Ramsey Jones.

"Christ," he muttered, looking away.

Here it comes. The justification. The implied criticism of the police. The theories that proved just how clever he was. How much smarter than the case's senior investigating officer. But Ramsey Jones kept quiet. When Mac looked back, Jones was watching him. Waiting.

"You believe that Lukasz Burksi had something to do with Amanda's disappearance?"

Jones nodded. "I also think I know what he did with her body. That's why I came to Edinburgh. To look at the area she was snatched from, but also to talk to you."

"I had nothing to do with that case," Mac said.

"But you know Doctor Cliodna Wray. So do I."

"Good for you. What of it?"

"She once did some consulting work for me. I was way ahead of you on the Celtic Killer, by the way."

Mac shook his head. There it was. People who thought they were clever could never hold it in for long when talking to a detective. He remembered awkward dinner parties when he'd been with Siobhan. Professional men and women whose eyes lit up when they found out he was a detective.

Then came the personal theories they'd come up with after a few episodes of a true crime documentary.

"At a count of ten. No, screw it, make it five. I'm going to break your nose and walk away. So talk faster," Mac said, teeth gritted.

"I heard about Adam Glebe's death and where he was found. I purchased the details because it was strange. That's how I work; I look out for the weird things. It was pure coincidence you were in charge of something linked to what I was already looking into. I followed you because I wanted you to listen to me. The forensics report matched Lukasz Burksi's."

"The PR team has a hotline for the public to provide information," Mac said, grabbing Jones by the front of his hoodie and hauling him half out of his seat. "Time's up, Jones."

"OK, OK, OK. I didn't want to just be an anonymous source. I wanted to be part of the investigation. Are you happy now? I thought I might get some insights by following you. Everyone knows you're a hands-on DCI. You don't just sit in your office and delegate."

Mac released him, shoving him so that he thudded into the driver's door. Ramsey Jones was a frustrated detective. Wanted to be in front of a camera showing the world how clever he was. Wanted to be the hero. It was pathetic. But Mac couldn't ignore another case that might be linked to his. He needed to know everything Ramsey Jones knew. He also needed to keep control of what information Jones was releasing to the public. Considering everything he was juggling, the last thing he needed was to be babysitting a bloody reporter. But at least he wasn't spouting conspiracy theories this time. He must be taking his meds.

Chapter Fifteen

ST AIDEN'S was a monstrous modern building of orange brick, square and brutal. Its lower level windows were barred and the surrounding grounds comprised open grass and broken concrete. The sign proclaiming the name of the church and the name of its priest had the look of something regularly scrubbed. Brown water of a canal lay to his right, crossed by a concrete pedestrian bridge from Hailesland Road. Verges were overgrown with daisies and takeaway containers. The church was reached up a steep, pot-holed slip road off the main road. En route, Mac had called Isla and asked her to pull all the information she could on a murder case involving a victim named Lukasz Burksi in Glasgow, June 2021, and to prepare a briefing for the team. Ramsey Jones had been visibly torn between coming into Brunswick Street to talk to Mac and caution born of paranoia. Caution had won, and Mac didn't have evidence enough to bring him in against his will.

Jones had agreed to meet with him somewhere public later in the day to share information. The thought that the sin-eater might be a serial killer sent a crawling horror through Mac. One killing could take weeks or months to solve for a team. But the pressure ramped up when it was a series. That meant potential future killings and as SIO, Mac couldn't help but feel that every new death was his fault. If he had just solved the case sooner. Found the evidence. The clue. Been a better detective. It was a fallacy; no police officer was to blame for the actions of a criminal. But it didn't change the feeling that the next victim would have been going home to their family if only he'd done his job more effectively.

He approached the church entrance, twin wooden doors protected by black wrought-iron gates. The gates were unlocked, swinging open with a creak. Mac tried the handle of one door.

He became aware of raised voices inside. Two men. One was shouting more than the other. A baritone voice with an Ulster accent. Mac paused, door open a crack, listening. The responses to the shouts were more controlled, voice raised only to be heard over the angry one. Hearing the clack of shoes on tiles, Mac pushed through the doors. A man wearing a fleece jacket with an open-collared shirt beneath, jeans and dark-coloured brogues was coming toward him. He looked to be late-fifties and red-faced. His hair was scarce and white where it still hung on. Mac found himself staring into a pair of bright green eyes and a mouth twisted into an angry grimace. They almost collided. Mac stepped to the side.

"Excuse me," he said.

There was no reply. The man slammed the door open and then sent the gate crashing closed behind him. Another man stood in the church's aisle, wearing the black of a priest. He was young with dark curly hair which fell to his collar. His face was long and careworn, creased into a worried frown. He had his hands clasped in front of him, rosary passing between his fingers. He looked to be in his late thirties, possibly as old as Mac. The frown he wore aged him and looked habitual.

"Father Neil Fitzsimmons?" Mac asked.

Dark eyes that had been looking at the doors now focused on him. A smile was forced.

"Yes, welcome to St Aiden's. How can I help?"

Mac took out his warrant card and Father Fitzsimmons approached, examined the card, then looked at Mac. They were of a height.

"DCI McNeill," Mac said. "We spoke on the phone earlier about one of your former parishioners, Adam Glebe."

The priest's eyes widened, then flicked to the door before turning back to Mac.

"Of course. I've been expecting you, detective. Please, take a pew, to coin a phrase."

He smiled weakly, indicating a pew to Mac's left. Mac took the seat and Father Fitzsimmons sat in front, leaning on the back with hands clasped and an attentive look on his face.

"We've had appeals out for anyone with information. If you knew Adam Glebe, why haven't you come forward?" Mac said.

"I'm sorry. I meant to. But there wasn't much I could tell you that would have been of value to your investigation. Only that Adam was a recent member of this congregation. That I took his confession and gave him the sacrament."

"When was the last time you saw him?" Mac asked, leaning forward in a pose that mirrored Father Fitzsimmons.

In response, the priest sat back a little, turning slightly away from Mac.

"Last Sunday evening," he said after a moment.

Mac's senses went to high alert. He didn't move, not giving away his excitement with a change of posture or body language. Instead, he nodded and remained silent. That silence weighed in the air. Father Fitzsimmons shifted in his seat. Cleared his throat. He glanced at Mac to find the detective staring right back.

"We were on a week's retreat. Not too far. Just outside the city, near West Calder. I run one every six months or so."

"When did the retreat start?" Mac asked.

"I started it when I took over this parish about five years…"

"No, no, no. I mean, on this occasion. When did you all leave?"

Father Fitzsimmons flushed. He stammered and played with his rosary.

"Friday evening. There were six of us, including me. Not too many takers for retreats these days."

"This Friday just gone?" Mac queried. "You said it was for a week?"

Father Fitzsimmons froze for a second. He glanced at Mac, then twisted away from his unblinking stare.

"We cut it short this time."

"Why?"

Father Fitzsimmons sighed and muttered something under his breath. Mac took it to be a prayer as he then crossed himself and kissed the crucifix on the end of the rosary he still clutched. Mac let the silence do its work, eating at Father Fitzsimmons' awareness, gnawing at his nerves. Silence would draw more words out than any amount of shouting or intimidation. It pulled like a magnet.

"There was an altercation between two of the attendees. It soured the experience, and I decided to cancel the whole thing and come home. I might never do it again. I'm looking for guidance..."

"Was Adam Glebe involved in the argument?" Mac asked, quietly.

Father Fitzsimmons nodded, then looked at Mac with something close to panic in his eyes.

"I'm positive his death had nothing to do with the row."

"Are you? How?" Mac asked.

"Because the man he argued with is a priest. And he's not a violent man. Could never be. He's been a missionary for G..." Father Fitzsimmons looked up at the statue of Christ on the cross and made the sign of the cross over himself. "Goodness' sake," he finished quietly.

"Who did he argue with?"

"Father Nathan. Nathan Flenders. He had a parish in Slateford. We became friends because we both had parishes in deprived areas. Both work with local children's homes and ex-offenders. We had a lot in common."

Mac nodded again, digesting, and not missing the priest's use of the past tense. Perhaps Nathan Flenders was no longer considered a friend.

"What was the argument about?"

Father Fitzsimmons shook his head. "I wasn't there. I had gone out for a walk and when I came back, it had all kicked off. Nick was trying to keep the peace, but Nathan and Adam were shouting at each other..."

"Nick?" Mac asked.

"Another priest," Father Fitzsimmons replied. "Anyway, things were said. Insults and...and things said in the heat of the moment that it's hard to walk back from, you know? We decided to call it quits. Nick took Adam back. Adam didn't drive. I gave Nathan a lift back. The other two men with us stayed on. They're still there as far as I know. I'm due to go out and collect them when the retreat is finished. I feel bad for leaving them there without a priest, but…"

"But you feel you're needed here more?" Mac prompted.

"Something like that. Maybe I'll go back sooner. I could probably use some peaceful contemplation."

"Who else was present at the retreat?" Mac asked.

"Father Nathan, of course. Father Nick, another priest. Joe Kimani and Leo Braddock. Leo was another ex-con who'd been through the Helping Hands programme the Church runs in HMP Edinburgh. Joe is a member of my flock who volunteers with us," Father Fitzsimmons said.

"I'll need contact details for everyone," Mac said, making notes on his phone.

Father Fitzsimmons nodded.

"When you were driving back with Father Nathan, did he not give you any idea why he and Adam were so angry at each other?"

"He refused to talk about it, and I didn't want to push. He has a…"

His mouth clamped shut so fast Mac could almost hear his teeth clack. He looked away, muttering again, eyes closed.

"A temper?" Mac said.

No response. Mac got up and walked into the aisle, crouching at the end of the pew next to the priest, who was looking down, refusing to make eye contact.

"Father…Neil, you seem a good man to me. Honest and compassionate. But you're not helping anyone by withholding information that might protect a killer. If Father Flenders has an anger problem, then I'm going to find out, anyway."

Father Fitzsimmons opened his eyes and Mac saw a haunted anguish there.

"He has a temper. He likes a drink. But he's not a killer. I swear it!" he said, desperately.

"I believe you," Mac assured him, lying.

"I think the reason I've been procrastinating about calling your hotline is because I know how bad it looks for Nathan. He's a good friend of mine. Have I broken the law?"

"No. You're telling me now."

Something else Father Fitzsimmons had said abruptly thumped into Mac's mind. He had been so fixated on the man Adam Glebe had argued with that he'd almost over-looked it.

"Wait. Adam was driven home by Father Nick on Sunday evening. What time?"

"We left just after six."

"Father Nick who?" Mac asked, standing up.

"Cass," Father Fitzsimmons said. "Father Nick Cass. He serves as chaplain at HMP Edinburgh."

"I know," Mac said. "We've met."

But Father Nick had never mentioned being the last person to see Adam Glebe alive.

"Have you spoken to Nathan Flenders since the retreat?" Mac asked.

"Oh, well, I've tried. Err, I've texted him a few times. Tried calling as well, but there's no answer. Come to think of it, he's probably at his caravan in Fife. Signal's terrible there."

"You've been?" Mac asked.

"No, but he's told me how he has to stand in a certain place outside to get any kind of reception."

"Whereabouts in Fife?"

"Not sure. I can't remember the name. He mentioned an outdoor swimming pool once, if that's any help?"

"He's got a pool at his caravan?"

"No, it's a public thing. A lido, I think it's called. A sea water swimming pool. I'll look up the contact details for everyone at the retreat. Can I email them or…"

Mac gave him an email address just as his phone sang out into the quiet of the church. Father Fitzsimmons jumped. Mac took it out. Saw Clio's name. He stepped away from the priest as he answered the call.

"Mac? Sorry to call you at work. It's about Maia."

Mac heard the worry in Clio's voice, and ice gripped his insides. He thought he had more time. Thought his ruse would have taken Musa longer to figure out.

"What's happened?" he demanded.

"She got into a fight and got suspended. The school called me to ask me to pick her up to take her home. But before I could get out of the door, they called back to say she'd left. Just walked out."

"And no-one thought to stop her!" Mac yelled.

"That's what I said. Look, Mac, she's got money, and it's broad daylight. Normally, I wouldn't be too worried, but…"

"I've put the fear of god into you," Mac said, glancing up at Christ involuntarily as he did.

The statue stared back mournfully.

"I'm just so paranoid now about her being out on her own."

Mac was already walking towards the entrance. Father Fitzsimmons was calling after him, but Mac had tuned out the priest.

"Where might she have gone?" he asked.

"There's a shop in the Old Town. We always called it the Witches' Shop. They sell crystals and incense and spells and things. Maia likes to go there and knows the woman who runs it."

"Where is it?"

"It's OK, Mac. It's close to me and there are a few other places in the Old Town I can look. I just wanted to let you know, in case she calls or texts you."

"Of course," Mac cut her off. "This is my fault. Look, I'm in Wester Hailes, not too far from yours. I'll head there now and let you know if she shows up. You do the same if you find her."

"No, Mac. I don't want you taking time away…" Clio sounded flustered.

"No arguments, Clio. I can do my job from the end of a phone. She's probably already on her way home. I'll let you know when I get there."

Mac could hear a door close and the sound of stairs taken in a hurry.

"OK, OK. Thanks, Mac," Clio replied.

"I'll speak to you soon," Mac said, pushing past the gate in front of the church entrance.

As he stepped onto the broken tarmac of the car park, he saw the man who had barged past him on the way in. He was sitting in a black Ford estate with splashes of mud on the wheel arches and a ten-year-old plate. Mac's Audi was two spaces along and as Mac hurried towards it, he met the man's eyes. He had been looking at a phone, but now he tossed it aside and gunned the engine into life. The Ford pulled out of the space hurriedly, forcing Mac to stop, wheels momentarily losing traction on a pothole filled with loose gravel. He drove away fast.

Chapter Sixteen

MAC HIT THE ROAD HARD, over and undertaking on Calder Road until he got to the bypass and then flooring it along the dual carriageway. He knew rationally there was no need. If Maia was home, then getting there in a hurry wouldn't make any difference. If she wasn't, then he was speeding to an empty house. But it was action, however pointless. A build-up of traffic at the Gogar Roundabout forced him to slow, and he fished out his phone, calling Mel.

"Mel, I've got a lead for us," he said by way of greeting.

"OK, guv."

"Adam Glebe attended a retreat with three priests and two other men on the weekend of his death. That's the holiday he told Angus Douglas about. It ended early and Glebe was driven home by Father Nick Cass on Sunday evening. He's the prison chaplain at Saughton and he's possibly the last person to see Adam Glebe alive. Something he didn't volunteer when Isla and I spoke to him at the prison. I'd like to know why."

"You want him brought in, guv?" Mel asked.

"I do. Invite him in this afternoon. Make it clear it's an invitation he doesn't want to refuse," Mac said. "And while we're on the subject of priests, look up a Father Nathan Flenders. He has or had a parish somewhere in Slateford. He argued with Adam Glebe shortly before Glebe's death and his friend and colleague seems to have fallen out with him over it."

"This case seems to be revolving around the Catholic Church. These are both Catholics, I assume?"

"Oh, aye. And they're as tight-lipped as any gangster."

"Do you want this Nathan Flenders brought in as well?"

"No, let's play that one softly, softly. He's got a bit of a temper and he might get spooked and run. Get his home address and see if he's there. Ask him about the argument with Glebe. He's also got a caravan in Fife. Don't know where, but it's near a public outdoor saltwater swimming pool. Get Kai and Isla onto it. Did you get hold of Glebe's ex?"

"Yes, called her and she couldn't have been more helpful once she realised I liked her for her ex-husband's murder. Wanted rid of us and him. She and her partner were at a fundraiser for the local boxing club. Started at about seven and they didn't get home until the early hours. A dozen witnesses say they were both three sheets to the wind by the end. I'll chase up the witnesses, but it's looking unlikely it was them, not if their condition was that bad."

"Did you ask about the alleged child abuse?"

"I did and was told, quote, 'it's a crock of shit.' Glebe was an abuser but not of kids."

"OK, cross them off the list," Mac said. "Let's focus on Cass and finding Flenders."

He was heading east now, along the Glasgow Road and into Corstorphine. Red sandstone houses filled the residential streets with boutique cafes and coffee shops along the main road. Lots of greenery and well-kept gardens. A nice area. Clio was lucky to have found somewhere so low down on the deprivation index. Mac suspected her dad had helped with the deposit. He was glad Clio had that relationship and Maia had a grandfather, an affluent one at that. He hadn't known his own grandparents, not on either side of the family. His paternal grandfather had been Struan McNeill and had owned the farm before Mac's father, William. He died before Mac was born. His mother's parents were from the mainland. Greenock, he thought. William McNeill had let slip in a drunken moment that Theresa Bailie, Mac's mother, had been cut off by her parents when she ran off with a crofter from Skye. He'd implied that the Bailies had a bit of money. He hadn't elaborated, and Mac had never looked into it.

Maybe he had family somewhere. Greenock maybe. Or maybe Theresa had been the only Bailie child. She was long dead. Mac had been twelve. Or was it thirteen? Had he started high school? It was a shock to realise it was all a bit hazy. He'd hardly attended high school anyway, spending most of his time bunking off and taking a hiding from his father when he found out. Mac reached Clio's house and turned into the driveway. Two strips of paving slabs laid over red gravel. The house was the same earthy red sandstone as the rest of the street with a pretty garden, now dormant but with a well-kept lawn. As he drove in, a dark saloon pulled away from the kerb opposite the driveway. Two men in the front, the passenger looking towards Mac as they drove away. The hairs stood up on the back of his neck and he ran to the end of the drive. The car was accelerating down the quiet street, then around a corner before Mac could get a close look at the plates. Clean though.

Shiny and with two passengers. Classic unmarked police car set up.

Anger surged in Mac. He knew why they were there. Sending a message from their boss. We're watching. But not you. We're watching the people you care about. The people we can really scare. He took out his phone and hit Musa's number. It went to voicemail. Mac stalked to Clio's front door, taking out the spare key she'd given him and letting himself into the porch area.

"Musa. Mac. I gave you what you wanted. Call your boys off or I'll be having words with Maggie about what she's holding on you," Mac spat.

He hung up; opening the front door with a second key on the keychain Clio had given him.

"Maia! You home?" he called out as he stepped into the hall.

It took less than a minute for him to go through the house, looking into each room and then the back garden. No sign of Maia. He sent a text to Clio to say so. Mac ended up in the living room, turning a slow circle, keyed up and frustrated. The case was moving, and he needed to be at HQ preparing questions for Nick Cass. That the prison chaplain hadn't seen fit to mention he'd seen Adam Glebe a matter of hours before his death was suspicious. That he'd been present during an argument between Glebe and Flenders was also significant. Maybe the argument had been about something Glebe had told Flenders. Something he'd done. Or was thinking about. And the priest had lost it. Nick Cass overhears and decides that Adam Glebe's soul needed to be cleansed. It sat even less well with Cass than it did with Mickey Plant. Mac wasn't naïve enough to think that killers couldn't be people who seemed amiable on the surface.

But instinct was an important tool to a copper, if an inexact one. And instinct told him Nick Cass was an unlikely killer. Still had some questions to answer, though. He went to the kitchen, checked the kettle, then filled it and turned it on. Took out a mug and tapped some instant coffee into it. The fridge was covered in pictures of Clio and Maia over the years. He stopped as he reached in for the milk, looking over them. He could see the Maia he knew in the face of the chubby toddler in some of those pictures. They looked happy. Self-loathing filled him at the thought his actions had put them in danger. His dishonesty. That's what happened when you started bending the rules. Innocent people got dragged in. He turned away from the happy pictures, forgetting the coffee he'd started to make. He didn't want to be inactive. Wouldn't allow himself to linger over those kinds of thoughts.

Striding back into the living room, he took out his phone, scanning his emails. One from Mel, the bright bold blue of unread. She'd titled it Lukasz Burksi, spelled correctly, Mac assumed. The name of the investigating officer was DCI Helen Cameron. It took Mac a moment to find her details on the Police Scotland internal directory. He called her mobile number first.

"DCI Cameron," came the prompt answer.

"This is DCI McNeill over in Brunswick Street, Edinburgh," Mac replied, and then to verify his identity, he quoted his badge number.

There was a moment of quiet, and Mac caught the sound of tapping on a keyboard.

"Right, DCI McNeill. What can I do for you?" Cameron answered.

Mac knew she would have been running the badge

number through the directory and then checking the number he was calling from against his entry.

"I can video call if you want to check," Mac suggested.

"That's OK, DCI McNeill," Cameron said.

"Call me, Mac."

"Helen."

"I want to talk to you about Lukasz Burksi. Do you remember that case?"

"Yes, I do. Throat cut in his flat in Drumchapel. Summer 2021. What about it?"

"You found breadcrumbs on the body," Mac said.

"We did."

"Did you ever establish a reason for their presence?"

A moment of silence.

"No. Other than someone stood over him after killing him and ate a sandwich. It didn't seem significant."

"Any DNA from those crumbs?"

"Too small and contaminated to get anything useful. What's your interest, Mac?"

"You hear about the Mary King's Close case?"

"Yes, I've seen it on the news. That's you? I thought it was a female DI—"

"Mel Barland. She's on my team. She's been handling the media for me. We didn't tell the press, but we found breadcrumbs and the remnants of beer beside the body."

"I see where you're going with this, Mac. But I got the man who did Lukasz Burksi, and he didn't kill your guy."

Mac frowned, scrolling down the case file that Mel had emailed to him.

"The case is still open."

"We got someone for it, but the case was Not Proven when it went to court. KC screwed it up. But I got him. Name was Kelsey Fuller. His sister was Lukasz Burksi's girlfriend before he went into Low Moss for a five stretch. For assaulting her and causing a miscarriage. Fuller is a full on Ultra. Union flag outside his house and Never Surrender tattooed on his neck. You know the type? Burksi was due to be deported back to Poland once he'd done his time, but Fuller wanted revenge. Had motive, means and opportunity. Got off on a technicality. Bloody travesty."

"Where's Fuller now?"

"Dead. Got himself run over. Couldn't have happened to a nicer man. Out of interest, what's the significance of the breadcrumbs to you?"

Mac sat back on the sofa, running a hand through his hair.

"Just a theory. Possible connection to a historical practise but nothing I'd take to the PF, eh? Did Burksi serve his full sentence?"

"I think so, can't remember off the top of my head. Probably got something off for time served. This helping your case at all?"

"Nae, but thanks anyway. Can I call you if anything else comes up?"

"Aye, just don't be making waves. As far as I'm concerned, the case is closed."

"Understood."

Mac hung up and tossed the phone onto the coffee table. He sat up and picked it up again after a few seconds, unable to remain idle for long. Accessing the Police Scotland mainframe was a pain without his laptop, requiring multi-factor authentication and passwords. Thank god his autistic brain was wired to remember this stuff. Eventually he was in, bringing up Lukasz Burksi's criminal record. An immigrant from Poland, back when EU nationals were welcome. Worked for a hotel chain as a barman. Then a gap in his employment history. Mac could fill in the gap easily enough. That was when Burksi had crossed the line, discovering it was easier to make money as a criminal. Links in the file to half a dozen known gangsters, all of them Polish of Lithuanian. All based in Glasgow. Arrests started in 2013; five years after Burksi arrived in the UK. Conviction for possession of Class A drugs, found with a personal stash of heroin.

Mac stopped scrolling. Fourteen months served in HMP Edinburgh, from 2014 to 2015. Burksi was out of Edinburgh for three months before he almost killed his then-girlfriend and did kill her unborn child. Both Adam Glebe and Lukasz Burksi had served time in HMP Edinburgh. Both found with breadcrumbs over them. Supposing Kelsey Fuller hadn't been Burksi's killer. Supposing that was the sin-eater. Identifying his victims from the population of the prison? Picking out those whose souls were most in need of saving, based on the severity of their crimes?

Chapter Seventeen

THE NEXT CALL was from Maia. Mac came out of his seat like a rocket.

"Maia! Where are you?"

"Oh, you spoke to mum, eh?"

"Aye. We're both pretty worried, pal. Where are you?"

"I'm really sorry. But, I'm scared. I'm in a cafe in town and I think someone is following me."

Mac left the house at a run, phone on speaker in one hand. The inner front door slammed closed. He didn't both with the porch. Keys beeped open the Audi.

"OK, Maia. You did the right thing by calling me. Are there other people there?"

Of course there would be. City centre cafe in the middle of the day? If Maia had realised she was being followed and went to the most public place she could find, she'd shown some good thinking.

"Yes, it's packed."

"Stay there. Can you describe the person following you?"

Mac had the engine running now and was backing out of the drive. A dog walker about to cross snatched their terrier back as the Audi emerged at speed. Mac barely registered their protest as he straightened and took off towards the Glasgow Road. It was the most direct route eastward to the city centre.

"It's a man. White with ginger hair. In his twenties, I think. He knew my name and mum's name. He knew yours too."

"Did he show you a badge?" Mac asked.

"Yes, and he said you'd sent him to find me. But there was something off about him. I ran away, and he followed me."

The Organised Crime Taskforce was big, and Mac didn't know every officer who had been assigned to it.

"I didn't send anyone. I wouldn't, you know that."

"I know. That's why I ran," Maia said, her voice tinged with panic.

"Is he still there?" Mac asked.

Maia was quiet for a moment. "No, I don't think… wait! Yes, he's outside," she swore, a word Mac would have said she didn't know. "He's sitting on a wall across the road looking at me. What does he want, Uncle Callum? Why is he following me?"

Full flooded panic.

"Maia, listen to me. You're safe in there. In a public place surrounded by people. No-one can hurt you."

"But if he's a policeman, who would stop him?"

"Even a policeman couldn't make a child go with them if that child didn't want to. There are people around you who will stop him if he dared to try. Most people don't like coppers anyway," Mac tried to assure her. "Just keep that in mind. He can't touch you."

"Why does he want me to go with him? Is he a friend of yours?"

"No. He isn't. And I don't know," Mac said, picking his words to avoid scaring her further.

Why tell a frightened fourteen-year-old that he was being stalked by a corrupt police officer with blood on his hands? A bent copper who would not blink an eye at murder.

"Where are you, Maia?" he asked.

"Waverley Station," Maia replied. "It's a Cafe Nero at the bottom of the ramp off the bridge. I just saw some other policemen go past, in uniform. Should I go to them?"

Mac thought for a minute. Two Transport Police officers not connected to Musa's team would probably be honest coppers. But all the plain clothed man had to do was flash his badge and pull rank. It was too risky.

"No. Just sit tight, kiddo. I'm on my way and your mum is even closer. Trust me. If that…" Mac used a word that he definitely shouldn't have said in Maia's hearing, "is still there when I get there, I'll throw him onto the tracks."

Mac was thinking miles ahead. The road he was on would lead him straight to Princes Street. It cut through Edinburgh east to west. But before he got there, the traffic would take hold and slow him down. Waverley would be almost impossible to approach by car. Murrayfield was passing on his right, appearing in between and above the houses. He kept his speed as high as the traffic would allow, higher than was safe.

"Maia. I need you to call your mum and get her to meet you. She went to the Witches' Shop looking for you, so she'll be somewhere nearby."

"I thought I should try you first, because it was a

policeman following me," Maia said, sounding on the verge of tears.

"You did the right thing, sweetheart. But I need you to hang up now and call your mum. You're safe where you are. Stay right there and wait for us, OK?"

Maia hung up as Mac was nearing Haymarket station. That's when he saw the patrol car parked outside. He swung the Audi across tramlines and traffic coming in the opposite direction, running through a red light and narrowly avoiding a taxi to screech into the Haymarket car park. There was a uniform sitting in the patrol car, getting out as he watched Mac's entrance, putting on his hat and looking ready to give him a bollocking. Mac kicked open the Audi door and held up his warrant card as he crossed to the officer.

"DCI McNeill, SCU. I have a vulnerable witness at Waverley Station in fear for her life. She's a minor. I'm in a civilian vehicle, and I need your blues and twos to get to her."

"Right, sir. Johnny's just gone into the station for a slash. I'll get him out."

The uniform spoke into his shoulder mounted radio in an urgent tone. Mac was already running back to the Audi. By the time he had it started another officer in Hi-Vis and a stab vest was running out. A minute later, they lit up the roof of the patrol car, and with Mac stuck to their bumper, shot down Morrison Street. It was Johnny driving, and Mac couldn't fault his skills. They wove between traffic on both sides of the carriageway, cut down side streets as they reached the Old Town, including a couple of one-way streets. Sirens wailed above the sound of wheels hurtling over ancient cobbles and at one point something clanged against the Audi's mirror, snapping it back against the body of the car. Mac ignored it, concentrating on staying close to the marked police car. When they reached Waverley Bridge, Mac followed the screaming vehicle down the long incline to the station level.

Mac screeched to a halt on the pedestrian crossing and the patrol car slammed on as they saw him stop behind. Mac left the Audi's door open as he got out and ran for the Cafe Nero a few yards away. When he got to the door, he saw Maia through the window. She was with Clio, the two of them sitting in a booth towards the back of the shop. His heart almost stopped, and he leaned on the doorframe with one hand, breathing hard. Heavy boots running on concrete reminded him of the cavalry he'd brought with him. He looked around at the questioning looks on the two officer faces. Then he scanned the crowd who were, even now, going about their business like nothing was happening. He saw the watcher immediately. Leaning against a wall opposite the coffee shop. Suited and booted. Ginger hair. Smirk on his face.

"See that woman and girl in there?" Mac pointed to where Clio was looking right at him, hand half raised to wave at him.

"Yes, sir."

"Escort them to my car and make sure no-one gets near them," Mac ordered.

No questions. Two snapped sirs and both men moved into the coffee shop with a sense of purpose. Mac crossed the open concourse between the cafe and a WH Smith, eyes locked on the bent copper who'd terrorised a young teenage girl. The man straightened and took a phone from his pocket. As Mac approached, he held it out toward him.

"The guv would like…" he began.

Mac grabbed him by his tie, pulled him forward sharply,

and brought his own forehead down at the same time. The phone dropped and the man's nose flattened with a crack, blossoming with blood. Mac let go, and he collapsed like his legs had turned to jelly. Mac turned and walked away just as the two uniforms came out of the cafe. They were watching the surrounding crowd, sharp and vigilant. Both clocked the man on the ground with his face streaming blood, but their eyes went past, looking for threats as they guided their charges towards Mac's car. They were professional enough not to waste time asking what had happened. Clio had her arm around Maia, who was turning her head to look at the man struggling to his feet.

"You think you can get away with that?!" he shrieked in a voice wet with the blood flowing down his throat. "You're dead!"

Johnny glanced at Mac. "Does he need dealing with, sir?"

Mac nodded. "But not by you, constable. Thanks. I can handle him."

Mac took out his phone and snapped a picture of the man, letting him know he knew his face, would put a name to it soon enough. Being a copper wouldn't protect him then. If Musa was playing dirty, then Mac wouldn't be sticking to the rules, either. Mac considered himself lucky he'd come across two honest coppers with the common sense to know how far the rules could be bent. When to turn a blind eye. There would be enough eyewitnesses to the assault he'd committed. Enough phones to capture it. He doubted Musa's man would press charges and Musa would be crazy to make a complaint. That would require explaining why his officer was stalking a fourteen-year-old girl. This had all been an exercise in terror. To keep Mac in line.

"Thanks, mate. You two did a great job," Mac said, offering his hand. "What're your names?"

"Johnny Franklin and this is Aiden Connor. We're based at Drylaw Station."

"I'll ring your guv'nor and let them know," Mac said.

He got into the Audi. Clio and Maia were in the back.

"That was so cool, Uncle Callum," Maia said.

"That was not cool, Maia," Clio reprimanded her. "That was assault."

"He had it coming," Mac muttered, executing a turn that had traffic in and out of Waverley blocked.

A black cab sounded its horn loudly and got a single finger salute in reply.

"Who was he?" Clio asked.

"A corrupt police officer," Mac replied, leaving the station considerably more carefully than he'd entered.

"Would he have hurt Maia?" Clio asked.

Mac glanced in the mirror. Maia was wide-eyed despite her attempts at being cool. Clio was looking right at him. She was asking her question deliberately. Wanting to show Maia this wasn't a game, maybe? Emphasise the danger to prevent a repeat of her behaviour? Mac glowered, feeling responsible. Feeling guilty.

"I don't think so. This was about intimidation. To get to me."

"And is it going to continue?" Clio asked, her tone challenging.

"Wait, is this why you moved in with us?" Maia suddenly said.

Her mum tried to hush her, and Maia threw off the arm about her shoulders.

"You knew this was going to happen?"

"No," both Clio and Mac said.

"I was just being cautious, that's all. Something you could do more of," Mac replied, after a moment's thought.

"I didn't know there were bent coppers after me," Maia said pointedly. "Maybe this is a lesson for the two of you about keeping me in the dark."

"You're a child…" Clio began.

"I'm a teenager, mum. I'm almost old enough to consent to sex. Or join the army. In three years, I'll be driving! Do you think I would have run out of school if I thought I would be in danger?"

She had a point, but Mac wasn't convinced it would have stopped her. The thrill of potential danger overcoming the allure of adventure.

"She has a point," he said.

Maia caught his eye in the mirror, the ghost of a smile on her face. Clio looked outraged.

"She does not. We are the adults here, Mac. I am her mother. She's a minor."

"Not for long," Maia replied.

"Enough. You are for now. That's all the matters. Mac, please take us home."

"That's where we're going," Mac put in.

"Good!" Clio snapped, looking out of the window to hide the tears welling up.

There was silence in the car for several minutes.

"Sorry, mum," Maia whispered.

"Mm hmmm," Clio said, hand over her mouth.

She reached out and Maia took her hand. Then lifted her arm and placed herself beneath it. Clio hugged her tightly. No-one spoke until they got back to the house.

"Go inside please, Maia. I want to talk to Mac privately," Clio said, wearily on the doorstep.

Maia looked about to protest, but one look at her mum's

face stopped her. Mac stayed quiet. He deserved whatever Clio was going to say next. Deserved to be told to leave and never come back. He'd brought this on them. If she pushed him away, he'd have to push back. Until he found a solution to this, they needed his protection. If that had to be from a distance, so be it.

"Mac, can you sort this out?" Clio asked, pointedly.

Mac thrust hands into trouser pockets, glowering into the middle distance.

"Look at me," Clio said, firmly.

He met her eyes.

"Can you?" she asked.

"I have to," he answered.

Clio nodded. "Maia has been suspended for a week. I'll speak to my boss about working remotely and take her away from the city."

"Not to your dads," Mac said. "That's too obvious."

"Ok. Where then?"

"Go online and find an Airbnb somewhere. Anywhere. Pick at random. I'll pay for it. Just choose somewhere you don't have friends or family. Somewhere you've never been."

Clio nodded. "Maia has always wanted to go to the west coast. Argyll. Skye. I'll look there. Is that far enough?"

Mac felt cold inside at the very mention of his former home. He couldn't imagine why anyone would choose to go there. It was so swathed in darkness for him, so corrupted by traumatic memories, he forgot it was a tourist attraction for everyone else. A beauty spot.

"Yes. Pick up a hire car in Glasgow and leave yours at the airport just in case anyone tries to follow you."

Clio shuddered. "Maia is going to love this. I don't know how I'm going to get through the next week."

"You'll be safe enough away from me," Mac told her. "For what it's worth, I really am sorry, Clio."

Clio just looked at him for a long, silent moment. "I know you are," she said. "You've got a week to make Maia safe."

Mac felt her fingers briefly entwine with his. Then she kissed him on the cheek.

"Thank you for breaking that creep's nose for her," Clio said.

Chapter Eighteen

"WHY AM I HERE, Detective Chief Inspector?"

Those were Father Nick Cass's first words as Mac walked into Interview Room 2. Mel Barland had gone in ahead of him. Cass looked straight past her to Mac. Interesting reaction. Sitting in a police interview room with a silent uniform by the door, having been informed that your presence is mandatory. Made to wait. And when the door opens, within seconds, you have the presence of mind to zero in on the one person you are most interested in speaking to, ignoring the others. Mac took a seat next to Mel, opposite Cass. There was no solicitor present. Mel did the usual housekeeping, setting up the recorder and introducing the participants. Cass was still looking at Mac, hands folded on the table in front of him, waiting for his answer. Mac looked back at him without expression.

"I won't deny I'm concerned. I can't think why you need to speak to me and do it here, of all places," Cass said.

"Is it a problem?" Mac asked.

"Being dragged to a police station and given no choice

in the matter? Yes, that's a problem," Cass replied, sounding a tad exasperated.

"Of all the people we need to speak to as part of this investigation, I had assumed you would be the most comfortable with police stations. Not that much different to a prison," Mac said.

"I'm paid to be in the prison. It's my job. This isn't. Now, are you going to tell me what you need from me that couldn't be obtained at home or over the phone?"

There was a hint of entitlement in Cass's tone now. It wasn't helped by his English accent. A Scouser or a Geordie could say something similar and Mac would take it at face value. A Southerner with an education and an accent that had money behind it, though, only sounded superior and pompous. Or like they thought they were. Mac wondered if he was the one with the issue, hearing a posh English accent and having a knee jerk reaction. He put aside the irritation that Cass's tone had caused and turned his head to Mel slightly. A signal.

"When did you last see Adam Glebe, Father Cass?" Mel asked.

"Adam?" Cass asked, as though surprised to be asked about the dead man. As though there was another reason for the police wanting to talk to him. "It was at the retreat," he said promptly.

He looked from Mel to Mac and then back again. Mac's eyes never left his face, watching for reactions or micro expressions. It was very difficult to lie close up. A lot of people underestimated that. Talked a lot of pish about poker faces. Mac had seen enough liars to pick up on things he didn't even know he was seeing. Like an unconscious lie detector. It was instinct, an intuitive sense borne from experience. Cass was projecting an air of injured innocence.

Genuinely unsure why he'd been picked on. Could be a front. Hard to say. But Mac was getting nothing.

"Who else attended?" Mel asked.

"Well, it wasn't as well subscribed as some previous retreats, but I was glad Adam was there..." Cass hesitated.

Mac saw the opening. A delay in answering and a deflection. Ask me about why I was glad that Adam was there. Mac wasn't about to bite. He couldn't think why Cass would want to go into that, but it was too obvious an invitation.

"Who else?" Mel prompted gently.

"Well, there was me. Adam. Father Neil Fitzsimmons," Cass said eventually.

"You last saw Adam at the retreat?" Mel asked. A repetition but designed to catch a lie.

"Yes," Cass said instantly. Then he stammered. "No, no, no, no. Actually, it was after. Sorry. Just after. I gave Adam a lift."

"A lift where?" Mac asked.

"From the retreat. At the end," Cass said.

"Home?" Mac asked.

"Not all the way, no," Cass replied. "Look, is there any chance of a cup of tea or a coffee? I'm parched."

Mac glanced at Mel.

"Interview suspended as DI Barland leaves the room. You wanting anything, guv?"

Mac shook his head. Mel left the room and Mac let the silence hang for a minute.

"Sorry about the mix-up," Cass said. "About when I last saw Adam. Hope that didn't count against me!" he laughed, forced and with a very slight hint of nerves.

Mac smiled. "Who remembers exactly where they were or when they last saw someone, eh?" he said.

"Yes, well, exactly. Hard to, um…hard to remember sometimes."

"I suppose we could have done this at the prison but didn't occur to me to ask," Mac said.

"Would have been easier probably," Cass replied.

"And you didn't volunteer the information that you were the last person to see Adam Glebe alive," Mac said. "By the way, have you seen Father Nathan since the retreat?"

He'd buried the question he really wanted an answer to behind one that seemed trivial, letting the first stab fester while Cass focused on the second. Let it get under his skin and unnerve him. If he had anything to hide, that is.

"He came to see me on…" a look up to the ceiling, trying to remember. Or over-acting, "…Wednesday I think it was."

"Social visit?"

"He wanted to apologise for his part in a row. All three of us look forward to those retreats and he felt like he'd ruined it for us all."

"Father Neil said he has a bit of a temper," Mac said.

"Nathan? No, no, no. You just have to know how to handle him. He had to act harsh at times. He was prison chaplain at HMP Edinburgh for ten years before me."

"Tough place to work. You don't strike me as the kind to survive there. No offence."

"None taken. Nathan was the hard man, born in Belfast. I suppose he had to be. I just tried to be myself. Easy going, approachable, but with no fear. I treated the guys as equals. They seem to respond to that."

"Must be burdensome, though, trying to help men who have done some pretty bad stuff, eh?" Mac said. "Rapists, child molesters, murderers?"

"All human beings, Inspector. All redeemable in the eyes

of God. We're all born sinners; the key is to find salvation before you reach the end of your life."

"What if you don't?"

Cass spread his hands, shrugging his shoulders. "That's why we give the sacrament as part of the last rites. To cleanse the soul."

Mac leaned forward, as though interested in the theology.

"What about the ones who don't want the last rites from a priest? The non-believers?"

"I pray for them," Cass said, flatly.

Mel came back into the room. Cass just looked at Mac. No expression. Lot of control going on there. Giving nothing away. Mel put the drinks down and took her seat, resuming the recording.

"Do I need a solicitor?" was the first thing Cass said.

Again, impressive reactions. For all his occasional stammering and air of doddery Englishness, Cass was sharp.

"Up to you," Mac said. "You're neither under arrest nor under caution. The tape is just for the record. We'd have it for a witness, too."

That was deliberate. Let Cass think he wasn't here as a witness. Make him think, well what am I here as if not a witness? A suspect.

"Which is what you are," Mel said.

Good cop.

"I didn't think I was here as anything else," Cass said.

"So, where were we?" Mac said briskly.

Cass wafted his hand over his cardboard cup, and then blew on it, looking over the rim at Mac.

"What can you tell me about sin-eating?" Mac asked suddenly.

"Could you repeat that, Detective Chief Inspector?" Cass asked. Carefully. Deliberately.

"You heard. Stop playing for time," Mac snapped.

"What? How…? I'm sorry, I didn't realise I was actually a suspect. I'm here to help you with your inquiry. This is beginning to feel more like an interrogation."

"That's exactly what it is because I caught you out in an omission. You didn't volunteer any of this stuff about retreats and arguments when I spoke to you at Saughton. Your pal Father Fitzsimmons did."

Mel glanced at him, one hand flattening against the tabletop. A signal between them. Cool it.

"I think you are extremely prejudiced, and it makes me think I should have legal representation, because I doubt I'm going to get a fair hearing."

Mac narrowed his eyes. Cass was deflecting, moving the conversation on from the original question. Why?

"The question was, what do you know about sin-eating?" Mel said. "Obviously, you have the right to a solicitor, but their advice would be not to withhold information if it doesn't incriminate you. Does this question worry you?"

Cass sighed, glaring at Mac. Mac gave it back in spades. Cass wasn't easy to intimidate. For all he looked as though the double act, good cop, bad cop, was getting to him. It didn't seem to change his statements. The agitation was skin deep.

"I see now why you were so interested in the last rites and cleansing of the soul. Sin-eating resides in that part of the Church we would rather pretend doesn't exist." Cass said. "It's a practise of historical origins which the Church has disowned. The feeling was that lay sin-eaters were undermining the authority of parish priests who had already delivered last rites and sacraments. They were feeding superstitions which the Church wanted stamped out."

"Sounds like you have some knowledge of this area," Mac said.

Then, recognising he had perhaps gone too far into an antagonistic role with Cass, he raised his hands.

"Just an observation. I'm not accusing you of anything. You might be quoting Wikipedia for all I know."

"I have an interest in ecclesiastical history among other subjects," Cass said. "I have read about sin-eating, although not in great detail."

Mac nodded, smiled thinly, and looked at Mel, giving the signal to get back to the agreed line of questioning.

"You last saw Adam Glebe, where?" Mel asked, frowning at her notes.

"In my car, well, getting out of the car at a petrol station," Cass replied.

"Which one?" Mac asked.

Cass looked up, narrowing his eyes.

"Don't know it. I'd probably be able to pick it out on Maps. I'm pretty good at that."

"Why not take him home?" Mel asked.

"He didn't want me to. Or rather, he changed his mind as we were driving," Cass replied.

"Why?" Mac asked.

"He was anxious and uptight, if you must know. Something happened at the retreat. It got closed early. Lots of drama. Adam was talking about it in the car."

"About what?" Mel asked.

"About this argument..."

"With who?" Mac cut across him, putting on pressure.

"Father Nathan Flenders," Cass said, glancing at Mac.

He didn't like being interrupted. The look directed at

Mac wasn't exactly beatific or spiritual. It was irritated. Mac could be like a rash when he wanted to be.

"What were they arguing about?"

Cass was silent for a moment. He sat back in his seat, staring at his tea. Then he looked around the room. Not much to see. Blank walls. Lights hidden behind ceiling panels. One way glass.

"I'm not sure I'm comfortable saying," Cass said cautiously.

Mac sat forward, hands flat on the tabletop, shoulders hunched. It was an aggressive posture. He hadn't slammed his hands down on the table, but his body language said he had. There was a slight scraping sound as Cass pushed his chair back. Mac didn't smile.

"Was it part of a confession? Or are you just choosing to be obstructive this time?"

"I'm finding your tone confrontational," Cass said, placing the heels of his hands against the edge of the table.

"The last thing I want to be is confrontational. What is it that's made you think that?" Mac asked with an innocence that fooled no-one.

"Is it because we're asking about the argument that Father Flenders had with Adam Glebe?" Mel asked, almost before Mac had finished speaking.

Cass's head whipped around. Mac pushed further.

"I can't think of a single legitimate reason for you not to tell us about that argument. Not in a murder investigation. I don't care how confrontational you think I'm being. I'm not here to babysit you."

He put force into his words, and Mel played her part of the good cop.

"Guv," she said warningly.

It was an act, but it got Cass's head moving from one to

the other, not knowing where the next words were coming from. The next attack. Put him off his guard, shake him up and see what comes floating to the surface. Mac had no direct evidence to suspect Cass of anything. But he had failed to volunteer what most people would think of as pertinent information when talking about a murder victim. And now he was stalling.

"Just tell us what the argument was about, Father," Mel said, placatingly.

Mac just stared, glowered. Cass licked his lips, glancing at each of them in turn. He leaned in, elbows on the table and hands over his face, dragging long fingers down until they covered his mouth. His eyes met Mac's.

"I could lose my job and my job is everything to me. I've been involved in a lot of different outreach and community projects for the Church, but working with the guys in prison has been my calling. So, this is extremely difficult."

"You think you'll keep your job if I have you charged with obstruction?" Mac asked.

Cass gave a bitter smile and looked aside, folding his arms tight, gripping the elbow of each. He muttered a few words under his breath, made the sign of the cross, then spoke.

"Father Nathan," he began. "Was accused of something. It led to him being taken out of his parish and moved while the accusations were investigated. I'm sure you know the kind of thing I'm talking about."

Those dark eyes beneath lowered brows held Mac's for a long moment. A lot passed silently between them. Mac understood the hesitancy now, wondered if the police had been informed or whether the church had closed ranks and were dealing with it in-house. A wave of disgust and anger rose within him and he tried to keep it separate from his opinion of the man in front of him. He was an individual priest, not the entire Catholic Church.

"I can imagine," Mac said.

"It's completely false. A man with a grudge making up stories about what happened to him as a boy. We didn't believe it for a minute. But the church is extremely sensitive to this kind of allegation. It acts first and investigates later. So, Nathan got treated as a pariah. Well, the subject came up on the retreat. Adam knew about it, goodness knows how. He didn't think Father Nathan should have been there and said as much to Neil. But Neil told Adam Nathan was innocent. I agreed. I hoped Adam would accept Neil's word and keep his mouth shut. Which was a vain hope as it turns out. Adam couldn't hold his water, and a huge argument ensued. End of retreat. We decided to call it a day. Nathan stormed off. I tried to talk to him, told him I would call him, but he said he was going to his caravan. He goes there when he wants to be off grid, you know?"

"Where's that?" Mel asked.

"Not sure. Fife coast, that's all I know. I've never been there," Cass replied.

"But he came to see you. Wednesday you said," Mac said.

"Yes, yes. He did. To apologise."

"And you haven't seen him since?" Mac prompted.

"No, I haven't. He was going to the caravan, and that usually means incommunicado. Because of the signal and how remote it is. There's only one road, and it's not passable for a vehicle. There was a landslide."

Mac nodded. Glanced at Mel, she brought the conversation back to where Mac wanted it.

"So Adam and Father Flenders didn't see eye to eye?" Mel asked.

Cass snorted. "No, they did not. Adam was disgusted by the allegations. Father Nathan said he was innocent. But according to Adam, there's no smoke without fire, the usual clichés. He just couldn't let it go."

"So, tell me again. Why did you drop Adam off and not take him home after the retreat?" Mac said.

"He said he wanted some air. Wanted to walk for a bit, think. Get himself a sausage roll and a Coke from the garage, I don't know. Look..." Cass stabbed a finger at the tabletop. "The truth is, I wasn't too happy with Adam's behaviour at that point. I don't believe the allegations against Father Nathan; I don't believe he's capable. I honestly don't. I might have been a bit short with Adam when we were in the car. Might have given him a piece of my mind."

He picked up his tea, blew on it, then took a few gulps.

"So, you argued with Adam too?" Mac said.

"Yes, yes, alright. Happy now? We argued. Check the CCTV at the garage and you can probably see me in the car having a go at him. I thought he was being unnecessarily judgmental and sanctimonious. There is no proof against Father Nathan, and I've known him for years. Alright?"

Cass was clearly becoming annoyed. He had to know that admitting to an argument with Adam gave him a motive and an opportunity given that he was one of the last people to see Adam alive. He knew that and admitted it. Belligerently and under a bit of pressure, but he admitted it.

"He went into the shop at the garage, came out with a plastic bag and just walked straight past me. And I just let him go. I just..." now there were tears in his eyes and he looked up at the ceiling, brows drawing down under a creased forehead. "God forgive me, I abandoned him because I was angry. Because I was disappointed, I didn't get my retreat. I let him go and thought, thought..."

He was getting choked, and Mac watched him closely. The emotion seemed genuine. Mel was pushing a pack of tissues towards Cass, always prepared.

"Thought what, Father Nick?" she asked softly.

"Go to hell!" Cass said, looking at her with bright, angry eyes. "I looked at him and I thought, just go to hell!"

Chapter Nineteen

"WHAT DO YOU THINK, GUV?" Mel asked when she caught up with Mac in the office.

Mac was at his desk, reviewing emails without really seeing the text on the screen. His mind was scrolling through text of a different kind. The interview with Cass, his reactions, his words. The account of the retreat given by both him and Father Fitzsimmons. The alleged predilections of Father Nathan Flenders. A lot of variables to add into the known evidence of the Adam Glebe case. It was a jumble. A whirl.

Nothing was fitting together neatly. It wasn't staying still long enough for the jigsaw to come together. He and Mel had spent the best part of four hours talking to Nick Cass, making him go over and over his account of Adam Glebe's last day, looking for inconsistencies or outright lies. At the end, Cass had agreed to provide a mouth swab for a DNA test, to eliminate his DNA from any found at the scene. Cass had done it, desperate to leave by that point.

"I think he's guilty one minute and innocent the next.

He does himself no favours with some of the things he says, but that tells me he's probably not our man. He would be more controlled about what he let slip if he was," Mac said.

"I think he's our best lead so far," Mel said.

Mac nodded slowly, turning the idea over in his mind.

"Aye, you're right," Mac said. "Let's run it down. Fast-track his DNA samples against any found at the scene. Nathan Flenders also needs looking at more deeply. Kai and Isla are on him. I want you to become an expert on Father Nicholas Cass. Deep background check, as much detail as you can. Let's see what we can find out."

"What are you going to do?" Mel asked.

"Check out Cass's home, his neighbours. See if I can find anyone to verify the alibi he gave us," Mac said.

Mel nodded decisively and moved halfway out of the door. Then she came back, hanging onto the door frame.

"Um, you good, guv?" she asked, overly casually.

Mac gave her a look.

"You want to know if I'm good?"

"Yeah, you just seem a bit..."

"What?"

"Distracted. We have a good lead and usually you're really zeroed in by this point. Sharp."

"Am I not sharp?" Mac asked, going still.

Mel recognised the danger she was in, but pushed on. Her need to check on Mac overriding her self-preservation. The mother's instinct. Mac felt the usual instinct to push back against any intrusion of the personal into the professional. It manifested as a flash of annoyance, the need to snap, a stillness of body and features. He knew he didn't communicate well, that what his face told the world was not always what his mind was thinking. Sometimes the words came out sounding different to his intention. At worst, this could alienate even longstanding colleagues. Colleagues like Mel who knew him better than anyone. He couldn't afford to lose Mel. He leaned on her, relied on her to manage people, freeing him up to pursue the detective work he was so good at. Mac forced a smile, hoping it didn't look that way. Tried for the rogue. Women always like that. Mel tilted her head and raised an eyebrow, pursing her lips.

"That usually works with me, eh?" she said.

Mac barked a laugh, leaning back on his swivel chair, running a hand through his rarely combed, shaggy dark hair.

"Aye. I just can't quite get a handle on this one as quickly as I'd like. It's reminding me of the Richard McCullough case. It's just... different. No obvious motive and a lot of muddy waters."

Mel nodded. "I know what you mean. I've been thinking the same thing. Cazzy has picked up on it. I'm not allowed through the door until I've left the office behind, so the baby doesn't pick up on it."

"And how do you do that?" Mac asked.

"On the drive home I give myself a count down. I leave something work related behind at each count until I get home completely unburdened."

She smiled like it was the easiest thing in the world to do. Mac thought about his own home. Unburdening himself of the office only to walk into an extension of it.

"I'll give it a try," he said.

"No, you won't. For a copper, you're a terrible liar, guv," Mel laughed.

"Hey, I've been in private psychotherapy for months now," Mac said. "I'm not oblivious to the toll our jobs take on our mental health."

Mel's face said she was surprised. "Good for you, guv. I

will stop trying to mother you then and get on with some work."

"Don't stop being the mother hen, Mel. I appreciate it," Mac said. "Even if it doesn't seem like it most of the time."

It was true, though admitting it felt like tearing off his skin. He smiled to back up his words and Mel actually blushed. She left the room and Mac looked back at the dozens of unread emails, feeling like something had been achieved. The emails shouted for his attention, probably a few hours' work to deal with them. Later. He stood up, locking his workstation and striding from the office, hands in pockets and head down.

"Later, guv," Mel called after him.

"Call me if you need me," Mac called back, raising one hand over his head.

———

THE ADDRESS NICK CASS had given them was in King's Haugh, across the train tracks from Wester Hailes, one of the city's most deprived areas. It was an easy commute from Saughton Prison, a small island of residential streets that turned in on themselves to end in cul-de-sacs and crescents. The houses were the familiar bungalow and one and a half storey houses that could be seen all over Scotland, but especially in the leafier suburbs of Edinburgh. The trimmed hedges and well-kept gardens made Mac think of a retirement village. Occasionally a trampoline was visible in a back garden or a bike left on its side on a lawn said younger families were also in residence. He took his time navigating towards King's Haugh Avenue, which lay at the centre of a network of streets, all beginning with the word King's Haugh. The houses there were older sandstone villas, clustered around a road and an open green space surrounded by wrought-iron railings. Once upon a time, this probably stood alone on the edge of the city, looking out over fields. Now it had been swallowed up by sprawling suburbia.

There was no car in the driveway of number 6, Cass's house. There were religious messages taped up in the windows, posters advertising God and the Church. Nothing too happy clappy but clear which house was the parochial one. Mac pulled up opposite, looking over the house. Nice place to live if you could afford it. He wondered how it worked. Did he pay rent to the church, or was it all taken care of? The numbers 1909 were inscribed over the doorway. He tried to gauge what it might tell him of its inhabitant. Privileged. Wealthy. Or was that just his own prejudices talking? If Cass was home, Mac would just find some more questions to ask him, though it would risk a harassment complaint. If he wasn't, then he would try the neighbours. In a street like this, they might be obnoxious 'my taxes pay your wages' types. Doctors. Solicitors. Chartered accountants. Money tended to make them feel that anyone obviously earning less wasn't much more than a peasant.

After a minute, he got out of the car. There was no sign of life from the house. He walked up a gravel drive to the front door, seeing a brass intercom panel next to it. There were two names on it. Cass - Ground, Rose - 1st. So the house was subdivided. Maybe Cass wasn't as well off as outward appearances. Could a parish priest be well off, anyway? Mac was perhaps making unfair judgments because of his well-spoken, Southern English accent. It sounded straight out of public school, but it looked as though Cass had maybe given all that up when he'd entered the church. He pressed the buzzer for Cass. Heard it sound somewhere inside. Waited. Nothing. Pressed again. The other buzzer came to life, a click, then the sound of breathing and finally a female voice. Young and husky.

"He's out at work. If you have a delivery, I can sign for it or just leave it around the back."

"Police," Mac said. "Can I talk to you, please?"

"Yeah, right, pal. Pull the other one. Now get lost before I call the real police."

Mac laughed. The intercom was cut off. He pressed the buzzer again for Rose this time. No answer. A female voice from somewhere above told him to go away using colourful language. It came from directly above the door, at the front of the house. Stepping out of the stone porch, Mac backed up the drive and held out his badge to the upstairs windows.

"DCI McNeill, Serious Crimes Unit," he called out.

The windows reflected the trees in the park opposite, but Mac thought he saw the shadow of someone moving behind them. Glancing at the houses on either side, he wondered if this was attracting the attention of any other neighbours. Maybe that would get him inside quicker.

"Hello!" he called out. "Police Scotland! Can I talk to you, please?"

He heard the click of the front door unlocking and strode into the house. The hallway was tiled, turning sharply to the right, and then running towards the back of the house. There was a door to the left with a crucifix attached to it. A staircase faced him as he followed the hallway round the corner. A passageway led past the stairs to the rear of the house. The walls were covered in vibrant abstract paintings.

"Come up, mouth!" came the female voice from upstairs. "Nicky will be raging when he hears you were shouting the odds."

Mac climbed the stairs. Above was a doorway standing open but secured with a chain. A woman stood behind the chain. In her thirties Mac Guessed, with blonde hair piled on top of her head. Wearing baggy joggies and a sweater that was covered in paint. She wore sandals and had a cigarette in one hand, the ash almost as long as the remaining cigarette.

Mac showed his ID again when he reached the top of the stairs. She puffed on the cigarette as she looked at it critically, then at Mac.

"I've got a stash, but it's legal. Personal use," she said, blowing out smoke.

"I don't care. Can I come in?" Mac replied.

She was English but had the sound of the north. Yorkshire maybe. Or Lancashire? Mac couldn't really tell the difference. The door was closed, the chain removed, and then reopened.

"Elizabeth Rose," she said.

Mac stepped into a flat that smelled of paint, cigarettes, and something floral and slightly spicy, like pot-pourri. It was decorated with multi-coloured throws, draped over furniture, the floor and hung from the walls. To the left was a kitchen in a sorry state. To the right, a living room with a bay window that reached from floor to ceiling. Decorative moulding ran around the edges of the tall ceiling and formed a floral rose at the central light fixture. Surfaces were filled with paintings in various stages of completion or else books. Or piles of laundry.

Mac put his hands in his pockets and looked at Elizabeth Rose.

"You're an artist?" he guessed.

"Yes. You're a good detective, I can tell," Elizabeth replied acerbically.

"I don't miss much," Mac grinned. "Can I talk to you about your neighbour, Nick Cass?"

"What's Nicky done?" Elizabeth asked.

She moved a pile of pants from a chair and sat. She didn't offer a chair to Mac, and he settled for moving a pile of large hardback books from one end of a sofa. The book on top had a black-and-white photo of a naked man on the cover.

"He hasn't done anything that I know of. I just need to ask about his movements over the last few days."

"Checking out an alibi, eh?" Elizabeth said, knocking ash from the end of her cigarette into her hand.

"He doesn't need an alibi. I just have to check on the veracity of a statement he gave. Standard routine."

"Sure. Well, ask away."

"Sunday night. Was he at home?" Mac asked.

Elizabeth scrunched up her face.

"Yes, he was. Well, he was here, actually."

"Here? In your flat?"

"It's an apartment, but yes, he was."

"From when?"

"Six."

"How can you be so precise?"

"Because he comes over for our Great Pottery Throw Down night at the same time every Saturday."

Mac frowned. "I'm talking about Sunday, though."

"Yes, this week it was Sunday. Usually it's a Saturday night. This week it wasn't but we always keep the same time," Elizabeth said, sounding exasperated. Mac nodded, as though that made everything clear.

"How long does your Pottery Throw Down night last for?" he asked.

"Anything from a couple of hours to midnight. Sunday's

was a marathon. We were catching up to get ready for the new season."

"What time did he leave?" Mac asked.

His heart was pounding, adrenaline sharpening his attention. This was the feeling he lived for, the thrill of an investigation moving.

"He didn't. He slept on the sofa, where you are," Elizabeth said, getting up to empty the ashes from her hand into a mug.

"What time did you last see him on Sunday night?" Mac asked.

"I went to bed about half two. He was already asleep."

Mac gave nothing away even as his heart sank. He'd been hoping Cass's alibi would have a gaping hole in it. That this eccentric woman would admit to not knowing where her house mate was. But, half two in the morning was too late to match the CCTV of the man getting out of the van and snipping the chain on the building site gates.

"And this is the man we're both talking about, eh?" Mac said.

He held up a picture on his phone of Nick Cass, taken from the HMP Edinburgh website. Elizabeth lit another cigarette and leaned in, frowning at the picture.

"Yes, that's him."

Chapter Twenty

"WHAT'S your relationship with Father Nick Cass?" Mac asked.

Elizabeth looked at him through the cigarette smoke, pursing her lips.

"What do you think?"

"That's what I'm asking," Mac countered.

"He's a Catholic priest, and he's gay," Elizabeth said. "So, we're just friends."

That was new. Mac hadn't got that from Cass. Not that he had any sort of gaydar, but it hadn't even occurred to him.

"How do you know he's gay?" he asked.

"Come off it. He's a celibate priest. It's well known that homosexual urges are common where celibacy is enforced. That's why so many Catholic priests end up fiddling with choir boys. They're hiding their sexuality."

"So, you think he's gay? Has he ever said as much?"

"Not in so many words. But we've circled the airport many times in a lot of late night chats. Plus, he's never so much as looked at me twice since I moved in. I offered it, you know? He's a good-looking man and there's something about forbidden fruit that's very alluring."

Mac wanted to laugh. Cass's neighbour fancied Cass and, because she couldn't seduce a Catholic priest, assumed he must be gay. She was attractive, though her obviously chaotic lifestyle would be an instant turnoff for Mac. Maybe it was for Cass, too.

"Maybe he takes his vows seriously," Mac suggested.

Elizabeth snorted. "Can I paint you?" she asked suddenly.

Mac raised an eyebrow. "No," he said.

"I'd like to do a nude study. I'm abstract, so no-one would know it was you," she persisted.

Mac smiled the rogue's grin and Elizabeth smiled back. It did work sometimes.

"No," he said, letting the smile vanish to leave no ambiguity. "So am I gay too?"

"Oh no," Elizabeth said. "I can see the way you're looking at me. Given time, I think I'd get you."

Her eyes were very blue and her stare very direct. The oversize sweater had fallen away from one shoulder, revealing tanned skin with no bra strap. She folded her arms beneath her breasts, letting them show against the baggy material. Mac held her gaze.

"Did Nick Cass ever tell you anything about his sexuality?"

Elizabeth rolled her eyes. "Not in so many words. There was a friend," she encased the word in quotation marks with her fingers, "a few years ago. He topped himself. And I've seen Nicky with someone recently."

"A man," Mac said.

"Yep. Nicky was trying to sneak him in last week. So,

no, he hasn't said in so many words, but I'm no slouch as a detective either when I want to be."

Mac didn't know if it was relevant. Probably not. A death in Cass's past was worth looking into though. Standing, he decided it was time to build a little rapport with Cass's eccentric neighbour. He looked over a canvas leaning against the wall by the sofa. Just making out the name Rose in a sharp scrawl in one corner.

"Is this what you do for a living, Elizabeth?" he asked. "It's OK to call you Elizabeth?"

"Beth. Call me Beth," she almost purred.

She walked over to Mac and picked up the canvas.

"From my blue period. An examination of the frailty of human existence."

Mac nodded, resisting the urge to turn his head to one side to try and make sense of the jumbled mess in front of him.

"Interesting," he said. "What can you tell me about Nick's current boyfriend?"

Beth sighed, resting one arm on Mac's shoulder. Her fingers were smudged red and blue from paint. Mac let her remain within his personal space, playing along.

"Not much. Younger than Nick. Maybe in his late twenties. Looks a bit rough if you ask me. Maybe that's what Nicky likes."

"When was he last here?" Mac asked.

"A week ago. Haven't seen him lately," Beth said.

With Mac not responding to her body language, she moved away, flicking her cigarette into a nearby ashtray and picking up another canvas. This was predominantly red.

"Your red period?" Mac asked.

"My oil period," Beth replied. "I've never been sure of this one."

"I prefer it," Mac said, picking it at random over the blue period painting. "More vibrant. Full of energy."

He was plucking words out of the air, but it seemed the right thing to say. Beth smiled, licking her upper teeth, and revealing a tongue piercing.

"You have unexpected taste," she said.

"So, how long have you known Nick Cass?" Mac probed.

There was a loud thump from somewhere downstairs. Beth glanced down. Mac froze, listening.

"Someone downstairs?" he asked.

"Can't be. I saw Nicky go out this morning, and he hasn't been back," Beth replied.

"What about the boyfriend?"

"I would know if someone had been staying for an entire week."

"Does he have a cat?" Mac asked.

"No, he's allergic," Beth said.

Another sound from downstairs, a creak. Like someone stepping on a floorboard. Mac started for the door.

"What's his name? The boyfriend?" Mac asked.

"Conor, I think. He's mentioned a Conor a couple of times. From work."

Cass worked in a prison so either Conor was a screw or an ex-con. And dating an ex-con while continuing to work as a prison chaplain would be frowned on. Apart from the whole being in the closet thing. Mac reached the bottom of the stairs and approached the front door of Cass's flat. He put his ear to it, listening. No sound. He rapped sharply on the door.

"Conor? DCI McNeill, Police Scotland. Could you open the door, please?"

Silence. Beth had half descended the stairs, leaning over the metal banister. Mac knocked harder.

"Is there a back door?" he whispered to Beth.

She pointed to the hallway.

"Key above the cellar door inside," she whispered back.

Mac went along to the low door under the stairs, opened it. There were electricity meters inside, as well as a mop and bucket and an old mountain bike. Feeling above the door frame inside, he found a key and picked it up. At the end of the hallway was a door leading out to an area of decking, then a lawn with metal drying poles sticking out of it, revealing something of the building's history. There was another door a few yards away, clearly a private back door to the ground-floor flat, added when the house was subdivided. Mac put the key into the lock and turned it.

The door flew open from the inside, and a man ran out. His shoulder struck Mac in the chest, knocking him off balance. He grabbed for a leg as the man stepped over him, running. He got a brief grip of denim, then a laced trainer. The man kicked out, catching Mac on the temple and breaking his grip. Mac rolled over, pushing himself to his feet and forward like a sprinter coming out of the blocks. The man was wearing a t-shirt and faded, ripped jeans. He had fair hair close cropped. He was sprinting down the garden towards the fence which separated the property from trees beyond. At that moment, there came the rushing roar of a train. Mac saw it in between branches, flashing past a hundred yards away.

"Conor!" Mac called out.

The man looked back once, telling Mac that Beth had the name right at least. Mac saw a boyish face. Mid-twenties. Enormous eyes, too big, the kind you only got after losing weight way too fast. As Mac got a better look at him, he could see the scrawny arms with the scars of track marks. Addict, or at least a recent addict. Conor took off after a second's hesitation, reaching the fence and jumping for the top.

"Hey! I'm not here for you and I don't care what you've done," Mac said, slowing to a walk. "Just stop, lad."

Conor turned, putting his back to the fence, and reaching behind his back for something. He came up with a knife, licking his lips.

"OK, that's got my attention," Mac told him. "You don't need it, though. I'm not armed and I'm not out to do you any harm. I didn't even know you were in there."

"Nick locked me in, eh?" Conor said.

"Locked you in? Why?" Mac asked.

Conor was looking in all directions, looking for an escape route. Mac stepped to one side of the lawn, leaving Conor the lion's share of the garden to run. He put his hands in his trouser pockets.

"I can't let you go carrying a deadly weapon. So throw it away and you're free to leave. I've got nothing on you," Mac said. "Unless you want to press charges against Father Nick Cass?"

"No, no. I don't want to do that," Conor replied. "I just want to go."

"Throw the knife away. That's not a chef's knife and there's only one reason to carry it. You'll get picked up inside of twenty-four hours if you keep hold of it," Mac said.

Conor looked at the blade, long and narrow, the switch-blade type.

"Yours?" Mac asked.

Conor shook his head and threw it aside into a leafy shrubbery.

"Can I go now?" he asked.

"Can I ask you something first?" Mac asked, hopefully.

"No. I don't talk to polis," Conor said.

Suddenly he was running, making a wide berth around Mac who just let him go. Beth stood in the communal back door. She said something, but Conor didn't stop. A fence separated the front of the house from the back, with a tall gate secured by a bolt. Conor hit the gate at a run, scrambling up it and vaulting over. Mac slowly walked to the shrubbery, gently moving aside long branches with small green leaves.

He saw the knife lying in the dirt and reached into an inside pocket for an evidence bag. Scooping up the knife with the bag, turning it inside out and wrapping the open end over carefully, he put it in his pocket next to the encrypted phone.

"That the man you saw with Cass last week?" Mac asked as he walked back up the garden.

"That's him. Bit of a chav, but that's what Nick likes, clearly."

"He's a junkie or used to be," Mac told her.

"No way! Nicky really does like a bit of rough then."

"As rough as it gets," Mac said.

He was peering into the private backdoor. Inside was a small room, not much more than a cupboard. A tumble dryer stood against one wall and some stacked plastic crates against another. A further door led into the flat. It was open, showing a hallway with an upturned laundry basket and clothes spilling out across the floor. Mac took out his phone and called Mel.

"Mel. I'm at Nick Cass's house. There was an intruder inside who fled the scene when I arrived. I'm going inside. Have a couple of uniforms head up here and a forensic tech. Suspected burglary. Also, see if you can get hold of Cass to let him know there was a break in."

"Right, guv. Is there a witness to the intruder?"

"Yes. Woman in the flat above saw the whole thing, so we're golden, eh?" Mac replied, knowing exactly what Mel was getting at it.

"Ok, guv. On it."

Mac hung up. Beth was at his shoulder again. He could smell the cigarettes and the paint.

"Stay out here, please," he said formally.

Entering, he closed the outer door almost on her face. He glanced around the utility room and then slipped into the flat proper, turning sideways to avoid touching the door or the frame. He stepped around the spilled clothes. The basket had obviously been sitting on a table against the wall and been knocked off by Conor. One of the thumps that had caught Mac's attention from upstairs. The flat seemed to be L-shaped, with bedrooms at the back of the house and a bathroom to one side. A front room took up half the house's frontage and incorporated a large bay window, mirroring Beth's flat above. A kitchen and office occupied the other half of the ground floor.

The place seemed tidy and well kept. Images of Christ proliferated on the walls as well as crucifixes and books about religion. One bedroom was meticulously tidy, almost like a room in an army barracks or a seminary. The other was dark, with curtains drawn and the bed unmade. A pile of dirty plates stood on a bedside table and a collection of beer cans and bottles, all empty, were strewn across the floor. At the risk of being prejudicial, he guessed this was where Conor had been staying. Correction had been imprisoned. Mac noticed a hasp and padlock halfway down on the outside of the door. It had been bust from the inside.

The padlock was still locked, secured to the door frame while the hasp had broken free of the actual door; wood where it had been screwed in was splintered. The living room was bright and airy, one wall dominated by shelving filled with books. A cursory examination revealed more ecclesiastical texts, as well as some biographies. Bowie, Cobain, Brian Clough, and Bill Shankly. Eclectic. The TV was modestly sized and had both video and DVD player next to it. Mac turned a circle in the middle of the room, looking for anything that might stand out. Nothing did.

He went through to the office. More books, all appearing to be related to Cass's professional life. Books on religion but also academic volumes on the subjects of childhood trauma, the effects of parents in prison on the child and Glasgow's vaunted Crime Reduction Unit, among other titles. Mac was getting the impression of a man with liberal social views. Someone who was trying to understand criminal behaviour in terms of adverse childhood experiences and trauma. Mac was aware of this kind of thinking and knew about the work that had been done in tackling gang violence in Glasgow.

He admired it, though found the parameters of his own job meant he couldn't allow that thinking in his own approach. His job was to detect, find the perpetrator and build the evidence that would see them successfully prosecuted. Maybe people like Nick Cass would one day make him redundant by reducing the need for so many police officers. It was a nice fairy tale. Mac knew there would always be men and women willing to do anything to each other for their own interests. He could only think in terms of good and evil. Black and white. You couldn't deal with the likes of John Lowe or Hance Allen in any other way. Not if you didn't want your throat cut.

There were some framed photographs on shelves against one wall. A young man, clearly Nick Cass, with an older youth who bore a passing resemblance. Another showed three men in clerical black. Nick Cass was one, Neil Fitzsimmons beside him. He assumed it was Nathan Flenders that stood behind and between both, arms around their shoulders. With gritted teeth, Mac recognized him as the man who had barged past him at St Aiden's. Older than the other two. He made a mental note to speak to Father Fitzsimmons again.

Another picture was of a young man, late twenties, possibly. He had raven hair that fell across his eyes and was squinting at the camera through dark, narrowed eyes. A scar made a shadowy patch to the left side of his chin. He was standing in a doorway, holding up a piece of paper. Despite the scowl on his face, he seemed to be smiling.

No sign of who or where it was. Mac picked it up, looking closely, trying to make out what was on the paper. He took out his phone and zoomed in. The image became blurry and out of focus for a moment until Mac got the distance between the picture and the camera just right. He could distinguish the larger text on the piece of paper. The words 'Tenancy Agreement' were clear, but that was all he could make out.

On a whim he turned over the frame and undid the catches that held the back in place. Shot in the dark. Some people wrote on the back of pictures that had significance to them. Dates. Places. Names. On the back of this one was the name Carl and a date. 13/09/20.

There was more, a scrawl that he could barely read. It looked like Sighthill Loan. Charming area to be moving into. The doorway in which Carl stood, whoever Carl was, appeared to be the door of a flat. A number 7 was just visible, partly obscured by the picture's subject. Mac replaced it, wondering who the young man was and what his connection could be to Nick Cass. A brother? A nephew?

Perhaps someone from a relationship before Cass took a vow of celibacy? A boyfriend? He replaced the picture on the shelf, careful to position it exactly as it had been. On the desk in a corner of the room was a stack of magazines. They seemed to be academic and all relating to the Church. He stopped dead as he read the cover of the first. It included a summary of the articles within. The first on the list was titled - A Brief History of Sin-Eating by Father Nathan Flenders.

Chapter Twenty-One

MAC FISHED a pair of gloves from his coat pocket and put them on. Then he picked up the journal, flicking through to the article by Nathan Flenders. It covered six pages, written in dense, small type. Skimming it, Mac saw it appeared to be exactly what the title suggested. He jumped to the end, looking for a conclusion, and read through it quickly. Flenders summed up the practise with references to Church doctrine and using theological language that Mac couldn't follow.

He felt like he would need a translator. He put the journal aside and picked up others. They all contained an article by Nathan Flenders, but none of the others seemed to cover sin-eating. They were opaque to Mac, using words whose meaning he could only guess at. Academic language combined with ecclesiastical jargon. It might as well all have been in Latin. At least he could have used his phone to translate that. Each article by Flenders was marked with a post it, stuck to the top corner of the first page.

"Now why are you so interested in what your pal is writing about?" Mac wondered aloud.

Was it coincidence that Cass was reading an article on the practise of sin-eating? Or how about the fact that the two men who were last to see Adam Glebe alive, had some connection to the practise, and one of them apparently having seriously fallen out with Glebe recently.

"Should I be looking more closely at you, Father Flenders?" Mac mused, flicking through pages.

He stripped off his gloves and took out his phone, sitting at the desk. Bringing up Clio's name, he was about to hit call when he stopped himself. He'd caused a lot of trouble for Clio. She was moving to the arse end of nowhere because of him. Skye might be a tourist attraction, but to Mac it was grey and dismal, a place lacking hope and flooded with desperation. It was dead. He tossed the phone onto the desk, throwing back his head and staring at the ceiling. Clio had done enough. He couldn't involve her further. Couldn't ask. The trouble was, he'd learned enough about academia from Clio to know that information on Nathan Flenders's academic work was likely to be locked away behind paywalls. Universities and academic publications shared knowledge with each other but guarded it jealously against the general public. And that included police officers.

Clio could look through anything Flenders had published while Mac's officers would be limited to abstracts or publishers summaries. He wanted to know what Flenders's academic interests were. Whether he was an expert on sin-eating. He rubbed a hand over his face, feeling a powerful urge to smoke. His mind felt muddy, working at half its normal speed. It didn't help that sleep came in fits and starts these days. Punctuated by nightmares that sank their claws into his mind and refused...

"Dammit!" he sat up and then swore again before picking up the phone and hitting Clio's number.

It rang three times, and he was about to hang up, telling himself he'd tried and that was enough. Then Clio picked up.

"Hi Mac."

Sounding like nothing was amiss, and nothing had happened. Everything normal.

"Hey, Clio. Where are you?"

Awkward. Not sure how to broach the subject of Clio being effectively on the run.

"We're here. It's a beautiful place. Maia is making a list of things to see. The Airbnb is amazing."

"Am I on speaker?" Mac asked.

Pause. "Not anymore. Maia's in the next room, anyway."

"I sent some money to you for the place," Mac said.

"And I told you, you didn't need to. I think I probably earn the same as you do now," Clio replied.

"Probably. Spend it on Maia then," Mac said.

"Thanks. I'll keep hold of it. Don't worry about us, Mac. We're fine. We're safe," Clio said.

"You are, but I'm going to worry anyway, eh? You know what it's like being a parent."

The words were out before he even had time to think about what he was saying. He wanted them back, but suddenly felt silly. He even blushed, gritting his teeth and screwing his eyes shut, swearing inside his head. His thoughts were too sluggish, like his head was full of treacle.

"Not that I'm...you know what I'm...I mean," blundered Mac.

"It's OK. That's sweet and Maia would be over the moon to know you think of her that way," Clio said gently.

"I misspoke. She's got a dad," Mac said.

"She doesn't, actually. He left us when Maia was a baby, as you know, and hasn't been back. She has me. And she has you now. Don't go all male on me and backtrack. You said something really lovely just now. I appreciate it."

Mac swore aloud. "I've never been good at the family stuff. Look, I called to ask for your help. I know I don't have the right to ask. You've done enough, and it's my fault you're in this..."

"Keep this up and we're going to fall out," Clio interrupted. "You're not responsible for the bad guys. It isn't your fault. It's theirs. Right?"

"Clio..." Mac began in a tone that said he was going to disagree.

"Right?" Clio said, firmly.

Mac chuckled after a minute of gritting his teeth. "You've been on some assertiveness courses for this new job, eh?" he said.

"Yes, actually," Clio laughed. "So, what do you need, Mac?"

"Nothing that's going to involve you directly in the investigation. I need some research and you're going to have more joy with your university credentials than any of my team. There's a Catholic priest called Nathan Flenders. Seems he's also a scholar, quite a few pieces published. I'd like to get an idea what kind of work he does."

"OK, I can search for the name in the university online library and any others we have sharing agreements with. I take it you can't just ask him?"

"Haven't found him yet. When I do, I will. Wanted to get a heads up before that, though."

"Mind if I get one of my graduate students to help? I'm still working, remember?"

Mac hadn't remembered, thinking of Clio as being on holiday. Of course she bloody wasn't. She was in hiding with her daughter, in fear for their lives, thanks to him. Couldn't just drop everything at a moment's notice and expect to keep her job. She was working from home, though she was actually working a couple of hundred miles away from home.

"Aye, fine. I'm not looking for anything confidential or sensitive. I'm particularly interested in any historical or theological papers he might have written or anything mentioning sin-eating," he said.

"Ok. I'll get onto it."

"Also…if your assistant could give me a summary of the works he's done, eh? It might as well be written in Latin for all I can understand what he's banging on about," Mac said.

"Sure. Alexis has a degree in applied philosophy, so she should be able to make sense of some theological tracts for you."

Looking through the window of the office, Mac could see a marked police car pulling into the drive.

"Clio, I've got to go. But thanks and…"

He didn't know how to finish that sentence. He wanted to say he was sorry. Wanted to tell her he appreciated her and that he'd meant what he said about caring for Maia the way a parent would. But the words weren't there.

"I know. Get back to work. Speak soon," Clio said, and the line went dead.

Mac went through the flat to the back door, not seeing a key anywhere to unlock the front. Beth was waving through two uniforms who had been standing at Cass's front door.

"It's locked. Back door was open," Mac said.

They both called him sir in acknowledgement, even before he produced his warrant card. He nodded, not placing their faces but sure he would, given time.

"A man came out of the back door. White, late twenties, average height. Had the look of a junkie and he was carrying a knife, which I'll log in as evidence. First name Conor. Fair hair. I'll notify the owner and get him down here to see what, if anything, was taken. We'll get prints and DNA," Mac said.

"Right guv," said the first, a female officer with dark hair and thick, straight eyebrows and an Italian complexion. Mac thought she was called Gail.

"This the owner coming now?" said the male officer with her, pure Edinburgh accent and a bent nose with a square jaw. Mac couldn't place him, but had a feeling he'd been present on at least one of Mac's crime scenes in the past.

Mac walked up the hallway to the front door of the house. A Toyota SUV had pulled into the drive and Nick Cass was getting out. He wore the Catholic blacks still and there was outrage on his face.

"What the heck is going on? What are you doing at my house?" he demanded.

"Burglar, Father Cass," Mac replied bluntly.

"What? What? When?" Cass said, crunching across the gravel, taking out his keys. "I've never had any trouble like that before."

"I came to speak to your neighbour and heard a noise in the flat. A man came out and ran away. It's lucky you weren't here. He was armed," Mac said, watching Cass for a reaction.

He got it. Cass's mouth flapped open and his eyes went

wide. Then he frowned, put a hand to his head, mouth still opening and closing like a fish.

"Shall we go inside? You'll need to tell the officers if anything is missing," Mac said.

"Well, was he carrying anything?" Cass finally said.

"Just a knife," Mac replied.

"Then how can anything be missing?" Cass shot back.

He took a set of keys from his pocket and unlocked the front door. He went through the living room, looking around with not much more than a glance. Straight for the back bedroom. He stopped at the door, looking down at the splintered lock. Mac held up a hand to stop Gail and her partner from going in. He followed Cass, waiting quietly behind him. Cass turned and looked at him.

"He said you were keeping him prisoner, Father," Mac said, quietly.

"It was for his own good," Cass said, his face anguished. "Conor wasn't a junkie before he went inside. He came out an addict. I got him into rehab. Nothing seemed to work. He was... he was too damaged. This seemed like the only way. Cold turkey."

The look on the priest's face was so desolate that Mac believed him. This wasn't a predator locking up a vulnerable young man. This was a man who'd given his life to helping others and had failed to help this one individual. Mac nodded.

"I let him go once he dropped the knife. Couldn't hold him since he had nothing on him that could have been nicked."

Mac omitted the fact he didn't actually believe Conor had been robbing Cass. He just wanted a pretext to get into Cass's flat and have a snoop.

"I know," Cass said, wearily. "Some people just can't be helped. That's what I need to learn."

"You met Conor inside? At Saughton?" Mac asked.

"Yes. He was doing eighteen months for taking without consent. Fifth time he'd been done for it. He had so much potential. He was clever, could have done well for himself with a few courses, some qualifications. But the drugs just took over." Cass gave an angry growl and kicked the door to the bedroom. "It makes me so angry sometimes. The men who sold him the stuff destroyed his life just for money. They might as well have killed him and had done with it. It just..."

He tailed off.

"I understand. I've seen the same thing," Mac said.

"Yes, but you just focus on punishing them, don't you? I'm trying to help them. Trying to..." again words seemed to fail the priest.

Mac watched the war being waged across his face. He felt a certain respect for this man now, seeing beyond the facade of the privileged Southerner that had so irritated the working class chip on his shoulder. But there was a question he wanted an answer to.

"When I asked you about sin-eating, you gave me a vague reply, but you know more about it than you let on, don't you?" Mac said.

Cass looked at him from behind a frown of confusion.

"Do I? What makes you say that?"

"I found a pile of journals containing pieces written by your friend Father Nathan Flenders. One of them was a history of sin eating."

"You went into my office?" Cass said, sounding outraged.

"I considered it my duty to make sure the property was

safe. There might have been someone else in here waiting for you."

"I hadn't got round to reading them. Nathan asked me to peer review for him. He often did. He probably asked Neil as well. So, no, I don't know as much about it as Nathan did. He was the expert."

Mac nodded, satisfied with the explanation for now. When he finally tracked Nathan Flenders down, he'd be able to verify it.

"Incidentally, how long have you had Conor locked... have you been helping him get off the drugs for?" Mac asked.

The question had been foremost in his mind since Cass had appeared, but he wanted an opportunity to catch him off guard.

"He's been here this last week," Cass replied without hesitation.

"Your neighbour seemed to think you sneaked him in a week ago but he hadn't stayed," Mac said.

Cass made a face, looking over his shoulder as if to check that she wasn't listening.

"Beth drinks, quite a lot. I ended up spending all night at hers a couple of nights ago to keep her from going on a bender. I think she's bi-polar."

"You're quite the Samaritan," Mac said.

"I'm a priest," Cass said with a touch of bite. "It's in the job description. Believe me, at times like this, I wish I could be as cynical as you. Sorry, that was uncalled for. I'm... I'm a bit on edge."

"I don't suppose you have the address of Nathan Flenders's caravan in Fife?"

"No. I told you this already. I've never been there. Sorry

again if I'm being a bit sharp. I'm just worried about Conor."

Cass's face was tense, eyes hard and constantly darting. He was drumming his fingers on the wall, staring about but seeing nothing. A worried man or a talented actor.

"You have a surname or an address for him?" Mac asked.

"Please, Detective Chief Inspector. If the police start looking, I'll never find him. Just let me search for him on my own, alright? Please. He's done nothing wrong. There's nothing you can possibly be interested in talking to him about. Please?"

Mac looked at him, letting the silence gnaw at the priest. Finally, he nodded. Even if Conor could be found, he would be no more reliable a witness as to Cass's movements than Beth. Locked up in the back bedroom, he wouldn't be able to verify the priest's whereabouts. It didn't matter. Mac was having a hard time seeing Nick Cass as the Sin-Eater.

"OK, Father Cass. I'll get out of your way."

Mac walked out of the house and back to his car. As he got back in, he took out his phone and called Kai. On the way over to Cass's house, he'd called and assigned Kai and Isla the task of physically finding Nathan Flenders.

"Any luck?" he asked by way of hello.

"Not yet, guv," Kai replied. "We checked at his house in Edinburgh first. It's owned by the Church and there was a housekeeper who confirmed Flenders was away to Fife but couldn't tell us where. There is a saltwater lido at Pittenweem. You did mention a saltwater pool, eh? We've been checking the big caravan parks around Pittenweem. So far, no luck. But we've got two more to go to. Isla is speaking with local estate agents and holiday lets to see if there are any privately owned caravans around that could be his. Or that he might be renting."

"Cass mentioned it being remote. A single road unusable by cars, partially swept away by a landslide. So, probably not a caravan park."

"Right, guv. That narrows it down. Still a lot of privately owned places to look through, though. Lots of little places that don't show up on Maps."

"OK, well, stay over if you need to. I'll authorise the expenses when I get back to the office," Mac said.

"Thanks, guv."

Kai sounded happy, though he was trying not to show it.

"Separate rooms," Mac said.

"Guv!" Kai replied, sounding hurt.

Mac hung up.

Chapter Twenty-Two

MAC WORKED LATE. He logged the knife as evidence, filing it against the Adam Glebe murder case. He wanted to know if the blade fitted the profile of the wound that had opened Glebe's throat. Long shot, but worth checking. Waiting for Kai and Isla to track down Nathan Flenders up in Pittenweem, he dove into the minutia of the case. In his office, he scrolled through statements taken from potential witnesses. Staff and customers at bars and clubs on Cowgate near the building site where the body of Adam Glebe had been taken. CCTV sourced by Kai and uploaded to the Police Scotland servers. DNA found at the scene and matched up to known sources.

Adam Glebe. Jacob Danzig, Mac himself. No match for Nick Cass. An unidentified sample found at the scene, still outstanding. Could be the killer. Could be a member of staff at Mary King's Close who hadn't yet been checked. Or a former member of staff. Lot of variables. A knock at the office door stirred him from a state of computer-induced hypnosis, scrolling through almost endless lists of files and folders into which every detail had been logged and filed, right down to the smallest.

Exhausting to wade through, but sometimes this was how a murder case went. Gather every piece of information and then go through it over and over, looking for anything you might have missed first or second time. He'd got lucky a few times, been assigned cases that were unusual in their rapid development. Mac wondered if that was the ultimate source of the success he'd had as a detective. Rising to DCI because of a few spectacular cases in which he'd got lucky. Now he was mired in one that didn't seem to have a clear cut solution. Maybe this was where he got found out.

"Come in!" he called out; blinking away the near sleep state he'd fallen into at a knock on his door.

"I'm knocking off, guv. I've sent you everything I could find about Nick Cass," Mel said.

"You look tired, Mel. Thanks for staying on. Get home to Cazzy and the baby."

Mel frowned, and Mac realised he'd been unusually personal. He felt like he was drunk.

"You look done in yourself, guv," Mel said. "Remember, it's a marathon, not a sprint."

Mac turned back to his computer screen. "I'm good thanks, Detective Inspector. I'll see you tomorrow," Mac replied, barriers back up again with a vengeance.

Mel laughed. "Can't hide the human from me, guv. Good night. Don't stay too late."

Mel left and Mac sat back in his chair, running his hands through his hair. He didn't relish the thought of going back to his flat. Facing the whiteboards and their crisscrossing red lines. The mess. Professional and personal. It felt like a toxic pit he wanted to bury. Seal it off. But he couldn't.

Driving rain made Mac's cheeks numb. His hair was slicked back against his skull and his suit was plastered to his skin. The road was pitted and in the dark he kept stepping into potholes, twisting his ankles painfully each time. Except the pain was a secondary thing. Most important was the young girl running ahead of him. She had dark hair, cut short and spiky.

"Iona!" he called out, but knew it wasn't her. "I can't keep up! Come back!"

But she kept going, sprinting, and looking back over her shoulder like she was being chased. Mac tried to run after her, but the potholes in the road made it impossible to get into a rhythm. Trees to either side of the road were masses of black, hills beyond invisible in the darkness. There was only the road and the inadequate streetlights. Ahead, in a pool of flickering orange light, a bus stop appeared. It was made of brick with a rotting timber lean-to roof. Maia stopped beside it. No, it was Iona. Except it looked like Maia. And there was a figure stepping out from the shadows behind the shelter, grabbing for her. Mac screamed, ran harder, tripped, and fell. His hands were lost in puddles of freezing water. He was blinded by it, blinking the rain from his eyes but unable to see what had happened to Maia. Only the vague shape of struggling figures. Two of them. One was lower than the other. On the ground. Moving slower. Succumbing. Mac screamed until he was hoarse. The sound of a car engine behind made him turn. It was bearing down on him, driving in the middle of the road. He was lying between the glaring headlights. The car was going to crush his head like a watermelon. He wanted to cover his head with his arms, put his face to the tarmac, and wait for the end. But that would leave Maia, no Iona, no Maia. It had been Maia! That would leave her alone at the mercy of Mark Souter.

Mac scrambled to his feet and jumped into the blackness beside the road. The car sped past. He picked himself up from the mud and sodden grass, running for the bus shelter where he could see a small body lying on the ground. When he reached her, there was a priest carefully placing a loaf of bread on Maia's chest. There was no sign of injury, but she looked pale and wasn't breathing. The priest placed a cup at her side, then looked at Mac.

"She's your daughter. You'll need to eat her sins so she can go to heaven."

"She's innocent," Mac protested.

"How can she be? We're all guilty. Just eat the bread. Take on her sins. Do it."

And now it was Iona. Slim and pretty, with long hair rendered jet black by the rain. Her face was peaceful. There was no hint of the violence that had ended her. The horror that had taken place in the dark so that Iona's last conscious thought was of terror and pain.

"She's innocent," Mac whispered, worn down by the grief and the weight of responsibility.

"She's a sinner. We all are, and we don't know when we're going to go. Do we? Isn't it better to send her on her way ready to meet her maker than to let her die with her soul unprepared?"

It was Father Cass now. He was breaking off a piece of bread and holding it out for Mac to eat. The bread was dripping and soggy. It was dark with the liquid it had been soaked in. The same liquid was oozing from a dozen places on Iona's naked body. Stab wounds, a frenzied cluster of them. The bread was engorged with her blood. Cass was chewing. He was smiling with blood running over his chin and offering a piece of Iona's dripping flesh for Mac to eat.

Mac jerked awake. His feet were up on the desk and printed sheets of paper spilled from his lap to the floor. As he lurched, he kicked the computer monitor, sending it toppling over the edge of the desk. His feet hit the floor with a thump and his office lights suddenly came on, activated by his movement. He was breathing hard, panting. He put a hand to his mouth, feeling wetness there and holding up his hand in front of his face, suddenly sick with terror. Clear liquid. Drool. Not blood. He'd fallen asleep at his desk with his mouth open.

Wiping his chin, he rose, ignoring the scream of protest from his back and knees. Planting his hands on the desk, he forced himself upright. Through the glass partition, he could see a cleaning crew just leaving the large open plan space his team used. They'd left him alone. Grabbing his coat and shrugging into it, he left, pausing only to make sure the encrypted phone was still there. As he rode the lift, he checked his own phone. Missed call from his therapist. He remembered he'd had a call scheduled with him that afternoon.

He set a reminder for the next day to reschedule, actually intended to do it. It felt like the dream was a recurring one, though he couldn't clearly remember having it before. It was just after half eleven. He'd started the day early. Needed to get some proper sleep. Put down the burdens for just a few hours. But the dream had left a bitter taste in his mouth, one he was reluctant to go back to.

Clio's house would be preferable to his own flat. But he needed to speak to Ramsey Jones first. See what information the journalist had, if any. He might be a waste of time, a wannabe amateur sleuth who fancied himself as Sherlock Holmes. Mac called the number Jones had given him. No answer. A few seconds later, Jones called him back.

"Sorry, Detective Chief Inspector, I screen my calls," Ramsey said after establishing it was Mac who had called him.

"Very smart. I'm sure a man in your position needs to take precautions."

"I've had threats made against my life, I'll have you know."

Mac grunted. "Fun, isn't it? So, where do you want to meet to discuss your information?"

"You can come to my hotel. I'll meet you in the lobby."

He gave the address of a hotel on Grassmarket. After hanging up, Mac considering his next move. Ramsey Jones was a journalist and a part of him was reluctant to rely on a civilian, an amateur. Let alone one who resorted to stalking, so desperate was he to get his voice heard. It all smacked of conspiracy theories and nutters. But if Jones had spotted a wider pattern that connected to Mac's case, then it couldn't be passed up. Frankly, he'd take all the help he could at this point.

Mac looked up Ramsey Jones online. Found social media accounts and a YouTube channel. Scrolling, he saw a succession of videos purporting to be in-depth investigations into official corruption, unsolved cases, cover-ups and miscarriages of justice. Mac sighed. Exactly what he hadn't wanted to see. He had a sinking feeling this would be a waste of his time. He felt slow, his brain mired, unable to process information as fast as he usually could.

Running a hand through his hair, he gave serious thought to cancelling on Jones. Could he really know anything of significance in this case? His online presence was just too garish. Too sensational for him to be a serious investigative journalist. Yet... Screw it. He'd give Jones half an hour and if he turned out to be a complete time-waster would put the fear of god into him about interfering in police investigations and bribing police officers for information.

The streets were slick from a shower that had descended while Mac was sleeping in his windowless office. Orange sodium streetlights reflected in puddles and cast an oleaginous sheen across the black tarmac. Grassmarket wasn't far from Brunswick Road. Leith Walk was busy with taxis and buses, crowds emptying out of the Playhouse, milling on the pavement. An endless succession of traffic lights made the drive a monotonous stop start. The city was a heart with clogged arteries, blood flow restricted to a trickle.

He turned down North Street, speeding up once through the congestion trap that was Waverley Station. As the road carried him south, crossing over the top of that buried, ancient part of Edinburgh sealed in when the bridges were built, he sped up. Ornate terraces glowered down, each with elaborately carved rooflines, doorways and windows. Those facades were now homes to chain restaurants and gift shops. Blair Street led him down to the Cowgate, passing beneath North Bridge. Tan coloured modern buildings faced the originals they were designed to emulate. The originals were stained, dripping black. Both were scribed with graffiti. Cowgate was a narrow canyon passing under pollution-eaten arches. Shadows ruled here, even with the streetlights.

After a few minutes, he was out onto the open expanse of the Grassmarket. The pubs and bars hadn't chucked out yet. People accumulated outside, surrounded by clouds of cigarette or vape smoke. Ramsey's hotel was the Pinnacle, on the other side of the road at the end of the Grassmarket. Beyond the hotel was the castle, atop its crags. Mac pulled into a car park behind the hotel, then walked to the front entrance, hands in trouser pockets and overcoat open.

Ramsey Jones was the only person in the foyer. Floor to ceiling windows provided a view out across the eateries and bars. The chairs were of the bucket kind, arranged in groups around glass coffee tables. Pastels ruled in the subdued lighting of the nighttime lobby. A night-receptionist had looked up as Mac entered and looked away again as he made straight for the seating area, showing no sign of needing help. Jones stood, rubbed his hand on his jeans, and offered a hand to shake. Mac took it perfunctorily, sitting down.

"Ok, let's hear it," he said brusquely.

"It started about a year ago," Jones said. "I came across a case of a homeless man found dead in Oxford. His name was James Kendrick. It interested me because of who the man was. The CPS had tried to prosecute for him murder. The trial collapsed due to police errors. I had been looking into the case as part of my channel on miscarriages of justice. Police screwed up his life. He lost his wife, job, home. Everything. Then was found dead."

"And?" Mac asked impatiently, seeing no connection and fearing an overlong ramble on Jones' skills as a detective.

"I bought the forensic evidence and noticed a reference to breadcrumbs on the body. Noted it as strange but irrelevant. Then a story came across my desk in the same part of the world, two residents in a care home. Both died of supposed natural causes and breadcrumbs were found at the scenes. I looked into them because they had both, years before, worked at a care home in Oxfordshire, which had been at the centre of a child abuse scandal. It's since been shut down. They had never been accused of anything. It didn't seem relevant then, but it was a strange detail that stuck in my mind."

"No connection to James Kendrick?" Mac asked, despite himself.

"None that I could see," Jones said, sitting forward in his seat. "I started looking for other cases in my spare time. Not knowing exactly what I was looking for, but working on the basis that all three men had proximity to serious crime.

Kendrick was accused and might have been guilty. The other two, Arnold Denton and Malcolm Fletcher, worked somewhere child abuse had been taking place."

Mac nodded, watching Jones intently. He was warming to his subject, nerves vanishing in his enthusiasm. Mac found it distasteful. He also knew that connections could be found between any two cases if you looked hard enough for them.

"Two deaths by natural causes. One that was…what? A murder accusation, unproven, you said? Was that also found to be natural causes?" Mac asked.

"Exposure and substance abuse," Jones offered.

"So far, no crimes," Mac pointed out.

"No, I know." Jones said. "And at that point, I had these cases filed away. Didn't think I would study them again. Didn't seem to be anything to find. I'd hit on Denton and Fletcher because I'd been tracing people who worked at the children's home that had been shut down. A separate story. But that random point about the breadcrumbs stood out for me."

Mac sighed, feeling his interest wane. This was clutching at straws and he was tired. Bone weary.

"Then there was Carl Hesten…" Jones was saying.

Mac held up a hand, regretting indulging him now. It might have opened up a can of worms, allowing this fantasist to feel validated by an actual police officer.

"I've heard enough," he said. "You told me about Lukasz Burksi, and I can't see anything to connect it to Adam Glebe. Breadcrumbs can come from a lot of places. It's not enough to build a theory out of, let alone a full police investigation."

"At least look at the evidence I've collated," Jones said, sounding desperate now. "I was right about the Celtic Killer, wasn't I? I made the connection to that boy's suicide. Just look at the data. Look at Carl Hesten."

He took out his phone and swiped hurriedly, tapping the screen, then looking up at Mac.

"Your email?" Jones asked.

Mac sighed, then gave it to him. A moment later, he felt his phone buzz to announce a notification. Mac didn't look at it. He almost told Jones to stop wasting his life and stop bribing police officers. He didn't have the energy to arrest him. Instead, he got up and walked away.

Chapter Twenty-Three

GETTING INTO HIS CAR, he drove out of the car park, aiming westward at first, towards Corstorphine and Clio's house. Then he changed direction. Driving south instead, he took out his phone and began scrolling through the contacts with one hand, glancing up every couple of seconds to check the road. He found the name he was looking for and the address. Not an actual address. Just a place Mac knew Scott Diggs could be found at this time of night. Where he did business from. The Patriot Bar had a union flag outside and bars on the windows. It stood on a corner flanked by a Chinese takeaway and a timber yard just off Niddrie Mains Road. Mac stopped fifty yards away, watching the scrawny man in a black tracksuit and Burberry baseball cap sitting on a bin outside the pub. He spoke to men who came out for a smoke and sometimes things changed hands. He looked up and down the street constantly, keeping one hand in the front pocket of his tracksuit top. Mac frowned. Scott Diggs was a coward. He didn't normally go about his business armed. That's why he chose The Patriot. If anything kicked off, the pub would empty like a kicked anthill.

Someone walked past the car, head down, but looking at Mac with furtive sideways glances. They said something to Diggs as they went past him into the pub. Diggs hopped off the bin and disappeared around a corner. Mac went into the Audi's glove box and took out a packet of cigarettes, putting them on the dash after considering the contents for a second. Less than five minutes later, the door behind him opened and Diggs got in.

"OK, Detective Chief Inspector. Drive. Back up though, eh? Not past the pub. Got a fag?"

Mac tossed the cigarettes over his shoulder and reversed the Audi down the empty road and around a corner into a side street. He took off at speed back onto Niddrie Mains Road and out towards the Royal Infirmary.

"Been a while," Diggs said.

"It has," Mac replied. "Since when are you carrying, Diggsy?" he asked.

"Since Lowe got killed. It's bad out there. Scary, eh? Thinking about going straight."

Mac laughed. "You always are."

"Aye, well, maybe this time I will. Bunch of animals out there these days."

"You know a user called Conor?" Mac asked. "Been staying with a priest out Saughton way. Prison chaplain from Saughton jail. Ring a bell?"

"Maybe. That's a bit off my patch. Might have heard about someone like that. Bummer is he?"

"Don't know. Don't think so. I'd like to find him though," Mac said.

He reached back into the glove box and took out a roll

216

of tenners, peeled some off and handed them back over his shoulder. They were snatched away.

"Might be Conor Taggart. Got some stick for being all pally with a priest. They're all benders. Housebreaker, eh?"

"Sounds like him."

"Might know someone who knows someone who hooked him up with some stuff when he was out of Saughton and strung out. I'll ask around."

"Just find him so I can go talk to him, eh? Not looking to do him any harm."

"Aye, course."

Mac paused, rubbed a hand across his face, and thought about the bloody bread. About Maia or Iona lying dead. About what waited for him when he went to sleep.

"You got anything for sleep?" he asked. "Like something to knock me out?"

"Course. Twenty and I got something that will send you off for the best night's sleep you ever had..."

"I don't want to get high. Mess me up and I will bury you and burn down the Patriot on top of you. Understood?"

"Loud and clear."

Mac twisted the mirror so that he could see Diggs's face.

"I pay you well and I want to carry on paying you for information. I just need one pill to make me sleep for a few hours. Got it?"

Every fibre of his being screamed this was wrong. This was a bad idea. He watched the sly, pock-marked face with bad teeth in the mirror. Knew he was putting himself at the mercy of someone who could never be trusted. But at that moment, he felt desperate. Haunted. He just wanted his mind to go blank. Just for a few hours.

"Cross me and I'll kill you, Scott," Mac said quietly. "I

was there when Lowe got a bullet to the head. Could have stopped it. Didn't. Get me?"

Diggs swallowed his grin, forced it back. Mac could see from his body language he was gripping whatever he was carrying for protection. Gripping it hard. And Mac had done that. Mac had put the fear of God into people like Diggs. The bottom feeders. He'd allowed the apex predator to be killed, and he'd wreaked havoc in the structures that had been keeping order. Now people like Scott were terrified, and what had been a business empire was just chaos. He held Diggs' eye, and the man nodded, looking pale and sweaty. Diggs reached into a pocket and took out a plastic bag with another one wrapped up inside. Tossed it forward onto the passenger seat.

"It's prescription. Legal in the US. Not here. But it's legit. Sleeping drug, eh? Nothing spicy. Safe. If you were American, you'd get that from your doctor."

Mac turned the car around, doing a u-turn in the middle of the road, getting flashed by an oncoming truck and ignoring it.

"Don't forget Conor Taggart, eh? There's another fifty in it for you," Mac said.

Chapter Twenty-Four

MAC SAT on Clio's sofa, staring at an innocuous, chalky blue pill. It had an imprint on one side, maker's logo. He didn't know how hard that was to fake. If it was even possible. But he trusted Diggsy's cowardice. If Mac ended up spiked or with something in his bloodstream that would fail a drug test, Diggsy knew what the consequences would be. Mac was known to be a hard man. It was known inside and outside the force that he was willing to bend rules, even if he wasn't actually bent. To someone as pathologically afraid of violence as Diggsy, that was enough to keep him in line.

"This is stupid," he told himself.

The clock said after one am. His body was crying out for sleep. He dreaded the dreams. Waking up after an hour, unable to go back to sleep. How long until that started to really affect his work? Mac swore and picked up the tablet. There was a killer out there. Maybe a two time killer and Mac had no clear idea who it was. Two of his team were chasing down a Catholic priest who may or may not be involved. He was neck deep in a game of cat and mouse with a corrupt and powerful police officer, the lives of his best friend and her daughter at stake. He had to be sharper. Had to be stronger. Mac swore again and shoved the tablet into his mouth, swallowing it dry with a toss of his head.

———

NO DREAMS. Mac woke on the sofa, still wearing his suit. He opened his eyes, the room bright. Sunlight spilled in through open blinds. He was in Clio's living room and the TV was on, the remote lying on the floor where it had fallen from his hand. An entire season of a seventies sitcom had streamed by while he slept. He remembered putting on an episode while he wondered if the pill would work and remembered little else. But there had been no dreams. His neck was sore and his back ached, but he had slept. With a groan, he levered himself up off the sofa, running a hand through his hair. He felt brittle, as though he was made of glass. In his head, there was a sharp clarity he hadn't experienced for a long time.

"Diggsy, you're a genius," he muttered aloud.

He went to the guest bedroom, where a couple of spare suits hung in a wardrobe. Stripping off the one he had slept in, he took a shower, feeling the aches, pains, and mental cobwebs from the previous night being rinsed away. There was no sense of impending doom that usually came with the running water. No panic attack waiting to overcome him. No flashbacks to Skye. Dressing was like putting on armour.

He felt stronger, more resilient. Was a good night's sleep all he really needed or was this the hangover from a narcotic that had knocked him out and left him with a sense of euphoria? Like he could take on the world. Either way, it was different from the feeling of carrying the weight of his burdens. Different from the constant ache of anxiety, the constant clamour of conflicting demands. He picked up his phone, fresh coffee in one hand, and sat at Clio's kitchen table. The time registered in his awareness. Almost ten! A string of notifications told him Mel, Isla, and Kai had all been trying to reach him.

He scanned through text messages, dismissing the automated ones that told him he had voicemails and missed calls until he saw a text from Isla.

Seconds later, he was calling her.

"Guv! We've been trying to reach you..." Isla said, tension alive in her voice.

"I was at the doctor's," Mac replied. "What do you mean Nathan Flenders is dead? How?"

Isla and Kai had both sent him texts, following up from calls. Both had said the same thing. Father Nathan Flenders had been tracked down. But he was dead.

"We found his caravan. A local estate agent sold him the plot it's on and he built it. We got there an hour ago, and he was inside. Forensics are in there now. Looks like suicide..."

Mac's mind was flying. "Looks like? How?"

"He was lying on his bed, naked. There was an empty bottle of painkillers beside the bed and a suicide note on a typewriter in another room. He said he couldn't live with what he'd done any longer and was surrendering his soul to God to judge. He named Adam Glebe and Lukasz Burksi in the note."

Mac's mind snapped at one particular fact in the string he'd been given.

"Typed? He typed his suicide note?"

"Yes. There was an old electric typewriter in the living room. The paper was still in the machine..."

Mac's perception was firing quicker than Isla could talk,

bringing up thoughts and ideas almost faster than he could perceive them himself. He knew he was cutting across her; it was as though she was talking in slow motion.

"Did he sign it?" Mac asked.

Isla took a breath. "No."

"Don't move it until I get there. Were the painkillers on a prescription? What was he taking them for?" Mac pressed.

"I don't know what they were for. I'll try to find out, guv..."

"Was there a sticker on the bottle showing Flenders's name and address and the details of the dispensing pharmacy?"

"Yes, there was. I've called them. They prescribed it," Isla replied.

"Were there crumbs on the body? Or traces of alcohol?" Mac asked, swallowing his coffee quickly and looking around for his jacket. He spotted his car keys in the hall by the front door. Isla hesitated and Mac stopped short of opening the front door.

"Isla?" he said, sharply, impatient.

"Not that we could see..."

"Did forensics find anything? Were they looking for it?" Mac demanded, striding down a set of paving stone steps through the front garden. The Audi was parked on the road in front of the house. Again, Isla was slow to respond. Mac hauled the door open and stopped again, his mind racing ahead, putting together aspects of the conversation. Isla's voice. The underlying stress that he'd put down to not being able to reach him with a dead body on their hands. Another potential victim. A flash of insight and he was thinking something else.

"Everything OK, Isla?"

Silence for a moment. The sound of her breathing. Mac

got into the car, pulling the door closed and starting the engine. He waited out the silence.

"Just a shock, that's all. Sorry."

"Don't be. It's normal. You're doing a good job, Isla. Seal off the scene, let forensics do their work. Who's the pathologist?"

"Someone called Carole Strickland. I'm not familiar."

"Used to work for Stringer. She's good. Make sure she knows about the bread and beer angle we're looking for. Stay close to her team and tell Kai to start canvassing. I want you to call the pharmacy and ask for the details of the prescribing GP practice."

"Done, guv. I've spoken to a doctor who's asked for a face to face before he's prepared to divulge patient information."

"Where?" Mac asked.

"Edinburgh. Colinton Road, just down from Napier," Isla said.

"I'll head out via there. Find out what he was prescribed them for," Mac said.

Typed suicide note. Typed. It made Mac think the suicide was staged. Typed because the killer couldn't replicate Flenders's handwriting. If the medication was strong enough to kill and had been prescribed by a doctor, Flenders must have had a genuine medical reason to have them. Didn't mean the killer didn't force an overdose, though. If that's what happened.

"OK, guv. I'll tell Kai to start canvassing."

"Well done, Isla. I'll be there shortly."

Mac was already out of Clio's street, heading west toward the Forth bridge, the quickest way over to the Fife coast which faced Edinburgh across the Firth of Forth. He asked for the address and put it in while driving. He was more than an hour away, but would cut that down. A fresh crime scene and a host of potential leads had his heart racing. The peculiar crispness of his thinking was still there. The new pieces were turning over in his mind, being tested against known facts. He didn't care where it had come from. For the first time in a long time, he felt he was ahead. That he was equal to the weight on his shoulders.

———

HAVING CALLED in to see Flenders's doctor beforehand, Mac was relieved to find progress was good on the north side of the Forth Bridge. Once he was out past Rosyth and Dunfermline, the roads were clear. A leaden sky gave occasional glimpses of bright sunlight. Where the road looped close to the coast, he saw blue water, Edinburgh lost to haze in the distance. Villages and towns with quaint names, unusual to Mac's ear, flashed by. The Audi was barely slowed by the narrow streets, devoid of the tourist hordes that would be here in summer. He sped past terraced cottages and bright signs for holiday parks. Country pubs and gift shops. In between wide expanses of apparently empty countryside. Following instructions from Isla, he drove straight through Pittenweem itself, passing signs for its outdoor tidal swimming pool. On the other side of the village, he glimpsed the familiar Police Scotland neon green and yellow through the trees. Around a bend, he saw a police car parked to block access to a single track road. A stationary van was further down, leaving squeeze room to either side for pedestrians. Mac stopped, and a uniform walked towards him. He took out his warrant card.

"DCI McNeill," Mac said, winding down the Audi's window.

"I'll pull in so you can get past, sir, but you wouldn't be able to go much further than the forensics van, anyway. The road is quite steep, dropping to the beach and part of it washed away last winter. We're having to get down there on foot."

Mac nodded. "How far?"

"About a quarter mile, I'm afraid, sir. At least the rain's off, eh?"

Mac grunted, not relishing a quarter mile of country roads. He wasn't a country vet, didn't carry a pair of wellies in the back of the car. He waited for the police car to move aside and then guided the Audi into the lane, stopping behind the forensics van. Its back doors were open and men in women in paper suits were coming and going with evidence bags. Mac got out and gestured to the nearest.

"Carole Strickland?" he asked.

"Still down at the scene," came the answer.

Mac reached into the van, grabbing a paper suit, shoe covers and a mask from an open box just inside. He squeezed past the van and started walking. The surface was muddy, with puddles lingering. Mac ignored the squelching and oozing as best he could, cursing the lack of decent tarmac. On his right, a grassy meadow sloped steeply down. At the edge, longer grass waved in the breeze. Beyond was the sea, a good distance below. The lane wound down the hillside, steep enough that driving would have been a nail-biting experience and getting back up would have taken a four-wheel drive.

On the last bend, the surface had been completely washed away. It was level enough to walk on, but Mac's shoes sank an inch into the churned mud as he crossed it. The inclination was steep enough that one foot was a good six inches lower than the other and he was forced to walk crablike. He glanced occasionally to the edge, a lot closer here. Bare rocks poked up through a pile of earth, vegetation, and stones. It looked like a bulldozer had just shoved it right to the edge, leaving it piled up there. The roaring hiss of waves breaking against the shoreline sounded loud down there. Ahead, he could see the caravan. The road was firmer and rose towards it. It was mounted on a large flat area that had been surfaced in concrete, now broken and cracked by weeds. Mac wondered how the owner had got the building materials all the way down here. No wagon was going to make it along the road he had just walked.

The caravan was the static variety and had clearly been added to over the years. It looked like at least three of the prefab structures had been stitched together to form a squared-off u-shape facing the sea. The view from its promontory was spectacular. On the far side, a rusty gate closed off another lane.

The only sign there had been a road there was the presence of hedges to either side. Any surface had been taken over by grass. It looked wider than the road currently in use. Mac guessed the materials to build the caravan in situ had probably been brought down that lane, once upon a time. It had then fallen into disuse, been allowed to become overgrown and impassable.

The result was perfect isolation. No-one would wander down here by mistake. If you found yourself here, it was because you were looking for it. Isla was sitting on a bench seat at a wooden picnic table, talking on her phone animatedly. She looked up as Mac arrived and hurriedly ended the call. Mac walked over, taking off his coat and suit jacket, then opening the plastic bag containing the single-use paper suit. Isla was still wearing hers; hood pushed back and mask hanging from her ears. Mac glanced at her as he dressed.

"Everything OK?" he asked.

"Yes, guv. Pathologist is still inside; she's being very thorough."

The answer was a bit too immediate, too rushed for Mac. Isla's phone was ringing again in her pocket. She reached for it, swiping at the screen to silence it, and put it back.

"You need to take that?" Mac asked.

"No, guv, it's nothing. So, I found the body. Spoke to an estate agent based in Elie, just a bit along the coast from here. He sold the plot to Father Nathan seven years ago. Didn't know what he'd done with the land. We came straight here. The door was locked, but Kai could see someone lying on the bed through a gap in the curtains. There was no response when Kai knocked, so we broke in, forced the door. I found the Father in the bedroom."

"I spoke to Flenders's doctor. He was suffering sciatic pain and was prone to migraines. Prescribed some heavy duty pain relief to manage it." Mac said.

Isla nodded.

"Recently diagnosed or...?" she asked.

Mac liked the question. Recent might mean accidental overdose by a man who didn't understand how potent the medication was. The kind of man who scoffed at instructions provided with painkillers and knocked back a handful, thinking it would work quicker.

"Over a year," Mac said.

"Long enough to know how to take them, then." Isla scribbled a note. The phone rang again.

"Just speak to whoever that is and then catch up, eh? I'm going inside," Mac said.

227

Chapter Twenty-Five

HE WALKED AWAY towards a door on the side of the structure that was open, evidence of a forced lock on the wall and the door itself. A crowbar leaned against the side of the caravan, a yellow forensics tag around the shaft to highlight that it had been used by police to gain entry. Inside the caravan felt surprisingly spacious. Mac could have believed himself in a bungalow.

To the left of the door was a kitchen that took up most of the length of one of the three caravans. To the right was a partition with a closed door. Opening the door revealed a bedroom with two single day beds facing each other. Everything seemed to be clean and tidy. Running a gloved finger over a windowsill, he could see no signs of dust or dirt. Recently cleaned then. By Flenders? A cleaner? He left the bedroom and stepped up and through another door, which would have been the external door of another caravan.

It had been orientated at right angles to the first and formed a wide living room. A leather sofa faced windows looking out over the sea. A bookcase stood under the window, another against a wall to the side of the sofa. And a flat-screen TV was mounted on one wall, visible to an armchair arranged to the left of the picture window. The chair didn't match the sofa. Mac moved into the room, taking in everything, letting the detail sift through his subconscious.

As he was halfway to the door at the far end, he stopped. Crouching in front of the bookcase, he looked along the row of books stuffed into the shelf space. Mostly fiction, with legal thrillers and police procedurals taking up the lion's share of the space. In a corner of the room was a camping table with a folding chair in front of it.

An ancient-looking typewriter sat on the desk, a single sheet of A4 paper sticking out of it. Mac went closer. Keeping his hands firmly clasped behind his back, he leaned in to read the neatly typed words on the page.

To whom it may concern,

I am sorry for my weakness and for my sins. God alone can judge me. The only way I can atone is with my immortal soul. I commend it to the judgement of the Almighty and am ready to serve my penance in hell. I deserve no better for the sins I have committed. It is a further sin that I seek to end my suffering here on earth. The Lord will be my judge. I confess to the murders of Adam Glebe and Lukasz Burksi. I consumed their sins and dispatched them to Heaven.

My own sins are scarlet. I hope in time they shall be as white as snow.

No signature. No typos in the short passage. Mac looked around for a wastepaper basket and saw none. He went back into the kitchen and found a pedal bin in a corner beside the sink. A figure in a paper suit was walking out through the kitchen.

"Have you finished checking in here?" Mac asked.

"Yes, we've covered in here," a man answered. "Carole's just finishing up in the bedroom. Everything else has been checked."

Mac opened a couple of drawers, found a wooden spoon. He took it out and began poking around in the bin. Empty packets of cooked meat with expiry dates from a month ago. A carton of fruit juice expired around the same time. A banana skin and some polystyrene takeaway containers. An empty plastic bag with a crumpled piece of paper at the bottom. It was a receipt.

Amongst other things purchased was a loaf of sliced white bread, a pint of semi-skimmed milk and packet of wine gums. No sign of scrunched up A4 paper in the bin. So Flenders had been a good typist, able to type up his suicide note without a single error. Mac crouched beside the bin for a minute, staring straight through it. The typewriter bothered him. It had done since Isla had mentioned it. Setting up the typewriter took time. So did inserting paper and then producing a clean copy while presumably in considerable mental distress. He shook his head. No real reason to doubt this was a suicide, particularly as he hadn't even seen the body yet. But *typing* something so intimate and personal was just jarring.

There was a door behind the sofa. Walking over to it, Mac saw a bathroom, a forensics technician working in there. He nodded as Mac poked his head into the room. It had a wet room shower and a chemical toilet. Finally, he reached the third of the three interconnected static caravans. This one was a bedroom. A bed without a headboard was positioned lengthways. A naked man lay on the bed, his head under a window which also looked out over the sea. Another bookcase beside the bed. Theological texts, judging by the titles. Hardbacks with long, complicated titles. Mac couldn't fathom what any of them were actually about.

A woman was leaning over the body, directing a photographer. She looked back over her shoulder at him. Mac saw a pair of bright green eyes.

"Detective Chief Inspector McNeill?" she said.

"Yes, Doctor Strickland. I remember you," Mac said.

"Likewise. The stabbing in Queensferry, wasn't it?"

Mac nodded. That case had been five years ago. It was still unsolved.

"What have we got here?" Mac asked, wasting no more time on reminiscence.

"On the surface, a suicide. There's a bottle of very strong opiate based painkillers on that bookcase, empty and with a prescription label dated two days ago. Not possible he got through that many in such a short time, so the working hypothesis is he took the lot. You saw the suicide note?"

Strickland made air quotes as she said 'suicide note.' Mac nodded, moving to the side of the bed to look down at the earthly remains of Father Nathan Flenders.

"I saw it. That and the bottle suggests suicide pretty strongly, doesn't it?"

"I presume you're being sarcastic? Of course, I can only comment on the facts as they are presented. I'll know more after the post mortem but, for what it's worth, it seems like we've been firmly pointed in that direction. I'm inclined to believe proven facts rather than inferences, though. So, watch this space."

"Cause of death?" Mac asked.

"Signs of cyanosis around the nostrils and lips. Indicative of suffocation but could also be caused by an overdose of certain chemical substances, so doesn't rule out suicide by overdose. No other obvious surface indicators."

"Any signs of breadcrumbs on or near the body?" Mac asked.

Strickland frowned briefly but answered promptly. "No."

"Alcohol? Any evidence someone had eaten or drunk near or over the body?"

"Again, no. The room was actually pretty clean. I'd say recently cleaned to a decent standard."

"I noticed the same thing in the en-suite. Professional standard?"

"To me it seems that way, but I'm a bit of a slattern when it comes to housework. My other half is much better at it. So, that's hardly an objective observation. Could be. Or he could have been a very conscientious individual."

"And how long has he been dead for?" Mac asked.

"About twenty-four hours. Which is corroborated by the date on the prescription."

"So, he picked it up from a pharmacy intending to use it to top himself."

"Possibly. Picks up the tablets then contemplates suicide for a day or so before finally plucking up the courage. The facts as they currently appear would support that," Strickland agreed. "My team's almost done here. I'll have a report sent over to you as soon as I've completed the post-mortem and I have a more definitive cause of death for you. Twenty-four hours, give or take. That work for you?"

"Yes," Mac said, looking across the body at the bottle of pills. "I noticed the bin in the kitchen was full, by the way."

Strickland stopped, rolling her eyes to the ceiling.

"My apologies, Detective Chief Inspector. That shouldn't have happened. I'll bag the contents personally."

Mac waved away the apology, turning his attention to the body on the bed. "Thanks, Doctor Strickland."

Strickland nodded, and Mac could see a smile under the mask. "Give me a ring if you need anything else, Detective Chief Inspector."

For the first time since entering the room, Mac really looked at the body. He'd seen the bruises, the evidence of lividity and rigor mortis. Seen the physical evidence but hadn't observed the body as a whole. Hadn't taken in the man this had once been. There was no sign of the ruddy complexion he'd briefly seen when Flenders had pushed past him on the way out of St Aiden's church. The man before him was milk white except where the blood had pooled at the lowest points of the body.

Chest and arms, clearly once well-muscled, were now flabby. He looked like an old boxer gone to seed. Glancing out through the window, he saw Isla was still on the phone. She was walking back and forth, gesticulating. He couldn't hear what she was saying through the double glazing, but her body language told him she was raising her voice.

Mac rapped sharply on the glass with a knuckle. She looked up, and he gestured emphatically with a thumb over his shoulder. Get in here. She paled, ended the call, and shoved the phone in her pocket, putting up her mask as she walked towards the caravan. Mac met her in the living room. She stepped through the door and stopped, breathing hard, eyes wide. Mac pushed back his hood and removed his mask. Strictly against protocol, but he wanted to get to the bottom of this and wasn't going to let Isla hide behind the face covering. Slowly, she did the same.

"Forensics have swept the place," Mac said. "Brief me. And I'm not talking about the body."

"It's…it's personal, guv. I'd rather not bring it into the office," Isla said, looking down.

"Too late. You didn't tell the forensics team to look out for bread or alcohol on or about the body. Doctor Strickland wasn't expecting it when I asked. Kai forgot as well, which makes me think he doesn't have his mind on the job either."

He sounded harsh, but he was angry now. Being told by one of his team that they'd taken their eye off the ball for a moment, even for personal reasons, he could forgive. None of them were robots. People made mistakes. They got tired. Stressed. He'd made a lot of them himself. Still did. But evasion made him reconsider the opinion he'd had of Isla. Her face was scarlet and her jaw was set. Shame, upset or anger. Mac couldn't tell.

"You're a good officer, Isla. I wanted you on my team for a reason. This isn't like you. Something's going on."

"It's my boyfriend. He tracked my phone. He didn't believe me when I said I had to work overtime and he came to the hotel last night. Kai and I were having a drink and… there was some trouble."

"What kind of trouble?"

Isla was practically squirming on the spot, looking anywhere but at her boss. Mac didn't want or need the distraction, but the longer this went on, the more distressed he could see she was getting. His mind raced ahead. He knew nothing about Isla's boyfriend, but he knew Kai.

"Is Kai looking at an assault charge?" Mac asked, quietly.

Isla bit her lip like she was about to cry. Then she met Mac's eyes. "It won't come to that. I'll speak to Greg. He won't press charges. Kai was defending me," she said defiantly. "It won't get in the way."

Mac wanted to bang both their heads together. In the middle of a murder investigation, what he didn't need was an affair between two of his team and a jealous partner in the middle. And Kai didn't need an AC investigation into his conduct. Mac wondered what strings he could pull. It would depend on how public the fight was.

"Anyone else see what happened?" he asked.

"There was no-one else in the beer garden. Only a couple of locals in the whole place," Isla said.

"Let's hope so, eh? Did this Greg hurt you? Want me to get him picked up?"

It was an empty promise, and Mac knew it. If they were relying on Isla talking her boyfriend out of pressing charges, then arresting him wasn't likely to do any good. Unless they could claim Kai was using reasonable force.

"No, guv. That would just put fuel on the fire," Isla said, reaching the same conclusion that he had. "Let me talk to him when he's had a chance to calm down."

"And is that safe for you?" Mac asked.

"He wouldn't dare. Kai was just being overprotective," Isla said. "Honestly, guv. I can take care of it. Don't worry about it."

That was enough for Mac. He gave a single nod. "So, initial thoughts when you came in here."

Isla took a second to bring her mind into focus. Mac admired the speed with which she shrugged off what was happening outside of work.

"I found him as he is. Lying on his back, arms by his sides, palms up. Legs straight. Eyes closed. I saw the bottle and looked up the medication. It's strong, so it's deadly in the wrong dose. Kai saw the suicide note. We didn't remove it. Both of us read it."

"And?"

"No signature. It didn't occur to me until you asked earlier. Typed and with nothing to say it was Flenders who typed it."

"I found old packets of food in the bin. Someone had been clearing out the fridge."

"I checked the kitchen. Clean as the rest of the place. Including the fridge. I could still smell the bleach."

"Would you care about cleaning if you were suicidal?" Mac asked.

"Depends. I might if I thought people would be looking around and judging me. Don't they say cleanliness is next to godliness? Maybe, considering what he's confessed to, he wanted to clean away the signs he'd been here? On earth I mean. Sorry, it sounds daft when I say it out loud. Or what if he was ending it because he had something terminal? He might have been in a positive frame of mind, just wanted to end the pain."

"Could be," Mac said. "Maybe I'm just suspicious, even when it's an open and shut case."

"The whole place was locked up."

"Where are the keys?" Mac asked.

There had been a hook attached to the wall beside the door that had been forced with a crowbar. The kind of hook that usually held keys.

"There were some keys on the floor. They might have been knocked off the hook when Kai broke in," Isla said.

She went into the kitchen and pointed to a set of keys on a worktop next to the fridge. A painted ring on the floor marked where they had been found. Mac followed, glanced at the lock of the door, then picked up the keys. There were four small keys on the fob, apparently identical. He tried one in the door.

"Too small," he said.

Then he went to the rectangular window above the sink. All the keys fitted.

"Window keys. Not door keys," he said.

Isla flushed, clenching her jaw. She'd overlooked that and knew it. Mac went into the living room, which had large picture windows. None of the keys fitted. Moving into the bedroom, he repeated the experiment. Again, the keys didn't fit the large picture window. The only windows the keys fitted were too small for anyone to climb through. Mac had a familiar feeling. The feeling that he had a live lead in his hand. It was almost electric, shocking his system into a heightened state of awareness. The caravan was locked, which made sense if Nathan Flenders locked the doors and then killed himself. But if that was the case, where was the door key?

Chapter Twenty-Six

MAC AND ISLA waited outside at the picnic table while forensics finished up. Mac checked that no keys fitting the door of the caravan had been found. As the last of the white paper-suited figures disappeared along the overgrown lane, he and Isla went back inside. If the keys couldn't be found anywhere, then it confirmed that Father Nathan Flenders had not been alone when he died. It didn't prove his death wasn't suicide; just that someone had been there and locked the door behind them when they left. No report of a dead body had been filed, no ambulance called. Which suggested to Mac that someone knew Nathan Flenders was dead, either that he planned to kill himself, had killed himself or...they had killed him. Whatever the scenario, Mac wanted to talk to them. They worked methodically from room to room, moving furniture, unplugging, and dragging out appliances, unzipping cushions and shaking out books. When it started to get dark, they put on the electric lights, ending up in the bedroom where the bed still bore the shape of the body. The work had gone on in silence, broken only when the door opened and Kai walked in.

"Guv," he said, looking wary.

"Kai, forget it. Isla told me what happened. You're in the doghouse, so don't try and justify anything."

"Aye, right, guv," Kai said.

Mac heard Isla about to speak, and so did Kai. He gave a minute shake of the head. Isla stayed quiet, and Mac let it do. Kai knew him well enough to know you didn't make excuses.

"I've been to every shop, cafe, restaurant, and pub in Pittenweem and no-one remembered seeing Nathan Flenders any time recently. Went to both churches, prods, and papers. They didn't even know there was a priest with a caravan down here."

Mac fished out the receipt and handed it to Kai.

"Go back to this shop and ask them about who made these purchases. It says cash, but there's a date and time and the name of the staff member who was on the till. Might be CCTV too."

Kai looked over the receipt, then back at his boss. Mac just stared at him.

"You want this done now?" Kai asked.

"You have somewhere to be, Sergeant?" Mac replied.

"It's a long walk and this'll be the fourth, no, the fifth time. I had to go back up to show forensics where we were. I mean, we've got a deathbed confession in here, that wraps up the Adam Glebe case, doesn't it?"

That was the difference between Isla and Kai, Mac thought. Isla took nothing for granted, assumed nothing, and followed the evidence. No key to a locked caravan meant another party was involved, which cast reasonable doubt on suicide and, therefore, the confession too. Kai assumed the suicide note was genuine and stopped looking for any other explanation. He could be sharp. Could be very blunt, too.

"We didn't see him write it, so we don't know he did. Just call it a leg day. Get it done," Mac said, shortly.

"Right, guv," Kai replied, careful to keep any hint of self-pity out of his voice.

This was a punishment, and they both knew it. Kai had lost control. The circumstances didn't matter. A police offer didn't lash out at a member of the public. If Isla was assaulted, Kai could make an arrest and use proportionate force. He hadn't done that. He'd just hit the guy. That was inexcusable. Mac thought about what he'd done to Musa's boy down at Waverley. Pot. Kettle. Black. The difference was that was a bent copper who would not be reporting Mac. He knew it was a double standard, and it was unfair. But at that moment, he didn't care. He didn't want Kai turning into a carbon copy of himself. Isla had occupied herself, shaking the academic books occupying the bookshelves in the bedroom. Kai left, but not before Mac clocked the look between them. He turned the other way, putting it aside for now, and went to help Isla with the books.

"It's not here, is it?" Isla said.

"Looking that way. You notice anything about these books compared to the ones out there?" Mac said.

"A lot heavier. In terms of subject matter, I mean," Isla said. "Not exactly light reading."

"The books in there have broken spines and folded over pages. They've been crammed onto the shelves with no thought of damage. These are stiff and neatly stacked," Mac stepped back. "In fact, there's a lot of space on these shelves. Why stuff the books in next door so that they're creased and so wedged in you can't take them off the shelf easily when there's plenty of room in here?"

He ran a finger along a shelf, clean as a whistle. Interesting.

"Maybe he liked to keep his academic books separate from his light reading?" Isla suggested.

"Mmm," Mac said, the explanation not landing well with him.

"It's funny. It reminds me of my dad but backward," Isla said.

Mac looked at her.

"He used to have this bookshelf in the hall with his readers digest classics he'd never actually read. Or books about the bible, encyclopedia's that sort of thing. Things he thought made him look intellectual. In the back bedroom he had the Broons annuals, his Partick Thistle programs and his Bond books. Out of sight of visitors, you know?"

Mac nodded. Isla had hit the nail on the head. The books showing Flenders's intellectual side were hidden away and any visitor would see an untidy shelf full of pulp thrillers and cheap paperbacks. But to him, they looked as though they'd been moved.

"Alright. Let's put ourselves in the mind of someone who wants to kill Nathan Flenders and make it look like suicide. They rearrange his bookshelves to make it look as though his preferred bedtime reading is dense books on theology. Why?" Mac asked, looking around the room.

Isla was staring at the bookcase, one finger against her lips. "I have no idea. Maybe the question isn't why, but who for?"

Mac smiled, glancing at Isla to share it with her. "That's good thinking. Us? If you're staging a suicide, you are expecting polis to be involved at some point. How does it benefit the killer to make us think these books were Father Nathan's?"

"I don't know. Without knowing who the killer is, we can't possibly know," Isla reasoned.

"Right. But, regardless of motive, the result is to create the impression this man was a scholar. Except we know he was a scholar. I've seen the articles he published."

He picked a book off the shelf at random. It was a hefty hardback whose title was a sentence in itself. Mac opened it at the back and skimmed through the index. Sin-eating was referenced on a couple of pages. He put it back and picked another. It also contained a reference in the index to sin-eating. He felt a stab of anger. This felt as though someone was trying to lead him around by the nose. Making sure there were plenty of clues pointing in one direction. As if the polis would be too stupid to find the evidence without some heavy and clumsy signposting. Isla was watching him. She picked up two books of her own, went to the index.

"Here too. Both of them," she said, putting one back.

Mac nodded. She was sharp. Very sharp. It was a pleasure to work with her. Not having to spell everything out, not even what he was thinking. She would be a DCI herself one day if she wanted to be. It would be a waste to go higher. Too much potential as a detective.

"Don't let an office romance hold you back," Mac said in a rush, looking at another book for references to sin-eating.

"What's that guv?"

Playing for time. She was standing next to him, she'd heard.

"Kai's a bit of a player, eh? If it's causing problems in your relationship…just don't let it. Not for Kai. You've got potential, a lot. I don't want to see it wasted."

Isla cleared her throat. To her credit, she didn't give any other sign of being embarrassed.

"Thanks, guv. I…he's a nice guy, but I don't see a future in it. I'm not looking for anything long term. My relationship with Greg has been in trouble for months. He just won't admit it. Kai was just a bit of fun. I didn't think it was going to kick off like this, though."

Mac shrugged, not as comfortable with the personal nature of the conversation as Isla seemed to be and not sure what to say next.

"If the PCC come along with a complaint or if he presses charges…we'll manage it. I'm not losing either of you, but just don't make it harder for me to protect you."

"Understood, guv. Thanks."

She had been turning over a book in her hands as they spoke and had opened it to the front. Now she was staring at it as though seeing it for the first time.

"Guv, I think this is a library book," she said.

Mac shoved the one he held back onto the shelf. There was a piece of white paper stuck to the first page bearing the name HMP Edinburgh stamped at the top in red ink. Below were two dates, again stamped in red. One of those dates was two weeks ago. Mac took out his phone and snapped a picture of the paper, then closed the cover over and took a picture of the front. Isla turned it so that the spine faced him. There was a piece of laminated white paper bearing a code of letters and numbers at the bottom.

"Nathan Flenders used to work at HMP Edinburgh, but not for a few years. Get onto the prison first thing tomorrow and find out who checked this book out," Mac said.

His mind was already racing ahead, following a path forged by this book. It all pointed to Flenders being the killer, committing suicide when his guilt became too great.

But if he believed in the sin-eating ritual, would he want to die without the same service being performed for him? That and the fact that the caravan was locked pointed to an accomplice. Or else Flenders wasn't the killer, but just another victim. Cass had access to the prison library. Had access to the articles written by Nathan Flenders. Did those articles contain enough information to recreate the sin-eating rite? Was Flenders killed because he'd discovered what Cass was doing?

Was that the real reason for the argument at the retreat? Had Cass and Flenders concealed the truth from their friends and colleagues to protect the sin-eater? No, that would require acceptance that Nathan Flenders would rather be thought a paedo than knowing anything about sin-eating. Ridiculous. He thought about the artist Beth Rose and her Pottery TV marathon, whatever show that had been. Usually a Saturday, but this time on a Sunday. A woman who Cass admitted needed to be supervised to stop her drinking.

"We need to talk to Father Nick Cass again," Mac said, thinking aloud.

"Wasn't he alibied?"

"Aye. But she may be lying to protect him. We'll need to speak to her again as well. Test the alibi."

"And he framed his friend to cover his tracks?" Isla asked, testing the emerging theory out loud.

"Possible. There had to be someone else here. Suicide or not. Could be they're in it together. Cass's neighbour seems to think he's gay…"

"You think he and Flenders might have been lovers?"

Mac shrugged. "Or conspirators. Each with a secret the other was keeping. I don't know. This is all just speculation. Let's keep it to the facts we know. The caravan was locked, but there's no sign of the keys in here. Which means someone else took them and locked the door when they left. Nick Cass is as good a starting place as any."

The sharpness he'd felt at the start of the day was waning. There was an exhaustion waiting behind his eyes, a sense of growing weight. The bag of pills was in the glove compartment of his car. There had been half a dozen when Diggsy tossed him the packet. He tried not to think about how much he needed them already. If he was tired, he should try sleeping naturally. Now the case was moving, there was one less burden to carry. But the usual excitement of a promising lead was muted. He ran a hand through his hair. Suddenly, he remembered the conversation with Ramsey Jones and the email he hadn't yet read. Carl Hesten. He swore. It had gone out of his head completely, quashed right back in his mind by the pills.

"What's wrong, guv?" Isla said.

"Something I overlooked. Don't worry about it. I'll handle it."

"You sure, guv?"

"Aye. There's not much more we can do here. I think a search of Nick Cass's flat for the key is warranted. I'll make a start on the authorisation request to Carmichael. Knock off for the night."

Isla smiled. "Right, guv. You coming too?"

"Aye, I'll be along in a minute. Get yourself back to your digs. Don't forget to chase up that library book first thing."

Isla nodded, leaving the caravan. Mac went through to the living room and sat down, looking at the haphazardly stacked paperbacks with their creases and faded covers. The overhead light was too bright. He watched Isla pass by the window, gave her time to get into the lane leading back to the main road. An intense white light marked her progress as she shone her phone torch on the ground she was picking her way across. When it was out of sight, he switched off the light, breathing a sigh of relief when darkness enveloped him. It felt like a respite after the glare. Outside, the sky appeared as a slightly paler shade of ebony than the trees. Gradually the noise of the sea reached him, a gentle, hissing rush of fizzing bubbles over sharp stones. He took out his phone, checking for messages from Clio. He typed one out, just checking in. Send. Emails were piling up again, and he skimmed through, looking for the background report on Nick Cass from Mel. Ramsey Jones' dossier, came up first, and Mac opened the email. The first attachment was a Word document giving a timeline.

If one of Mac's officers had pulled together something so slipshod and amateurish, they'd have been giving directions to tourists on the Royal Mile within the hour. Mac skimmed the document, seeing a man clutching at straws, trying to find a conspiracy where there wasn't one. Despite himself, he opened the next attachment. A biography of the first "victim" Jones had identified. Nothing of significance that Mac could see. An ordinary life, tinged with tragedy and bad luck. Ending with an anonymous death on the streets. There were millions like it. Mac saw a name on the next attachment. Carl Hesten. He remembered Jones' insistence that Mac remember the name. He opened up a search engine and typed it in. Then put his phone down in frustration. He had actual police work to do. A background check on his chief suspect. A review of all the evidence and statements collected so far, stepping back to see if anything stood out. Authority from Carmichael for a search warrant. Mac's eyes were heavy. He put his head back, closing his eyes for just a minute. The relief of surrender hit him like heroin. He was asleep inside a minute.

Chapter Twenty-Seven

Iona ran ahead of him through the sheeting rain. It stung Mac's skin, freezing it. The ground beneath his feet was thick mud. Iona seemed to skip above it, but Mac couldn't get a proper rhythm to run. He slid and slipped, hand sinking to the wrist in the mire when he fell to one knee. Invisible branches whipped at his face. There was no moonlight. The trees choked the illumination of streetlamps. It fell into a black mire. But he could see Iona running, tried to call out to her to wait for him. The need to hold her hand and keep her safe was unbearable. It choked him, brought blinding tears into his eyes. If he could just catch up, then he could change things. Stop her going. Stop her from leaving him. Then she was gone and Mac was alone in a Stygian wood. He knew the place, yet didn't know it. A place that was familiar while being utterly alien. The paths he expected were not visible, and he had no way of knowing which direction to take to keep up with his sister.

Then his phone was ringing. He picked it up.

"Iona!" he shouted.

"Mac!" Clio replied. "Where are you? Where did you go? We've been waiting for you…"

Mac remembered he had promised to come back in just a minute. Back to the farmhouse where Clio and Maia were trying to avoid the body of his father lying dead in the chair, with blood and vomit mixing with the foam drying around his mouth, and half his head blown off. Bone and brain matter oozing down the wall behind him.

"I'm sorry, Clio!" Mac cried. "I'll be there in a minute."

"Where did you go?" Clio asked, plaintively.

"I had to go to work," Mac replied.

He was turning a circle, wondering which direction led back to Clio. He couldn't remember. Then Clio was screaming. Maia was screaming. Not the instinctive cry of fright, the kind that came after fear, a distress call to anyone who might hear. This was the visceral sound of two people in pain and losing their minds. Mac ran, desperate to find the way back to them. Iona was gone. Clio and Maia were being taken away. What was left? The dark woods and the mouldering body in the old, ruined farmhouse. The ghosts.

MAC OPENED HIS EYES. His heart was pounding, but he didn't make a sound. Didn't move. Couldn't move. The dream was at the back of his throat, clinging to his skin. He swallowed, staring into a dark room of unfamiliar shapes overlaid with the cold smell of forensic chemicals. But it wasn't the dream that had wakened him. Something in the real world had wrenched him from sleep early. Grogginess lasted only a few seconds, but it felt like ten minutes of blinking, swallowing and staring. Then the aches of a body forced to slump in an uncomfortable position on a sofa too small for it made themselves known. The stiff neck, the aching back, the cramped muscles. Then the noise that had first wakened him; the sound of a foot scratching against gravel. The scuff of a stalker trying to be quiet. There was someone outside the door.

The door was pulled, handle useless after Kai had

broken in, and it swung, free-falling but caught before it could slam into the wall. As Mac's eyes adjusted to the gloom, he made out the darker shape of a person against the muted black of nature outside. He froze. Not out of fear, but from the hunter's instinct. Movement would spook his prey. He wanted whoever it was to come in. The figure was lower than him, not yet stepped up into the caravan. Mac could see the outline of head and shoulders, detail smoothed out by a hood, taking away any definite shape. It stepped into the caravan slowly. Two deliberate steps. Then head turning, body still. Listening. Then coming into the room, moving with increasing confidence and turning rapidly into haste. It appeared to be looking for something. A drawer opened and then closed. Moving over to a book-case and then away. Opening a cupboard, closing it.

No, not looking for something. Looking for somewhere. Each place was discarded without a second glance. As though being tested for suitability. The figure was coming closer to the sofa, reaching for a cushion against one arm at the opposite end to where Mac slumped. Even in the dark, they couldn't help but see him now. As the hand reached the cushion, Mac pushed forward and grabbed the outstretched wrist. The dark figure yelped. Yelped. Male voice. Scared. Already on edge from the situation. Now terrified. A villain would have enough experience of street fights to lash out with a fist at the face that must be beyond the hand gripping their wrist. An amateur unused to solving problems with violence would panic. Thrash, tug. Try to escape. This person panicked first. Mac got to his feet quickly, keeping hold of the thin wrist. Then they mastered the panic. The free hand was pulled back. Mac reached up to stop the inevitable blow, but it came too quick. Something stabbed into the meat of his shoulder at the top of his bicep. Not the quick clean delayed pain from a blade sharp enough that the body didn't realise it was hurt for a few seconds. This was the dull, sickening pain of a blunt weapon forcing its way through skin and into muscle.

Mac screamed. Pain and rage. The stab was reversed and something wet flicked across Mac's cheek. It came in again. This time, he caught the hand. Felt the key sticking out between clenched knuckles. That's what had punctured him. Mac swore and jerked his head forward, catching his assailant on the side of the temple. The attacker fell back but grabbed the front of Mac's shirt, pulling free of Mac's grasp on his wrist. He fell back and then swung and pushed. Mac found himself flung to the floor. A knee came down into his stomach, winding him. The man was on his feet, running for the door. Mac grabbed a trailing leg, clinging on, trying to avoid being kicked in the face. His grip slipped from a calf to a foot, fingers digging into laces, trying to use them as a handhold. For a second, it felt as though the shoe was coming away at the heel. Then the pressure was lifted as the man stopped fighting, came back towards Mac, and stamped down on his head. Mac was quick enough to get a hand up to cushion the blow, but another stamp followed. Then another, and Mac had to use both arms over his head to prevent a fractured skull. The blows stopped. The man was running.

"Police!"

One day someone would stop in their tracks hearing that and come quietly. Mac was already on the move. He took the steps in one leap, hit the ground hard, and almost fell. He turned himself toward the sounds of flight, remembering the direction of the lane that led back to the road. Ignoring the instinct to slow when he couldn't see where he was putting his feet, Mac sprinted. He felt mud and grass beneath his feet, entered a greater darkness as the shadows of trees enveloped him. The first fall sent him to hands and knees, then straight back up. The second time, he landed on a stone and numbed his leg from the knee down. Trying to run pitched him onto his side and the stab wound in his shoulder. Nausea flooded him. But anger overrode it. He pushed himself to his feet and staggered a dozen paces. There was a lighter patch ahead where the trees stopped. It was the section of lane that had been swept away. Below to the left was the sea. Breathing hard, he stopped, no longer able to hear his quarry ahead. Maybe they'd stopped too, realising that without sound they could blend into the darkness even if they only stood a few feet away. Mac put his hands to his knees, bending over, letting the waves of sickening pain wash over him.

"I'll get you!" he shouted.

Then he turned and limped back to the caravan. One of Musa's boys following him? But looking for what? Planting something? Evidence? Something to incriminate Mac? Or was this all to do with Nathan Flenders? Mac couldn't say for sure it had been Nick Cass he'd just wrestled with, though the build and height were similar. But he wouldn't have expected Nick Cass to retaliate so viciously. Didn't think he was capable. Unless he was already capable of a lot worse. Mac's shoes squelched. He was soaked through one side of his body. He reached the caravan and staggered inside, briefly hesitating as he thought about forensics. But only briefly. He put on a light and immediately saw the door key lying in the middle of the floor.

Unknown male returns to the caravan with the key he accidentally took when he left Nathan Flenders. Which meant that Flenders's death was unlikely to be suicide. Otherwise, why the urgent need to bring the key back? Why take the risk? Unless you knew the absence of the key cast doubt on the suicide and you wanted to remove that doubt. Put the key somewhere it might be missed by forensics.

Mac looked for a bag in his pocket, but didn't find one. He rooted through kitchen drawers until he came across a pack of sandwich bags, not yet opened. He took one; turning it inside out, he picked up the key and tried it in the door. It fitted though the mechanism had been damaged too badly when Kai had broken in and Mac couldn't turn it beyond a few degrees. He sealed the key inside the bag, noting his blood staining the surface of the metal. He put the bag in his trouser pocket and focused on his wound.

It was impossible to see the puncture properly through the ragged hole in his jacket and shirt, so he stripped to his waist and washed it over the kitchen sink, hissing as the hot water and soap stung the open gash. Wadding dishtowels against the cavity, he applied as much pressure as he could stand, then wound the lot with a roll of masking tape he'd found under the sink. Where the hell were the local police to keep the crime scene sealed? Gingerly he shrugged back into his ruined clothes, taking a moment to fight back the nausea and light-headedness before stomping back up the same lane he'd chased his attacker along, tiredness dragging at him. He didn't think he was going to make it back to Edinburgh, would probably crash in his car where he had parked it. Emerging onto the road, he saw a marked police vehicle pull up and two coppers get out.

"About time," Mac griped. "Someone just tried to get into the crime scene. A man. In black and wearing a hoody."

"And who might you be?" one copper asked. He sounded young and stood with the attitude of a prick.

"Detective Chief Inspector McNeill," Mac spat, brushing past the young officer.

"Sorry, sir."

"We'll keep an eye out for anyone, sir," said the other.

"Forensics will be back tomorrow," Mac said, walking to his car. "No-one in or out." They acknowledged his order, and he got in his car, closing the door against them, and putting his head back against the rest. The dream came back to him then, or rather the bitter taste it left in his mouth. As though it had been merely screened by the sudden need to fight. Now that his pulse was calming and the adrenaline was leaving his system, his mind returned to the nightmare. Until his phone rang. He fished it from his pocket and looked at the caller's name. Carmichael. Detective Chief Superintendent, acting anyway. And until Kenny Reid admitted he was being pushed out and actually retired, Mac's boss. It was a video call. Carmichael liked video calls. Mac ran a hand through his hair, felt wetness. Accepted the call.

Chapter Twenty-Eight

"SIR."

"DCI McNeill, good of you to answer," Carmichael said, his voice dripping with sarcasm. Mac could already feel his blood pressure rise in response.

The DCS had round, boyish cheeks. He looked like a squirrel who'd stuffed his cheeks to the max with nuts, though there was nothing about him to suggest fat. The youthful face was contrasted with black eyes and touches of grey in his otherwise dark hair. He was sitting at a desk in shirtsleeves, camera slightly above him. Behind was a shelving unit, books sharing space with framed family pictures, photos of handshakes with dignitaries, and a couple of awards.

"I have wasted my time twice today joining a call to which you were invited, but didn't even respond to, let alone show up," Carmichael said.

His voice was calm and controlled, pure Kelvinside accent.

"I'm in the middle of a murder investigation, sir," Mac said.

"I'm aware of that. It is your job. So is joining planning calls set up by your superior officer. I regard strategy implementation and prioritisation calls as crucial to my senior leadership team. Which you as a DCI are part of. In turn, I expect you to chair your own meetings to discuss, prioritise, and execute action plans that sit within your own team. I know this isn't how DCS Reid ran things, but it is how I run them."

"Understood, sir. I will prioritise your meetings in future."

And let murder investigations take a back seat while he watched presentations about budgets and PR. Mac was suddenly tempted to tell him where to shove his job. If Mac wasn't polis, then Clio and Maia wouldn't be under threat. No scrap that, they still would be. The only thing that would change would be their protection. Mac couldn't protect them as a civilian the way he could as a copper. So he forced a polite smile, tried to lighten the glower and swallow the rising anger his acting commanding officer usually evoked.

"I understand we have a confession in the Adam Glebe case," Carmichael said. "I saw the preliminary report from Doctor Strickland."

"The suicide note," Mac said.

Carmichael paused to sip from a mug.

"Go on."

"Father Nathan Flenders. Found dead, cause of death to be confirmed, but powerful opiates were found next to the body and a suicide note claiming responsibility for two murders. Adam Glebe and a killing in Glasgow a few years ago."

Carmichael nodded, shifting a piece of paper, reading one beneath.

"Lukasz Burksi?"

"Yes," Mac answered.

"Motive?"

"Circumstantial evidence that Flenders was familiar with a historical practise called sin-eating where the sins of the recently deceased would be consumed to allow them to go to heaven. Forensics found traces of bread on both bodies, which I believe was consumed over the victim as part of the sin-eating ritual."

"Impressive, Detective Chief Inspector. So, Flenders was a madman who committed murder and then saved the souls of those he killed. Very good. So, we can close this case then?"

"No," Mac said.

Carmichael paused, face unreadable.

"No?"

"I think the suicide was staged in order to provide us with a credible suspect and a confession."

"Based on what evidence?"

"The fact the victim was found in a locked caravan with no sign of a key. We had to break in."

"The key could have been lost. Overlooked," Carmichael suggested.

"It wasn't. My DC and I searched after forensics..."

"Forensics had been through the place, then you and your DC? You can rule out absolutely this key is not inside the caravan somewhere?"

He didn't raise his voice. Didn't speak aggressively, but there was a challenge there. Carmichael was part of a new breed of copper. University educated and corporate minded. The kind of policeman who knew what mission statement meant and talked about core values, stakeholder management and the bane of Mac's life, optics. Mac remembered when good policing was giving a ned who was making a pest of himself a slap followed by several threats. Kenny Reid had solved cases by sitting down with gangsters like Hance Allen making a deal for one of his men who had stepped over the line and turning a blind eye to something else. Some called it corruption, but sometimes being a copper couldn't be black and white. Couldn't be battle lines or existential threats. Sometimes you needed to let the sprat go to catch the mackerel.

"Yes, I... " began Mac, about to say he could guarantee the key wasn't in the caravan because it was currently in his pocket, but he got no further.

"Deathbed confession is robust evidence. Strong enough for the procurator fiscal to consider the case closed and Nathan Flenders posthumously guilty," Carmichael said.

"And good PR for Police Scotland."

"And for you, Mac." Carmichael had never used his nickname before. "You're practically a legend because of the cases you've solved. There aren't many police officers below the rank of Chief Constable who the public could name. I'd say you're one. This would be the feather in your cap."

"I'm not much of a hat person," Mac retorted.

Carmichael had sat forward, looking into the camera earnestly. Now he sat back and picked up his mug again. Mac wondered if it said Number One Detective Chief Superintendent on it.

"Then become one," Carmichael said with a suave smile. "I think this case is closed. I'd like you and your team to focus on wrapping it up. Final reports to me and the PF's office. Have your DI announce to the press the usual teaser.

A person of interest in the case of a deceased man found in Mary King's Close recently has been found dead. Police do not consider the circumstances suspicious. More to follow, etc. etc. You know the script."

Mac looked away from the screen, biting back his frustration, forcing a smile that felt like a snarl.

"Sir, I was going to submit a request for divisional approval to search the property of Father Nicholas Cass."

Carmichael frowned. "Another priest? No, I don't think that would be appropriate. Once news about one Catholic priest committing murder and some kind of ancient ritual leaks, any others whose name ends up in the public arena will become the subjects of witch hunts. I won't cause that kind of hysteria."

"But, sir, I have good reason to believe..." Mac protested.

"You have a confession. A deathbed confession. An open and shut case solved by Scotland's greatest detective. How about that? Promotion board is meeting in a couple of months. This could be a springboard for your career..."

"Screw my career! You've got the wrong man. Someone just tried to break into the caravan to plant the key back inside. Look at the state of me! I had to chase him through a swamp. Why would they risk breaking into a crime scene if Flenders killed himself?" Mac shouted.

"McNeill, drop it. That's an order. We have our man. He's dead, so no-one's going to plead not guilty. Easy one for us. Now, I also wanted to talk to you about a complaint I've had across my desk today. One of your team assaulting a member of the public?"

Mac froze, watching the screen and waiting for the quid pro quo.

"But that can wait for now. Flenders was our man. Get

some sleep. Get back to the office tomorrow. Debrief your team and do your paperwork," Carmichael ordered.

He looked away from the screen, then back. Mac sensed there was more to come. Carmichael moved closer.

"There's another reason for speaking to you out of office," he said. "I wanted to fore-warn you. Word has come down from the Chief Constable's office. Reid is being fast tracked out. Full pension with severance. Not a stain on his character."

"He'll be happy. Why tell me?"

"Because you're his friend. God knows how, the man's an intolerable dinosaur."

"That'll be why then."

Carmichael snorted. "A pair. This is an unofficial word for you to pass on. So he does nothing stupid that either ties our hands or embarrasses us. Akhtar is going to be too busy to worry about him. He slips away quietly, never to be heard from again. Understand?"

"Got it, sir. I'll pass it on."

"Good. And well done. Murder case closed in a week. Excellent work."

The call ended. Mac whipped the phone across the car with a slash of his arm. It clattered against the passenger window and fell to the footwell. He put his hands on the steering wheel and lowered his head. There was a killer out there and Mac felt on the verge of catching him. To let him go, take the path of least resistance, and not question Nathan Flenders's death was letting the killer win. Mac couldn't do it. Wouldn't do it, even if it cost him his job. Suddenly, he felt utterly exhausted, down to the very core of his being. As though there was not a single unburned calorie left in his body. No cell that hadn't been wrung out. He was conscious of the two local uniforms he'd ordered to secure the caravan, wasn't about to fall asleep in his car in front of them. But the idea of an hour and a half or more on the road back to Edinburgh made him cringe. He stared at the blank screen of his phone. Woke it, intending to scroll through the contacts to Clio's name. The urge to speak to her was strong. She might have the information he was waiting for on Nathan Flenders's academic record. That's what he told himself. Wasn't about to admit, even in the privacy of his own mind, to needing another person.

Clumsy fingers hit the wrong app, and his last search filled the screen instead. Carl Hesten. The first match cut through Mac's fatigue like menthol through a blocked nose. A blast of icy air scythed through his mind and the fatigue shrivelled. It was a news story in the Daily Record. The headline was stark.

Sighthill man found dead in his flat.

Coroner rules suicide was cause of death for Sighthill man.

Scanning down the list, he saw more.

Hero priest fights for life of Sighthill man

Catholic priest questioned in death of ex-con

Mac hit the first story, scrolled past the ads, and consumed the story in a few seconds. Carl Hesten was dead. He'd already known that. Ramsey Jones had included him in his conspiracy theory. An ambulance had been called on the 3rd of October 2020 by a Catholic priest visiting a flat in the Sighthill area of Edinburgh. He'd found Hesten bleeding out from multiple knife wounds. Hesten had died before paramedics arrived. They'd found the priest performing CPR, but the blood loss had been too great. The priest was named in the story, Father Nicholas Cass, prison chaplain at HMP Edinburgh. Mac was staring through the bright screen now. Looking into his memory at the picture he'd examined at Cass's flat. A picture labelled September 2020 of a man holding a tenancy agreement for a property in Sighthill. Carl, it had said on the back of the picture. No picture of Carl Hesten featured in the Daily Record's story. But an Edinburgh Daily entry further down the search results showed his police mug-shot. Remanded for actual bodily harm and possession with intent to supply. A string of convictions dating back to pre-adolescence. They'd really gone in on the criminal angle. In contrast, Nick Cass was depicted as not far off being a saint, fighting for the life of one of his flock.

An article from the Catholic Times focused on Cass too. A priest dedicated to pastoral care who followed up on those he worked with in prison. Cass had helped Hesten find work and digs when he'd been released from prison. There was a tingle running through Mac. An instinct that told him he'd just fitted a puzzle piece snugly into the mystery. Everything led back to Father Nicholas Cass. Carl Hesten and Adam Glebe had both done time at HMP Edinburgh. So had Lukasz Burksi, though, before Cass's time there as chaplain. Could he have known about Burksi by other means? Mac wondered if breadcrumbs had been found near Carl Hesten's body. What had happened that night? Had Carl really killed himself, or had he been murdered? And if he had been killed, why had Cass remained at the scene?

A high-risk strategy for a killer, trying to double bluff. Unless he'd been cornered and decided bluffing was the only way out. That took a lot of nerve. He needed to talk to

Nick Cass. Wouldn't get a warrant authorised by Carmichael. Couldn't bring Cass in, Carmichael would get wind of it and shut him down. Mac would have to go to Cass at home or work. Try and catch him off balance. He went to contacts, picked out Mel's name. Began a text but stopped. He needed Mel as cover in the office, co-ordinating the final report to Carmichael, leaving him free to do what he had to do. He changed what he had been about to send. Asked her to look into Carl Hesten and run, as a matter of urgency, the DNA sample provided by Cass against those found at the scene of Adam Glebe's murder. Then he added in Flenders. Might as well eliminate them both if they could be. He scrolled on to Kai. A chance for his DS to make amends. Kai would be keen and never took much persuading to bend the rules. He typed out a text and sent it. Then he started the engine and began the drive back to Edinburgh.

Chapter Twenty-Nine

"SMILE, Maia. Come on; don't be too cool for your mum. Smile!"

Maia stood in front of a row of multicoloured terraced buildings. Yellow, pink, blue, green. Craft and gift shops, a pub, a restaurant. Behind them, framed by trees, was a church. Maia stuck out her tongue.

"I'm going to send it to Mac," Clio said.

Maia smiled. Clio snapped the picture she felt like she'd been waiting to take since they'd arrived in Portree. And all she'd needed to say was the magic word, Mac.

"He'll love it," Clio said.

Would he? Clio had chosen Skye for their forced holiday because she and Maia had never been, but had always wanted to. Mac seemed to blame the place for the death of his sister and his father. Not the person who had killed Iona, but the entire community. It was all tarred with the same brush as far as he was concerned. As Maia crossed the road to join her mother, leaning against the harbour wall and looking at the picture Clio had just taken, Clio wondered if this had been the best decision after all. She could have chosen the highlands. Cornwall or Devon. Wales.

"I like the different coloured houses," Maia said, taking the phone and scrolling through filters and options that Clio hadn't even known were there. Soon the picture looked like it had been taken by a professional. Clio was impressed.

"That's amazing, Maia. I like them too. So picturesque aren't they? And peaceful. I love this place."

Maia shrugged, having already volunteered a genuine emotion in front of her mum and with a nascent teen reputation to maintain. Behind the row of houses, the sun was rising. It was before nine in the morning.

"Will Uncle Callum come up here to visit us?" Maia asked.

"He used to live here, so it's probably not as much a novelty as it is for us."

"He must be due some holidays soon though, right?"

"I don't think Mac fully understands what a holiday is. It's not that kind of job," Clio said.

She shivered. There was a stiff breeze whipping small whitecaps on the top of the rollers coming into the harbour. It had a chill to it but oddly wasn't as cold as Edinburgh would be. It was out of season in Portree and most of the people they saw were locals, rather than backpack wearing holiday makers. The house she had rented was at the end of the spit of land that enclosed the south side of the harbour. A set of steps rose behind the rainbow parade of buildings, and their turn of the century fisherman's cottage was the first of the houses running along the road that led to the church.

Clio picked up one of the plastic bags of shopping they'd filled during their second walk down to the small supermarket. Maia had skipped ahead, peering over the harbour wall at the grey water beneath.

"Maia, this isn't all for me," Clio called.

She came back, picked up her share, and they walked along together. Clio lifted her head as though appreciating the bracing sea air, but glanced to the side, surreptitiously watching her daughter. Maia didn't have a smile on her face. Not quite. But Clio knew every twitch of her daughter's face. Every micro expression. She could see contented neutrality.

"Beats being in school," she said.

"Yep," Maia replied. "And work."

"I'm supposed to be working, though," Clio admitted.

She hadn't done much, attended a few video calls and peer reviewed a couple of papers. Not as much as was expected, but this place had that effect. It made the rest of the world seem distant and unimportant. Trivial almost.

"Do you think we could go see where Callum used to live?" Maia asked as they reached the end of the harbour and turned to begin the climb up the ancient stone steps, made safe for modern times by a steel, municipal hand rail down the middle.

"I'm not sure where it is," Clio admitted. "It's outside of Portree. It used to be a farm."

"We could ask at the hotel tonight."

They'd survived on takeaways for the last few nights, and Clio had decided they would try a proper cooked meal tonight. The Pier Hotel, one of the pretty pastel coloured buildings they had just passed, had been recommended.

"Maybe," Clio said.

She hoped Maia would forget about her obsession with seeing parts of Mac's past. Clio knew it was a sinkhole he didn't want to venture near. She walked on up the steep steps, head down and puffing. She wouldn't be half as insistent if she knew just how traumatic his past had been. But to Maia, Mac was a superhero. She didn't know half the stuff that had gone on since her mum had been asked to consult on a murder investigation. But she knew he had cool colleagues, a married lesbian with a non-binary friend Maia had met. Mel Barland had taken Maia to Pride and the Fringe. Mac himself had been the knight in shining armour. He could do no wrong and was utterly fascinating to Maia.

"I think it would be cool to see where he grew up," Maia added from up ahead.

"I think you should ask him then," Clio told her. "It would be rude not to. We don't want to intrude, Maia. He didn't have a happy childhood."

"OK."

Clio hoped that would be the last of it and tried not to regret her choice of hideaway. Tried to convince herself it would be the last time Maia asked. Sometimes you just had to bury your head in the sand and hope. But she knew how tenacious her daughter could be. Perhaps it would be better to speak to Mac and let her get it out of her system. They reached the house, a white-washed stone cottage with small windows set into thick walls. The front rooms had flag-stone floors and dark timber beams supporting low ceilings. Walls were white painted or just bare stone. The rear had been extended and refurbished around principles of light and air, creating a multi-level room that opened out onto a terraced rear garden. As Maia was putting the shopping away in the American-style double fridge, Clio opened her laptop on the island that divided the kitchen from a bright, open-plan living room. Alexis, one of her graduate assistants, had finished her task for Mac, checking up on any publications by Father Nathan Flenders. Clio scanned the email and looked through the half dozen email attachments and hyperlinks to the works Alexis had found referencing the name. The last link made her pause. She scrolled to the top of the webpage, checking the author name, date and the name of the publication. She knew the works of both author and publication. Trusted both.

"Here's your chance, kiddo," Clio said as she picked up her phone. "I'm calling Mac right now. If he picks up, you want to ask him?"

Maia turned and made a face as though weighing up pros and cons.

"Maybe."

"Better be sure."

Clio had received a text from Mac the night before to which she hadn't yet replied. She didn't know what or how he was doing. He wasn't volunteering anything. As though the threats to Clio and Maia had made him paranoid, affecting even the way he thought of her. Made him determined to keep his distance both physically and emotionally. Mac picked up quickly. She was video calling, which he often declined, switching to voice only. This time, he appeared on the screen. His hair looked wet, like he'd not long showered and was just letting it dry. It gave his face an even harsher look, angular and hard. His eyes were intent, but there was a smile lurking at the corner of his mouth.

"Hey," he said.

"Hey, yourself," Clio replied. "You look bright eyed."

"A good night's sleep," Mac replied.

"Really? It was the opposite before we left."

Mac shrugged, looked away from the screen.

Clio wondered what or who might be in that direction and glanced to where Maia was chugging fruit juice directly from the container. Clio looked back to Mac, and a raised an eyebrow. Mac shook his head, grinning, the rogue's smile.

"Nothing like that," Mac said.

"OK, well, I have some information for you. You wanted to know about the academic career of Nathan Flenders," Clio said. "My grad assistant came back to me. Don't know if it's going to be useful to you or not. I have the name of about half a dozen publications he's authored. None before 2018 and none after 2020. I've just sent you the list."

Mac's eyes left the camera, roamed the screen.

"I see it," Mac said. "I've seen these already. There's nothing else?"

"Nothing we could find," Clio said.

"What does that tell you? As an academic," Mac asked.

Clio spent a moment gathering her thoughts.

"I would say he wasn't a serious academic. Academics live to be published. Not to teach. I know plenty who didn't publish until later in life, but usually because they were engaged in a long-term project and there were significant time restraints or they were curtailed by an NDA. But none who just quit completely. There is something else that came up on the search, though that might explain why he stopped."

Mac raised an eyebrow, sitting back. Clio could see he was sitting on the sofa of his bare bones living room. There was a muted roar of discordant noise in the background, present but not loud enough to interfere. The counter top behind him was spartan, and the kitchen was immaculate. It looked the way she imagined the flat had been when he first viewed it. Empty and stark, waiting for a personality to imprint itself. It had got Mac and remained impersonal.

"Several of his works cite the same references. Professor Phillip Patrick Cass and Father John Christopher Cass."

Mac felt a spike of excitement. The thrill of facts finally fitting together, giving a larger view of the whole.

"Can you tell me who they are?" he said.

"I can. Professor Phillip Cass was an Oxford don. He died. Fellow of Christ College and professor of Theology. Father to Nicholas, was divorced before he died at his own hand in his mid-sixties. His wife was a Spanish national, an interior designer. Alexis couldn't find anything about Father John. Apart from the honorific, which suggests he was a cleric, there is a book mentioned which Alexis hasn't been able to find online, written in the '20s. It's probably in the British Library, but she'd have to go to London for that. Obviously, the name suggests he was a relative of the Professor."

Mac sat forward, lacing his fingers together, staring at and through the screen.

"Was that any help?" Clio asked.

"Aye, it was," Mac replied, distractedly. "I'm thinking maybe Flenders wasn't the author of the works his name is attached to, wasn't academic at all actually, and this was nothing but a smokescreen to divert attention."

"Hi, Uncle Callum," Maia chimed in suddenly.

"Hey, Maia. How are you liking Skye?" Mac said, smiling brightly.

"Good," Maia replied. "Would you mind if mum and I..."

Clio made silent motions for Maia to stop talking, but she ignored her mother and barrelled on.

"... went and looked for your old house?"

Mac's smile faded slowly. He looked serious, but after a moment his lips twitched once.

"I sold the house and the land after my father died. I inherited it all. Feel free. Show me a pic when you get there. Be interesting to see what it's like after all this time."

"Are you sure, Mac?" Clio asked.

"Aye, I'm sure."

Clio watched his face closely for a moment and Mac watched her back. He gave nothing away. She felt a flash of irritation. If it was a problem, he should just say so instead of getting angry and suppressing it. If he said there was no problem, they were entitled to take that at face value. Mac's lips twitched again.

"I mean it, Clio. I wouldn't be so keen if I was there with you. But I'm not. See it and tell me how ordinary it looks these days. In my head it's hell. Probably good to find out it's been turned into an Aldi, eh?"

"We will," Clio promised.

"I've got to go. Enjoy. Any issues?"

Clio was caught in the middle of signing off and stopped.

"No," she said, conscious of Maia's presence. "Everything's been fine. Everyone we've met has been really welcoming and friendly."

Mac gave a thumbs up and reached for the bottom of the screen. The call cut off.

Chapter Thirty

MAC STARED out of the windscreen as rain spattered across it. He was waiting for Kai, having arranged to meet in a supermarket car park in Newhaven. Kai had a flat in a complex not long completed, looking out over the docks and the Royal Yacht. Mac's mind was a trap, locked tight on the throat of Nicholas Cass. The key was being walked through forensics by Isla while Carole Strickland had sent a small team back to Pittenweem to check for DNA from the intruder who'd attacked Mac. One skin particle or drop of fluid would place Cass at a place he'd said he'd never visited. Any alibi he tried to give would be ripped apart. Mac would not stop now he was seeing to the heart of the case. Cass asked Flenders to put his name to articles so he could publish on a subject he knew well but didn't want to be publicly associated with. Just in case someone made the connection to sin-eating and started looking for experts on the subject. Cass was the real academic, son of an Oxford don with a grandfather, presumably, who was also a published author. What he couldn't get his head round was why Nick Cass had mentioned them in the first place if he wanted to keep his involvement a secret? He obviously hadn't been able to resist for some reason. Was it ego? A desire to see his family name in print? Some sort of skewed justice for a father and grandfather who were no longer alive? All of the above? Aye, that was possible. Cass and Flenders could have been in it together from the beginning. Either the suicide was real and Cass helped facilitate it or it was staged. But whatever the hell was going on, Mac was going to get answers.

The only distraction was Clio and Maia and the fact they were planning to visit the McNeill house. It was a constant shadow at the back of his mind, and Mac didn't want them tainted. Wanted to keep them free of the horrors of his past. He released his hold on the wheel, realising he'd been gripping it tight enough to numb his fingertips. Forcing his shoulders down, he let out a breath, opening a window a crack to let in some cold but fresh air. The rain didn't help, but at least he was free of the dreams now. Just so long as long as he took the pills. Kai emerged from the square block of sand coloured flats, hurrying along a paved path across waterlogged grass strewn with litter. He opened the door and got in, hair heavy with rain.

"Morning, guv," he said warily.

"Morning," Mac replied, starting the engine.

"What's the plan?"

"Isla's liaising with forensics. Mel is checking Cass and Flenders's DNA against a previous crime scene. We're going to talk to Father Nick. My gut tells me he knows more than he's telling. He's now the last person to see Adam Glebe alive and had reason to want him dead. Glebe believed the abuse accusations made against Flenders, who was a friend of Cass. Maybe Cass was afraid Glebe was going to go public. Or tell the wrong people, drum up a witch hunt. And if Cass is the sin-eater, he also has a motive to kill Flenders."

"What's that, if Flenders was his friend, I mean?" Kai asked.

Mac gritted his teeth. He'd got used to Isla's quick mind, reaching conclusions at the same time as his own.

"Because he'd also come to believe, though he didn't want to, that Flenders was a paedophile. Didn't want to circulate the information, but couldn't let him live knowing what he'd done. However, he wanted to make sure his friend went to heaven with his soul cleansed," Mac replied.

Kai nodded, taking it in.

"There's just too much evidence building up. Cass seems to be linked to three victims so far, four if Nathan Flenders didn't top himself. Adam Glebe, Lukasz Burksi and a new one, Carl Hesten. Cass was found with Hesten's body performing CPR. There's evidence at two of the scenes of the sin-eating ritual. And I think he's an expert, unable to avoid gloating about his knowledge and with an egotistical need to see his words in print, if not his name. He tried to hide it by having his pal put his own name to academic publications on the subject."

"So we need to break his alibi and then break him," Kai said.

Mac looked at him, gauging his DS' resolution. Was this how Strack had felt once, looking at PC Callum McNeill and assessing how far he'd be willing to bend the rules?

"Yes," Mac said.

"Let's do it," Kai said, then he paused, took a breath. "Guv about…"

"He's already made a complaint," Mac said. "And Carmichael has seen it."

Kai swore, made as if to punch the dashboard, but stopped himself, remembering whose dash it was.

"We'll manage it," Mac told him. "But that's why we're splitting the team up. I can't afford to make waves with Carmichael. He needs to think I'm following orders. For your sake. He also doesn't want PCC or AC sniffing around."

The complaint would be with the Police Complaints Commission but could turn into an internal disciplinary if they upheld it. Which would fall to Anti-Corruption. Carmichael was making a case for staying in his DCS role now that Kenny Reid was about to retire. He wouldn't want the bad press associated with an internal investigation. Mac was relying on Carmichael's political skills to keep Kai out of the brown stuff.

"Thanks, guv. It won't happen again," Kai said. "Last time I chase after a lass in the team. I swear."

"You're bloody right it won't happen again, Kai. I don't want to lose either of you, but if you're a couple, it's not going to work. One of you is out," Mac said, firmly. "We'll go after Cass first. I can't bring him in without risking Carmichael shutting us down. Call Saughton prison and ask them if he's working today."

It was Sunday but Cass's job as chaplain in the prison didn't have to be a Monday to Friday role. It wasn't as if the prisoners all had the weekends off. Besides, Sunday was a traditional day for the absolving of sins. Kai made the call as Mac headed for the Ferry Road. West to the Gogar Roundabout, cutting across the northern fringes of the city, then south on the bypass which circled Edinburgh to west and south. Quicker than trying to go straight as the crow flies from Leith to Saughton, even if the journey was longer in miles. Kai's call was brief.

"Father Cass hasn't been at work since Thursday. Is that significant, do you think?"

Mac grinned. "We had a tussle last night at the caravan. Can't prove it was him, but if his DNA is there, I'll have him for assaulting a police officer on top of everything else."

"What was he doing there?" Kai asked.

"Trying to return the key he must have taken without thinking. He must have realised how suss it made the suicide look. Which Carmichael can't seem to see," Mac replied.

"Bloody eejit," Kai said, shaking his head.

Mac wasn't sure if he was talking about Carmichael or Cass. It applied to both.

"I take it you got no bites with the receipt?" Mac said.

"I got a grainy CCTV image of a man in a hoody with a baseball cap under the hood. Never looked up enough to get his face on camera and the girl on the tills said she couldn't be sure it was Cass when I showed her the picture of him."

"Let's push that when we speak to him. Make him think we have an eyewitness," Mac said.

"Aye, we'll shake him and see what rattles loose, boss."

THERE WAS a car parked outside Cass's house at Kingshaugh. The curtains were drawn in the downstairs windows. As Mac got out of the car, he caught whiffs of weed coming from the open upstairs windows.

"Look out, it's the narcs!" Beth Rose called out from somewhere inside.

Kai glanced at Mac with an eyebrow raised as they approached the front door.

"Neighbour and friend of Nick Cass. An artist named Beth Rose," Mac told him, an idea occurring to him. "Go up and talk to her. She's a bit of a flirt. She's Cass's alibi for the night Adam Glebe was killed."

He spoke in a low whisper as he pressed the buzzer for Cass's flat, then the one marked Rose. The front door clicked open, though it was unclear which of the two had opened it. Kai gave him a grin and headed for the stairs. Mac went to Cass's front door and rapped on it sharply. There was silence for a moment, broken only by the sound of Kai taking the stairs two at a time. Then movement, which Mac responded to with another sharp rap. A chain was drawn as Kai knocked upstairs, the sound reverberating down the staircase. The door opened enough to show Nick Cass. He wore sweats and his hair was dishevelled. A dark stain of stubble marked his jawline, and a bruise blossomed on his temple, dark and slightly swollen. He didn't look like he had slept. Mac smiled brightly.

"Father Cass."

"What do you want?"

"Can I come in?"

"Why?"

"Doesn't matter to me either way. I'll happily have the conversation out here, but your neighbour might be a bit too interested in what I have to say," Mac replied, flippantly.

He was being obnoxious, which he didn't find difficult. It hit the mark with Cass, though, whose face had stilled. He opened the door wider and stepped aside. Mac walked in, heading down the hall to the living room. Along the way, he glanced into the office. There was no sign of the journals, but the picture of Carl Hesten was still visible. Cass caught him looking, tried to see what had caught his attention, but Mac turned away and took a seat on the sofa. He crossed his legs, putting his arms across the back of the sofa. Made himself at home.

"Can I get you anything, Detective Chief Inspector?" Cass asked. "Tea, coffee?"

"Beer and sandwiches," Mac said, still smiling, then immediately added, "don't worry. I'm fine."

Remarkably, Cass hadn't reacted to Mac's thinly veiled jab. He took a seat in an armchair and appeared to be quite composed. He had the air of a psychiatrist waiting for this patient to begin talking.

"Where were you around ten pm last night?" Mac asked while Cass was folding his hands over his knee.

Cass froze for a microsecond before coughing into his fist and holding up a hand.

"Sorry, Inspector," he cleared his throat. "I think I'm starting with the flu. Ten pm last night, you said?"

Mac didn't respond. Or smile. Or move. He just glowered. Cass looked to the ceiling and made a long, umming sound.

"I was here. I might have gone out for a takeaway at some point. There's a rather good Chinese just five minutes down the road and they give a discount if you pay cash and collect…"

"Can anyone verify that?" Mac interrupted.

"No, I was alone. I mean, Beth was in. She might have seen me go out or come back. She might not…oh the takeaway, if they remember. They get busy on Saturdays."

"You pay by card?"

"No, as I said, it was cash. You get a discount."

Mac nodded. A simple test for a lie. See if the details stay the same when repeated.

"Any calls during the evening? Any parishioners visiting?" Mac asked. He hadn't blinked, hadn't looked away from Cass once.

"No, my parishioners are all locked up. And no calls. I get a lot of calls, but usually not late at night. I can check my phone."

"Please do."

Cass nodded and remained seated, waiting for the next question.

"Oh, you mean now?" he said, after a minute.

Mac gave a curt nod. Cass got up, patted his pockets, and then went into the office, returning with the usual black plastic and glass rectangle. He jabbed it a few times.

"I'm sorry, Inspector. I dropped it last night. It was still working but seems to have given up the ghost."

Mac held out a hand, but Cass didn't bite.

"Are you asking me for my phone?" he said, sitting.

"Only if you volunteer it."

"I don't think I do."

"Your prerogative. How well did you know Carl Hesten?"

Cass's eyes darted to the door that led to the study. That confirmed for Mac, the Carl in the picture was Hesten.

"I worked with him at HMP Edinburgh. Helped him with his addictions and the trauma he'd suffered through his life. We became good friends. I sponsored him and it helped him get a job with Timpson's and a flat of his own when he got out."

"And you found his body," Mac said.

Cass didn't reply at once, staring straight through Mac. "Yes. I went to see him and I…I found him."

"You had a key to his flat."

"I did."

"You must have been close."

"We were."

"As close as you are to Conor Taggart?"

Cass shifted in his seat, tapping fingers against his phone, which he'd placed on the arm of the chair.

"I…yes…somewhat. They're both young men in need of help and guidance."

"How does a Catholic priest manage with celibacy?" Mac asked, aiming for another disruptive question. "Your neighbour seems to think it causes homosexual urges for want of a better expression. That true?"

"No, it is not. And I manage it through devotion to my vocation. The demands of the body are fleeting. Have you ever smoked, Inspector?"

"Ah, I see. So, you're not queer, eh?" Mac said insolently.

"None of your damn business!" Cass snapped. "Why am I sitting here letting you speak to me like this? I should be…"

"Sitting there letting a senior police officer speak to you like this!" Mac snapped back. "I'm investigating a murder, pal. How did you get that bruise on your head?"

Cass's mouth opened and closed like a fish. He stood up, hand going up to cover his head.

"I bumped it on a cupboard door…"

"I nutted you," Mac replied, remaining seated.

"What? That's ridiculous."

"We're checking the key you left for DNA. How did you kill Nathan Flenders?" Mac asked, voice dropping in temperature.

Cass stared at him.

"What did you just say?" he asked.

"How. Did. You. Kill. Nathan. Flenders," Mac said, emphasising each word.

"Nathan..." Cass swallowed and sat down heavily. "Nathan's not dead."

It was a good act. The slack mouth, the wide eyes, the shallow breathing. Mac even felt a momentary chill of fear. Fear he'd got this completely wrong and Cass was innocent. Aye, a good act. But not perfect.

"Nathan's dead. His suicide note was typed. That's a bit of a giveaway. Who does that, eh? And pains were taken to make him look like an academic, even though he clearly wasn't. I mean, take you, for instance, you could be an academic. You have a dedicated office. You have a lot of academic books and they've obviously been read. Repeatedly. Your dad was a respected academic and your grandfather was a published author. Nathan's books didn't look like they'd been touched. Except for the library book."

"Get out! I want you out!" Cass hissed, putting his face into his hands, and shaking his head.

"Want all you want. I'm staying. The library book, Nick. The one checked out of HMP Edinburgh's library. My team is checking who borrowed it last. You remember that book, Nick?"

Cass made an inarticulate noise of frustration, running a hand through his hair.

"I could check your shoes and clothes for traces of mud, which forensics can match to the Pittenweem crime scene. But I don't think I need to, eh? Why did you kill Nathan Flenders?"

"I want you out of my house. I'm going to make an official complaint. This... this is harassment," Cass cried out.

Mac's phone buzzed. He took it from his pocket. A text

from Isla. Replacing the phone, he looked at Cass and grinned.

"You checked out the book, Nick. Four weeks ago. I'm thinking you put it in Nathan's bookcase, forgetting it was a library book. You wanted to make it look like he killed Adam Glebe. That he was the sin-eater. Then you killed him. Ate his sins and sent him on his way to heaven."

Father Nick Cass burst into tears.

Chapter Thirty-One

MAC STAYED QUIET, sensing the pivot point of the case, the chink in Cass's armour. He felt the urge to hold his breath, prayed that Kai wouldn't choose this moment to barge in.

"I was there at the caravan," Cass said, brokenly. "I found his body. Read his note. I couldn't believe it. He was my Father Confessor. He absolved me of my sins, I confessed to him. Confessed everything. And here he was..."

Mac remained still, not wanting to risk derailing wherever this flow was going.

"You knew about the caravan in Pittenweem?" he said softly.

Cass nodded.

"Why did you go there?"

"To talk to Nathan. To check on him."

"To confess?"

Cass nodded.

"Confess to what?"

Cass was staring at the floor. It was a thousand-yard

stare into something that horrified him. His hands were clenched between his knees, knuckles white. His head shook slowly.

"I needed to confess my sins," he whispered. "They were weighing me down. I was dragging them like chains."

"What sins?" Mac probed. "Did you kill Adam Glebe to save his soul?"

Cass looked up and Mac thought he had gone too far, pushed the priest out of his guilt stricken state and back behind his walls.

"No, Inspector. I did not. I wanted to confess to...my feelings for... another man."

His mouth firmed, brows drew down. He looked angry at having to confess something so personal. Mac watched him without expression, waiting for the story to be told, reading Cass's face, looking for the signs of deception.

"I'm...I'm...gay," Cass said, with the last word delivered in a hoarse croak, as though his body was attempting to prevent its utterance. "It's a sin according to the faith I have dedicated my adult life to. I cannot reconcile it with my God and the Church."

"So, you sought your friend Father Nathan in order to make your confession. You told me you didn't know where the caravan was. That you had never been there," Mac said.

Cass nodded. "It was a lie. I've been there a few times. I knew how bad it would look for me if I admitted I was there. Because I behaved so stupidly. Reacted so stupidly." His voice finally broke.

He put his face in his hands and sobbed. His shoulders shook. Mac sat forward, hands together and eyes on the priest. At any moment, he expected the man to peek between his fingers to see how his performance was being received. Mac said nothing. He wanted the performance to continue, wanted the story.

"How did you react stupidly?"

"I saw the note. Found his body. I ate bread over him, drank water. Took on his sins. I don't believe in the rite, but Nathan did. It was important to him."

"He told you that?"

"Yes. He told me he had traced his family tree back to the last sin-eater in Britain. It had been passed down through his family as this dirty little secret. It was the least I could do. But afterwards I locked the door behind me. It was automatic. When I realised what I'd done... I panicked. Tried to put the keys back but..."

"I was there," Mac said.

"Yes. And then I was just in such a state I thought my heart was going to stop. I honestly thought I was about to have a heart attack or a stroke."

Mac let out a long breath. "I understand what you're saying. You found him and panicked. Did some stupid things. You didn't kill him."

Cass nodded, rubbing his hands up and down his face. It was all to cover his expression. Hide his eyes and his facial muscles. Mac could see straight through it and wanted to tell him he didn't believe a word he'd said. But that would put Cass back into defensive mode. Probably lead to a lawyer being brought in. Cass might not know how precarious Mac's case was, but he was intelligent. He had to know his DNA would be found in the caravan. That it would be on the key. Mac's blood might also be on the clothes he'd worn. So Cass was confessing to something he knew wouldn't lead to heavy legal consequences. Failing to report a dead body in the context of friendship with the deceased and good standing in the community probably wouldn't go anywhere. The PF wouldn't be interested in pursuing a prosecution. Assaulting a police officer? Cass would argue he thought it was an intruder. That Mac didn't identify himself as a police officer. But he wanted Cass to believe himself out of the woods. Wanted him in a false state of security.

"We will need a full written statement from you given under caution, Father Cass," Mac said, putting an edge of weariness into his voice. The disappointed bloodhound.

"All of it?" Cass asked, swallowing.

He was laying it on thick now. Mac wanted to hit him. Give him a matching bruise on the other side of his lying face.

"All of it. I need to know why you were there and why you performed the sin-eater ritual, including how you knew what to do. Trust me, being gay even for a priest is nothing compared to being a murder suspect."

"But my statement will be confidential," Cass said.

"Of course," Mac said.

"Ok, when do you want me to do it?"

"Do you have pen and paper to hand?" Mac said, struggling to keep the edge from his voice now. Cass's tears had evaporated. His broken voice had miraculously healed itself. Mac was seeing a manipulative and intelligent man. His mind was already running along routes that would lead him to evidence. Cass would not be browbeaten into a slip. Would not be tricked into incriminating himself.

"Is that allowed? Do I need to do this at the station?"

"Do you want to go to the station?" Mac asked.

"Well, obviously not, but I want this done properly. I don't want any further comeback."

"My sergeant and your neighbour will witness it and you will sign and date it. Beth doesn't need to know the contents of your statement. Just that you are helping us with our inquiries," Mac assured him.

As if on cue, there was a knock at the door. Cass's head whipped round and Mac stood, walking out of the room and letting in Kai. He peered over Mac's shoulder and then stepped close, lowering his voice.

"She's a flake. She doesn't know what day it is. I even suggested to her that the day Cass was with her was Monday. She thought about it for a minute and then swore blind he was with her on Monday evening, not Sunday."

Mac nodded. No alibi. At least not one that would stand up to a good KC.

"Doesn't matter now," Mac whispered back.

Kai frowned but didn't say more as Mac turned back to Cass, who was hovering in the living room doorway watching them.

"I'll take your statement to my commanding officer and he'll decide if it needs to be taken further, if it needs to go to the Procurator Fiscal's office or not. You may be required to come into the station for further interviews."

Cass nodded, standing awkwardly as though unsure what to do next. Mac walked back into the room, followed by Kai.

"Kai, could you get us paper and pens? Father Nick, I will record you writing your statement on my phone as further evidence if that's OK with you?"

Cass sat, literally on the edge of his seat. He wiped his palms on his trousers, licked his lips. Mac took his seat as Kai rummaged for pens and paper. Then Mac cautioned Cass and took out his phone, opening the camera. A number flashed on the screen, one he didn't recognise.

"Kai, do the honours, will you?" Mac said, gesturing to

where Cass was settling down to write. "I want a record of this."

He walked into the kitchen as Kai set up his own phone to record.

"McNeill," he answered.

"Detective Chief Inspector? It's Father Neil Fitzsimmons here, from St Aiden's. You remember?"

The voice was halting, catching as though he wasn't sure how to introduce himself, how much detail was needed.

"Yes, I remember. It was the day Nathan Flenders barged past me after a heated conversation with you. Even though you insisted you hadn't seen or heard from him. You lied to my face, Father Fitzsimmons."

There was a lengthy sigh from the other end of the phone. Mac gritted his teeth, knowing what was coming.

"I apologise, Detective Chief Inspector. I was, and still am, bound by the Seal of the Confessional. It is my duty…"

"Fine," Mac said, cutting him off. "What can I do for you?"

"You gave me your number the other day in the church, said to call if I heard from Nathan?"

Mac experienced a momentary swirl of unreality, thinking he'd stepped into the twilight zone.

"Don't tell me he rang you?"

"No, no, I haven't heard from him since. Did you find him?"

"He's at his caravan. Pittenweem," Mac said.

"Of course. I remember the name now. Anyway, I wanted to ring you about... well, I feel foolish. It might be something and nothing... I just..."

Mac glanced through the open kitchen door, along the hallway. He'd closed the door of the front room when he left, wasn't sure how much could be overheard. He tried the backdoor and, finding it unlocked, stepped out into the back garden.

"Just tell me, Father," he said with the impression of patience he didn't feel. Cass was playing the system, and it made him angry, made him want to catch him in a vice and split him open, scoop out all his secrets. But for now, he had to take what he could get.

"Remember, I said that two of our party had stayed on at the retreat? That I was thinking of joining them for a bit?"

Mac wracked his brain.

"Joe and Lee? No, Leo," Mac recalled.

"That's right, well today I went up there, to West Calder. They were gone, packed their bags, and left. Neither of them drives. I assumed they'd got a bus or something, but it was odd neither of them sent me a text first. Especially Joe. He's an active member of the community here at St Aidens. Anyway, I was a bit... well, put out to be honest, so I text them. No answer. Unread. I called, and it went straight to voicemail. I even spoke to Leo's partner. He has two kids with her. She was surprised to hear from me, thought Leo would be at the retreat for another week. She hasn't seen him."

"Maybe they left today and they're still travelling," Mac suggested, his mind still on Cass.

"The caretaker said he's seen no one up there for nearly a week. He remembers seeing Joe leave, but not Leo. That was Monday."

"Are you concerned these men are missing?" Mac was losing his patience.

"No, I don't think so. No. I just. Well, yes, perhaps. I just have a very odd feeling about it all. It's out of character for both of them. And I can't think where Leo would go for a week other than back to his family."

"Do you think they're still together?" Mac asked.

"They were friends, so perhaps, I just didn't know if it would be serious enough for the police, but it's been nearly a week and since you'd asked me about them the other day..."

Mac had asked, had wanted to know about the retreat and had meant to get Mel to follow up on the two men. He swallowed his irritation. It had to be investigated, and Father Neil had done the right thing. Mac knew he was angry because Cass had outmanoeuvred him. Knew with a feeling of absolute certainty he was being played. He even wondered if Cass somehow knew of Carmichael's pressure to close the case.

"I'll look into it. You did the right thing. I'll be in touch," Mac said.

He hung up the phone and walked back into the house. Kai looked up, Cass didn't. He kept writing, head down and one hand combing his fringe out of his eyes as he leaned over the paper. Diligent and cooperative.

"Have you spoken to the two guys who stayed at the retreat?" Mac asked.

Cass looked up, frowning.

"Joe and Leo? No, I don't think so," Cass said.

"Were they part of the argument?"

Cass shook his head. "No, they kept out of it."

"Father Neil just called me. They left the retreat early."

"Oh, well, that's understandable. It was ruined."

"That must have been annoying, frustrating at the least," Mac said.

"Very. It's a release for all of us. A chance to reset. Yes, frustrating is an excellent description."

"You wanted Adam to go to hell. You must have blamed him for the failure of the retreat," Mac said, taking a seat and not breaking eye contact with Cass, who put the pen down, placing his hand flat on the page he had almost filled.

"I did blame him. I've known Nathan for a long time. He was my predecessor at HMP Edinburgh. He taught me a lot."

Mac nodded slowly, as though processing this.

"Of course, we had very different approaches. I wanted to treat the men as equals, understand the trauma that had shaped them. Treat them as human beings. Nathan believed in punishment and saving those who wanted to be saved. He was a hard man. I think he believed firmly that most of the men he worked with were going to end up in hell. Hell was a very real place to him."

"It's not real to you?" Mac asked.

Cass stared at him for a long moment, then looked down at the page again and picked up the pen.

"Do you believe in hell, Father?" Mac persisted. "Is Adam Glebe in hell? Is Nathan Flenders?"

The silence extended. Mac had an instinct, a growing feeling this was a chink in Cass's armour. Would he lie about something that must be fundamental to his beliefs? If he was the sin-eater, then could he pretend to be otherwise?

"No, they're not in hell. Their souls were saved," Cass said.

"How?"

"Because they embraced God, they cleansed their souls. I wouldn't expect you to understand," Cass said shortly, pen hovering over the paper.

"How were they saved? Did they make confession before they died?" Mac asked.

"Yes!" Cass snapped. "Nathan was flawed, but he was a

good man and he confessed his sins. Not to me, but I know he did. Conor... I mean Adam was, too. He confessed to me the last time we spoke."

"You wanted him in hell the last time you spoke," Mac pushed.

"It was an expression! I was angry, so was he! I wouldn't wish hell on anyone."

"But you did," Mac said, leaning closer. "Even if just for a moment. And now you're confessing. You're cleansing your soul, confessing your sins."

"I am," Cass said, breathing out. "All of them."

He looked Mac in the eye and there was a hint of a smile. Mac had pushed as much as he dared. He wanted the confession Cass was giving and didn't have enough evidence for anything else. He needed Cass to think he was winning.

Mac caught Kai's eye and nodded his head towards the kitchen. Kai followed as Cass resumed writing.

"I don't know how long we're going to be able to stay on him, but everything tells me he's the one. Everything. Carmichael is not going to take this confession as grounds to open the case. He wants closure."

"So, we're going rogue? Suits me," Kai said. "What do you want me to do?"

"Keep Cass under surveillance. I want to see what he does next, where he goes. Let's just do this as long as we can. I would do it, but he's going to be watching for me."

"So is Carmichael," Kai said.

"Exactly. Look, Kai, officially I can't ask you to do this. You've got enough on your plate without getting on Carmichael's bad side..." Mac said.

"Guv, enough. I don't care about that. I just want to get this scumbag."

Mac nodded, looking back into the house.

"Get going when we've finished here, but not too far. You know the script; keep an eye on the street so you can pick him up if he leaves. Just watch him, where he goes and who he meets. It might be a boring few hours, but I think he's the kind who will think he's safe, be congratulating himself."

"And when he makes a mistake, we'll have him," Kai said with satisfaction.

Chapter Thirty-Two

CASS TOOK two hours to complete his statement. Mac read it, keeping his face still, masking his growing rage. It was a statement of self-importance. Cass sat opposite, one hand across his mouth, legs crossed and eyes occasionally wet. It was grief as a performance. Mac signed it and handed it to Kai, who read and then witnessed it. The phone recording was saved and emailed to Mac. Kai, took the pages and went upstairs to have them witnessed by Beth Rose. She could come down and have Cass confirm his authorship personally if she wished.

"Will there be any further action taken?" Cass asked.

"That's not up to me, Father," Mac replied. "I'll speak to my boss and the Procurator Fiscal to decide if any crime has been committed. Don't be surprised if we have a few follow-up questions for you."

"Just ask. Any time. I want to be completely transparent," Cass said earnestly.

Mac forced a smile.

"Thank you for your co-operation, Father Cass."

He and Kai left. Mac drove out of Kingshaugh and pulled in around the corner from Cass's road but in sight of it. Kai got out of the car and walked back to the corner, where he would have a view of the priest's house. Mac took out his phone and brought up Isla's name with the fingers of one hand.

"Isla, things have changed. I've just been to see Nick Cass. The DNA just became less important. We have a signed confession he was at the caravan and found Flenders's body, but he didn't kill him. He knows he can't deny being there, so he's confessing to the lesser crime of concealing a death. The DNA will add to the validity of his confession, but it's not needed urgently anymore."

"What do you want me to do, guv?" Isla asked. "Mel said Carmichael has been into the office a couple of times asking after you and Kai."

"Kai's with me. Currently on stakeout, in the event Cass leaves his house. Can you arrange for his car to be delivered ASAP in case Cass drives off somewhere?"

"Will do, Guv. What about Carmichael?"

"He wants the case shut down. Has Mel announced it to the press yet?"

"She's meeting with the PR team now," Isla said. "I think they're getting the press to HQ in about an hour."

"If Carmichael asks..."

"Tell me what I'm working on and that's what I'll tell him."

"You're chasing up witness statements from the last people to see Nathan Flenders alive. He can't object to that. It's a loose end that the Procurator Fiscal will expect to be cleared up. It's also going to potentially help us nail Cass."

"Got it. Where am I going?"

"Nowhere alone. Grab a uniform to back you up. In

fact, you can kill two birds with one stone and deliver Kai's car at the same time. You'll need to pick up the keys from him first. I have an email from Father Neil Fitzsimmons giving the addresses of the two men who were at the retreat with him, Flenders, Glebe and Cass. They left last Monday and haven't been heard of since. He's tried to get in touch with them but hasn't got an answer. Start with their home addresses," Mac said.

"Can't get in touch with them? Is this something to be concerned about?" Isla asked.

"Who knows? We don't know enough yet to say. Father Fitzsimmons is concerned, though. We're following up in the absence of any other leads."

Mac heard a beeping on the line and glanced at the screen. Melody Onayemi. For a moment, he looked at it blankly, trying to place the name to someone on the force. Then remembered the mental health crisis specialist who'd been sent to assess Jacob Danzig, the vampire. The first suspect in the Adam Glebe killing.

"I have to go, Isla. I'll send you the addresses. Get there as soon as you can."

Mac hung up and picked up the call from Onayemi.

"Ms. Onayemi, how can I help?" he said.

"Detective Chief Inspector, call me Melody," she replied.

"Mac."

"I thought you should know Jacob has become lucid. They have suppressed the violent personality that makes them so dangerous and are managing that side of them- selves. They are keen to help with your investigation. I think this is an opportunity for you to ask the questions you have, but I don't know how long he will remain rational, so the sooner the better."

Mac felt a surge of excitement.

"Do they remember that night?" he asked.

"They have been talking to me about their experience. They see it very much in the third person, as though they were a captive to the darker side of their personality, observing but not able to take action. I cannot relay what they said, as it occurred within the context of confidential counselling sessions. Ask the right questions, though, and you'll get the information you need for yourself."

Mac suppressed a frustrated growl, knowing it wouldn't go down well with Melody Onayemi. He felt as though this case was full of people who knew things but were hiding behind false constructs of confidentiality. Conventions created by people which enabled a murderer to unburden themselves of the guilt of their actions without taking the responsibility. He couldn't feel empathy for a priest who knowingly allowed a killer to walk the streets. Or a psychiatrist, or whatever Melody was. But at least she'd stuck to her promise to call him.

"Am I going to need to dress up in my sergeant's gym kit again?" Mac said, his resentment leaking to the surface before he could stop it.

"No, that was an aspect of the violent and paranoid personality that lives within Jacob. It's currently suppressed, so they should not react to your suit."

"Where are you?"

"Mental Health Crisis unit at the Royal Infirmary. We have an annex just off Little France Crescent," Melody said.

"I know it. I'm on my way."

He hung up and took stock of where he was, mentally mapping the route to the Royal. The phone buzzed again as he put it on the passenger seat beside him. Glancing at it, he saw Clio's name. It would have to wait.

———

THE MENTAL HEALTH CRISIS team was housed in a red brick building in landscaped grounds of verdant grass and hardy shrubs behind the sprawling Royal Infirmary. It was screened from the road, a sign bearing an NHS logo on gates which barred entrance. Mac spoke to someone through an intercom and the gates opened electronically. It was a sign of the security operating here despite the signage announcing it as a hospital. Parking in front of the building, he entered through sliding doors to a reception area manned by a young woman with a blond ponytail, a round face, and sporting blue scrubs. Mac showed his ID.

"DCI McNeill. I'm here to see Jacob Danzig."

He was asked to take a seat on a pale green sofa, partially screened from the rest of reception by a jungle of potted plants. He waited impatiently, hands clasped, fidgeting. Melody appeared through a door beside reception, an ID card on a lanyard. She spoke to the receptionist and was given a second card with a large red V on it. She smiled briefly as she approached Mac, offering him the visitor pass.

"Thank you for letting me know, Melody," Mac said.

"I am passing on a request from Jacob. They are keen to be of help, and I considered it important for their continued recovery."

Mac nodded. Swiping her card against an electronic reader beside the door she'd come through, Melody led Mac along a corridor with floor to ceiling windows on one side and a row of doors on the other. Each door had a sign taped to the reinforced glass window announcing its function. She led him to the last door; the sign announcing it as Meeting Room 3.

The room was carpeted and furnished with a couple of

armchairs and a beanbag. A shelving unit held a random assortment of books and board games. A small window overlooked a garden, but the view was spoiled by the wires threaded between the panes of glass, reinforcing the window against breakage. Jacob Danzig sat in one of the armchairs. He was wearing a thin dressing gown over pyjamas with slippers over white socks. His hair was pulled back tightly into a bun and his face was pale. His hands draped loosely over the arms of the chair and one leg dangled over the knee of the other.

Mac took a seat opposite him as Melody shifted a third chair to a position between them both.

"Jacob, thank you for meeting with me," Mac said.

Jacob glanced at Melody, who nodded, giving him a small, encouraging smile. Mac sensed how fragile Jacob's peace was. Felt the violence that lurked not far beneath the surface. He wondered what had happened to produce this man. What trauma had turned him into this unstable person who believed himself to be a vampire, living in subterranean passages beneath the city?

"I am currently seeing things clearly. I recognise the need to share with you what I know before my memories become clouded by the other," Jacob said.

"The other?" Mac asked.

"The one who lives within me. He who wants to kill and hurt others. The vampire," Jacob said.

Mac nodded, as though what he had just heard was perfectly reasonable. As though he met people claiming to be inhabited by vampires regularly.

"Do you want to tell me about the night we met?" Mac asked.

"I saw two men. One was dragging the other. He carried him at first, crossing an area of derelict ground and partially into the tunnel before it became too small. He then dragged him. I followed at a distance. I was convinced this was the Master. A source of evil. I thought he had summoned me to witness this act, but I didn't want to get too close. I was afraid of what would happen if the Master noticed my presence," Jacob said.

He hugged his knees to his chest, resting his chin on top. Melody reached out and put a light hand on his arm. Mac waited, holding his breath, waiting for the signs of impending violence. Of losing the opportunity to get answers.

"I followed him into darkness, following his sounds. Then we reached the chamber and there was light. He had a torch and put it on the ground, then knelt beside the body. It shone under his face."

Mac watched Jacob's pale, twitching face. His eyes looked haunted. Melody shifted, and Jacob glanced at her. Mac braced himself to be told that the interview was over, that the violent other was rising. He felt so close.

"I'm OK, Melody. I'm OK," Jacob said.

"Can you describe him?" Mac asked.

Jacob shook his head. "Dark hair, dark eyes, white skin. He glowed."

"That's all?"

"Yes."

Mac wanted to shout in frustration. The evidence he needed was locked up in the damaged mind of Jacob Danzig. There must be a way to access it.

"If I brought one of our artists here to ask you about the face you saw, would you be willing to talk to them?" Mac asked, carefully.

Jacob nodded sharply. "I will do my best."

"Thank you, Jacob," Mac replied.

"There's more," Jacob said. "I took something from him."

"Took something?"

"When he left the chamber, he saw me. There was no room in the tunnel for him to pass me, so I ran and he caught me. I lashed out. I thought I was going to die. During the struggle I... I grabbed at his hair. Some of it came away."

Mac's jaw dropped. He recovered quickly; clamping his mouth shut as Jacob put a hand into the pocket of his dressing gown and produced a handful of dark hair. Without looking away, Mac put a hand in his pocket and produced a bag.

"May I?" he asked carefully, holding out the bag.

Jacob nodded, holding out his hand and dropping the clump of hair into the evidence bag.

Chapter Thirty-Three

MAC STARED at a picture on his phone. It was part of a series. A woman crouched at the side of a road in front of a tall, wooden fence. The picture was taken from fifty yards away. Mac could see fair hair, a bag over one shoulder, jeans. It was framed by the window of a car; the photographer taking it through the open window. Another followed, closer. The car hadn't moved. Mac could tell that the camera had been zoomed in. There was deterioration in the image quality, but Mac could tell now the woman had large earrings and a leather jacket.

Another picture. Another zoom. The woman was turning. Facing toward the camera, but not looking at it. Mac frowned, squinting at the image. It looked as though there was some disfigurement on the right side of her face. A reddening. Possibly burn scars or a birthmark. It might have been the quality of the image, but he thought not. Kai could get the picture enhanced on the quiet. Mac sat back in his desk chair, zooming into the picture.

It had been taken by Clio outside what she believed was the site of his childhood home. He called her.

"Hi, Mac," Clio answered on the third ring.

"Clio, just looking at the pictures you sent me."

"I thought it would be easier to show you than describe it."

"You're sure that was where the farm used to be? I heard it became an outdoor pursuits thing after I sold it."

"It's where you said it was, as near as we can tell. As we were driving up, we saw this woman. The whole site is fenced off and there are signs up by some developer announcing housing to be built," Clio said. "We drove past and then turned round, and that's when I got some pictures for you. Do you recognise her?"

Mac shook his head, then remembered the call was audio only.

"No. Did you get a good look at her face?"

"Yes, she has some kind of birthmark or scarring on the right side. I couldn't tell which."

"What was she doing?"

"She was leaving flowers and a bottle of rum. We waited until she'd gone and went to look."

"What kind of rum?"

"It was called Sailor Jerry," Clio replied.

Mac laughed, but there was no humour in it. It was a sound of bitter regret, the presage to tears he had no intention of letting out.

"That was Iona's go to drink. Sailor Jerry and coke," he said.

"Maybe this woman knew her?"

"I can't think of anyone we knew that had a scar or birthmark. Unless it's something that happened after. I thought maybe it was a burn."

"Could be."

"She didn't leave a card? Just flowers and booze?"

"That's all."

"Did she see you?"

"I don't think so," Clio said. "We stopped a suitable distance away. I thought she looked at us, but I don't think she could see us from where she was."

"If you could see her, then she could probably see you," Mac pointed out. "Just be careful. I don't know who this person is, but she clearly knows something about Iona and what happened. If she's not a friend from the old days, then who is she and what's her interest in my sister?"

Mac brought the picture back up, the closest one. He scrutinised the mark on the side of the woman's face, tried to place her in his past. She was a stranger. Except how could she be? She knew Iona. If she knew Iona, then she knew the McNeill's, knew Mac. Who the hell was she?

"Should Maia and I come home?" Clio asked.

"No, not yet. The house is paid for until the end of the month."

"Yes, but you're now asking me to take care. Is this woman a danger to us?" Clio said, responding to his curt tone.

"I don't know. I don't know who she is." Mac was exasperated and couldn't help showing it.

"I didn't ask to be in this situation, Mac," Clio snapped. "We're in danger in Edinburgh. Now you're saying be cautious here on Skye? It was only supposed to be a week and now you're talking a month? I just want my child to be safe!"

Mac could hear the tension just beneath the surface, now breaking through. He put the phone down, closed his eyes, fighting down his own frustration. He felt powerless.

There had been no sign from Musa that he'd taken the bait Mac had left for him. That he believed the name he'd been given. If Musa was still after him, then Clio wasn't safe. But how dangerous was this woman? What threat to Clio and Maia was someone on the island who knew about Iona's death?

"I'm sorry. Clio, I'm... I just didn't expect this. I've buried Iona. Been trying to bury her. I didn't think you being there would dig her up."

"Neither did I. If coming to Skye was going to be a problem, we could have gone anywhere else."

"It's not. It shouldn't be. I've no idea who this is and why she's leaving flowers for my sister, and I want to know. Want to find and ask her!"

His voice was going up, anger at being so helpless driving him.

"Christ, I'm sorry, Clio."

"I'm sorry too. I knew I should have just ignored this woman..."

"No, I needed to see this. It's just a shock, eh?" Mac said, trying to put the conversation on a friendlier footing.

Suddenly, he felt vulnerable, alarmed by the fact he might be alienating his best friend. Along with the frustrations of the Glebe case, it was an uncomfortable sensation, leaving him feeling out of control of every aspect of his own life. He ran both his hands through his hair.

"Thank you for this, Clio. Are things OK otherwise?"

Clio sighed. "Yes, they're fine. We've been on boat trips and we're seeing more of the island away from Portree today. We're at Loch Treaslane. Do you know it?"

"Aye, I've been there," Mac said.

He remembered a trip there with his dad, brother, and sister.

"One of the few times my dad was sober, all of us piled into his van one summer's day, me and Iona sliding about in the back without seatbelts or seats. We were hysterical. Dad singing Sinatra at the top of his voice. We ended up at the loch. Didn't happen often. Hard to take holidays when you're a farmer."

"Sounds like a fun day."

"Dad got into a fight with a guy on holiday from Glasgow. Got himself arrested for drunk and disorderly. Connor drove us back. No license or insurance but, you know..."

There was a silence. With anyone else, it would have been awkward.

"Mac, you should come out here and see us," Clio said. "It's time you exorcised some of these atrocious memories."

Mac snorted. "You saying my childhood was atrocious?"

"Not every day of it, you clot," Clio replied. "There must have been some good times?"

"Aye, but I can't remember many, eh?" Mac replied, feeling the dark mood lifting somewhat. Clio had that effect. She could speak to Mac in a way no one else could. And with an effect no one else could achieve.

There came a sharp knock at the door of his office and Mac could see through the glass who it was.

"Got to go, Clio. Take care and stay in touch," he said, hanging up.

Carmichael opened the door. He was in uniform, as always, but held his hat under his arm.

"DCI McNeill, do you have a minute?" he asked.

"Yes, sir."

"I've just been sitting in on the press conference with DI Barland about the Adam Glebe case," Carmichael said. "There will be a lot of positive media coverage for us because of solving that case."

Mac nodded but made no reply, looking at the screen of his laptop, scrolling through emails that he wasn't seeing.

"I know you have doubts about the outcome, but I believe we have the right man, and this works for us politically as well. However, in future, I would like you to lead the press conference backed up by your DI. I looked for you beforehand, but you were... AWOL."

Mac looked at Carmichael and bit back his first reply.

"There were a couple of witnesses I needed to secure statements from," he said.

"That should have been done earlier in the investigation. By a subordinate," Carmichael said. "Look, now is not the time for a post-mortem of the case. There will be a review and we can address any issues that arise and formulate action plans to implement in the future. I would like to say DI Barland is a credit to you. She handled herself very well, a natural on camera. I was very happy with her performance."

"She's an excellent officer," Mac said.

"And with skills I don't think are being fully utilised by working for you," Carmichael said. "I'm considering offering her a place on my HQ fast track programme."

"She's an excellent detective. I would hate to lose her. Personally, I think she'd be wasted in an office when she should be out working cases and getting tangible results," Mac said, letting out his irritation like a safety valve releasing dangerously high steam pressure. Carmichael was eating into his team, working away at the keystone. Mac wanted to tell him to back off but was forced to smile, trying to take the edge off his words.

"She has untapped potential," Carmichael said briskly, putting an end to that part of the conversation. "On another subject, I had a case for your team, but on the way back here, I got an email from Ben Musa. He made a case for it sitting with the OCT and I'm inclined to agree."

Despite himself, Mac wanted to know more. His head was full of Iona and Cass. Now Mel Barland was added to that. But the idea of Musa poaching his cases still kicked his ego.

"What's the case? I would have appreciated a look at it in case I don't agree with Musa."

Carmichael's face was still, eyes fixed on Mac. He didn't like being questioned or challenged. Reid would have sworn, called Mac all the names under the sun he could think of, and slammed the door, but would have returned and listened to Mac's opinion whether or not he agreed with it. Carmichael stored grudges.

"A low level enforcer from the John Lowe organisation was found dead near the airport. Shot twice in the back of the head and tortured before death. Interrogation and execution..." Carmichael began.

"Who?"

"Douglas Griffiths."

Mac was silent for a moment. He offered up a silent prayer to the ghost of Dougie Griffiths. He deserved everything he got, but he'd been killed for something he was innocent of. If Musa had had him killed, then it meant he'd taken Mac's tip-off seriously. It also proved just how dangerous Musa was. Whether he still believed Griffiths was Mac's informant was another matter. Mac hoped so. It was a ray of light.

"I'd agree. Classic gangland. Musa should have it."

"Good. Glad you see it my way," Carmichael said. "Let's get the Adam Glebe case over the line. Finish the paperwork and send it to my office before it goes to the PF. We need to make sure of the detail."

He left and Mac repressed an urge to throw something at the door. He glanced at his phone. Three hours since leaving Cass's house. Below the time, the screen was still showing the woman paying tribute to Iona.

Chapter Thirty-Four

MAC LOOKED at the Glebe crime scene boards. Hands thrust into trouser pockets, he let the images wash over him, not concentrating on anything in particular but taking it in as a whole. The clump of hair was with forensics; Derek Stringer himself was supervising the comparison with the sample provided by Cass. He at least wasn't going to put politics before evidence. Kai was following Cass. Would the confession lead the priest to do something stupid, or was Kai just following him to his local Chinese and back? Would Kai be cursing Mac for having to sit out in the east-end of Edinburgh all night? Probably. At least it would keep him away from Isla.

Mac had handpicked the police artist to introduce to Jacob Danzig. A woman with twenty years' experience who produced likenesses that, more often than not, actually ended up looking a lot like the suspect. Would it point to Nick Cass? Mac knew the pieces were all there, they just needed to be slotted together. He needed the right edges and corners in the right order. But what if he was wrong?

What if the hair wasn't a match and the police artist came up with a completely unfamiliar face? But as far as Carmichael was concerned, it was solved anyway. Chalk up another success for DCI McNeill. It would be a chance for the likes of Ramsey Jones to pick apart on his YouTube channel and call a miscarriage of justice. Mac wondered if Cass was done now after coming so close to getting caught. Would he consider it a lesson and keep his head down, or was he already planning the next kill, the next sinner, the next ritual now he thought he was in the clear?

"Guv?" Mel's voice.

Mac turned round. Mel was entering the office.

"Mel, good job today. Thanks for having my back. Carmichael was impressed."

"Sorry, guv," Mel said.

"Why?"

"The case. We got the wrong man."

"Not exactly. Thanks to Carmichael, we announced too early and named the wrong man to the press, but there's forensic evidence linking Cass to Adam Glebe's crime scene with Derek Stringer right now for DNA comparison and a potential eyewitness."

Mel gaped at him, breaking into a smile.

"Guv! You mean we got him?"

"Maybe, if it passes the evidential threshold and if the PF thinks it is stronger evidence than a deathbed confession. I can't prove Flenders didn't die by suicide. I can't prove that Cass killed him or what his motive was. It may not be enough, but if it is, Carmichael is going to hate me."

"Do you care? When Reid is back..." Mel said.

"He's not coming back, Mel. They're fast tracking his retirement to avoid an expensive and politically damaging investigation. He's gone. We're stuck with Carmichael."

Mel swore vehemently. It was odd hearing language like that coming from her motherly face. Mac smiled.

"My feelings exactly, eh?"

"Want me to look at vacancies for security guards?" Mel said, grinning.

"I'll let you know. By the way, Carmichael thinks you're management material. I think you're detective material, but no pressure."

"Aye, he said the same to me. Wants to poach me for his fast track programme."

"You thinking about it?" Mac asked.

Mel looked uncomfortable, glanced away, and fidgeted with the back of a chair. Mac turned, pretending to look at the boards again. He had expected Mel to immediately say she wasn't interested. She was a copper, not a politician. Her skills as a detective would be wasted at a desk, managing budgets and hosting video conferences.

"It's a lot more money. And Cazzy and I would have a lot of uses for it. You know, with the baby." She sighed. "I don't know, guv. It's not the kind of job I joined the police to do and I would probably hate it, but the increase in salary..."

Mac nodded. "Hard to turn that down, I know. I'd be gutted to lose you, but always happy to see a member of my team doing well."

Mel snorted. "No, you're not. You'd hate having to recruit a new DI and then train them up on how to deal with you. You'd be cursing me every day."

Mac laughed. "Aye, very true."

"Anyway, it's a big decision and I'm not making it now, so you won't have to replace me anytime soon," Mel said.

"Good. Look, I've got Kai following Cass, seeing what we can find out about him. I'm going to catch up with him.

Why don't you knock off for the day? It's not far off time, anyway."

"Thanks, guv. And seriously, I haven't made any decisions yet and I won't without talking to you first," Mel said.

Mac gave a corner of a smile and jerked his head towards the door. Mel left and Mac stared, unseeing, at the boards again. At Adam Glebe. He took out his phone and called Kai.

"Guv, nothing to report. I haven't moved from Kingshaugh since you left. He's been in the house the entire time," Kai said, frustration rife in his voice.

"I'm on my way to relieve you."

"I'm OK, guv," Kai protested.

"It's fine, Kai. I want to do it. Get yourself home, eh?"

As Mac left the office for his car, he called Isla.

"Hi guv, no sign of Leo Braddock at the address you gave me. His partner and kids were there, and she is not happy with him. Apparently, he's gone off for days before, usually on a bender with his mates though since he started going to church again, he's supposed to be sober. Has been actually for the last six months. But she thinks he's fallen off the wagon. Thinks the retreat was just a front. She's given me a few names and addresses for his friends, but she's already spoken to them and they've not seen him. I'm going to check a few local pubs that he frequented."

"What about Joe Kimani?" Mac asked.

"Haven't got to him yet, guv. Want me to move on to him or stay on Braddock?"

"Check Kimani's address. He works for a charity linked to the Church, so he seems less likely to be the type to go on a bender. If there's a chance Braddock is pished somewhere, let's not waste our time, eh? Keep me posted and check in regularly."

The dark mood that had swept over him after his conversation with Carmichael was lifting. He switched the radio to CD mode and some classic Norwegian Black metal filled the car, spiked riffs, and screamed vocals suddenly cutting to atmospheric keyboards and faux orchestration. It was somehow soothing and energising at the same time. His fingers tapped the wheel in time with the furious drumming. Carmichael could only deny the evidence to a point. Then even he would have to admit he'd got the wrong man. Whose face the egg got splattered on was another matter. Cass wouldn't be able to stay sitting in one place forever. If Mac had to watch him for twenty-four hours, he would. Serial killers were arrogant. They were also dopamine addicts. Whatever the motivation for killing that drove Cass, however theological or high minded it might seem to him, it was still the dopamine rush that he craved. That's what made him unable to stop. That's what would make him move once he thought himself safe.

HE PULLED in behind Kai's car. Kai was walking back from the junction of Cass's street, shaking his head as he saw Mac get out.

"Still at home. No lights in the house except upstairs, so maybe he's visiting Beth Rose. Car's still in the drive. According to Maps, there's nowhere he could go out the back. A fence, some scrubland and then a burn and the railway."

"Get yourself home, Kai. I've let Mel knock off early."

"You sure you don't want company for the stakeout?" Kai asked.

"I'm good. Get on your way. See you tomorrow."

Kai nodded, went to his car. Mac went to his and when Kai had pulled away, he moved his own car forward. Then he switched off the engine, folded his arms and watched the entrance to Cass's street. He'd stopped on the way for snacks and drinks. They were in a plastic bag in the passenger footwell. He didn't feel the need for anything just now. How long since he'd done this? Not since he'd been a DI probably, so a few years. It wasn't something a DCI would be expected to do. But Mac wanted a direct hand in the investigation now, wanted personal control of it. He could have tracked down Joe Kimani and Leo Braddock, but he was reluctant to delegate anything relating to directly to Cass. The man was taking on nemesis like proportions in Mac's mind.

———

THE SKY WAS ORANGE, the streetlights bleaching out the stars, when Cass's car emerged from the junction. Mac had been dozing, despite coffee and Pro Plus, lulled by boredom. The headlights from Cass's car might as well have been directed straight into his brain. His eyes went wide and his attention became focused. As Cass turned away from Mac and drove down the road, Mac started his own engine and followed, keeping a reasonable distance so Cass remained in sight, but it wasn't too obvious he was being followed. The brief sweep of headlights over Mac's car shouldn't have revealed too much, not if Cass had been checking both directions before emerging. Mac switched his car's dash display to the built in sat nav, glancing at it occasionally to keep fixed in his mind where they were in the city. Simultaneously, a mental map was rolling, placing Cass and his route in context with other places of significance in the case.

Like Mary King's Close, the retreat at West Calder and the prison.

Cass was heading east; from the roads he was taking, it appeared he might make for the city bypass. Mac allowed another car to join between them, keeping the priest in sight. Cass went to the Gogar Roundabout at the eastern edge of Edinburgh, then turned south onto the bypass. At Hermiston Gait, he joined the M8, heading west towards Glasgow. Mac was surprised. He hadn't expected Cass to be leaving Edinburgh. He sat back in the slow lane, two cars behind his quarry, occasionally drifting into the middle lane to check the position of Cass's SUV. Mac's target was driving sedately, less than seventy and not stirring from the slow lane, slowing down further behind a lorry, not trying to overtake.

Mac's phone rang, and he glanced at it. Isla. He answered via the Bluetooth connection, hitting the on-screen phone icon on the dash display.

"Guv, you sure about the address you got for Joe Kimani?" Isla asked

"Read it back to me."

Isla did so.

"Yep. That's the address I got from Father Fitzsimmons. Why?"

"Because it doesn't exist," Isla said. "That number on that street is a reclamation yard in Saughton. There's a portacabin inside the gate, but it was all locked up. I found a mobile number for it online and spoke to the guy who runs it. He'd never heard of Joe Kimani. In fact, I could have arrested him for racially aggravated hate speech for what he said when he heard the name."

Father Neil hadn't said so, but Mac had assumed that Kimani was Black with African heritage, or of a country within the African continent. There was no reason for Father Neil to give a false address. And if Kimani worked for a registered charity sponsored by the church, then he couldn't just make up his address, either. They would have governance rules in place, especially if they were hiring non UK nationals.

"It could be some kind of immigration scam?" Isla said, "I don't want to assume his ethnicity or nationality, but..."

"I think it's a reasonable assumption. I don't have the name of the charity he works for. Check on that tomorrow. Get back to Father Neil and double check the address. If it is correct, then we need to speak to his employer and see what they have on record for him. Probably nothing to do with our case, but we need to get to the bottom of it," Mac said.

They were approaching the exit for Bathgate, and Mac saw Cass's indicator blinking.

"Isla, I've got to go. Good work. See you tomorrow."

He hung up quickly, indicating and following Cass onto the slip road. No-one else exited there, but it was now dark enough that Cass wouldn't be able to distinguish Mac's car or see him over the glare of his headlights. Cass turned into an industrial park just off the roundabout at the end of the slip road and pulled into the car park of a self-storage business. Mac drove past, turning a corner and stopping in front of the locked gates of an automotive body shop. Getting out of the car, he walked back around the corner, keeping close to the tall, grey metal railings that surrounded each of the estate's units. Low shrubs decorated with drinks cans and takeaway containers grew at the base of the fencing. It was beginning to rain, but Mac barely noticed. He was in time to see Cass hurrying to the entrance of the storage facility and going in. Mac leaned on the railings, waiting.

Cass hadn't looked to be carrying anything in with him, or if he was, it was something small enough to fit into his pocket. In which case, what was the point of putting it into storage rather than a safety deposit box if it was valuable? Surely, you used places like this for things you didn't have room for at home, or when you didn't have a home to keep things in. Cass did, and it was spacious enough. It could have been bias, most likely was, but Mac found himself wondering what Cass was hiding. That was another use for a place like this. The rain became more persistent, a steady, fine curtain. It ran into Mac's eyes and he had to keep wiping his face, pushing his hair back from his forehead. He put his hands into trouser pockets, ignoring the open overcoat that meant his shirt got soaked. If this turned out to be Bathgate's red light area, then he risked someone reporting him. But instinct told him Cass wouldn't be in there for long. Then another car pulled in and parked. It was an old estate, square and boxy. Volvo probably and at least twenty years old by the look of it. Mac could smell the exhaust fumes from where he stood.

A man got out, baseball cap on his downturned head as he ran to the entrance. Mac moved as soon as he saw the doors close behind the newcomer. He dashed along the pavement and into the car park. Taking out his phone, he took pictures of the Volvo's number plate, then switched on the torch and shone it into the interior. The back was full of fast food containers in the footwells. A tartan blanket covered the back seat. The front had a crucifix hanging from the mirror. There was nothing else to see. He crouched behind the car, looking over the boot towards the door leading into the building. Watching for the Volvo driver, he rang the Police Scotland dispatch number, requesting an

ANPR check. He read out the number plate phonetically, waiting while the operator input the details into the system.

"Registered to Joseph Kimani," she said and gave Mac an address which differed from the address he'd given to Father Neil. Mac put the phone away, wiping his hair away from his forehead so that it was slicked back against his head. Pieces were falling together. Something was happening tonight. This was not a coincidence. Cass thought he'd got off scot free and a potential witness turns out to have been lying about his address. He knew he should go back to his vantage point and wait for Cass to leave. Follow him again. But he couldn't tail both of them, and he would likely need a warrant to get access to the storage units inside. Carmichael would block it. It only took Mac a moment to reach a decision. He stood, walked quickly across the slick, puddled tarmac to the double doors that led into the storage facility, and pushed them open.

Chapter Thirty-Five

THE CORRIDOR beyond had neon strip lighting. The floor was scuffed from years of footfall, leaving the lino dirty and worn through to the concrete in places. To the left was a lit window with an ancient intercom next to it. Mac approached. A man sat in the room beyond a bank of CCTV monitors in front of him. A cardboard cup, steam rising, sat next to a black keyboard. He had a pockmarked face and tattoos on his neck, visible above the colour of his corporate branded polo shirt.

"Alright, mate," he said.

Mac held up his warrant card.

"DCI McNeill, Police Scotland Serious Crimes Unit. I need to know about the two men who just came in."

"What?" the man asked.

"Can you see them on your cameras?" Mac asked.

The man turned on his swivel chair and looked, jaw working a piece of chewing gum.

"Yeah," he replied.

"Can you let me in? I need to see them."

The man hesitated.

"Look, this is a murder investigation. So, let me in there to have a look at your CCTV," Mac said, using bullying to get what he wanted faster.

"I don't know. I should call my manager."

"Are they here?" Mac asked.

"No, they're in Hamilton."

"Those men might be dangerous. I don't know what they're doing, but I think they have at least two deaths on their hands. If you want me to go away and leave you with them...?"

The man gulped, swallowed his chewing gum, and then pressed a button on the wall beneath the window. He jerked his thumb towards a door to Mac's right that had just clicked.

"It's open."

Mac stepped in, picking up the odour of recently made noodles, seeing a kettle in the corner and a microwave. The man wheeled himself back from the desk in front of the monitors. Mac moved closer, looking at the displays. Each one was divided into four images and there were eight displays.

"Big place."

"Five hundred units. It's a maze down there," the man said in an accent straight out of Livingston.

"Where are they?" Mac asked, eyes quickly becoming lost in the myriad of tiny displays.

"The system's motion sensitive. Look for the lights. They switch on with movement."

Mac zeroed in on a dozen screens showing a lighted corridor. All were empty.

"The lights stay on for about a minute after activating," the night manager told him.

One by one, the lighted corridors went dark until only one was left. Mac assumed it was the one that had sensed movement last. He pointed to the display.

"Where is that?"

The man dug out a binder filled with laminated pages, flipping through it.

"G corridor, row fifty three," he pointed to a map on the wall above the monitors.

"That's us and G corridor is..." he pointed to a section. "There. The rows cross the corridors, they're narrower. They're numbered left to right, low to high."

Mac tried to take in the map but knew how easy it would be to become lost in what was likely to be dark corridors of identical rows of storage units. He glanced around the office.

"What's your name?" he asked.

"Craig."

"You have any kind of radio, walkie-talkie, that sort of thing?" Mac asked.

"Yeah," he opened a drawer that got stuck halfway and had to be kicked to get it all the way open. Inside were two small radios. Mac took one, pressed an obvious power button. A display lit up blue.

"Watch me on the display. If I get lost or if you see those two come out, give me a shout on the radio, ok?"

"Are they dangerous? Maybe you should have backup or something, mate."

"No time. Just keep me right and keep the door locked, eh?" Mac told him, watching the monitors.

The last light had gone out. The view on the display switched to the monochrome green gray of night vision.

He left the office and went through the inner doors. He faced a corridor running left to right, with others running off it, all designated with a letter on signs hanging from the ceiling panels. Bright overhead lights came on as Mac moved looking for G corridor. After a minute, the lights behind him winked out. It was unnerving in such a cavernous space, but he put it from his mind. At least no one could sneak up on him.

He had to pass through a couple of fire doors before he got to G, then he proceeded along it. Lights preceding him while darkness followed. Craig was right. He knew he should call Kai and Isla in as backup. It was the thought of being wrong that stopped him. Mel was already mulling over the idea of leaving the team; he didn't want the others to think he was losing his touch. If this was something inno-cent, no-one else would know about Mac's embarrassment. He wanted to keep it that way.

The radio in his hand crackled.

"Officer, they're coming out!"

Craig's voice sounded loud and panicked. Mac glanced at the numbering on the wall at the nearest crossing row. Twenty-seven. Could they have heard from where they were?

"I think they heard me!" Craig was definitely losing it. "One of them is running. The other went back inside. No, the first one is stopping. Looks like they're arguing!"

Mac sprinted down the corridor, counting off the inter-sections and hoping there was only one way in or out of the facility. One exit, but with all these corridors, there were any number of routes to get there. He was running too fast for the motion sensors to track properly. Lights flashed on as he was passing, giving him a fleeting glimpse of the numbers on the wall. Then a light came on ahead of him. He had company. Mac slowed and braced just as a tall, Black man in a hoody and sweats appeared. He had a backpack over one shoulder and was clearly just as prepared as Mac. He ran forward, head down. Mac had time to drop his shoulder just before the man ploughed into him, carrying him to the floor. Continuous punches rained down: ribs, chest, stomach. The man was trying to overwhelm him, preventing Mac from getting to his feet, not letting him get the upper hand. All Mac could do was try to shield his body as his attacker got to one knee, pushing Mac down, preparing to run. Mac closed his fist around the small plastic radio and swung, slamming it into the side of the man's face. It wasn't much of a weight, but as the plastic cracked sharply, it was disorientating enough for Mac to shove upward, pushing the man off balance. Mac kicked up hard, connecting between the man's legs. He fell against a wall, clutching himself but still hobbling, trying to get away.

"It's over, Joe," Mac said, getting to his feet. "I'm polis. We know you lied about your address. Know you're helping Cass. It's all over."

Kimani's eyes went wide, and he snarled, lashing out. But he had neither the breath nor the strength to hurt Mac. Mac shoved his shoulder into Kimani's chest, slamming him against the door of a storage unit. Pinning the other man's shoulder with one hand, Mac swung with the other, putting all his anger into a blow to Kimani's stomach. He folded up, trying to suck in lungfuls of air, then vomited. As accomplices to serial killers go, he was a pushover. Maybe even a killer himself. Mac couldn't help feel a tad disappointed.

"Stay there. Do yourself a favour, eh? The guy in the office has locked down the building and the polis are outside."

Mac had no idea if Craig could actually lock down the building and he sure as hell knew there were no cops outside. He backed away from Kimani as much as the cramped corridor would allow. For a moment, he put his hands to his knees, breathing deeply. Kimani kept his head down, slumped against the wall. The lights went out. Mac had forgotten the motion sensor. He pushed off the wall, hearing the scramble from the man opposite him. The lights came on and Mac slammed into the wall where Kimani had been a split second before. He was sprinting down the corridor. Mac looked in the opposite direction, down the dark row of storage units Kimani had come from. No motion down there.

"Cass, I know you're down there. Let's not make this harder than it has to be. I have DNA evidence proving you were at the scene of Adam Glebe's death. And an eyewitness. It's over."

Darkness remained. But Mac heard a small sound. It might have been laughter. It might have been weeping.

"Your pal has legged it. He's looking at assaulting a police officer, at the very least. He won't get far."

Mac started to walk along the row. There was no hint which of the storage units contained the man he was looking for. None showed light under the door or around its edges. None were open. A sound came from behind him and he whirled, heart racing, ready for another attack. Instead, he saw a door swinging open. Light came from within. Stark and white. Mac approached cautiously. When he reached the door, he pulled it open further and peered inside.

The unit was the size of a shipping container, lit by harsh strip lights caged against the ceiling. At one end was a shelving unit of thin, grey metal. Plastic crates were stacked against one wall. Against the other was a rolled up sleeping bag and assorted plastic bags which seemed to be full of clothes. And there was Father Nick Cass. With a body. Cass knelt beside the corpse of a middle-aged man, whose arms were covered in tattoos, cheap looking line drawings and inscriptions. His hair was cut short, and the body had a few ugly looking scars. The kind you got from improvised blades or broken bottles. Mac could tell this wasn't the body of a chartered accountant. Cass was eating, the remnants of a sliced loaf in a plastic bag beside him. On the other side of the body was a can of lager. Cass looked at him, tears pooling in his eyes as he ate the last of the bread. When he'd finished, he stood.

"This is Leo Braddock," he said. "And thanks to Joe and me, he is guaranteed a place in heaven with the Lord. He is cleansed."

"You've eaten his sins," Mac said.

Cass nodded. "I don't know why Joe reacted like he did. He was the one that introduced me to this ritual. His father and grandfather were sin-eaters in Ghana."

"You and he were doing this together?" Mac asked.

The calm of the situation was surreal. Cass leaned against the wall of the storage unit, wiping crumbs from his front.

"No. Joe did nothing illegal. Well, I think he was in this country illegally, but he came from a desperate situation at home, so I'm not going to blame him for that. All he gave me was information. Stories. We were just shooting the breeze, as the Americans say."

"About?"

"About the ritual my great grandfather was a practitioner of. He was one of the last in this country, as far as I can tell. Father John Cass, parish priest and secret heretic."

Mac crouched beside the body of Leo Braddock.

"How did you kill him?" he asked.

"I went back to the retreat. He and Joe had gone to bed.

I went into Leo's room and used chloroform. He didn't go down easy, put up quite a fight, actually. Some people don't want to admit their sins. But he eventually succumbed. Afterwards, I realised he wasn't breathing. Heart attack, I presume."

Cass sounded almost dreamy. He was poised, detached and without emotion despite the signs of recent grief. Any tears were long gone. His face was sad as he looked at Leo Braddock's body.

"Joe was woken by the noise and found me with a cloth clamped over Leo's face. I thought he would report me, but he didn't. I explained about the secret that had been handed down through my family for years and he understood. He agreed to help me hide the body. This storage unit is his. He was living here. Sad, isn't it? And very wrong. Joe has so much good to give. He works for a charity helping the poorest and most desperate people in our society and comes from a place where he would be tortured to death because of his sexuality. But because he came here illegally out of sheer terror, he has no chance of a decent life. Yet people like Adam Glebe and Leo Braddock and Nathan Flenders..."

He trailed off, the first signs of genuine emotion appearing. Anger. His brows drew down. Tears gathered, but there was no sadness in his face now. Mac stood, readying himself for violence. But Cass noticed him and his face cleared. He grinned, scrubbing at his face.

"You're not in danger, Detective Chief Inspector. I won't try to get away. And I'm not going to attack you. I killed Adam Glebe. Nathan Flenders, Leo Braddock and...and...my Carl."

Now his voice did break, he covered his mouth.

"Carl Hesten?" Mac asked.

Cass nodded, incapable of words, eyes tight shut. Mac gave him a moment, hands in his pockets to avoid touching anything until forensics could be brought in. He watched Cass, waiting patiently.

"I loved him. Met him inside and fell in love. How stupid! How pathetic! He was half my age and a little ned. A crook. But I was taken in. I thought he wanted to change. Thought he was a victim of the system. Of our sick society. I took him under my wing. I helped him get out early. Helped him find a place to live. Thought we would... but he was using me. He started blackmailing me. Threatened to go to the papers. Can you imagine? Gay Catholic priest grooming young male inmate? I was so...so...angry. I confronted him, told him I wouldn't pay. He came at me with a knife and in the struggle..."

"You turned the blade on him."

Cass nodded, rubbing his nose with the back of his hand. "I stabbed him several times. I have never been so angry. Not just at him, but at the society that made him. The careless parents. The incompetent schools. The callous prison system. At God even! After, I stood there looking, and I realised there was one thing I could do for him. What my ancestor did. I performed the ritual. And it was as though I could feel the darkness lifting from him and moving into me. I could almost see his soul ascending. It was... miraculous!"

"The newspapers made you out to be a hero," Mac said, contempt in his voice.

Cass shrugged. "It wasn't difficult to assume the pose for the paramedics, Inspector. Everybody saw what they wanted to see. After all, who would suspect a priest of murder?"

"Me."

"Ah, yes. You, I hadn't counted on."

Chapter Thirty-Six

BRUNSWICK ROAD, Police Scotland Edinburgh
Headquarters, Interview Room 2. Mac sat opposite Father
Nicholas Cass, wearing a pristine dark suit and white shirt
with an open collar. Cass wore blue, a paper suit to replace
clothes taken for forensic analysis. Two steaming plastic
cups sat on the table between them. Two pairs of eyes
watching through the curling steam. Cass looked relaxed.
Facially and in his posture. Mac did not feel triumphant.
Did not feel he had beaten his nemesis. There was no
victory because there was no sense of defeat coming from
the man opposite. Mel Barland sat next to Mac, a bottle of
water in front of her. A faceless solicitor, working pro bono
as Cass didn't have legal representation of his own, sat next
to his client. Mac had been told the Bishop of Edinburgh
had dispatched a top solicitor, but Cass had refused to speak
to him. A duty solicitor had been sent for.

Mac glanced at Mel, who opened a binder. A copy of
which was in front of the solicitor and Cass. Cass didn't look
at it.

"Carl Hesten, Lukasz Burksi, Adam Glebe, Nathan Flenders, Leo Braddock," Mac said, tonelessly. "You are confessing to the murders of all five?"

"Correct," Cass said.

As Mac listed the victims, Mel was producing pictures from plastic wallets at the front of her binder. Each held the picture of a body. The solicitor looked at his copies, pushed them towards Cass, who didn't.

"We will need to go into the details of each death," Mac said.

"But why, Inspector," Cass interrupted. "I admit to taking the lives of all of them. I have written my confession as requested..."

"I've had a written confession from you before, remember? That you found Nathan Flenders *after* he had killed himself. I can't take the word of a liar."

Mac could see the words stung the priest. He'd assumed he could just put up his hands and confess. It spoke volumes about the man that he would feel slighted at being called a liar, but not at being called a murderer. Cass frowned, picking up his tea and taking a sip.

"I only lied because I wasn't ready to give myself up then. I hadn't finished," Cass said.

"And now you're finished? If I hadn't stumbled onto Joe Kimani's storage unit, you would have just handed yourself in. Is that what you're saying?"

"Perhaps," Cass replied, annoyance on his face.

It was as though the mask had slipped now he'd been caught. There was no more pretence. He was arrogant. Believed himself superior. Intolerant of questions. There was a cold, hard man staring back at Mac. As cold and hard as Mac himself.

"I doubt that. There's no shortage of sinners to cleanse.

For a start, there's a prison full back at your work. Why stop with Leo Braddock?"

"Inspector, my client is voluntarily confessing, therefore sparing the police time and resources that would otherwise be spent trying to prove his guilt. Saving the court system both time and money. I don't understand your need to be so adversarial," the solicitor said.

"Because I do not like your client," Mac snapped. "And if I want to pick a fight with him, I will. Now, as you say, he's confessing, so you don't have to say anything. Be quiet."

The solicitor couldn't have been too experienced because Mac's bark made him go pale and turn away. Mac looked back at Cass, who was smiling.

"What has happened to Joe, Inspector?"

"We haven't found him yet. When we do, he'll be charged with being an accessory to murder, obstruction, and assault. He'll do time and then be deported."

"Where he'll die," Cass said, the smile dissolving.

"So, I understand. I'm not responsible for government policy on small boats. He helped conceal a murder."

"Because he believes in sin-eating. He knows some people won't allow themselves to be saved. Won't confess their sins even at the moment of their deaths. Leo Braddock wouldn't confess to the deaths he caused through selling heroin mixed with cement dust. Lukasz Burksi wouldn't confess to the unborn child he murdered when he beat its mother half to death. Adam sexually assaulted his partner and Nathan was a paedophile. They deserved to lose the privilege of life in this world, but they were all God's children. They were entitled to the chance of redemption, to go into their next existence with their souls cleansed. Everybody is."

Mac sipped his own bitter, stewed coffee.

"So that's why you killed them? All of them?"

"It started with my father. He was the one who told me about my great grandfather. I went back to Oxford because Dad was ill. We had been estranged until then. We had a rapprochement, and I discovered the accusations made against him by a young male undergraduate. Dad was of a generation that regarded homosexuality as something shameful. As do I, because my faith says so. I chose God over my sexuality, but Dad couldn't bear the shame and hung himself. I performed the sin-eating ritual because, as a suicide, I knew he would go to hell otherwise. He didn't deserve that."

Cass was talking calmly, matter of fact. He didn't look away from Mac once as he spoke. Voice level. Face still.

"I met Joe a few years later. This young, terrified, starving man appeared at the church, seeking sanctuary. He'd hiked and hitch-hiked from the south coast. Lord knows how he made it as far as he did. I think he was guided to me. I knew at once what he was, where he had come from. He tried to hide it at first, thinking I would turn him in. But, I didn't. From Joe I learned a lot more about sin-eating, about the theology behind it, the history. The men in his family had practised it for generations, since before Christianity found them even. Joe is a remarkable scholar. I saw the rightness of it. How it could help save so many who were walking into damnation with their eyes tight shut. I brought him with me when I secured the post of Chaplain at HMP Edinburgh. It seemed the perfect place to begin."

"Why did you pretend Nathan Flenders was the author of your academic works?" Mac asked. "It was something that stood out a mile to me. It connected you to Flenders and was clearly faked. I might not have looked too closely at you, but for that. Moving the books in the caravan was a mistake."

Cass spread his hands, allowing himself a smile.

"I should have left the books alone. I realise that now. As to Nathan being the author, I thought it would keep attention away from me if anyone ever made the connection to sin-eating. I'm surprised a man like you did."

Mac scowled. "I have a lot of layers."

"I told Nathan I wanted to remain anonymous. He didn't question it. He had an ego you wouldn't believe."

"Why would you include such obvious links to your father and grandfather when it would lead back to you?"

"Why wouldn't I? It's important to keep the history alive. The ritual. For future generations. The Cass's were practitioners and experts. An academic publication would have to include them. It would look odd otherwise. It doesn't matter who was named as author of the contemporary works, it happened a long time ago. The interest was from a purely historical point of view."

The conversation went on. Mac asked fewer and fewer questions. Cass talked. Told his life story and went into detail on every murder. Mac checked against the pathology reports as Cass talked. His accounts matched the findings of forensics in each case. He knew things about the three scenes and the bodies that had not been made public. Cass was proud of himself. He wanted to tell his story. It didn't change the fact that the only killings to which there was any evidential link between Cass and the bodies were Hesten, and Braddock. For Lukasz Burksi, Adam Glebe and Nathan Flenders, they had Cass's word alone. Mac could prove Cass had entered the caravan with a key, then tussled with Mac. He couldn't prove Cass killed Flenders. But he was hopeful the imminent DNA results would prove Cass had been at the scene of Adam's murder.

After two hours, the interview was suspended when there was a knock at the door. Isla entered. She bent to whisper to Mac.

"Stringer's office just issued DNA results on the sample you got from Danzig and we got the artist impression through. Carmichael has seen both. He's next door. He wants a word."

Mac glanced at Mel and stood abruptly.

"Probably a good time for a comfort break. Interview suspended," Mel said, reading off the time.

Cass looked up as the two officers stood, a question on his lips. Mac knew he was unhappy at being interrupted in full flow. He left the room without a word, entertaining a brief daydream of overturning the table and smashing Cass over the head with a chair. He went into the small observation room next door. Carmichael stood there, a piece of paper in hand.

"Shut the door," he snapped.

Mac complied, and the paper was thrust towards him.

"The artist impression you requested from Jacob Danzig. Your eye witness at the scene of Adam Glebe's death. A witness you saw fit to say nothing about while I went to the media telling them Nathan Flenders was the killer!"

"Jacob Danzig is a paranoid schizophrenic who believes he... sorry, they are a vampire and the man in this picture is probably Count Dracula. Or King of the Vampires or something. His evidence wasn't reliable enough on its own..." Mac said, not looking at the image.

"No, but if the DNA linked Nicholas Cass to the crime

scene, it might have been the clincher!" Carmichael roared, uncharacteristically angry.

"I told you I believed Nick Cass might have been the killer. You dismissed it!" Mac retaliated, stepping up to Carmichael as though this was a confrontation outside of a pub.

"Because I didn't know there was DNA evidence and an eyewitness! I had a deathbed confession which any judge will tell you is pretty bloody convincing to a jury. What the hell were you playing at keeping this from me?"

Mac gritted his teeth, biting back his instinctive reply. A reply that would have landed him with a suspension. Another one.

"And let's talk about that DNA evidence, shall we?" Carmichael hissed.

He stood the same height as Mac, though slimmer. Clad in the armour of his rank, he probably thought himself looming over Mac. He didn't know the depths of anger seething through his subordinate at that moment. Anger at the arrogant, sociopathic serial killer in the next room. But anger that was also being directed at the politician in front of him who was scheming to take away one of Mac's best officers and only friends.

"I was cc'd on Derek Stringer's DNA sample update. Hair found at the scene of Adam Glebe's crime scene, yes?"

"Yes, obtained by Jacob Danzig and kept as some sort of relic in his eyes," Mac said, forcing his anger out with each breath, recognising the danger he was in.

"Not Nick Cass's DNA," Carmichael spat. "Not a match. Zero percent. It does not tie your suspect to the scene."

Mac found his mouth open. He stared at Carmichael.

"Look at the bloody artist's impression," Carmichael said. "Thank god I caught this before it got any further."

Mac looked at the paper he had been given but, until now, hadn't even glanced at. It was a stark black and white ink drawing of a man. He had receding hair and a strong, square jaw. His brows were straight and his nose flattened in the middle, as though once broken. His lips were full. It looked nothing like Nick Cass. Not even close.

"Christ Almighty! Cass is covering for someone," Mac exclaimed. "Or he's an accomplice. There's two of them!"

"No!" Carmichael snapped. "Absolutely not! I will not humiliate myself in front of the media again. This is an election year for the Police and Crime Commissioner. We don't want the embarrassment of police being duped by two confessions to the same crime. The public won't trust us again. If Cass wants to take responsibility for it all, let him. PR will work something out regarding your previous gaff with Flenders's confession. This goes no further."

Mac stared at him, unable to believe what he was hearing.

"You're not thinking... sir," he added the honorific reluctantly, wanting to get Carmichael onside. "Blame it all on me if you need to. But if the actual killer is still out there, we can't close the case. What if they kill again?"

"I'll live with it, and so will you. That is an order, McNeill. Like you said, Danzig is a paranoid schizophrenic psychopath. He could have got that hair anywhere. He could have conjured that face from his sick imagination," Carmichael emphasized the pronoun as though to communicate his contempt for Danzig's gender choices. "It proves nothing."

Mac shook his head. "I won't have more deaths on my conscience."

He turned away, but Carmichael caught his arm.

"Don't be a bloody fool. You think it was coincidence I offered your DI a place in the fast track programme? It wasn't. I was preparing your team to be taken apart if you didn't toe the line and start working as part of a team rather than running off on your own, making yourself look good. There is no room for a renegade DCI in my unit, McNeill. I will not have it! Do you understand? I can send your team anywhere and you too if I choose. Barland is just the start. You want to be a DCI in the Serious Crimes Unit? You could learn a lot from Ben Musa. If not, I'd be happy to send you to the Transport Police. Or the Highlands and Islands."

Mac had never been so close to hitting someone without going through with it. He thought about Clio and Maia. About the protection afforded them by the thin blue line. His lips peeled back in an approximation of a smile. Or maybe just a snarl.

"Yes, sir," he said.

"But in case your plan was to blurt this evidence out in front of Cass and his brief. DI Barland will finish the interview. You can take some much needed leave and I will inform the media of this latest turn of events. And I will make sure you get full credit."

Mac savagely pulled his arm free and yanked open the door. Mel was standing outside the interview room, waiting for him. Carmichael followed.

"DI Barland. Please finish the interview. DCI McNeill has some urgent business to attend to. Thanks for your help with this, Mac."

Barland looked to her boss, and Mac gave her the rogue's grin.

"Sorry, Mel. Can you handle the rest?"
"Sure, guv. Everything, OK?"
"Everything's fine, Mel."

Chapter Thirty-Seven

"YOU'RE LOOKING WELL," Mac said.

"Feeling well, son. Now I've got my pension coming to me. In full. No questions asked and that jobsworth Akhtar off my case," Reid said gruffly.

They were sitting together in a bar tucked away at the end of the Royal Mile. Away from the gaze of the tourists, a place for locals. It served craft ales and had no pool table or Sky Sports. Mac sat opposite Reid at a circular table. Small, barred windows let in as little natural light as possible. The walls were covered in pictures of Edinburgh, past and present. The stale smell of tobacco told Mac the landlord probably flouted the law on smoking in public places, at least while he was hosting lock-ins. Reid wore an open-necked shirt under a blazer that had probably been fine tailoring in the eighties. His navy overcoat was flung over the back of a chair. He supped from a cloudy pint with a thick head, leaving traces of it on his upper lip. Mac had an empty pint glass and a full whisky tumbler in front of him.

"So, I hear congratulations are in order. You screwed

over my replacement and closed another serial case, eh, son?" Reid said, eyes sparkling.

"Aye, well, there's more to it than that. A lot more. But it's out of my hands now. Carmichael was too quick to close the case for the good PR. He's embarrassed, but he should have been open to my theory about Flenders's suicide," Mac said.

"A bloody idiot could have seen through a typewritten suicide note. Come on, I ask you!" Reid agreed. "He got what was coming to him, but he's going to want blood from you. Make no mistake, son. He'll blame you for being embarrassed in front of the press and he's a vindictive little..." Reid swore eloquently and profanely.

"I don't care," Mac said. "It's finished. Cass has copped for the lot and he'll go down for it without a trial. Guilty on five counts of murder. I'm done with it. I'm concentrating on this phone and finding the man who knows about Iona."

Reid took another swallow, smacking his lips. "Did it ever occur to you, son, that Lowe was pulling your chain? That he would have said anything to persuade you to save his life. He'd have put his hands up to killing Iona himself if he thought you'd believe him."

Mac scowled into his whisky. It had occurred to him. Of course it had. He wanted to believe Lowe knew something. But in that desperate situation, with his life on the line, Lowe would have said whatever he needed to stay alive. Thinking about it left a yawning emptiness inside Mac. It put him back to square one after months of believing he was finally closing in on Iona's killer.

"John Lowe built his business on knowing everything he could about his enemies, and that includes you and me, son," Reid said, leaning close. "He knew all about Skye and your past. It would be easy for him to lie, get you to save him. He made sure he had the leverage on both of us. I don't think that phone is going to lead you to what you need to know, lad," Reid said kindly.

Mac tossed back the whisky in one fiery swallow. He slammed the glass back, returning Reid's gaze fiercely.

"I think you're wrong," he snapped.

Reid shot him a look that said he wasn't about to take that attitude from Mac, even if he was retired now. Reid had lost weight since Mac had last seen him. Still looked like a boxer gone to seed, but also like he could pack a punch if he wanted to. Or drink Mac under the table.

"Aye, son. You always were a stubborn wee prick," Reid told him. "But you'll come around because you're no' daft. Do the right thing, son. Leave the past where it belongs and think about your future. Anyway, I didn't invite you for a drink so we can resume our professional relationship. I'm done with all that aggro. Not good for the blood pressure."

Mac snorted, then laughed long and hard enough to bring tears to his eyes. The idea of Reid being tired of aggro was priceless. He lived and breathed confrontation and antagonism.

"Watch it, son," Reid told him, but with a ghost of a smile.

"So, what are you going to do with yourself now you're one of the little people?" Mac asked.

"I've got some irons in the fire. I'm talking to someone about opportunities in consultancy work," Reid said.

"Consultancy? What do you know enough about that anyone would want consulting on?" Mac said.

"I know about scumbags who break the law. And I know how to catch them. I was a better detective in my day than you are, son. I just didn't have quite so many cases that made the papers, or the chiselled good-looks needed for the TV, that's all. Anyway, early days. But I'll be alright."

The door to the street outside opened and Mac saw Kai step in, followed by Isla. Kai raised a hand in greeting, and then mimed drinking. Reid looked over.

"Aye, same again over here, son. Two pints of best and whisky chasers, right?"

Mac looked at Reid questioningly.

"I wanted to celebrate," Reid said by way of explanation. "And I don't actually have any friends. The wife stole them all. The last wife. Closest I have is my team. Your team. So I invited them. And do you know what, Mac? Despite your moody presence, they all accepted."

Kai brought over the drinks and pulled a couple of chairs to the table.

"Greg's dropped the charges," Isla said suddenly.

Kai beamed, and Isla blushed.

"He did, did he?" Mac asked innocently.

Isla opened her mouth to speak, and it stayed open.

"You didn't..." she began.

"Mac wouldn't have done anything like putting the frighteners on your ex-boyfriend to protect his team, hen. Now, if I'd been in his place, well..." Reid said, conspiratorially. "But your guv is far too professional."

"Of course," Mac said, sipping his fresh pint.

"I'm saying nothing," Kai said.

"You were lucky to get away with suspension for a month," Mac said. "I can't put the frighteners on AC. Akhtar was always going to want a suspension for punching a member of the public."

Kai shrugged. "I was always happy being a sergeant, anyway."

Mac saw him reach across under the table and briefly squeeze Isla's hand.

"So, what are you planning for your time off, guv?" Isla asked, after the moment had passed.

"Mac, time off? You going soft, son?" Reid laughed.

"Carmichael made me an offer I couldn't refuse," Mac said. "I'm going to Skye. To meet up with some friends."

His phone buzzed in his inside pocket, and he stood.

"Friends? Since when do you have friends?" Reid asked.

Mac ignored him. "I have to see a man about a dog."

He walked towards the gents, taking his phone out of his pocket, and swiping it awake. There was a text message from a number that wasn't on his contact list. He opened it as he pushed open the door of the gents and then stopped dead. The message was simple.

My sins are scarlet, but in time they will be white as snow

There was a picture below the message. A naked, black man lying on his back, arms by his sides. His throat yawned bloodlessly. It was Joseph Kimani. On his chest were sprinklings of white, on his right was a tumbler of dark liquid. Danzig had been right; it was someone else at Mary King's Close. A man with a strong, square jaw and a previously broken nose.

Abruptly another message arrived. Mac blanched. This time it was a video clip. He took a deep breath and hit play.

Instantly, Sandie Shaw's breathy voice came through the speakers. Puppet on a String was playing, but the face was Billy from the Saw movies. Mac's blood ran cold as words scrolled along the bottom of the screen;

Did you really think you were in charge Detective Inspector McNeill? Maybe you can do better next time. Ready to play round two?

With shaking hands, Mac swept aside the text message and brought up Clio's name. He sent a single message.

Stay there. I'm coming to Skye.

Next in the DCI McNeill Crime Thrillers Series

vinci-books.com/ThePriceOfBlood

The past won't stay silent. Justice demands answers. But can he live with the truth?

Haunted by his sister's murder, DCI McNeill returns to Skye to confront the past. But when Clio vanishes, he discovers some secrets kill—and the truth may claim him next.

Turn the page for a free preview…

The Price of Blood: Prologue

HE WATCHED, breathless with anticipation. Ignoring the frigid wind that numbed his cheeks. Ignoring the rain that stung his bare fingertips, poking out of woollen fingerless gloves. Hand knitted. Water runs down his forehead, biting his eyes. He didn't dare blink. Because if he blinked, then the man he watched might move. Might shift into deeper shadow. Might appear behind him. He shivered, and it had nothing to do with the frigid temperature of Skye in autumn. That man down there was vengeance. The watcher feared that dark-haired, gaunt face, so much like his brother's. And there's the true fear. Born out of vicious games and sadistic torture. Born of years in which he was the oppressed, under the dubious protection of a different bully. Accepting a milder form of torture to spare him the more extreme cruelty.

His mouth was the only dry part of him as he recalled the events of the past few months, specifically the soft, vulnerable body. The alluring, teasing, taunting... he gritted his teeth as his thoughts spiralled into the usual recriminations against the woman, the woman who was the ultimate victim but whom he still blamed.

"Brought it on yourself. Brought it on yourself. Why did you make me do it?" he whispers, barely audible.

It's a mantra he's learned to distance himself from the void in his memory. Just ten minutes when bodies clashed to match the ferocity of the waves below them. When violence was born out of passion. When fear was smothered by love. Life crushed out by lust. Now, from his vantage point, he saw the old brick bus shelter. Across the road was an impenetrable tangle of trees and bushes, concealing the sheer drop to the road. A few houses down there and then the grey water.

In the distance, back towards Portree, the pub, old brick and paint, broken concrete, and signs advertising Sky Sports. The kind of place the tourists drive past because of the local neds sitting on the picnic tables outside, smoking, vaping, and being intimidating. All gone home now. Too late for them, except for the one weaving his way down the road.

Mark Souter. God, what a mess! He used to be the bollocks. What happened to him? She happened to him. Broke him. He was hunched in an old bomber jacket, thin as always, but now looking like he was on chemo. Or smack. Probably was. The watcher couldn't be sure these days. Mark had never hit the hard stuff before. He always scorned those members of his crew who had fallen into that trap. Now? Now he was leaving the last pub in Portree, kicked out of the lockup, and wasn't done for the night. He was looking for somewhere quiet where he could finish his cliff dive into oblivion. How had Mark ever seemed like someone to admire? How had he ever seemed like a leader? What the hell had Iona ever seen in him?

Heart racing faster now because the other watcher, down there in the shadows, had seen Mark too. For a moment, he lost sight of Callum McNeill and experienced a moment of panic. Then Callum moved out of the dark, just a little, lit up momentarily by a weak streetlight. The denim jacket is blue but now almost black with wet. The collar turned up. Dark hair slicked back. Jeans and work boots from his last job on a site. Moving back into the shadows once he'd made sure Mark was heading his way.

Oh God, it's happening! Would Mark scream? Beg for his life? Would Callum kill him? Stamp the life from him with those steel toe caps. Callum wasn't as bad as Connor. Hadn't been as bad. But the watcher had seen him descend after his sister's murder. The sickening plummet of a plane that's lost its engines and wings simultaneously. Falling like a stone. Into hell. The watcher licked his lips as Mark wandered closer to his nemesis. They were almost level now; Mark was occupied with lighting a roll-up. God, he was just a ned, wasn't he?

Callum was moving, and the watcher felt terror on Mark's behalf. He had to clamp his jaws shut around the warning he suddenly wanted to shout. Callum was holding something white. A bag. It went over Mark's head. The watcher wished he'd used a bag. Then Iona wouldn't have seen his face. Wouldn't have known who was attacking her. Maybe she wouldn't have had to die. Then he could have replayed that night in his mind every time he saw her. Relive that moment when she was completely in his power. His property.

Callum was dragging Mark off the road and behind the bus shelter. In the distance, a car was turning onto the A87, heading along it towards the pub, the bus shelter, and the attempted murder. It swept by with a rush of sluiced rainwater, lights painting the bus shelter but not penetrating the darkness beyond. Callum was methodically destroying Mark Souter. Punching. Kicking. Spitting. Stamping. In silence. That made it all the more terrifying. Mark was innocent, but the watcher found the idea of being in his place enough to bring on a wave of nausea. To have so much control that you didn't shout or scream when you were beating your sister's rapist and killer to death meant you could control the pace of that death. Stretch it out. Make your victim suffer. Like the watcher had done to Iona, prolonging the suffering to delay the gratification. Even the thought aroused him as he watched the misplaced vengeance being meted out below.

Callum was stepping back, taking something from his pocket and tearing the bag from Mark's head. Mark was cowering. Pleading, one hand raised. And Callum was lifting his hand, too. The one that held the object from his pocket. Holding it high. Knife? Rock? Do it! Do it now! The watcher held his breath, thinking of power and control, seeing it manifested in the tableau below him. Wanting the climax.

No. Callum was stepping back, tossing something away. No! He was shaking his head. His power was gone, and his shoulder slumped and then shook. Mark was foetal, head covered, and shaking. Callum was running, staggering away into the dark.

The Price of Blood: Chapter One

MAC WATCHED the rain dribble down the windscreen of his Audi. Beyond was a wall of grey rock punctuated by the dark green and bright yellow of gorse. Mac knew little about botany, but you couldn't grow up on Skye and not recognise gorse. He looked to the passenger seat at the phone encased in its tough case of hardened rubber. It had been raining that night as well. The night that had stayed fresh in his mind for nearly three decades. He could still smell the leaf mould and the mud. The stale smell of urine and vomit from the old bus shelter.

But not as fresh as it was in his nightmares. He thought he'd got them under control, brought out into the light by his therapy sessions, the terror shrivelled by the daylight. But this trip had reanimated them.

"I'm not sure you're ready to go back to Skye, Callum," his therapist had said at their last session.

"I just need to get away," Mac had replied. "Clio's there. Never thought I would say it, but I feel like I need to be among friends. Well, friend, singular. I don't have a lot of choice."

"And that shows growth. When we first met, you would never have admitted to needing another person. Not in that way. But I don't think you can tell me, honestly, that you've done the work needed to process how you feel about Iona's death."

"I've done everything you've asked me to," Mac had protested.

"Have you?" gentle smile, raised eyebrow.

Resentment. Defensiveness. Reptile brain snapping into action.

"I'm going," Mac had said flatly.

Now his chest felt tight. Heart was racing. Behind him, over the road and across the water, was Skye. Dark and looming, shrouded in low cloud. His eyes found it in the rearview mirror and skated past it. He picked up the phone. First things first. An important piece of procrastination. Then he would cross the bridge. After a coffee. And a vape. Irritated at his weakness, he almost kicked open the door, slamming it and thrusting the phone into a pocket of his jacket. Hands in jeans pockets, holding his waterproof coat open. It left the fleece beneath exposed to the rain, defeating the object of the expensive hiking jacket he'd bought just for this trip, but he'd always hated hunching away from the weather. He wouldn't acknowledge cold or wet.

The only people out in this weather wore brightly coloured waterproofs, hiking boots, and rucksacks. Mac had chosen the most muted tones for himself, refusing to walk about in bright orange, Day-Glo green, or red. He strode along the road towards the bridge. The wind picked up his dark hair, which had grown longer than usual since he'd taken time off. When he reached the middle of the first stretch, where the bridge connected the mainland to the small island of Eilean Ban, he leaned on the railing and looked north across the Inner Sound.

Dark shapes rose in the distance, shrouded in mist and cloud. Desolate places. Below him, the water was lead. It was also desolate, but hiding that beneath its opacity. The railing was no barrier to jumping into that murkiness, to being swallowed by it. And the height probably wouldn't be enough to kill. Cold would do that later. The dark water would stream into him and be welcomed by the greater darkness already there.

"Christ, what am I doing?" Mac muttered to himself when he realised he was leaning over, both hands gripping the slick metal. Drivers passing by would assume he was thinking of jumping. Someone would call the police. That would be fun. He put a hand in his pocket that was already losing feeling because of the needle-like pricking of icy rain. He found the phone and brought it out to look at it.

"Are you in there, Iona?" he whispered, and then hated himself for being so indulgent. She couldn't hear him. He didn't need to speak aloud to understand his thoughts. The phone contained a lot of intelligence. The inner workings of a criminal empire. Mac had used it to burn that empire, tearing through it like a barbarian at the gates of Rome. And it had put his best friend at risk. Kenny Reid had urged him to get rid of it. It couldn't hold the information Mac had been promised. It was too far-fetched. But Mac's fingers dug into the rubber case, refusing to let go.

It might be true. The name of the man who had claimed knowledge of Iona's killer might be in there like the phone's owner had promised. The owner who had been staring death in the face. His only hope to escape it was

Mac. Winning Mac to his side. Offering him a bribe because he'd known a police officer's duty wouldn't be enough to save him. He would have said anything, wouldn't he?

"Course he would. Bloody idiot," Mac said.

The phone left his hand at speed, arcing high before falling into the water. Mac thrust his hands back into his pockets, staring at the spot it had struck, imagining the phone sinking into the depths, the seawater finding its way in eventually, ruining the delicate circuits, purging the data, and rendering it a useless brick. Mac turned away, walked back to the Audi, and was crossing the bridge at speed moments later.

After nearly thirty years away, he was finally returning to Skye.

The Price of Blood: Chapter Two

"MAIA! GUESS WHERE I AM!"

Mac had felt the urge to hear Clio's voice as he'd crossed the Skye Bridge and returned to the island for the first time since he was eighteen. The trees that hemmed the road seemed to get closer, tightening their grip, leaning over to hide the grey morning sky. Mac recognised the beginnings of a panic attack that had been signalling its own arrival for the last hour. He'd called Clio's phone, and Maia had answered. Her voice was a bright light. It forced Mac to push life into his own voice, shoving back the tension and disengaging the lizard brain.

"Hi, uncle Callum! Are you here yet?" Maia asked.

Her voice had dropped a bit, a touch deeper, more adult. Mac wondered when that had happened.

"Not yet. I think I'm about an hour away from Portree, but I'm on the island at last."

"Good, can't wait to see you. Mum's on the loo," Maia replied unashamedly. "Will you show us some places you used to hang out when you get here?"

A flash of tension through the middle of him. Stomach clenching. Mac's hands tightened on the wheel.

"Maybe, if they're still there. It was a long time ago, remember? Twenty-five years. More, in fact."

"Yeah, but like where you went to school and what pubs you and your pals went to. That sort of stuff," Maia said.

"My pub was usually a quiet bit of woods with some booze from the offie," Mac countered. "And your mum would kill me if I showed you that."

"Hi Mac, what have you been telling her?" Clio came onto the phone.

"Hi Clio, sorry I caught you on the loo," Mac said.

"Did she say that? Maia, I told you to say I was outside hanging up the washing!"

"Won't tell a lie, mum!" Maia's voice in the background.

Mac laughed and was surprised to find it a genuine emotion. The tension was easing, and emotions flowed smoother without the jagged peaks and troughs of fight-or-flight responses. He forced his shoulders down, shifting in his seat, and relaxing tensed legs.

"So, how are you doing?" Clio asked.

"I'm doing good. Here on Skye and on my way to you."

"Great. So, how are you doing?" Clio asked again without a change in her tone.

"Clio, I'm ok," Mac said.

"It's okay not to be," Clio replied. "I know this place must be loaded with memories."

"Have you been talking to my therapist?" Mac asked.

"I'm not stupid, Mac. I've been through my own demons, and I know how hard it can be to go back to a place with so many negative associations."

"Jeez, Clio. You have been talking to my shrink."

"I've been reading a lot," Clio replied.

"Because your mental friend is coming to stay?" Mac asked.

"Yes. And for Maia's mental mum as well. We've all got stuff to deal with. Don't flatter yourself that you're the centre of my world, officer."

Mac chuckled. "You've done more than I have then," he said.

"I can imagine. I bet your therapist is pleased with that."

"He gave me a telling off."

"And how did he feel about your coming to Skye?"

"Thinks it's a great idea. Cathartic is what he said."

"Bull," Clio said. "I agree with what he probably did say. I don't think you're ready, but when did anyone ever change your mind once you'd decided?"

"Because once I've decided, it's usually the right course of action," Mac replied.

"Because once your autistic mind is on a certain track, it doesn't like to be diverted," Clio pointed out.

"What would I do without your insights, Clio?" Mac said in what he hoped would be a disarming way.

"I fear for the people of Edinburgh in that case. Maia's glad you're coming, though."

"I'm glad too. What I need right now are the two of you. See how easily I say that out loud?"

Clio laughed. "I do. Well done. No, I mean it. Joking aside."

Clio's voice had become warm and motherly, switching from the acerbic, dry humour that coloured their usual conversations. Clio could say things to Mac that would have been extinction-level events to another friend, but Mac knew her well enough to see through the barbs.

"Thanks. Look, I know I'm pushing it by coming to

Skye, but I want to be somewhere as far from work as I can right now. Never thought I would say that. And Maia has made your holiday on Skye sound so... magical that I can't help myself. Joking aside. Seriously."

"Right. Ok, face value then. I'm glad you're here too. I have missed you."

"Me too,"

"And... the problem back in Edinburgh. The reason we're here on an extended holiday?" Clio asked.

"I'm working on it," Mac said.

"We can't stay here forever, Mac. I wish we could."

"I know. Just a week," Mac said.

Clio stayed on the phone as Mac drove along Skye's coast towards Portree. He was glad of her voice as he passed through the green desolation. The mountains and hills peeked from around bends in the road, always shrouded in mist and cloud. Moorlands on one side, empty. Grey water, on the other. Hidden depths. Mac would have given a lot for a betting shop, a tanning salon or a pound shop. A soulless concrete tower block, stained and dripping. He hated nature. Clio's jokes and chat kept his mind off the oppressive limbo he was driving through. The hinterland.

Edinburgh wouldn't be allowed to get too far from his mind, though. His phone lit up with another call incoming. The screen told him it was Ben Musa.

"Clio, I've got to go. It's another call. I'll see you in half an hour. I'm just coming up to Sconser. Not far now."

He didn't wait for a reply. Hung up. Took Musa's call.

"Mac, how's the holiday?"

"What do you want?"

"Ok, straight to business. No small talk. You could benefit from a course on interpersonal relationships, you know. Make you less abrasive as a colleague."

"Book it. We can do the course together, eh?" Mac said.

Musa chuckled in a deep, rich voice. Calm. Powerful. "Thought you would want to know, Mac. Dougie Griffiths is dead. Had you heard?"

"No."

"Karma, I'd say. Someone worked him over. Made a real mess of him. My team has the case because of the underworld connections. He was connected to Lowe and now has links to the Russians, who are trying to fill the power vacuum."

"His wife will be happy."

"Won't she? I know he wasn't your informant, Mac."

"You do, eh? He was a gold mine," Mac replied.

"No, Mac. He said nothing about being a snout for you. And with what he went through, he would have. Told just about anything else."

"You torture him yourself?"

"Me? I'm a copper, Mac, like you. I don't break the law. You?"

"Bent it a few times," Mac said.

"Right. You pull the trigger on Lowe yourself or just stand back and watch?"

"Did everything I could to save him. It's all on file."

"'Course it is, pal. And so is the account we got of Dougie Griffiths' last hours. Got an excellent source. So, if he wasn't your snout, then who was?"

"I told you. It was Dougie." Mac took a deep breath.

Musa was a shark, circling Clio and Maia. Mac had to draw him away with a show of vulnerability and give him blood in the water.

"You scared me when you mentioned Clio. Ok? I'm not messing around. You wanted the name, you got it. Now he's dead there won't be any more leaks because he was the source. You're in the clear. Just leave it."

The word please stayed clamped behind his teeth. He felt bad for not bringing himself to say it, but there were limits.

"We'll see. Where are you off to, anyway?"

"Cornwall," Mac said. "On the motorway now."

"I could get your phone tracked, but I don't want the scrutiny from Anti-Corruption. They've got all kinds of flags set up on the mainframe for mentions of you and Reid. Searches, files, you know."

"Doesn't surprise me. Akhtar doesn't like to lose any more than we do."

"Oh, I really hate it. I'll be in touch."

Musa was gone. Mac clamped the wheel to keep from throwing his phone out of the window. It wouldn't hurt Musa, but it was the proxy target for his anger. He bared his teeth, biting back a scream of frustrated rage. He didn't know how he was going to solve this, how he was going to put Musa off a second time, how he was going to keep Clio and Maia safe. If he still had the phone, he could have handed it over. Or found a name in it with more substance than Dougie Griffiths. But that ship had sailed.

"Stupid! Stupid! Stupid!" he roared, hammering the wheel with the flat of his hands.

The Audi lurched into the middle of the road, and an oncoming car sounded its horn. Mac swerved back, receiving another angry blast and a gesture from the passing driver. Sligachan was racing past, a small village, a handful of houses, and some tourist traps next to the road. Car park full of caravans and camper vans. Mac sped up. The car threw itself toward brown hills that seemed devoid of life beneath clouds that looked as angry as he was.

There was something else he was trying to keep out of his head. It kept sneaking under the door he kept it behind like smoke. Choking him. There was a killer out there. Mac had arrested that killer's accomplice. Or follower, acolyte. Mac wasn't sure of the relationship. He'd put his hands up to all of it and then Mac got the evidence there was someone else. Someone larger and darker. Someone truly messed up. But the case had been so public that Detective Chief Superintendent Carmichael didn't want the truth getting out. Was actively suppressing it. Mac clamped his jaw shut painfully, grinding his teeth. Muscles stood out on his neck like cables.

He forced himself to relax. The weight was as heavy on him as it had always been. Musa. The killer. Carmichael. Anti-Corruption. Iona. Jesus Christ, but he wanted to toss it all aside. As the road wove into those hills and up, Mac knew he was on the last stretch. Portree was up ahead. Twenty miles maybe. The ground levelled, and he was tearing over moorland. Evergreen trees on one side were as opaque as the water surrounding the island. Hiding things. Bodies. Victims. Killers. Musa would have to be dealt with. When Clio went back, Mac could stay on Skye. Tell Musa where he was. Lure him in. Kill him. No other way.

Mac felt scared by his own resolve. It had been a long time since he had thought himself capable of taking a life with his own hands. Letting a man be shot, standing back and doing nothing, that was different. He picked up his phone, scrolling to a streaming app, looking for some music to drown out his thoughts. His eyes were off the road for a second. When he looked back, a black van was on his side of the road, speeding towards him. Mac had a clear view through the windscreen of the oncoming vehicle. The man had receding hair and a round face. Creased. Worn.

Looking down into his lap. Classic driver looking at his phone pose, which everyone seemed to think a copper couldn't spot. Another driver would have been dead. They'd both have been dead. Mac's reactions saved them both.

He slammed his hand onto the boss in the middle of the wheel, sounding the horn long and loud. At the same time, he wrenched the wheel to the left. Bloody dangerous. Nothing but trees close to the road there. Instant death if he hit them. But he had to clear out of the van's way and he couldn't swerve right. When the van driver heard his horn, he swerved back into his own lane.

Mac had a brief glimpse of terrified eyes and then the van was passing him with a squeal of tires. No impact. Mac hammered the brakes, swerving back as pine trees reached for him. Branches scraped the window and a fence post went down under the car. The speed took him back across the road. Thank god there was no one behind the van. The Audi launched itself across the other lane and then dropped into the drainage ditch beyond it. The airbag exploded, punching Mac in the face.

Grab your copy…
vinci-books.com/ThePriceOfBlood